1929

AN UPPERCLASS AFFAIR

* * *

Margaret Chai Maloney

ISBN: 1-4392-3667-4
ISBN-13: 9781439236673

Visit www.booksurge.com to order additional copies.

For more information on the book and period, visit the website:
www.1929anupperclassaffair.com

Cover photograph of Dorothy Knapp by Alfred Cheney Johnson, Courtesy
of The Ziegfeld Club of New York, www.nationalziegfeldclubinc.com and
www.alfredcheneyjohnson.com and with the assistance of Nils Hanson and the
very talented Robert Hudovernik

DEDICATION

To my loving husband, inspirational parents,
darling daughters, dearest family and friends – without
whom this would not have been written.

Thank you,
MCM

CHAPTER I

Josephine Baxter-Browne, eager for a new adventure, waited just long enough to hear the unmistakable sound of her father snoring before she raced down the marble staircase and into the fragrant air of the night. *This* time, she remembered to take off her shoes first.

Once outside, under the bright glow of the evening moon, Josephine slipped on her favorite pair of Ferragamos before looking back at the townhouse to make sure her activity had gone unnoticed.

Content at what she found and the view around her, she paused for a split second in the cobblestone street to savor the quiet, dark stillness and the unusual night air. Serenity reigned over New York City's upper eastside in this hour just before midnight. Not a car passed nor a person walked in the street. Few windows within the towering apartments and impressive homes lining the area were illuminated. For most, peaceful slumber marked the hour and the silence.

But to Josephine – free at last – the darkness of the night brought exhilaration. Like a newly released inmate, the striking girl twirled around the street in a flimsy white silk dress – more of a petticoat than an evening gown. She knew thus attired she'd raise eyebrows, but she didn't care; it was what *she* wanted to wear.

The outspoken spirited girl had a knack for getting herself into trouble and regularly having to talk her way out of difficult situations, many of which were exacerbated by her own acerbic wit.

None would have predicted she of all people would become society's "*It*" girl – *the* debutante of 1929. Dismissed by dance instructors and social arbiters alike as a bony, sharp-tongued tomboy – a difficult child who squirmed when she should sit still, laughed when she should be silent and was too opinionated ever to be considered a proper young lady, Josephine, had been viewed for years as a real disappointment to her socialite mother. Perhaps that Josephine blossomed into such a desirable catch shocked her family most. Even her adoring father joked that he had encouraged her education out of the fear that her lack of interest in society and short fuse necessitated it. At times, the social pressure and familial guilt engulfed her, but more often, the young flapper managed to lead a carefree life embracing the times. She believed that she represented a new generation – a different society filled with the infinite possibilities of life, dedicated to the pursuit of pleasure, so sheltered, so privileged, so totally unaware of fallibility and consequences.

But even the most celebrated socialites could not infinitely delay the inevitable. After glancing at her Cartier watch, Josephine knew she needed to dash. While she briskly walked down 5th Avenue, she heard the clicking sound of her heels hitting the hard, stone pavement, a hallow echo through the empty streets. She would have hailed a cab, but since none were in sight, she strode as fast as she could towards her destination while enjoying the distinct, smell of summer drifting out of the luscious, green spaces and woods of Central Park, filling the street with a matchless, sweet fragrance.

It was the last day of the summer, 1929. Few had any inkling of the tempest to come.

* * *

While summer and the sweet scent silently slipped away, debutantes like "Josie," as she was known by those closest to her, snuck out simply to amuse themselves by making shocking statements and behaving outrageously at taboo places, they called familiar haunts.

As arranged, Geraldine Ashley, Catherine Thompson and Rebecca Stanley, Josie's three best friends from childhood, met at the corner of 54th and 6th Avenue. Predictably, the ever-dependable auburn-haired Geraldine arrived first and waited nearly a half an hour for the others. Catherine and Rebecca appeared almost simultaneously on the scene. After spotting the petite Rebecca making her way towards the meeting place, Catherine ran the last hundred yards to beat her. Born and bred to be competitive, the perfectly put together, tall socialite couldn't stand losing, even to her sweet natured, diminutive friend. Before Geraldine had a chance to comment on the matter, Catherine spotted Josie making her way towards the group as quickly as her heels permitted. Geraldine thought Josie's flushed face only made her look more attractive.

Together, they gathered at an intersection in midtown that they knew so well from so many other nights. Under the dim light of the flickering street lamp, the young flappers planned yet another escapade to break up the tedium of endless rounds of croquet, tea parties, and overly formal stuffy affairs.

Her eyes sparkling with the promise of the night, the thrill-seeking Josie said before even catching her breath, "Game for giggles?"

"I certainly need a drink," muttered the towering Geraldine. "I've spent the last week at my grandmother's cottage in Newport."

"I didn't know your grandmother was a teetotaler," replied the naive Rebecca innocently.

Geraldine explained, "She isn't. But my great aunt is and she was with us. *Grange* is probably celebrating my aunt's departure right now with a bottle of gin and a lot less tonic."

As the girls laughed, they saw several well-dressed young men cross the street and head towards Texas Guinan's club.

Pointing to the men, Josie said to her friends, "Shall we?"

"I'm game!" replied the usually proper Catherine, as she looked the group over. Ever fashion conscious, she noted she liked the look of their Argyle sweaters even if their Oxford bags were "decidedly dated."

"I'll just take a drink," said Geraldine as she nudged her friends towards their favorite hot spot.

While the girls walked into Texas' *new* Texas Guinan Club, they stood behind the group of boys wearing Argyle sweaters and Oxford bags who had walked past them earlier. Enthroned on top of the grand piano that dominated the room, Texas stopped smoking a thin, long cigarette in an even longer ivory holder just long enough to greet them with her infamous phrase, "Hello, Sucker!"

Considered one of the best speakeasies in the city, Texas Guinan's club was always a spectacle. It certainly was *the place* to see, and be seen. On any given night of the week, but especially on weekends, starlets of the stage and silver screen, mingled with top tier politicians and the denizens of Wall Street. And at Texas' they could mingle undisturbed by all, except of course by the ebullient, Amazon owner. The buxom blonde considered everyone fair game at *her* club, but particularly the men.

Texas' new Texas Guinan Club had opened four months ago with great fanfare after the old joint had burnt down following a particularly wild night of debauchery. Even as the speakeasy had gone up in flames, Texas had continued the party in the street until dawn. A few of her more celebrated guests like New York City Mayor James J. "Gentleman Jimmy" Walker and Will Rogers had been quietly whisked away just before the police and fire patrol arrived on the scene. The mayor had been having such a good time; only a slap on the bum by Texas and a bottle of rum convinced him that he really had to leave to prevent the press from having a field day.

Wood paneled throughout; the atmosphere of the latest Texas Guinan speakeasy was clubby and intimate. Somehow the flamboyant proprietor managed to compactly arrange the tables and chairs in the main rooms to maximize occupancy without sacrificing aesthetics and leaving just enough room for her suggestively clad chorus girls to shimmy amongst the patrons.

Although just getting in to the club was a challenge to many, notables had their favorite tables. While Walter Chrysler, Harry Payne Whitney and banker Otto Kahn could be seen at tables 2 and 3 respectively, Irving Berlin, Al Jolson, Rosamond Pinchot, and Peggy Hopkins Joyce, sat at various times at table 10 and journalist Heywood Broun and playwright George Kaufman apparently preferred table 22. Josie's favorite spot in the joint was near the back where Texas had designed two alcoves out of storage spaces. These hidden areas were tucked away behind seemingly endless yards of thick, red silk drapes that the doyenne claimed had been rescued from a dilapidated theatre where she had once performed. Josie and her friends also thought the ladies' powder room with its whimsically decorated walls plastered with pages from *College Humor* was the "Bee's Knees." The girls had heard that the men's area was wallpapered with erotic European prints. Although Josie always threatened that "next time she would go and see for herself if the rumor was true," she always got distracted from her "mission" by the time she was seated.

The last time the girls had been at Texas', Geraldine's colorful cousin had driven his brand new Phantom into the fire hydrant immediately in front of the club – spraying jets of water all over the queue of patrons awaiting entry and into his car. He summarily jumped out of the vehicle, promised to buy new clothes for the soaked victims, nonchalantly handed his top hat and walking stick to the doorman, and partied inside until dawn. He gave the girls rides home that night in a new car that he impulsively had purchased later from another patron at the speakeasy.

No one seemed to know what actually happened to the crashed vehicle. All Josie could recall from the evening was that it had been removed by the time they left and a staff member had driven the new car, fully equipped with champagne and caviar, up to the entrance for them. The last that she had heard about Geraldine's cousin was that he had just divorced his fourth wife and crashed his twelfth motorcar with great fanfare during the Peking to Paris rally. Josie vaguely recollected Count Nasogrande, an egotistical spurned suitor of hers, making a grand statement during the summer about being impressed with Geraldine's cousin, who seemed to treat both his cars and women equally as disposable luxuries. Geraldine ruefully acknowledged the point but with the caveat that despite her personal views on the general superiority of her own gender, his choice thus far in women rendered them far inferior to the quality of the handmade cars he crashed. When Rebecca wistfully began asking questions about the playboy as Geraldine and Josie discussed his whereabouts and speculated what his next outrageous feat would be, a horrified Geraldine immediately changed the subject.

Knowing very well when to play the coquette and when to be demure, Catherine wasted no time singling out the most eligible of the Argyle attired preppy boys and exchanging formalities. As Geraldine laughed with wry amusement at Catherine's predictability, the sight of so many attractive young men in the club quickly dispelled any thoughts Rebecca had of Geraldine's cousin.

Taking in the scene for the first time in several months, Josie said with exhilaration, "I've got a good feeling about tonight."

* * *

Izzy Einstein and Moe Smith stood outside a poorly lit brownstone on an unremarkable residential block. At first glance, it seemed almost identical to its neighbors. But Izzy and Moe knew better. As the pair waited in front of the brownstone's basement entrance, Izzy calmly applied more lipstick while Moe tapped his foot impatiently. When Izzy asked him to stop because it was annoying, Moe ran his fingers through his greasy black hair and played with his untrimmed mustache. Finished with the lipstick, Izzy pointed out a stray nose hair that dangled out of Moe's left nostril.

Furious, Moe told Izzy, "Mind your own business!" Then after he looked at his watch, he fixed his suit, straightened his tie and firmly banged his fist on the heavy oak door.

"Shush. Not so loud! We don't need to draw unnecessary attention," scolded Izzy like a ruffled mother hen.

"I know, I know," grumbled Mo. He warned, "Just don't nag me!"

Izzy protested, "I wouldn't if you listened!"

As he turned his back to the door to glare at Izzy, Moe said in exasperation, "There you go again. You're just like my mother!"

Izzy retorted, "I look like her tonight, don't I?"

"Don't insult my mother," snapped Moe.

Izzy countered, batting her eyelashes in a parody of what she'd seen countless times in the movies, "I'm wearing her clothes."

"But you certainly don't have her face," replied Moe as disgusted by the suggestion as by Izzy's efforts to appear like a silver screen siren.

Izzy muttered under his breath, "Thank God for small miracles."

While the pair exchanged dirty looks, a trap window in the large wooden door slid open. A rough faced man peered through the opening. After he gave Izzy and Moe a hard look, he requested the secret password for entry.

Without hesitation, Moe handed over an admittance card. Then, as he grinned broadly to reveal a mouthful of crooked teeth, he stated confidently, "We've come to try some of Grandma's homemade cookies."

The door immediately opened.

Moe smiled at Izzy when the doorman informed the middle aged, heavy-set couple that the cover was back up to twenty dollars per person. Based upon the price, they knew it was a good night. When business was slow, as it had been last week, Texas charged as little as five or ten dollars for admittance.

Izzy and Moe could hear the band playing *Ain't We Got Fun* as they were led through a narrow, dark hallway into a boisterous, packed room. Moe gave Izzy a dirty look as Izzy started singing.

Shrugging, Izzy said defensively, "I like the song."

"You're off key," growled Moe.

Soon Moe found something musical to appreciate. As the couple stood for some time waiting for a table, Texas' dancing girls started performing on the floor stage below the proprietress' piano. Moe greatly enjoyed the show and the opportunity to make a mental sketch of the place.

Several tables were vacated and filled before Izzy and Moe were offered seats. Texas's headman considered these patrons, unlike the young socialites, bad for business. They were in fact, one of the homeliest couples he'd ever seen. Moe was dressed like many of the rag merchants; his suit was cheap and didn't fit well. One glance at his stout companion was more than the headman wanted. He couldn't imagine that Izzy ever looked attractive – even on her wedding day. The headman thought that the only thing worse than her heavily made-up face with the double chin was her body.

Finally putting them in a most discreet table in the far corner of the room, the headman said as Moe made a half-hearted effort to pay for a better table, "Don't bother. Trust me."

As the headman passed their waiter, he said pointing at Izzy and Moe, "Some people shouldn't have children."

The unattractive couple snickered in the corner. Their act was working even better than usual.

* * *

By one in the morning, Texas Guinan's was jumping. The club was so loud; Josie thought the walls must have been reinforced to prevent the noise from being heard from the street. The piano continued to bang out popular songs and every now and then Texas' police whistle and noisemaker competed with the music, the roar of the patrons, and her splendidly, although scantily, attired troupe of dancing girls.

As the debutantes looked around, they could see there wasn't a spare inch in the joint. Josie suggested they head for the bar, located in the rear of the club near the kitchen. Several months had passed since they had been together in New York, so the girls had a lot of catching up to do. While Josie was in Europe, Rebecca and Catherine summered in Martha's Vineyard and Nantucket respectively and Geraldine divided her time between Southampton and Newport.

On their way to the bar, the girls filed past a table of boys who tried to convince them to join their group. Noting the unfolding events, Texas, shouted, "Give 'em hell girls!" From her piano perch, Texas interacted with everyone in the club. As the girls walked past her, the nightclub hostess launched into her own rendition of the popular song, "Ain't She Sweet." Motioning towards Josie and her friends, Texas sang, "Just cast an eye in *their* direction – Oh me oh my! Ain't that perfection! Now I ask you very confidentially, Ain't *They* Sweet."

Before they got to the bar, the fashionably dressed girls encountered several men who agreed with Texas' sentiments. Male admirers gawked as the tall, blonde, willowy, confident Catherine and the perfectly proportioned, petite brunette, Rebecca, walked by. Then, they saw Josie, 1929's most celebrated debutante follow her attractive friends towards the back of the room.

While her friends spent hours learning how to apply make-up and fix their hair, mimicking the fashion icons of the day, Josie, had a very different look. Although she loved beautiful clothes and cared about her appearance, she rarely spent much time doing her hair and putting on make-up, largely because she found the experience so frustrating. While her mother effortlessly was graced in these feminine arts, Josie seemed incapable of enhancing her own looks and believed from all too many painful experiences that the more time she wasted attempting to improve them, the worse the outcome. More interested in just having a good time, except on the special occasions when others did her up, over time she fully embraced a simple, natural, classic look that actually quite suited her.

As Josie strode past the men, her pale complexion and full red lips were most striking against her dark, bluntly cut hair and arresting black eyes. She had an unmistakable defiant air in her walk and in her smile, just a hint that she could be wickedly funny. There were those who claimed 1929's most celebrated debutante was more striking than beautiful, but regardless, even they could not deny Josie had a most unusual look that made people stare, ask who she was and wonder how they could get to know her.

Pushing past the tables to catch up with her friends, the five foot ten, 180 pound Geraldine quickly destroyed any fantasies the male patrons now entertained about Josie, Rebecca, and Catherine. Geraldine's glowers made it perfectly clear their feelings about her were reciprocated and more importantly, in order to get near her attractive friends, they'd have to get past her first.

* * *

Izzy and Moe had to wait over three quarters of an hour for a waiter to appear at their table. But the couple didn't seem to mind. They knew the speakeasy was extremely busy. They also understood the staff considered them lucky to be admitted. For this, Izzy and Moe would make them pay. When their waiter finally appeared, Moe claimed he was hard of hearing. Then he requested that the man go through the entire menu before he made up his mind. The rag merchant expressed outrage when he was informed a pint of whiskey was ten dollars and a bottle of champagne was priced at twenty-five dollars. The waiter was about to recommend that the couple try another establishment when Moe finally settled on "two glasses of your finest water."

The waiter narrowed his eyes. From experience, he knew he should have known better. The longer people took to order, and particularly whenever they inquired about the drinks other patrons ordered, the cheaper they usually were. Moe had asked about everything. What was the most popular drink in the house? How many people ordered tonight? Who was the couple at the corner table and what were they ordering? What were the names of the girls who just walked by? Every time the waiter thought Moe finally was ready to order, the rag merchant had launched into another litany of questions. Glancing at his watch, the waiter figured he'd wasted a good ten minutes on these two. And they weren't even good looking.

Izzy and Moe burst out laughing. They loved winding people up to get the information they wanted. The waiter thought he'd punish them by taking his time bringing the drinks. This just gave Moe a chance to walk around and do the other things he had to do. Moe located the table he was looking for at the other side of the room. Around it, sat five of the most powerful men in the New York underworld, including Dutch Schultz, Larry Fay and Owney Madden. Together, they controlled most of the bootleg empire from Wall Street to 57th Street. What Capone was to Chicago, these boys accomplished in New York City. After carefully noting the number of men they had with them, Moe rejoined Izzy at the table. Their "water" had just arrived.

Taking just one sip of the "water," Izzy and Moe had the proof they needed. They slipped covers over the glasses containing moonshine before placing the alcoholic drinks in Izzy's oversized handbag and then split up as planned.

* * *

At the bar, the girls began giving each other a run down on their summer holidays. After telling several stories each, all felt thirsty. Rebecca not only had a dry throat, she also the hiccups from laughing so hard at a story Geraldine had told. Desperate to quench her thirst and do something about her friend's hiccups, Josie looked around for staff. Finally she spotted a good-looking young man go behind the bar. Harried, as he grabbed a few glasses, he ignored the four girls who sat on the barstools.

As the fresh-faced, blonde man with almost unruly, wavy hair, started briskly to walk away, Josie called out to him. "Hey, you! What does a girl have to do to get a drink?"

The barman immediately responded.

Although arrested by her words, the barman seemed equally affected by her looks.

Geraldine couldn't help smirking. It wasn't the first time *this* dark-haired beauty had attracted a man's attention.

Not giving the barman a chance to make small talk, Josie summarily ordered lots of water and a round of Manhattans and Boomerangs for her friends.

While the barman prepared the drinks, Geraldine wandered over to a group of women she said she had recently painted – all in the nude. Although she sketched and sculpted as well, the titian haired, Geraldine was absolutely *mad* about painting. Taking her talent seriously, over the summer she had converted a guest cottage on her parents' Southampton estate into an art studio.

As soon as Geraldine was out of earshot, Catherine expressed shock at her friend's behavior.

Catherine said, "I can't believe Geri has gone bohemian."

"She always has been avant-garde. She's just raising her profile now," replied Rebecca kindly.

"You know her parents had to pay off the Southampton police after she got caught in a ménage-a-trois on the beach," gossiped Catherine.

Josie frowned. Then out of loyalty to Geraldine, she corrected Catherine. "She was painting the group in the moonlight. She wasn't a part of it," She emphasized, "From what I understand, there were no complaints from either the police *or* the participants."

Catherine insisted, "That's not what I heard."

As the barman handed the girls their drinks, Josie said, "A few weeks ago Geri sent me a picture commemorating the event."

"Really?" replied Catherine suspiciously.

"Yes," maintained Josie. "Unfortunately, she didn't put it in a thick envelope and my parents saw it before I did."

"You didn't tell me about this!" sputtered Rebecca as she choked on her drink.

"What's there to tell?" replied Josie innocently. "Except, of course, my mother knew all the subjects."

"You can't be serious!" exclaimed Catherine aghast.

"Who were they?" inquired Rebecca suddenly very interested. "Anyone we know?"

Leaning closer to her friends, Josie whispered, "Let's just say Geri has a special relationship with Gloria Vanderbilt and the Halsey boys."

"It was one of the most wonderful summer days," interjected Geraldine, as she took a luxurious puff from a recently lit cigarette and rejoined the group. She had just finished with her "friends" and had a big smile on her face. She waved a little card with names and numbers on it as she continued explaining the event; "Gloria was in town briefly. She stopped over for a dinner party before heading up to visit Reggie's family in Newport *and* she was bored. Can you believe it?"

The girls laughed because it was common knowledge that "Glorious Gloria," wife of the late Reginald Vanderbilt and mother of little Gloria, found American society, particularly certain members of her late husband's family like Gertrude Vanderbilt Whitney, at times quite tiresome and certainly very difficult.

Catherine said, "I heard she's been seen with some Spanish aristo who's biding his time until he can restore the monarchy."

Geraldine assured them, "She wasn't with him on this occasion! All through dinner she flirted with the Halsey brothers, both of them, and I might add, raised a few eyebrows doing so. When I offered to show her my studio, she was more than happy to escape." As she fingered the base of her silver cigarette handle that was embossed with the words, *Cherry Popper*, Geraldine said, "For the record, it was her idea to do a Greco-Roman period scene with the boys."

Catherine shook her head in shock and looked stunned. "She must have been very, very drunk."

"Not particularly. Just *very* attracted to the Halsey boys," replied Geraldine.

"Who isn't?" inquired Rebecca. As Catherine looked at her derisively, she added defensively, "They are the most eligible bachelors in Southampton, aren't they?"

Geraldine retorted, "I assure you, from personal experience, they're not to everyone's taste." As she smoked, she said reminiscing, "But thanks to them, we had quite the romp!"

"Geri, I just hope you don't have any pictures of me," said Rebecca with a sigh.

"Don't worry. I only *do* subjects I'm attracted to." said Geraldine pointedly. After taking several sips of the cocktail that the barman finally handed her, she offered more kindly, "Besides, I know your taste." Motioning to a group at a table in an alcove, she stated, "Right now, I have a few boys you'd like, who I can tell would be delighted to meet you, Catherine and Josie." Smiling broadly, she explained, "I know them quite well."

"*That's* what concerns me," replied Catherine warily.

As the girls got up to join the male group, Josie noticed the barman had been leaning against the bar, eavesdropping on their conversation. It seemed to her that he had been more interested in what they had to say than in the cocktails he had mixed for them. She had been so involved in the conversation that she hadn't taken a sip of her drink yet.

Taken aback, she handed her Boomerang to the barman and said saucily, "Unless you've attended one of Geraldine Ashley's parties this summer and have something to say about the event, you'd better re-mix my drink."

"I've never disappointed a woman before," the barman shot back with a smirk as he slid her Boomerang across the counter towards her.

Slapping down the money for the drinks, Josie, a former Seven Sisters Conference Debating Champion, retorted, "Get used to it."

Noting the evidence of a sinewy body underneath his tight white shirt, Geraldine said licentiously as she settled back down comfortably in her chair, "I think we should see what he's got."

"You mean how much he's willing to reveal?" Catherine chimed in.

Geraldine responded with a wicked look in her eyes "Both."

While the girls spoke about the barman as if he were an item on an auction block, he started walking away. He didn't bother picking up the money Josie left. The expression on his face made his feelings clear.

Realizing they had gone a bit too far, Josie stopped him. She offered a form of apology that said more about her class than any indication of regret. Oblivious of just how far he would take matters, but fully aware that he was a mere barman – a member of the serving class that she had been reared to see as simply existing to service her set's pleasures she explained, "Look now, you really shouldn't be offended. We're just having a fun night out."

Demeaned and doubly insulted by their condescension, the barman's reply was full of contempt, his blue eyes piercing. "I've been a lot of places, but I've never met a group of more self-absorbed spoiled bores than the four of you." Making his disgust clear, he told them in no uncertain terms, "Your behavior is indicative of just what's wrong with society!" Then he demanded to know, "Who are you to view everyone else as objects to be used when you deign to notice anyone else at all?"

While Catherine and Rebecca gasped at the affront, Geraldine contemplated sitting on him and Josie verbally retaliated. Haughtily, she replied, "If you were worth noticing, we would have taken note."

"Well if I thought *you* were worth the effort, I would have made sure you noticed me," retorted the barman cockily.

Trying to deflect the tense situation, Geraldine said, "C'mon Josie. He's not worth it."

Rebecca and Catherine agreed, "Let's just go."

But Josie was determined to put the barman in his place.

While her friends joined the corner table of boys, Josie and the barman continued their heated exchange. Finally Josie had enough. She got up from her stool and downed her Boomerang.

Turning to the barman she said coolly as she handed him her empty glass, "I'll give you this, although you do nothing for me, you mix a decent cocktail."

Handing him her calling card, she said insultingly, "I'll recommend you to my mother. At the rate she goes through servants, she's always looking for more help."

Letting Josie's card fall to the ground, the barman said icily, "I'm not interested in servicing either you or your mother."

Furious, Josie reached over towards the barman to slap him. Just as her hand was about to hit his cheek, he stopped her. He only agreed to let go when she stopped fighting. Grinning, he asserted, "You know if you were serviced more often, you might not be so uptight."

Enraged at his audacity, Josie shot back as she deliberately looked him up and down, "Don't flatter yourself. I don't feel like slumming tonight."

"That's good because I wasn't offering," retorted the smirking barman.

Fuming as much from his words as her own growing attraction to the first man who had ever put her down effectively, Josie said as she stood up and upped the ante, "I've always been open-minded, but after meeting you, I understand why there should be class barriers."

The barman stopped Josie with his stinging words. "Just because you come from the right background doesn't mean *you* have any class."

After pushing her back down onto the stool, the barman stood directly in front of her, in order to say, "At least this way I can enjoy the full view even if you don't have anything worthwhile to say."

As Josie colored, the barman moved closer. His eyes penetrated her. She wanted to look away but the intensity of his gaze overwhelmed her. Her heart raced and her breath shortened. She had the distinct feeling he was about to kiss her when they heard loud noises and the sound of police whistles.

The joint was being raided.

* * *

Josie and the barman weren't the only patrons of Texas' joint caught off guard by the police. Even some of the authorities weren't ready. As the party crashers bashed through the doors, Izzy screamed and Moe cursed. The law enforcers were ten minutes early, trapping them inside the joint as well!

Izzy Einstein and Moe Smith were the best dry agents in New York City and arguably the most respected in the nation. Since the Prohibition of Alcohol became law in 1920, the pair managed to maintain a perfect record in busting joints that served illicit beverages.

As a result, they sent 4,932 patrons to jail and had confiscated fifteen million dollars worth of alcohol. They were good at what they did and grudgingly respected in all quarters for their creativity and honesty – even by bootleggers and club owners. They had panache.

Disguising themselves as patrons, Izzy and Moe cased out joints for weeks before the actual bust. They always dressed to fit into the neighborhood. Speaking Yiddish, German, Hungarian, Polish, French, Russian and even a bit of Chinese, there wasn't an ethnic enclave where Izzy couldn't get a drink. Occasionally he also got into joints by playing his trombone or violin.

Since couples usually attracted less attention than a single man, the diminutive Izzy usually donned a wig and went as a woman. Izzy had dressed as everything from a dancing girl to a washerwoman. Once, he even busted a speakeasy in drag as a Dowager Empress. Moe was a little concerned the act was too good when his formidable "wife" got them the best table in a place that was reputed to be a mobster haven. He was delighted, however, when it turned out to be a blackjack table. Izzy and Moe not only won $10,000 that night, but also managed to put away almost every goon in the Lower Eastside for six months. The night was particularly satisfying when the police discovered a basement full of bad moonshine. Had the patrons drunk this liquor, many would have been at the very least violently ill from the contents. Since Prohibition, alcohol poisoning had risen dramatically. There had been thousands of hapless victims, many of them young and poor, and almost all totally unaware of the potential, deadly repercussions of their actions. More than anything else, that is what kept Izzy and Moe in the business.

The cross-dressing dry agents had been casing out Texas Guinan's for over two weeks before the actual raid. It was such a popular and profitable joint that they noted the club's deliveries had to be made twice a day. One was made in the afternoon in a bakery truck and the other well into the night. Izzy had been watching the deliveries for the past week. The second truck always came be-tween two and two thirty in the morning. There were usually two men in the front and another six who rode with the hooch in the back and did the unloading.

Ever cognizant of the importance of timing in their missions, the dry agents had every intention of ensuring that the greatest number of perpetrators got caught. But they also were extremely wary of blowing their covers during the bust and had always man-aged to get out before the police entered. When the second de-livery truck ran late, the pair became concerned but not alarmed. They were experienced enough to have expected the scenario and had built in enough time. What they hadn't expected was an over eager police chief.

As Texas' patrons drank and danced the night away, the pair had done their usual round of observations and checklist. Izzy marked out all the exits while Moe continued to watch for the delivery truck. Izzy inconspicuously circled the bootleg table once more. Then he examined the "food" bar. He saw no evi-dence of edibles but a lot of glasses and alcohol. As he had prepared to leave, he had overheard part of an animated discus-sion by the bar that made him smile. He found the attraction between the young flapper and her male companion undeni-able. He thought she looked familiar and was certain he had seen her before.

When Moe rejoined his partner, he enlightened Izzy on why he thought he knew the girl. Pointing towards Josie, he had elaborat-ed, "She's always in the papers." The agent had chortled, "But may-be tomorrow there'll be another headline: *Debutante Detained!*"

After glancing at his watch, Izzy had replied, "Yeah, but that won't be the only headline if we don't get out of here in five min-utes." Izzy and Moe knew of too many prohibition agents who had become department statistics by hanging around too long.

As the pair headed towards the exit, Izzy had stopped to take one final look around the place. His well-trained eyes focused on a corner table. He had spotted a large, young woman sketching. Izzy had thought he felt someone watching him earlier. Walking over to Geraldine's table, he had said, "I don't like to have my picture taken."

"I'm not taking it," Geraldine had retorted. "I'm drawing you."

"I'd rather you didn't," the agent had stated forcefully.

She asked half joking as she had continued sketching, "Why not? Are you on the lam?"

Izzy had replied as he roughly grabbed the paper from her hand, "Let's just say, I don't have time to explain."

She had shouted, "Hey, you can't do that! That's mine! Give it back or I'll make a scene you'll never forget!"

Forcefully gripping Geraldine's arm as he leaned into her, Izzy had threatened in a deep, low voice as he looked meaningfully into her eyes, "Don't be a fool."

Stunned by his grip and words, Geraldine knowingly looked at his face, "You're not a woman! No woman grabs like that!" As she had backed away from the agent Geraldine muttered softly, "Keep the sketch."

As Izzy and Moe had headed towards the door, Geraldine had grabbed Rebecca and Catherine and said, "We've got to get out of here – NOW."

Before the girls had had a chance to settle the bill, the police arrived blowing their whistles, waving batons, overturning tables, sending glasses crashing to the floor. In the main room, screaming patrons, musicians, and workers pushed and shoved, desperate to get out, but there was no place to go. Based upon Izzy and Moe's surveillance work, the police already had blocked most of the exits. The law enforcers even had sealed off the kitchen and side entrances, leaving violators with only one alternative.

Trying to remain calm, Geraldine had attempted to re-assure her trembling friends. Telling them to edge towards the back, she had explained, "As long as we're one of the last to be plied out, we may stand a chance."

While the girls made their way to the far end of the club, Geraldine wondered where Josie was.

* * *

As the police barged into the club, Josie froze. For a moment she was too stunned to react. But she quickly recovered from the shock. Looking her companion straight in the eyes as she forcefully gripped his arms, she said in a firm but calm voice, "We've got to get out of here."

Grabbing her hand, the barman pulled her up and said, "C'mon. I'm sure there's a trap door somewhere in the back."

Despite the urgency, she paused for a moment to look around the room for her friends. Reading her mind, the barman said, "They could be anywhere." Prodding her along, he continued, "We don't have much time. In a few minutes every exit will be blocked."

Frantically pacing back and forth while she continued to look, she said emphatically, "I'm not leaving without my friends."

The barman knew his chances were better if he left her to her own devices and principles, but he admired her loyalty. Reluctantly, he said, "Okay, I'll help you find them."

Luckily, a few minutes later, just as the police chief entered the smoky room, Geraldine spotted Josie.

While the chief ordered those left in the place to line up, the barman and the girls made a run for the storage rooms. All they had to do was follow the group of other fleeing patrons from the alcoves that also rushed in the same direction. The barman and the girls soon found themselves at the end of a line. When they finally got inside the dark room, they were overpowered by the smell of recently emptied alcohol and the odious scent of vomit from some of the more ossified patrons who had tripped over the emptied containers that littered the floor. All eyes were on the trapdoor with the rickety pull down ladder that was situated at the far end of the workroom. The anxious in line cursed those going up the ladder for not moving faster. They feared that at any moment the police might bust into the room and arrest those left below.

Finally it was the girls' turn to climb. One by one, slowly, Catherine, Rebecca and Geraldine made their way up the wooden rungs to the upper room that led to a passageway and more staircases that would lead to a fourth floor fire escape. As Geraldine made her way up, the ladder creaked and heaved, threatening to break. The barman sighed with relief when she finally made it to the top. With her friends and the barman urging her, Josie prepared to make the ascent.

Just as Josie was about to start climbing, a man who yelled, "Get outta my way, you dumb Dora," roughly shoved her against the wall.

Although he was only of average height, her attacker had a pockmarked face and the most menacing voice she had ever heard. She shivered as she realized in all probability he was one of the underworld thugs who delivered the bootlegged alcohol to the speakeasy.

While Josie struggled to get up, the barman immediately reacted. After checking to make sure she was all right, he went after her attacker. The thug was half way up the ladder before the barman managed to pull him down.

Josie gasped as a small gun slipped out of the goon's pocket when he fell to the ground. She went after the weapon as it slid across the floor. While the barman jumped on top of the thug, he urged her to make the ascent to safety. Reluctantly she complied. As she climbed up, all the while holding the gun, she saw the goon get in a few good punches before the barman knocked him out.

Just as the barman made it to the top, they heard police whistles. The law enforcers rushed into the storage room as Josie and the barman pulled up the ladder and bolted the trap door. They could hear the police shouting for back up and shooting at the trap door while they ran through the passageway and up three more flights of stairs to rejoin Josie's friends and find safety. Knowing the lock on the trap door wouldn't hold, Josie and the barman raced up as fast as they could. Moments later, as the girls climbed outside onto the fire escape, they heard the police climbing up the stairs. In order to give the girls more time, the barman offered to hold them off. Given Rebecca was trembling and Catherine was afraid of heights, Josie knew this might very well be necessary. Just to get Catherine to make the descent down the fire escape, Geraldine and Josie had to put her between them and use Rebecca's scarf as a blindfold.

When the girls finally reached the bottom, they didn't have time to wait for the barman. A group of policeman who had just finished emptying the speakeasy spotted them as they jumped down the last rungs. With a grin as wide as his girth, a particularly vigilant lieutenant informed the society violators that there still was room left in the wagon for the four of them.

While Josie urged them to make a run for it, Geraldine caught a glance of Izzy and Moe peering from behind the bars of the window in the back of the police wagon. The artist would have laughed at their predicament if the girls themselves weren't in such jeopardy of joining the incarcerated dry agents. Instead she made a mental note of the scene in order to sketch it as a cartoon she'd submit to the *New Yorker*.

For her part, as she started off with a few amused, burly policemen in pursuit, Josie took one last longing look at the fire escape. She wished she could get another glimpse of the barman, but he was nowhere to be seen. Several blocks later, as the police shouted after them, the girls continued to run like thieves, escaping into the dying night.

By the time Geraldine, Rebecca, Catherine and Josie had reached the upper eastside, the sun had just started to come up and the milkman was almost done with his rounds. He nodded fondly at the girls. The milkman had seen them slipping back into their homes frequently over the last few years.

An hour later, as she lay in her comfortable bed trying to get a few hours sleep before the rest of the house woke up, Josie couldn't get the barman off her mind. She didn't even know his name. The one thing she did know for certain was that she wouldn't be seeing him at Texas Guinan's anytime in the near future. After last night, she knew Texas's would be closed for some time.

* * *

CHAPTER II

James Ellison DeVere nursed a terrible hang over. The dark haired, desirable bachelor drank like a fish and was often drunk, but rarely suffered like this. It took serious amounts of alcohol mixed hideously to affect the tall, fit, blue-blood in this manner.

James greeted Bentley, his proper English houseman, with growls when the man brought in the morning papers and the mail. The servant just managed to duck in time to avoid a champagne glass James threw to prevent him from tying back all the red silk damask drapes in the wood paneled bedroom.

While Bentley pulled down the duvet covering James' ornately carved Tudor bed and set out his master's clothes, he said provocatively, "Sir, perhaps you'd be more pleased to see me if I brought you another glass of *Champers* this morning? Isn't that what you call it?"

As he rolled over, James muttered, "Go to hell."

"Abuse me verbally as you will, but you know you have to get up," stated the houseman unemotionally.

In response, Bentley's handsome, groggy master retrieved the duvet and covered his face with a down pillow to block out the sunlight streaming through the windows.

Knowing from years of experience how difficult it could be to get James up, Bentley positioned himself at the foot of the imposing oak bed. He had a tired look on his face and sighed heavily at the lump under the covers. While he waited, the houseman thought that at least he could enjoy the view of one of the four massive seventeenth century Delft school tapestries that adorned each bedroom wall.

After a few minutes as he attempted to remove the duvet again, Bentley said brusquely, "It's half twelve sir and if I'm not mistaken, you have to be downtown to meet Mr. Morgan at the Exchange Luncheon Club by one." The houseman resumed his duties knowing what he just said would generate the desired reaction.

While he crawled out of bed, James moaned, "I feel sick."

"It's no wonder, sir," replied Bentley as he helped James into his dressing gown.

While Bentley shaved his master's face, he said half amused, "Do you remember anything about last night?"

James thought he remembered quite a bit. He informed Bentley he had had a most delightful night with all the old boys. The evening had started at the Yale Club with drinks. Each Skull and Bones boy had brought a bottle to mix into the drinks at the club. There had been quite a lot of toasting so that by dinnertime, most of the chums loudly belted out the school drinking songs – oblivious and in some cases indifferent to the distraction they caused to others.

Dinner was held at James' favorite club, the Metropolitan, where they had ten courses to symbolize the time since their graduation from Yale and the number of years that the group had met up in New York. Twenty boys had gathered – a few were "honorary" members.

The food was delicious but played a secondary role to the sconcing. As was the case in college, any boy had the right to sconce another as long as he willing drank the same concoction he proposed. Punishment for not finishing the drink was the administration of another in which every member of the table added an ingredient. By four in the morning, James had imbibed in some mixture that began as port but included red and white wine, a cigar stub, a cigarette, two rose petals, a raw egg and cream, sugar, salt, pepper, a spoon full of dirt, and three drops of cod liver oil. James hardly could keep himself from gagging as he stood up and downed the atrocious drink in one horrific gulp to a cheering audience.

By dawn, several had passed out. James remembered stumbling into the street and cursing at the milkman for inconsiderately making so much noise.

After yawning and washing away the sleepy dust from his blue eyes and the remaining shaving cream from his face, James said proudly, "I made it home and into my bed all right!"

Handing his master an Appenzell monogrammed towel, Bentley replied, "Just about, sir."

James cocked an eyebrow at his houseman inquisitively.

While the servant helped James into his clothes, he explained, "I found you asleep."

"Yes?"

"In the Whitney Straight's entrance hall very early this morning." The houseman made it clear, "I brought you home from there."

Appalled, James' jaw dropped. For close to thirty years, Adele Whitney Straight had reigned as New York society's grand dame. James had been to a number of her parties but never spent the night. The woman was close to seventy.

Looking at his master wearily, the houseman explained, "Their butler rang me this morning *after* Mrs. Whitney Straight fainted when she found you.

Quickly recovering, James wryly smiled and retorted, "Well, at least you didn't find me in her bed. I certainly would have fainted at her sight."

Bentley sighed heavily. For once, his British sense of humor failed him. As he dressed his master, he wondered how he would have managed over the years to put up with the imp without his humor. Bentley had served the DeVere family for close to forty years and James almost since his birth. He attributed most of his gray hair to his young master.

Just as Bentley finished his duties, the men heard the hallway grandfather clock announce the time. James counted the dongs. Then he exploded. "It's only eleven now! Damn you Bentley! You lied to get me out of bed."

Quietly dismissing himself, the tall, calm, distinguished looking Bentley claimed as he left the bedroom, "I must have made a mistake." He emphasized, "*Terribly* sorry sir." Bentley smiled as he closed the door. The houseman looked forward to a big breakfast that he was sure Cook would prepare for him after she learned what he had done.

James smashed another glass against the wall. Then, picking up his mail, his mood changed as he opened an invitation. John D. Rockefeller III requested his presence at an upcoming dinner party he planned to host for Winston Churchill. Pleased, James smiled. Without a doubt, all the best people would be there. His smile broadened as he read the extra lines J.D. had handwritten on his invitation. "Do come. You won't be disappointed. A certain Josephine Baxter-Browne will be in attendance as well."

* * *

Geraldine slept most of the way from New York to Detroit. Her mother had prodded her to enjoy the beautiful scenery along the way, but nothing could keep her eyes open. She wished her best friend, Josie, could have come along for the trip. With Josie, even the most mindless social occasions ended up being a laugh. Over the years, the girls had tried the patience of their parents while taking the piss out of the most uptight socialites and somehow managing never to get caught doing the things that were really bad. Geraldine still chuckled every time she thought of how she and Josie had put a fish head in the mailbox of the most obnoxious girl at school and how her friend had sent anonymous love letters to a bully who had made Geraldine's life miserable for years in order to ultimately humiliate him by setting him up publicly with a date with a cow.

Geraldine smiled as she thought of the wild night she and her friends experienced at Texas Guinan's. As she went through the events, she started to drift off. She heard her father say to their companions, "Must have been some party!" Then she surrendered to the seduction of the movement and sound of the locomotive and she drifted into a much needed, deep sleep.

Geraldine and her parents, Lord and Lady Ashley, sat in Charles Schwab's personal railway car, with the steel titan and his wife. They were among a select group of government leaders, tycoons and society luminaries whom Henry Ford had invited to celebrate the commemoration of the fiftieth anniversary of the invention of the light bulb.

Lord and Lady Ashley numbered among the most prominent socialites. Geraldine's mother was born into one of the wealthiest industrialist American families. She had been sent to school in Europe, where she met Geraldine's father. Until the Great War, the couple divided their time between Lady Ashley's vast family holdings in America as well as Lord Ashley's estates in England. Wherever there was a glittering party, the social columns inevitably noted Lord and Lady Ashleys' attendance. Geraldine's earliest childhood memories were of the fancy dress parties that her parents hosted at Wolverstone Hall, one of her father's country estates.

Everything changed after World War One. Like many of the British aristocracy, Lord Ashley's family suffered from the conflict. His father's unexpected demise after a heart attack was compounded by the death during the war of his two older brothers within two months of each other. Lord Ashley never forgave the government for the heavy death duties imposed, even though the losses resulted from heroic action for King and country. Henceforth, Lord Ashley vowed never again to call England home and the Ashleys turned their full attention towards socializing in America. Following the war, the couple also embraced the avant-garde. Geraldine's friends thought her parents threw some of the best parties since they always had a good mix of people. In addition to the expected financial and social notables, a typical Ashley gathering included: African American writer Langston Hughes, social philanthropist and lawyer Clarence Darrow, Broadway funny girl Fanny Brice, Mayor Jimmy Walker and before she passed away, dancer Isadora Duncan.

The Schwabs and Ashleys disembarked from the private railcar minutes after President Hoover got out of his in Detroit. Joining his motorcade, the socialites followed the President as he headed towards Dearborn. Hoover sat in an open top vehicle, shivering as rain pelted down upon him. Although they too were soaked through, the crowds that had gathered hours before didn't care. The locals were just delighted to get a glimpse of the President who now presided over the greatest economic boom in the history of the country and had been lauded for his humanitarian efforts both abroad and stateside.

Orphaned at the tender age of nine, the President who had achieved early success as a mining engineer after graduating from Stanford University had become an international celebrity first through his successful evacuation of 120,000 Americans in Europe at the start of the First World War. His reputation grew through his unprecedented relief work during and after the war, when he administered the distribution of over 1 ½ million tons of food to 9 million war victims. Over-riding prominent members of his own party, he ensured that all those in need were helped regardless of their politics. More recently, when he had served as Commerce Secretary, Hoover aggressively promoted American business interests abroad, especially Hollywood films. But many of those gathered on the streets of Dearborn were more appreciative of the fact that the President had launched the "Own your Own Home" campaign which had made ownership attainable to people like them across the country.

All along the route, bands played while the crowd cheered the popular President's motorcade. Hoover continued to smile and wave despite the inclement weather. By the time he reached Ford's house, he resembled a drowned river rat more than the President of the United States. Ford shuddered when the saturated Hoover embraced him upon arrival. The industrialist didn't like getting physically close to people, let alone wet ones.

By the time the festivities began, a flicker of sunlight shone through the cloudy day. Since a large part of the activity took place outside, Geraldine and all the other guests were relieved. Henry Ford painstakingly had re-assembled an entire village in which his guests could mingle. The area included Edison's actual laboratory where he invented the light bulb, Ford's own boyhood home, the village in which he had grown up, and numerous other buildings of historical value. Geraldine brought a sketchbook so she could capture this momentous occasion.

A few hours later, Geraldine sketched President Hoover while he pontificated about the strength of the American economy in Ford's reconstruction of Philadelphia's Independence Hall. As he prepared to toast the great inventor, microphones were turned up so radios simultaneously could broadcast his prophetic words in households across the country. The room was silent with antici-pation as the President stated, "Mark my words, as we move into the next decade – America will build upon the promise of the past to create one of even greater wealth and abundance for all mankind."

While she stared at the President, Geraldine started giggling. To get a better view and make sure her eyes weren't deceiving her, she leaned over the dignitaries who sat in the row in front of her. She couldn't believe she was the only one who saw it. Embarrassed by her daughter's behavior, which attracted the unwelcome glares of those around them, Lady Ashley narrowed her eyes at Geraldine as she pinched her arm hard and whispered frostily, "What's your problem?"

Geraldine pointed to the President. Her mother feigned a frown as she now too saw the bulbous shaped, yellow booger dangling in the corner of his left nostril. With great difficulty Lady Ashley kept a straight face as the President claimed, "Due to modern science and human invention such as we have seen here today, the economy of America in the 1930's will be remembered for unimaginable growth and financial security."

For her part, Geraldine felt obligated to record the moment for posterity. Sketching the President as quickly as she could, she labeled the piece, "The Presidential Booger declares the economy sound." As she put the sketch away to listen to the rest of the speech, she hardly could wait to show her friends. The young artist smirked, noting even when Hoover was on the home stretch, the booger stubbornly hung onto the side of his nose despite his animated gestures.

The President ended his speech with a standing ovation as he called upon the guests and the whole world to join him tonight by turning off their lights so they would fully appreciate how much Edison's invention changed the world. Then the 31st President honored the great inventor, "by declaring it Thomas Alva Edison Day!"

Geraldine noted that Edison also had noticed the booger and tried to give Hoover the hint by gesturing to his own nose. But Hoover didn't understand. Geraldine wondered what else the President didn't get.

* * *

To commemorate the fiftieth anniversary of Edison's invention of the light bulb, Henry Jay threw a bash for those New Yorkers who preferred *not* to go to Detroit.

As Josie approached Henry Jay's upper eastside, Chateauesque style mansion that had been designed at the turn of the century by Richard Morris Hunt, she was struck as she often was, by its magnificence. Even from across the street the debutante could hear the music and laughter emanating from the illuminated, limestone city residence. Confidently she walked through the imposing iron gates onto the crimson red carpet that Henry had servants lay over the pathway from the sidewalk to his front door. Before each party, he always selected the plush runner that most fit the evening's theme or his mood.

Before picking up the heavy doorknocker, Josie glanced at her reflection in the glass surrounding the majestic door that once graced the estate of Louis Philippe Joseph, Duke of Orleans. After some consideration, she had decided to don one of her new bias-cut, Madame Vionnet ball gowns that had been designed for her over the summer, at her mother's insistence. It had taken twelve agonizing fittings and twenty-eight pairs of hands to complete the stunning ankle-length ensemble with a V-neck, low cut back, and uniquely designed scarves and flounces that created a sexy, fluid effect, like a shimmy. She adored the feel of the sheer black silk and crepe de chine dress against her skin as much as she loved the way the garment looked. It was covered in iridescent sequins, bugle beads and silver and gold embroidery that she had been told had been hand stitched in a remote province in India and originally prepared for a maharaja.

To complement the outfit, Josie wore dangling black onyx pendant earrings and a sequined bandeau with a gold aigrette. With her matching Perugia ankle strapped pumps decorated with sequined vamps and gold heels that her mother had selected for her, she should have been ready to dance the night away.

But as she stood at the door, staring at herself, she yawned. Josie had not yet recovered from her escapade the previous night at Texas Guinan's. Finally, she perked up as she thought about the barman. She applied a little more lipstick as she thought that since Henry always hired extra help for his parties, there was a small chance she might run into him serving drinks tonight. Although the only make-up Josie normally wore was lipstick, she wished she now had cosmetics to get rid of the bags under her eyes and add a little more color to her cheeks. Not only did she want to look good in case she saw the barman, but also she liked to look her best for her Henry, who was her godfather. She knew Henry had impeccable taste and noticed everything.

Josie loved the old codger dearly and tried hard not to disappoint him. Although not related by blood, Henry and the Baxter-Brownes behaved as though they were kin. Henry bought his goddaughter her first pony and gave her, her first glass of champagne. He also had the distinction of introducing her at Ascot and ensuring she was invited to all the right parties held by the *Bright Young Things* in England. Catherine and a few of the debutantes in her year sniped that her social success resulted chiefly from Henry's unforgettable coming out party in her honor. Undoubtedly, his frequent campus visits during her college days at Mount Holyoke gave her legitimate excuses to break the curfew and solidified her reputation in the beautiful set. But what Josie cherished most was their frequent Sunday afternoon walks in Central Park and endless discussions of culture, art, history and philosophy. She was the first to admit much of her knowledge in these areas came from the strong foundation her godfather gave her.

Now, as Josie stood outside Henry's mansion, she knew no matter how tired she was she could look forward to a memorable evening. After putting her lipstick back in her black and gold sequined handbag, brushing her hair away from her face and smoothing down her dress one more time, she reached for the iron knocker. From the doorstep she heard the band cheerily strike up, "*I Wanna Be Loved By You*," from within the museum-like edifice and she started to move to the rhythm. By the time the door opened, she was ready to party again. But as Henry's butler ushered Josie into the grand hallway, she doubled back, unable to breathe from the heavy cigar smoke that hung over the room, permeating every pore, engulfing her. Just as she started coughing, Henry Jay emerged, his black, silk top hat angled jauntily on his head. A large Havana cigar dangled from his mouth as he twirled a silver-handled, elaborately carved, ebony walking stick while tossing off his signature white silk scarf.

Henry, also, just had arrived. The dashing, gallant New York social set icon made a point of never turning up to any party sober, or on time – especially the ones he hosted. As usual, he was dressed impeccably in a colorful waistcoat and finely cut tails. After handing his hat and walking stick to his butler, he offered Josie his arm.

Henry's adoration for his godchild and heir was apparent to all. As he escorted her around his party, Josie thought her godfather was the most engaging, debonair man she knew. Six foot four, with broad shoulders and a firm body that defied his age, Henry Jay was far more attractive than many men twenty and even thirty years younger. While he showed off his darling godchild to his glittering guests, few would believe if they didn't know from experience, this that warm, droll, accommodating host with blue-green eyes that twinkled with grandfatherly pride had a killer instinct when it came to acquisitions of any kind.

Accepted in every social and business circle, Henry came from the renowned Jay family. His progenitors had been extremely prominent financiers during the American Revolution and the early years of the Republic. Throughout his 30,000 square foot limestone mansion that nearly took up an entire block, there was ample evidence of this. The portraits, silver, and furniture all bore the signature Jay family marks.

Not content with merely enjoying the family's reputation, Henry not only consolidated the family's vast holdings, but also he actually tripled them during the second half of the last century. Outwitting Rockefeller, Morgan, Gould, Vanderbilt and Carnegie in a number of deals, he grudgingly earned their respect. No matter what industry he chose, Henry Jay emerged on top.

Unfortunately, his personal life had not been as successful. Married three times unhappily, Henry gave up looking for love after his last acquisition – a wife forty-five years his junior - committed suicide in the South of France. Since he had no children, he now spent his time expanding his sizable art collection, improving his stable of racing horses, and throwing memorable parties in New York City and at his Saratoga estate. By the fall of 1929, Henry's reputation as New York's most prominent hedonistic host was unquestioned. His greatest challenge actually lay in outdoing his own fetes.

This evening as Hoover toasted Edison for his invention of the light bulb; Henry's tastefully decorated New York City mansion was illuminated entirely by candlelight. Josie had never seen so many candles before. As she basked in the glow, Henry informed his goddaughter that it had taken a staff of a hundred and five, ten hours and twenty minutes to assemble the 6,525 candles around the place. When Josie looked enquiringly at Henry, he joked as he pointed to the guests, "They think I did it for Edison, but frankly it's easier on the eyes – the old bats look better this way."

Josie laughed as she looked around the scene. As far as she could tell, there were more people there her age, than his. In fact, the only old bat she noticed was Mrs. Whitney Straight, a woman Josie considered amusing and strikingly attractive given her age. Josie knew Henry only invited two sorts of guests: those who were entertaining or those who were good-looking. Although he preferred his partygoers to have both qualities, he occasionally sacrificed beauty for jocularity

Invitations to Henry's wild events were prized. It was common knowledge his parties were outrageous and went on well into the wee hours of the morning. His annual Venetian Masquerade and Arabian Nights Ball often went much later, ending with a survivor's brunch the following day. Looking around the townhouse's Ballroom, Josie was sure tonight would be no exception.

The host provided entertainment for every taste. Before his arrival, Henry had a concert organist play Vierne and Bach on the twenty-four rank pipe organ in his first floor Louis XIV-style Music Room. There, at various times of the night, guests also could hear Gershwin's latest tunes; their old Ragtime favorites and even arias performed by opera singers. To please the flappers, the host raided the Cotton Club. Henry had Ella Fitzgerald and Bessie Smith singing and Jelly Roll Morton and Duke Ellington and his band jamming in the rococo style Ballroom. He also opened up his downstairs Drawing Room, Billiards Room, enclosed Courtyard and Garden to his guests.

In the Drawing Room, the host set up a mini-casino where he offered baccarat, two blackjack tables and roulette. Groups of guests crowded around the tables to watch each other almost as much as to play. The gasps and cheers from roulette occasionally even could be heard above the sounds of the band. In the same room, women played mahjong as their husbands put together X-rated puzzles and their daughters had their fortunes read.

Several times during the evening, in the Drawing Room, Josie demonstrated how to make a cutout of a naked man from an orange peel. She sat on an Italianate, marble, inlaid table with her legs crossed so the large group could all view the process, as she explained holding up the figure to great applause, "Credits go to Joy Kenward-Edgar of London who taught me during the Queen's birthday party this year."

Throughout the night, obscene quantities of alcohol were consumed. Twelve bars were set up around the house and forty-five staff members charged merely with topping up glasses. Plates of imported delicacies were offered to everyone – even the dancers and the band members. Following their evening performance on Broadway of *The Cocoanuts*, the Marx brothers arrived to depict a spoof of Edison's noteworthy experiment that led to electricity in the Ballroom. To great applause Groucho Marx announced at the end of the performance, "Thankfully for all, this is the first and last time for the Marx brothers that electricity will shock their audience."

As the party raged, Henry held a private formal dinner with six courses for twenty-five of the guests in his private second floor quarters. At the same time, several immense buffet tables were arranged in the Ballroom and the Courtyard for the rest of the guests to enjoy. Afterwards, Henry led Josie into the Ballroom to start up the dancing again. The host requested a slow fox trot as the first number. In Henry's arms, Josie floated around the floor. All eyes turned to Henry and Josie as the normal chatter of the party subsided. The magical moment lasted the entire dance. Together they made such a striking couple that even the drunks took note – and there were a lot of them. When the last note of the fox trot gently waned, the band struck up the Charleston. Instantaneously, Henry and Josie swung into motion, as the 120 foot dance floor became crowded with guests.

While the band played, guests gambled, smoked, drank and danced the night away fully knowing that tomorrow morning more money would be made at the market.

* * *

James Ellison DeVere had looked forward to Henry Jay's party. Before leaving for the event, he had paused in front of his three-way mirror to admire himself. With his dark hair and tanned complexion, James could have passed for a Hollywood movie idol off the set of one of the Sheik sequels. He knew few men looked more attractive in white tie. To maintain his physique, he swam two hours every day and played court tennis and squash regularly at New York City's exclusive Tennis and Racquet Club.

James walked briskly towards Henry Jay's townhouse. He was later than he planned to be. Since he moved to New York a few months ago from Pittsburgh where he oversaw his family's concerns, he quickly learned that despite his age, Henry Jay always managed to collect the most attractive people in New York. This was incredibly important to James because he had a gargantuan appetite for women. As he walked into Henry's marble entrance hall, James spotted three ladies with whom he'd already spent the night. He got wet kisses and private invitations from each of them. Recently dubbed the *Most Eligible Bachelor in New York,* James rarely had to spend a night alone. For the most part, he preferred beautiful women who didn't challenge him – except in bed.

Interested in what else he might find before settling for a previous conquest, James headed towards the Ballroom. He paused in the enclosed Courtyard to get a drink and to admire the prominent statue of Bacchus atop a twenty-foot marble fountain with water rushing out of the intricately carved tiered centerpiece. He thought the artistic sculpture reflected most dramatically against the room's glass paneled walls. It was only upon closer inspection he realized that tonight the specially lit Bacchus fountain featured flowing champagne and not water. After topping up twice with this unique set up, James stood for a moment, in one of the open arched, Gothic-styled doorways that separated the Ballroom from the Courtyard. As he took everything in, he thought, this was a perfect setting for the perfect evening – the lights, the music, the over abundance of opulent wealth and most of all, New York's *beautiful people.* Henry Jay had not disappointed him. As he sipped his third glass of champagne, James found it difficult to make a choice since he saw so many attractive girls. Just when he was about to select a bubbly blonde in a gold lame evening dress with a plunging neckline, he saw *her* enter the Ballroom with Henry Jay.

Losing interest immediately in the blonde and everyone else in the room, James took a long sip from his champagne flute and stared. As difficult as it was to believe, she was even lovelier in person than in the newspaper photographs he had seen.

To James she seemed hauntingly beautiful, her features and body evocative of a poet's inspiration. He saw no evidence of the feistiness and deliberately shocking behavior that characterized her speakeasy jaunts. What he did notice was that she was tall and thin, with delicate features and a fine bone structure. Polished and poised, her inner confidence transcended her little flaws, making her simply radiant. With her reputation, he thought, she certainly could have graced the covers of the *London Illustrated News* or *Vogue* magazine, if she had been so inclined.

As James stared at her, Josie gazed up at her godfather, clearly fascinated with what he was saying. New York's most eligible bachelor wanted her to look at him with those adoring eyes. While Henry guided Josie across the dance floor, James was transfixed. To him she was the embodiment of the ideal woman. When the handsome couple finished their dance, New York's most desirable bachelor was filled with jealousy towards Henry Jay since the old codger monopolized *her* attention.

As she prepared to leave at three in the morning, accompanied by Henry's trusted butler, James knew he had to make his move too. Patiently, like a panther, he waited for the ideal moment to pounce. At just the right time, he took Henry aside and asked for an introduction. James then took full advantage of the opportunity when several fawning guests whom he had instructed ahead of time, distracted the host for a photo.

When Josie extended her hand to James, he kissed it. Then he stated with the confidence of a man who has had a great deal of experience, "You are a most beautiful woman." For just a moment, his hand lingered on hers before finally letting go. Noting that as he touched her, she had held her breath and her cheeks had colored despite her best efforts, he whispered just loud enough for her to hear, "I think we would be very good together."

Like most women of her class, Josie wasn't easily flattered. All of her life, men had complemented her – some she knew even actually had meant what they said. But there was something about James that Josie felt was different. She couldn't help taking note. He put her on edge. He certainly was one of the best looking men she had ever met and one of the few who had managed to leave her off-balanced. Although she had thanked him for his complement, there had been an awkward silence afterwards that she couldn't quite overcome. He could have continued the conversation but somehow he had the gift of making her feel as if she should have said something more; for once, she didn't know what that something should have been.

Josie had hoped he hadn't noticed and was relieved by her godfather's return by her side so that she that she could make her excuses and head out the door. But as was often the case, it would take two more enjoyable dances with Henry, a glass and a half of vintage champagne and many hugs and kisses before she finally pulled herself away from her godfather's fete, accompanied by his personal butler and driven home by his driver.

Later, as Josie replayed the highlights of the evening, she lay awake unable to sleep. She tried to assure herself that perhaps she was just overtired. Normally she knew exactly what to say and how to say it to achieve the desired response. Politeness and putdowns readily flowed from her mouth. She always had been nothing other than extremely quick witted but somehow with James she had lost her tongue. She realized that she had felt this way once before – the other night at Texas Guinan's. James had the same effect on Josie as her barman.

After Josie left, James wasted no time. Picking up another glass of champagne, he looked for *that* blonde. She was standing with a pretty brunette and a few admirers. He thought he could blow the other boys out in a matter of minutes. To be sure, he gave her a look from across the room to see her reaction. She melted.

Confidently, James strode over to her. Without so much as an acknowledgement of the gentlemen in the group, James put his arm around the blonde as if he was familiar. He said, "Darling shall we?" The blonde didn't have to be asked twice. She thought James was the "Cat's Meow."

As they started leaving, her brunette friend came running after them. Also attracted to James, she begged the couple to let her join them. The girls were flattered by James' attention. Of course they knew who he was. They had been watching him all night. The blonde had been sure he was interested in her earlier – as he had been before he saw Josie. She cursed the boys who had surrounded her afraid their presence had put off the desirable bachelor. When he came up to her and whisked her away, she was more than ready.

James gallantly requested the women's cloaks as the party broke up. As he helped the blonde into her patterned lame evening wrap trimmed with fox, he noticed she dyed her hair. He didn't care as long as the rest of her was real. As the group left Henry's, James suggested moving on to an afterhours place.

James figured that after a few more drinks, he'd be able to do whatever he wanted with the pair. He took the girls to Belle's pleasure palace. It was a noisy, wild speakeasy – just the kind of environment he sought since he didn't want to have to make small talk. Sometime after four in the morning, he brought them to the Pierre Hotel. Regardless of his companions, he insisted on comfortable, plush surroundings.

James gave the receptionist a little extra to check into a room under another name because he was slightly embarrassed by his companions' behavior. Both women had become quite demonstrative. He knew he didn't need to give them any more alcohol. As they rode up in the elevator, he feared the blonde already had too much. She was hanging on him and talking embarrassingly loudly to the elevator operator.

Sticking her hand out to the man, she said with a goofy voice in an overly friendly way, "I'm Mary and this is my friend Elizabeth." Then as she pointed towards James, she said her voice piercing, "Do you know who he is?" James frowned.

He sighed in relief when she said, "He's gonna marry me."

James had played into her naïveté. He told the blonde she should think of what they were doing as a preview to their wedding night. When she inquired about her friend's presence, he claimed, "This is just the rehearsal."

The brunette was too splifficated to object. She just kept smiling dumbly and repeating the same words as she pointed towards James, "I think you're cute."

Bored with their drunken conversation, James wasted no time when they got into the room. Pulling down his pants, he ordered the brunette to go down on her knees.

Grinning, he said as he pushed her head down, "Meet my special friend. He's cute too." Then he tore off her clothes.

* * *

CHAPTER III

James woke up early the next morning. Even though he only had a few hours of sleep, he felt refreshed. Seeing a flicker of bright light peeking through the curtains, he dressed quickly. He didn't bother to wake the still sleeping women since he had nothing to say to them. In truth, he couldn't even remember their names. He hadn't been with them for the conversation.

After his nocturnal activities, New York's most eligible bachelor looked forward to a big breakfast. His appetite was sated next door at the Metropolitan club where he also read the morning papers. For once, he didn't see anything of great interest in the *Wall Street Journal*. Turning next to the *New York Times*, he first looked through the international news section. James rolled his eyes as he read the headlines. The Jews and Palestinians were fighting again in the Middle East, the Germans were complaining about reparation payments and some guy in India named Gandhi was protesting the British salt tax. James turned the page quickly. He couldn't believe anyone who dressed in sheets would prove much of a long-term problem for the British Empire. In any case, since the situation didn't affect his interests, he didn't really care. Before he tossed aside the paper, he found one useful piece of news. Given only several lines and buried well inside the publication was an item that James considered potentially explosive. A troubling case of foot and mouth disease had surfaced this week in the Midwest. He gleaned more cases were expected. Given the likely impact on livestock prices, the savvy businessman immediately made arrangements to buy futures before the market opened.

* * *

After showering and changing at home, James walked over to 59th Street, where he crossed 5th Avenue and headed towards the West side. A few minutes later, he entered the Carnegie Hall tower and went directly to the suite occupied by astrologist Evelyn Maker. James had consulted the clairvoyant on various matters since 1927. Like numerous Americans, he was impressed with her track record of uncanny, accurate predictions and roster of noteworthy clients.

Miss Maker predicted Lindbergh's solo flight to within minutes. She also foretold of the 1923 Tokyo earthquake and pinpointed Rudolf Valentino's death to the day. But for many of her clients, what made this fortuneteller most unusual was her understanding of the financial world. Among others, Mary Pickford, J.P Morgan, the Prince of Wales and even steel tycoon Charles Schwab repeatedly had relied on her powers for these matters. Their pictures as well as a number of other luminaries lined the walls of the richly decorated waiting room like some great portrait gallery, creating credibility and even respectability.

Richly decorated in every way, the plush waiting room was designed to placate her clients for the often-long period they spent there as well as to provide visible proof of Evelyn's success. Clients frequently commented on how the furnishings befitted royalty. In fact, everything other than the stock ticker and the clairvoyant's newsletters came from the collection of a Russian nobleman who did not have the benefit of the Great Seer's predictions in 1917 and subsequently relied on the astrologist's star gazing for the best sale price of his heirlooms. As a result, Evelyn acquired the entire lot: twelve Faberge eggs, four gigantic urns, two Persian carpets, sixteen red velvet upholstered gilded chairs and four matching sofas for less than the month's rent for her office.

As James surveyed the room he wondered how many of the clairvoyant's clients were suckers? He could tell several clearly had made their money in the market. It annoyed him to see these paper millionaires dilute the power of his class – the old wealthy. He bided his time for the day of reckoning. James smiled to himself as he thought how 1929 already had proved more turbulent than the last few for investors. Even though the general market gains had been unprecedented over the last few years, he thought stocks had spiked too high too quickly and a serious correction was inevitable. He couldn't believe how many people didn't – even from his class.

James knew one member of the power elite, who wouldn't get hurt - former President Coolidge. The young businessman had been informed by a very reliable source that the popular official had chosen not to seek re-election because he had believed that the economic good times were near an end and had advised those closest to him to sell their stocks.

After fifty minutes, Evelyn's secretary finally invited James into the seer's inner sanctuary. The simplicity of the room where she individually met with her clients and consulted the stars starkly contrasted with the grand waiting area. The clairvoyant's private chamber was sparsely furnished only with early American furniture. Barren and cold, James always thought the uncarpeted room purposefully was designed to make her clients uneasy. Like the seer herself, James found the room rather creepy.

Evelyn's inner sanctum had one small round table and two American Windsor chairs in addition to a Goddard block-front desk and a Cromwellian styled sideboard that displayed the tools of her trade. For consultations, the chairs were positioned opposite each other. The client chair faced Evelyn and a wall lined with bookcases stacked with titles portending to astrological matters. Occasionally the astrologer would get up mid-session to consult one of the well-worn bindings in Greek, Latin, Sanskrit, and other languages not known by most of those seeking her aid. While her clients' viewed the overwhelming evidence of her knowledge in the form of the bookcases behind the clairvoyant, for her part, as Evelyn worked, she had a perfect view of the wall with the room's only fireplace and more importantly, the small nineteenth century clock on the mantel piece. Without her clients' knowing, the seer always could gage the time.

As he peered down at the already seated severe-looking woman dressed entirely in black, James thought he wouldn't have been surprised if she had claimed that in a past life she had been convicted as a witch.

After he sat down across from the seer, James channeled all his energy towards her. He focused entirely on her, making her feel like the most important person in the world. Just when he had her eating out of his hand, the fortune-teller snapped out of the trance he had put on her.

Concentrating on her job, she got a hold of herself. As she put on her glasses, she saw through the handsome rogue in front of her as clearly as any of her predictions. Sharply the clairvoyant said to James, "You're not a very nice man." Evelyn was angry with him but even more upset with herself for finding him attractive. She stated to him as much as a reminder to herself, "Don't think you'll get anywhere with me!"

Caught off guard by her assertion, James replied indignantly, "As if I'd have any interest!" Realizing too late that he had been offensive with his statement, he attempted to smooth things over with his next move. Leaning across the small mahogany table with spider-like legs that separated them, as he looked deeply into her green eyes and covered her hands with his, James whispered almost intimately as if his words were those of affection, "I am here to learn from you."

Evelyn couldn't deny there was a certain truth in what he said. Softening, her face and body relaxed.

Taking advantage of the situation, he continued playfully, his eyes expressive, "You know I do believe you owe me. My reputation and looks are such that they are financially beneficial to you."

Aware of his numerous indiscretions, Evelyn laughed. She retorted in the spirit of their light banter, "Quite the contrary, my dear sir. Any association with you would cost me dearly!"

Pretending to be surprised, James replied, "Surely I don't know what you mean."

"Don't be tedious!" exclaimed the clairvoyant. She gave him a knowing look as she asserted, "We both know I'd lose more business from young ladies who wish they'd never met you!"

James countered, "But if you hung my portrait in your waiting room, you'd attract so many more women to your establishment who haven't yet had the opportunity."

"Well, at least we agree that those who have met you wouldn't make the mistake twice," replied Evelyn tartly. Then, lifting her eyebrow at James, an amused Evelyn asked out of curiosity, "And just where should your picture be?"

Cockily he stated, "Although I'd prefer a wall to myself, I could settle for being placed between J.P. Morgan and Edward Windsor." Ignoring the clairvoyant's gasp, James asserted, "After all, I have the business acumen of Morgan and the taste and appeal to women of the Prince of Wales."

"I'll give you this, you don't have any humility," retorted Evelyn.

Then, as she started to consult her tarot cards she said, "Come now. Time is short. Let's see what the stars' divine." Taking a deep breath, Evelyn said frowning as she reviewed his choices, "It seems other women are not as bright or privileged as I am." After she further compared his cards to his charts and made several notes, she said, "Within a year and a half you will possess the woman of your dreams."

While James grinned at the thought, Evelyn muttered under her breath, "God help her."

* * *

CHAPTER IV

It was nearly eleven in the morning when Josie's mother pulled open the antique rose drapes in her Marie Antoinette inspired bedroom. As Claire Baxter-Browne kissed her daughter on the forehead, she said, "It's time to go."

Josie smiled, then rolled over and went back to sleep in her elaborately canopied satinwood state bed. Twenty minutes later, her mother returned armed with a few pieces of ice. Throwing back the pale pink satin bedspread, blankets and Egyptian cotton sheets, she placed the ice on Josie's feet. As Josie jumped out of bed screaming, her youthful mother laughed.

As Claire walked out of her daughter's room, she said, "Meet me in the hall in five minutes. Michael has already brought the car to the front."

Josie quickly threw on a Chanel jersey suit, ran a comb through her hair and bolted for the stairs to meet her mother. She was in such a rush that when she tossed her silk gossamer Callot Soeurs nightgown onto the bed and it instead fell onto the Aubusson carpet, she didn't bother to pick it up.

Ten minutes later, the Baxter-Browne women, who looked more like sisters than mother and daughter, strolled into the Palm Court at the Plaza Hotel. In his social column, Maury Paul noted that New York's comely, slender grand dame, *the* Mrs. Whitney Straight, the fetchingly attractive, petite brunette Stanleys and the shapely Ashleys joined the Chanel clad Baxter-Brownes. While the social columnist and fashion commentator noted the dowager's navy Molyneux suit and fetching Madame Agnes turban and complemented Rebecca on her new, shorter shingled hair style and Suzanne Talbot cloche hat that made her appear taller, he found Geraldine's Nile-green, georgette dress with a gypsy girdle "did nothing for her."

While a quartet played Mozart's "Four Seasons," Maury Paul prepared his column and the ladies lunched. He noted Catherine Thompson and her mother, Gertrude Thayer Thompson (Mrs. John R. Thompson), would have joined the group as usual if they had been in town. Unfortunately, the unexpected death of Catherine's Great Aunt, who lived in Paris, meant the Thompsons were not able to attend the weekly luncheon. The social columnist wrote that New York society looked forward to the imminent return of the Thompsons who would be coming back shortly by way of Cunard's luxury liner, the *Berengaria*.

After ordering lunch, Mrs. Whitney Straight proposed a toast. "To the glorious stock market!" She explained that she had just returned from her broker's office and wanted to celebrate another record performance for her portfolio.

Beaming, the grand dame announced that by buying and selling stocks, she had made several million dollars in the last year alone. As the conversation turned to money, Mrs. Stanley, a delicate, hazel eyed, former southern belle from a once prosperous planter family, looked at Mrs. Whitney Straight disdainfully.

Euphoric about her earnings, Mrs. Whitney Straight remained oblivious to Mrs. Stanley's response and continued gleefully, "My stock earnings now allow me to have financial independence from my husband."

Appalled, Mrs. Stanley said aghast. "Adele! I can't believe what you are saying. Are you contemplating a divorce?"

"Not at all," said Mrs. Whitney Straight. "I adore Mr. W.S., but I also love my economic independence." Unable to resist making the comment, the grand dame then explained as her eyes twinkled, "The main reason I enjoy earning my own money is so I don't have to listen to how *hard* Mr. W.S. works for his."

Finding her friend's logic as incomprehensible as her humor, Mrs. Stanley stammered, "But you have your own money! Your family left you with a trust."

"Inheriting money is just not the same as earning it." Mrs. Whitney Straight insisted, "Self-sufficiency is empowering."

"I think money-making is a sordid business," countered Mrs. Stanley adamantly. After an awkward silence, where even she realized her denunciation fell on deaf ears, she spluttered almost apologetically, "It's positively *boring!*"

"You also thought voting was too difficult a task for women before we got that right!" retorted the unmoved suffragist who was the first New York socialite to cut off her locks and one of the first to embrace the super short Eton crop.

Making it clear where she still stood when it came to enfranchisement, Mrs. Stanley who still coiled her long hair in a chignon asserted, "I still rely on my husband to tell me which candidate is the right one for us."

Exasperated, Mrs. Whitney Straight rolled her eyes.

Diplomatically Claire Baxter-Browne tried to change the subject by asking, "Is anyone planning to attend the Huntsman's Ball this year?"

"We live in the age of the automobile. Horses are passé!" exclaimed Mrs. Whitney Straight sourly.

"I think it will be *the* event of the season," countered Mrs. Stanley. Frostily she stated, "I am on the committee."

"I meant no offense by my comment," said Mrs. Whitney Straight quickly.

"No offense taken," replied Mrs. Stanley just as promptly.

Mrs. Whitney Straight graciously offered, "I will, of course, support you by taking a table."

The proud chairwoman asserted, "No need Adele. We are over-subscribed."

"Already?" replied Mrs. Whitney Straight clearly impressed. Having chaired the first Huntsman's Ball forty years before when horses meant something and so did the money of the Old Guard, the dowager knew only too well how difficult it could be to fill a charity event.

"I heard you sold more tickets this year for the ball than in the entire history of the event. Is that right?" inquired Lady Ashley.

"Indeed it is," acknowledged the current chairwoman. "Although I will admit there are a few responses that I do not wholly approve."

"Oh really?" replied the women leaning closer for an explanation.

"Yes, you know, '*new*' money," whispered Mrs. Stanley confidentially.

While Mrs. Stanley gossiped about the offensive people to Lady Ashley and Claire Baxter-Browne, Mrs. Whitney Straight had more interesting matters to discuss with the girls. She explained, "From my experience, playing the market is really simple. Anyone can do it. Every day fortunes are made by ordinary workers and the middle class!" Half joking, the salt and pepper haired, grand dame of society informed the girls, "Between us, I think the only reason men haven't wanted us involved in business is because women would realize we actually don't need them."

Seeing the girls clearly were interested in what she had to say, Mrs. Whitney Straight enthusiastically said to Josie, Rebecca and Geraldine, "Times are changing. It's very important for you girls to be exposed to business." Enthusiastically she offered, "If you like, I'll take you to my brokerage after lunch."

After settling the bill, Mrs. Stanley declined the offer. Taking Rebecca by the hand, as she got up to go, she said coolly, "My husband is handling our finances very well. I think the act of making money is simply - vulgar - and I don't see any need to expose my daughter to such a working glass mentality." Emphatically the diminutive woman stated, her voice pitching higher and higher as she got emotionally worked up until she practically screeched, "My Rebecca has been raised to be a lady in society – not to mingle with shop girls and secretaries!"

Having witnessed Mrs. Stanley's hysterics on a number of occasions and noticing that Rebecca was getting increasingly embarrassed by the situation, Josie squeezed her friend's hand under the table to let her know she felt bad for her. She often thought Rebecca's mother was extremely vocally opinionated without reason. Although she herself often disagreed with her own mother, at times like these, Josie considered herself lucky that however disappointed or angry, Claire found it much more effective to put pressure on her headstrong daughter in private.

As Rebecca and Mrs. Stanley left to go shopping at Bergdorf Goodman, Lady Ashley said, "I've had no interest in money, but a visit to your brokerage would be a laugh."

Also game, Geraldine picked up her sketchbook and prepared to go.

Claire Baxter-Browne said sheepishly, "My husband runs a bank, but I haven't the slightest idea what he really does. He tried to explain things to me once, but it was all rather confusing. Perhaps with your help, I might understand a bit more."

Delighted with the exposure, Josie thought that the trip could be quite enlightening. She asked the concierge at the hotel for some stationary and a pen to take notes in case she saw something worth committing to memory. Tapped by *Vogue* magazine to serve as a social commentator, Josie had great fun going to parties and writing about her friends. Occasionally she also submitted articles to other magazines on more serious topics.

Considered the darling of the English department and a Glascock Poetry winner, after graduating from Mount Holyoke with high honors the previous year, Josie had expected she'd have no trouble becoming a regular contributor to the *New Yorker* while she worked on her first book of poetry. To what degree her hopes were dashed by her success as a debutante as opposed to the fact that there simply were many other far more talented writers wasn't clear. Regardless, her attempt to join the literati's Algonquin Round Table certainly only could be viewed as a spectacular failure culminating in a highly publicized scathing putdown by Dorothy Parker who described her poetry as sophomoric – "just what you'd expect from a deb – pretty to look at but lacking any substance."

Depressed, dejected and infuriated by the criticism, Josie shed endless tears over the snub but nonetheless forced herself to continue writing her social diary for *Vogue* and to submit the occasional article for other periodicals – even the *New Yorker*. The aspiring writer tried hard not to take the rejection personally. Her friends claimed Dorothy Parker was jealous of her – that the literary world's doyenne simply didn't want an attractive, younger competitor in *her* inner circle. But, true to herself, Josie also knew Parker's talents, unlike her own, were beyond question. For better or worse, the Algonquin Table rebuff led to her loss of interest in writing poetry.

For several months, Josie remained dispirited. Her social prominence magnified her own doubts. After the build-up leading to her crowning as the debutante of 1929, she knew the gossip columnists and other girls and their mothers looked forward to publicly broadcasting her failings. Growing up, she had witnessed this vicious cycle dozens of times. Although Josie generally didn't care what others thought of her, the attack on her proposed career and sniping in her own circles hurt more than she expected. In the immediate aftermath, she had to force herself to attend events merely out of the necessity to appear unaffected.

By hiding her hurt behind a veil of frivolity and flurry of social activity, during this time she managed to get Maury Paul and

Cholly Knickerbocker to focus not on her shortcomings but rather on the Junior League events she suddenly took unprecedented interest in chairing. Privately she had nursed thoughts of confronting Dorothy Parker and telling the woman exactly what she thought of her and what pain her callous remarks had caused. But for once she had curbed her natural impulsive nature, reckoning upon reflection it only would lead to another acerbic attack by the seasoned writer. Still, never one to accept defeat easily, Josie put her ego aside to see a potential opportunity in the setback. The socialite even considered asking the acclaimed critic to become her mentor. On three occasions she actually walked down to West 44th Street and stood outside the Algonquin Hotel in the hope of intercepting the formidable woman. But after reading more of Ms. Parker's reviews, learning more about her personality and seriously thinking about what she enjoyed writing most, Josie thought it wise to give up her pursuit of becoming Parker's protégé.

Not one to sulk too long or to be dismissed by one rejection, eight months after the humiliation, Josie enthusiastically embraced a new literary venture. With the help of Geraldine, she established a humorous magazine entitled *Twenties Humor*, where she and other "mediocre" writers poked fun of the literary establishment that lambasted them as well as social conventions, religious zealots and other hot topics that appealed to the just over twenty crowd. Although panned by critics as just an extension of *College Humor*, a publication to which Josie had frequently contributed as a student, no one could question its appeal. Drawing initially first on the talents of her friends and a few recent graduates, due to Josie's stature, determination, and promotional efforts, within its first year, the publication became the most popular satirical rag for the Flaming Youth.

Although there were still times when she'd feel low and then subsequently angry when gossips took potshots at her for her failure to become a "serious writer," Josie countered that she had more fun with her writers' clique that was composed of people *her* own age who wrote things that interested *her* generation specifically than she would have done if she hadn't been an Algonquin Table reject.

By the time the ladies finally left the Plaza, Josie had scribbled down a few angles and specific questions she planned to ask the lady investors for *Twenties Humor.* She noted she found it quite irking that when she attempted to walk into one of the traditional brokerages at the Plaza for a comparison, she was not even allowed to do more than peer inside the doorway because of her gender.

Once outside the hotel, Mrs. Whitney Straight stopped the Baxter-Brownes and Ashleys from ordering their cars and suggested instead that the ladies all went in hers. As she got behind the wheel of her Silver Cloud Rolls Royce, she shocked her friends by bombastically announcing, "I'll drive."

"But you had the most marvelous driver before," replied Lady Ashley. "What was his name? Bigford? What happened to him? He came from Suffolk around the same village as my great grandparents."

Her gray eyes twinkling with laughter, Mrs. Whitney Straight said, "*Bigford* is the one who got me into the market."

"You don't say!" chimed the women together.

Then Lady Ashley inquired, "How so?"

The grand dame explained, "When Bigford turned in his notice, naturally I asked him what he was going to do. You know he had been very happy with us, so I was quite surprised when he decided to leave."

"Who's he working for now?" inquired Claire.

The women looked confused at Mrs. Whitney Straight when she replied, "For himself."

As they set off she explained, "Bigford made an absolute fortune in the market by buying on margin. He started small after the slump of '21 and now has several million dollars. He's been a great teacher! You should see his place!"

"Where does he live on Park – over one of the little shops?" inquired Lady Ashley kindly.

"My dears, he's at 1040," stated Mrs. Whitney Straight. Confidentially she informed her friends, "He has a ten room apartment on the top floor."

Lady Ashley gasped, "Your old driver has a penthouse?"

"That's right," replied the grand dame. Then shocking her friends even more, she said, "He's just across from the Nasts."

Josie giggled as her mother gasped. 1040 Park Avenue was considered one of the most exclusive, grand apartment buildings in New York. A lot of the old families had sold their townhouses and had taken spacious residences in this complex. They both knew Mrs. Stanley would be destroyed if she learned Bigford lived at 1040. Last year after the Stanleys were robbed, they had seriously considered moving into the building, and it hadn't even been on one of the top floors.

Thinking of the impact of the stock market on the social breakdown of the Old Guard in New York, Josie said, "I wonder if Bigford saw that article by John Jacob Raskob's in *Reader's Digest*. If I remember correctly, Raskob asserted that the average American could become rich just by buying stock. I guess he's right. If Bigford can move into 1040, everyone in America has the potential of becoming a millionaire through *this* market!"

Several minutes later, as Adele Whitney Straight pulled up in front of the Waldorf Astoria, attentive valet attendants opened the doors for the women and parked the automobile. Once inside, the women headed to the private suite on the second floor. The sign outside read: "Ladies Only."

Geraldine picked up her pad and started sketching. The blue velvet drapes with matching valances and tiebacks were drawn and the lighting kept dim. Otherwise, the wall-papered lounge resembled the sitting rooms found in the dorms of any of the seven sister colleges. From the gilded mirrors and crystal chandelier hanging from the decorative ceiling rosette, to the inlaid tables, comfortable overstuffed chairs and antique sofas, the décor of the Ladies' Brokerage seemed very familiar to the upper class women. To those not born into the elite, the suite offered them the chance to learn what it was like if they had enough money to open a sizable account.

There was only an hour left before the exchange closed. The clients were so busy following the ticker that few looked up to acknowledge Mrs. Whitney Straight and her guests. Periodically, a burst of delight was emitted by one of the ladies when a sizable profit was made. Glasses clinked and Turkish cigarettes lit up.

Mrs. Whitney Straight showed her friends the ropes. Using the ticker, they found several of the grand dame's stocks by their symbols and calculated how much money she made during the day. With Anaconda Copper up over five points, Steel up four and GM near its all time high, without even calculating her more speculative holdings, Mrs. Whitney Straight had made a paper profit of $35,153 as they lunched. The women were highly impressed with how easy it was to make money from stocks.

After the market closed, Josie talked with several clients. She was surprised to learn that one of the most sophisticatedly dressed women was a former Midwestern housewife who had left her abusive husband on their pig farm after an investment tip in an auto stock led to an overnight profit of over $67,000. Since then, the woman had bought mail-order houses that netted her close to $550,000 in the past year alone. Now the investor informed Josie she was bullish about National City, a stock that traded at over 500 points per share. Josie and Geraldine soon heard numerous tales of former seamstresses, washerwomen, divorcees and even grand dames like Mrs. Whitney Straight, who daily made vast sums through investing in stocks.

While Geraldine and Josie looked around the suite before leaving, Geraldine said, "There's one problem with this place."

"What's that?" inquired Josie.

Geraldine asked, "Why should women have to buy stocks segregated from men – in suites like this – why can't they trade on Wall Street?"

"Perhaps women would rather not subject themselves to a group of egotistical men smoking cheap cigars," Josie replied jokingly.

The girls laughed. Geraldine added Josie's comment as the caption to her sketch of the place. The girls decided to submit the piece to the *Vogue* as well as printing it with Josie's article in *Twenties Humor*.

With close to 5,000 ladies only brokerage offices in the United States, female investors had become ubiquitous and a source of interest for the *Vogue's* readers. The editorial staff immediately selected the sketch and printed it in one of the hottest issues focused on the flapper scene.

Josie thought it was time she found out even more about the market.

A week later, the stock market was still on Josie's mind as she sat between Randolph Churchill and Warren Bates during J.D. Rockefeller's dinner party in honor of Randolph's father, Winston. Josie was having a wonderful time. What she did not know was it had not been planned that way.

* * *

CHAPTER V

J.D. Rockefeller went all out for his fete in honor of Winston Churchill. New York's business, political, and social elite vied for invitations to the gala evening. Several who were not included unabashedly lobbied to be on the guest list. Others simply took the slight as a personal affront, refusing to understand how the host could consider the dinner party a success worthy of the notable Englishman without their presence. J.D. heard one bitter uninvited guest subsequently declared to anyone who would listen that Churchill's career was finished anyway!

But with so many prominent people of arguably equal status from the social register in attendance, J.D. found the seating arrangement for his fifty guests equally challenging. While he wasn't certain even moments before the dinner if he had gotten his arrangement right by placing the Raskobs near the Baxter-Brownes, Bushes, and Kahns and not next to the Morgans, Ashleys, and Astors, he was sure he had made one guest happy by deliberately placing Josie between James and Warren Bates.

Since Warren was a crashing bore, J.D. figured James would have ample opportunity to chat up the attractive socialite. He knew his friend would appreciate the gesture since New York's most desirable bachelor frequently told his jibing friends he would settle down if he found the right woman. J.D. suspected James and Josie would get on very well together. When James arrived, the grinning host took him aside to say, "Just wait until you see who I put next to you!"

As James spotted Josie from across the room, he smiled knowingly. But while J.D. and James exchanged pleasantries, Winston's rascally son, Randolph Churchill, switched his seating card with the one belonging to New York's most eligible bachelor. Like James, Randolph also had noticed the stunning beauty that wore a sleek silk Lucille gown and a fashionably long triple strand of pearls. Winston Churchill's son had been so taken by her that he requested an introduction as soon as he saw her arrive with her parents. The cheery cheeked, young blond man who appreciated his double brandies almost as much as beautiful ladies, enjoyed conversing with the engaging debutante so much before dinner that he decided to ensure they continued their discussion.

Randolph barely kept a straight face as the party moved into the American Empire styled dining room. While he led Josie to her chair and sat down next to her, the college student watched with great amusement as James' confusion turned to exasperation when he realized he not only was not seated by Josie but he had been put right next to Adele Whitney Straight!

Randolph found it doubly amusing when James, who was unaware of the switch, cursed J.D. instead of him. James fumed thinking his old school friend had not only successfully wound him up but also apparently knew about his embarrassing incident with the grand dame. Much to his chagrin, New York's most eligible bachelor had plenty of time to stew about the situation as Randolph busily entertained the girl James wanted to seduce. Although he was clever enough to ensure that no one at the table was aware of his feelings, it took two courses before his mood improved.

James initially feigned interest in the light table conversation and in his quail egg and caviar starter as he strained to listen to Josie and Randolph's discussion. But when those around him started discussing the market, New York's most eligible bachelor regained his appetite for other things. Always one to make the best out of a situation and come out on top, James now set a new goal.

Taking advantage of his close proximity to J.D.'s talented uncle Percy, the scion did his best to impress the man. He planned to be financially rewarded for his efforts with an invitation to partake in a pool organized by Michael Meehan in which J.D.'s uncle was rumored to be involved.

Josie found Randolph such an engaging companion that with the exception of his father, she hardly paid any attention to the rest of the party. For the duration of the dinner, Randolph monopolized Josie with amusing accounts of his American tour. Winston's son regaled 1929's most celebrated debutante with his tales from the Churchill coast-to-coast trip where the men were the guests of some of the most notable Americans. Josie listened with keen interest as he recounted their visit to newspaper tycoon William Randolph Hearst's castle San Simeon, described the beauty of Lake Louise in the Canadian Rockies which he suspected his father would soon paint in brilliant colors upon their return and told her how they nearly were caught red-handed by American prohibition agents as they crossed the border between the United States and Canada with lots of hooch. When Josie told him about her night at Texas Guinan's, Randolph laughed almost as hard as she had when he described how his father stuffed the illegal drinks in his bags. As the evening progressed, the young couple realized they had quite a lot in common. While Winston's son was much more interested in politics than Josie, they shared an interest in "the truth" and both were aspiring journalists.

Occasionally, as Randolph spoke about the critical issues of their times, she noticed how the young man's eyes would catch his father's, from far across the table, as older man periodically checked on the son he fondly called Chumbolly. Josie thought they had the same mischievous, twinkling blue eyes, reddish complexions, round shaped faces and general body types with broad if slightly stooped shoulders, although Winston was clearly shorter and more portly and Randolph still had a full head of hair. Given the Ex-Chancellor of the Exchequer's reputation, Josie would later tell Geraldine how shocked she had been by just how short he was. She reckoned he only was about five feet six inches tall. Yet despite his age and size, by the end of the evening she would understand why this remarkable man was renowned for his commanding presence that rarely failed to captivate those assembled.

Although Josie had been to Europe over a dozen times, she had never traveled to the American West Coast or into Canada. Curious, she asked Randolph as they paused between courses, "What have you enjoyed most?"

More interested in pleasing his dinner companion, Randolph replied flirtatiously, "You!"

"Very funny!" retorted Josie as she laughed at Randolph before grilling him like the most seasoned journalist.

Understanding this debutante had a brain as well as a noteworthy body, he said seriously to Josie, "Aside from you, I've enjoyed the natural beauty of America. My father's friend, Bernie Baruch – well, you know him – was kind enough to lend us his private railway car for traveling. As a result, I've been privileged to see a great deal. So much of your country is simply breathtaking."

"And what do you think of Americans?" inquired Warren, as he finally managed to join the conversation.

"Since my grandmother was an American, I'm quite a fan of American ladies," replied Randolph as he meaningfully gazed at Josie. His eyes twinkled with the mischief he knew he was causing. Randolph could tell he was irritating the infatuated Warren. The prankster enjoyed winding up the bore. Although years later she would remember sensing irascibility in his nature, at the time Josie couldn't help but laugh. Randolph, like his father, had quite a way with words.

While Warren glumly picked at the remnants of his food, Randolph planned his next move. J.D. had arranged a break between the main courses and dessert for those who danced. As the servers cleared the plates the twelve-piece orchestra started play-ing a tango.

Busy discussing his family's midtown development project, an art deco complex called Rockefeller Center, with Winston, Albert Baxter-Browne, John Jacob Raskob, Prescott Bush and their wives, J.D. was oblivious of the music.

Quickly realizing J.D.'s grandiose designs would pre-occupy him for some time, Randolph didn't wait for his host to dance the first number. He decided J.D. wouldn't mind if he even noticed Randolph's disregard for etiquette. Refusing to take anything oth-er than yes as an answer to his request for the first dance and every single one after that, Randolph filled Josie's dance card and took her hand in his, leading her onto the parquet floor.

While Josie and Randolph danced, J.D. finished providing de-tails about his family's massive undertaking and John Jacob Raskob proudly described his construction plans for the tallest structure in the world, a project he dubbed the Empire State Building. To make room for his steel skyscraper, Raskob informed the group he had to demolish the old Waldorf Astoria hotel. J.D. also ac-knowledged the Rockefellers' planned to knock down a Vander-bilt mansion and a number of other structures for their complex. As the men discussed the doomed sites, it became clear to those seated that the new buildings would forever change the city's sky-line. With this knowledge, a hushed silence came over the table as the diners contemplated the world they were building.

To those seated, the monumental changes that symbolized the sweeping technological innovation and progress of the century unquestionably were awe-inspiring. But to a few, especially the Vanderbilts, these buildings on some level were unsettling.

The elite gathered had an unspoken understanding that change of any kind, even progress, came with a price. None knew exactly what this meant only that it was inevitable. Several silently questioned whether the crowning achievements of the gods of mechanization and industry represented an impersonal, cold new age where technology could dominate the human spirit.

As they pondered the future, the adults at the dinner table gradually became aware of the popular music in the background and the ingenuous young couple who now confidently danced the Black Bottom. The innocent youth moved almost with reckless abandon, making the most of the moment, not knowing what tomorrow would bring, not even caring, just accepting without a question or thought, their life of leisure and prosperity that came from the greatest economic boom in the history of the world.

While some at the table worried that the Flaming Youth and the industrialist developers together represented an egotistical, decadent lot not seen since the last days of the Roman Empire and a hallmark sign of troubles to come, most were more sanguine.

As the quiet businessman Prescott Bush looked at Josie and Randolph, he murmured almost to himself, "America's future is in her children."

Later, when the reserved but warm Albert and Winston exchanged smiles as they looked at the photo of Prescott's young son, George Herbert Walker Bush. Albert thought the good-looking brown haired boy from Connecticut certainly had been baptized with an impressive string of names with almost dynastic pretensions. When the proud father mentioned he hoped to become a member of Congress one day, Winston imagined little Bushes running the nation's capitol.

Politics was far from their minds as Randolph and Josie smiled and laughed, dancing number after number. Their movements had not gone unnoticed by the younger generation that was present. Both James and Warren watched Josie intently as she confidently moved across the floor. Making a list in his head of all of Randolph's real and imagined shortcomings, James rationalized that as much as New York's most celebrated debutante clearly enjoyed Randolph's company, the debutante's radiance had more to do with the fact that she just loved dancing.

Determined to spend time with the girl with whom he had expected to spend the entire dinner and confident in his own dancing abilities, New York's most eligible bachelor purposefully strode onto the dance floor with the intention of interrupting the couple. Unfortunately for James, Randolph spotted him and had no intention of relinquishing his partner to the arrogant, handsome suitor. Turning Josie around to avoid his competitor, he passed her onto his father, who had noticed the enfolding events with some interest and secretly looked forward to the opportunity of dancing with this dark haired American beauty.

Taking the partner switch in stride, Josie easily adjusted to Winston's step as they resumed moving across the room. She was mightily impressed when the music changed that he wasn't thrown off and managed to shimmy almost as well as his son, despite his claim of not being much of a dancer.

When Josie told him as much, he replied drying, "I had rather hoped you'd say I was a bit better."

While they danced, Josie asked the former Chancellor of the Exchequer about his current interests. Although Mrs. Whitney-Straight and Lady Ashley had warned her that Winston was a conversation hog, as he spoke about his fondness for painting, polo playing, and his Marlborough progenitors, she couldn't imagine wanting to interrupt him. As Josie later would tell her friends, his boundless energy and enthusiasm coupled with an occasional brilliance of thought and a delivery quite unrivalled made him one of the most fascinating people she'd ever met.

Having heard from Randolph and others about his jaunts to the casinos in the Riviera, and thinking of stocks as a safer bet than gambling since her visit to the Ladies' Brokerage, Josie asked the former Chancellor of the Exchequer if he was playing the market.

Charmed by the lovely girl whom he regarded as almost the same age as his older daughters, Diana and Sarah, he replied, "Miss Baxter-Browne, you are so delightful, I wouldn't mind anything you asked me!"

"Of course that doesn't mean you'd give me an answer," retorted Josie in good humor.

Churchill chuckled as he remarked, keeping in the spirit of the light banter, "For an American, you have great wit!"

She acknowledged, "From the British standpoint, that doesn't take much."

Swinging her around, Winston replied, "Perhaps not. But you certainly are highly sophisticated and unusual in a most delightful way."

While Winston led Josie back to the table for dessert, he admitted he was quite involved in the American market. Honestly, he admitted, "I'd like to take credit for my financial prowess, but in fact I owe my earnings to American genius." As Winston smiled at several of the men at the table, he asserted, "With the help of Bernie Baruch and a few other chaps, I've done pretty well." He noted wryly, "In fact, based upon my stocks' performances in comparison to the abysmal results from the last election in which the British public told those of us in the Conservative party to sod off, I think I should consider retiring entirely from politics and playing the market."

"But you can't do that!" protested Josie.

Winston stated adamantly, "I can." Then, as he lit a large, Cuban cigar, he said firmly and quite deliberately before taking a puff, "But I won't because I still believe Britain needs men like me."

"Here Here!" came the resounding response from the dinner party guests.

Feeling it was an appropriate time for a toast in honor of the guest, Josie's father, who was considered by many to embody the

ideal physical and personality characteristics of an American gentleman descended from Puritan stock on both sides, stood up to
reveal a tall, lean frame that towered over the former Exchequer
and to proclaim in a deep, steady voice with his blue eyes full of
warmth: "To the beacon of light in the Conservative Party – Winston Churchill."

As they sat down, Winston explained to Josie that he expected
his stock positions to enable him to concentrate fully on helping the Conservative Party regain control of Parliament and not
worry about his finances. She laughed as he jokingly admitted,
"Of course I've been wrong before. I thought we'd win this last
election in England too!" When they both stopped laughing at his
dark humor, he reasoned, "Still, on balance, I think my odds are
better playing the market! So before I leave America, I'm going to
the Stock Exchange to see it firsthand."

After his erstwhile dance partner informed him that she
thought it would be a truly interesting experience, Winston graciously offered to take her along.

Thrilled at the prospect, Josie flattered the ex-Chancellor of
the Exchequer's with her heartfelt comment, "Churchill men
make the most memorable escorts!"

Josie truly was delighted by the prospect of getting a first-hand
look at the famous stock exchange from the member's gallery almost as much as she looked forward to spending more time with
the former Chancellor of the Exchequer.

Since Winston and Randolph were resuming their travels for
the next couple weeks, the former Exchequer invited her to accompany him to the New York Stock Exchange upon his return.
He explained, "I believe we'll be back in New York on October
24th."

As Winston kissed Josie's hand goodbye, he said, "It'll be an
honor to accompany you and watch Wall Street in action together!"
Although Randolph would have to return to England before then

to attend Oxford, Winston promised Josie he would try to be at least as entertaining as his son had been during the dinner party.

As the party broke up, Winston warned Josie not to expect market excitement. He thought October 24th would be just another uneventful day at the New York Stock Exchange.

* * *

As the *Berengaria*'s whistles blew, Catherine Thompson stood smiling wistfully on the crowded promenade of the ship. Many of those around her waved and blew kisses to loved ones left behind. Others threw flowers as they departed Cherbourg. Catherine remained on the deck long after the other passengers retreated to the comforts of the interior of the ship. After the stuffy ordeal of her Great Aunt's funeral, she couldn't get enough fresh sea air — nor could she get her mind off all the parties she had missed and the social drudgery that loomed below deck.

It was at moments like these that Catherine wished her friends were with her – especially Josie. As competitive and jealous as she occasionally became with her old school friend, she depended on Josie's humor and spunk. Of the four friends, in many ways, Catherine and Josie had the most in common. Both came from old New England families with mothers who had been *the* debutante of their respective years and had married extremely well. They also had responsible, loving fathers who were successful bankers that relinquished all social and household decisions to their society-focused wives. Catherine always thought Josie had a better deal because her mother was so much younger than Gertrude Thompson. Claire had gotten married at eighteen and had Josie the following year, while Gertrude had been older and spaced her two children a decade apart. By the time she had Catherine, she had been considered an elderly primer. Josie frequently assured her friend, despite the closeness in age, the Baxter-Browne women's mentalities truly were of different generations.

MARGARET CHAI MALONEY

While Catherine modeled herself on her mother and generally conformed to the roles expected of her, earning credit with social arbiters to the relief of her proud parents, Josie had always been a bit of a rebel. She often threatened that she would never marry if it meant she had to commit herself to a life of tea parties, nagging gossips and doing whatever her future husband deemed appropriate. Certainly she avowed no interest in marrying for any reason other than love and seemed to take great pleasure out of threatening her mother that if she ever did the dastardly deed, she would run off with a romantic hero like Lawrence of Arabia or follow an adventurer like Shackleton to Antarctica and might never be seen alive again! Until that time, she delighted in verbally taking apart potential suitors and scaring her mother senselessly about what crazy new fad she might next embrace. From dance marathons to rally driving and everything in between, she tried all with zest, amusing her friends endlessly while giving herself plenty to write about in her private diary entries and under her nom de plume in *Twenties Humor*. While Henry Jay and Albert Baxter-Browne knew half of Josie's fun was in the shock value – deliberately winding her mother up - even they on occasions thought she pursued life with a slightly worrying wild, recklessness. Despite Albert's best efforts for the sake of family peace, more than once the Thompson's servants had gossiped about how the Baxter-Browne staff had whispered about "another incident." Albert seemed as powerless as his wife in getting his daughter to stop the antics that caused such friction. Both Baxter-Browne women were incredibly stubborn and strong-willed. Neither wanted the other to boss. Given the dynamics and Josie's temper and vocal nature, there often were major disagreements in the household.

Peering out at the disappearing sunset as it gradually faded into the horizon, Catherine thought about what she and Josie would have been doing if her friend had been on board *Berengaria*. She imagined they would have been accused of being louches by their parents. The girls would have slept most of the day in order to recover from their late night chats and secret rendezvous with boys they'd have met on board. Whenever possible, Josie and Catherine would have wandered the decks and lounges claiming to be novelists or psychologists practicing Sigmund Freud's techniques. Once they even had pretended to be mail-order brides from Eastern Europe. Two summers before when the Baxter-Brownes and Thompsons had taken the *Olympic* back from Cherbourg and had ended up in Boston, Josie had half of the ship convinced she was a professional golf player and the other half sure that she had been a gypsy king's daughter making her way to California to launch a movie career. The fun continued until the day before the ship docked when a friend of Claire's overheard passengers speculating about her daughter's future. Just thinking about these past exploits, as she stood on deck, clasping the cool steel railings with her finely manicured hands while the trade winds gently blew through her loose hair, improved Catherine's spirits. Thus, having gotten her dose of freedom, just as the last streak of light vanished from the darkened sky; the willowy blonde went below, prepared and willing to *be* what was expected. It was a half an hour after sunset, but Catherine knew she had needed the time and the space.

Of course, when she returned to her family's suite there was hell to be paid. Upon entry, her mother literally threw an evening dress at her and demanded to know, "Where have you been?" Gertrude Bayer Thompson explained, "Your father has been looking for you everywhere." As she helped her daughter into the pink Schiaparelli gown and the custom made Pietro Yantourny shoes that had taken close to two years to complete, she berated Catherine because they were going to be late for cocktails.

Kissing her mother on both cheeks, Catherine ignored the comments. She knew sea travel made her extremely nervous. Gertrude's parents and brother had been on the *Titanic*. As the famous ocean liner went down, her father was last seen sitting in the first class smoking lounge drinking a brandy with John Jacob Astor and Benjamin Guggenheim. Gertrude's brother Robert had survived the disaster only by clinging to an overturned boat he reached after plunging into the frigid ocean as the ship sank.

To mask her own personal grief, Gertrude made light of the situation. She told everyone she knew that if she had been stuck on board, she would have gone down instead with a glass of champagne in her hand. Gertrude's friends found the statement extremely funny for a variety of reasons since the Bayers were renowned alcoholics. In fact, while Gertrude's mother neglected to bring any of her jewels with her, she had taken several bottles of red wine to her lifeboat. As *Titanic* sank, she had passed the bottles around to the other new widows.

While the Thompson women made their way to the first class dining room, fellow passengers looked at them admiringly. To complement her daughter's cubist Schiaparelli ensemble, Gertrude had chosen to wear a stunning, chemise Poiret gown with an oriental theme. John Thompson proudly watched his wife and daughter make their way to the table. He thought he had the most ravishing women on board. At fifty-nine, Gertrude still looked fabulous and Catherine, who had resembled *Alice in Wonderland* as a child, had grown into a sophisticated beauty. Glancing around the room, John could tell other people thought so too. Tall, blonde and blue-eyed, Gertrude and Catherine certainly were conventionally attractive women. But what really set them apart was their keen understanding of what enhanced their looks and a willingness to work hard and spend a great deal of money to do so. The Thompson women also benefited from the fact that what was deemed fashionable and most stylish in the roaring twenties suited their long, thin bodies and angular faces perfectly.

As they walked past several tables, the family could hear passengers whispering in awe, "The Bayer Thompsons." Everyone knew them at least by reputation. John and Gertrude had been in the public eye since their marriage when social columnists had dubbed their union *The Wedding of 1890.*

The Thompsons sat down to dine at the Captain's table. While her parents talked with the Captain, Catherine demurely watched, like a pretty ornament on display, just as she did at all formal dinners with her family. Minutes later, other members of the ship's elite joined them. Tonight, in addition to the Thompsons, the Captain had invited the Warburgs, Prince Mikhail Stravinsky and his companion, Helena Rubinstein, and her financial advisor Davenport Pogue.

"Who's wearing *Shalimar?*" inquired Helena Rubinstein in a commanding voice as she took her place next to John Thompson.

"I know this will surprise everyone," said the Captain seriously with a straight face. As the table leaned forward in anticipation, he continued speaking as he broke out into a smile, "I'm not."

The group laughed. Captain Rostron was known to have a splendid sense of humor and occasionally even to enjoy the art of a prank.

After the laughter died down, Helena continued to sniff around the table inquiringly.

"I prefer Lanvin's *Arpege* and that's what I have on tonight," said Catherine.

"My dear, it suits you," replied Helena expertly.

Leaning confidentially closer to the women, Gertrude Thompson whispered, "But Miss Rubinstein, you're right. Someone really does smell *quite* odiously."

"It's perfectly ghastly!" exclaimed Helena quite annoyed. Throwing her napkin on the table, the doyenne of the cosmetics world got up from the table with a determined air stating, "It's putting me off my food."

Satisfied that the offensive odor did not come from her group, Helena started circulating around nearby tables to the amusement of all. The cosmetics queen was merciless once she found the perpetrator seated several yards away.

Although the girl couldn't have been over twenty, excess was the one word that described her. She not only wore too much perfume, but she also was overly made-up, wore jewelry that could only be described as gaudy, and had on the flashiest gown that could have been taken straight off the stage from of one of the dancing girls in the most over-the-top production of Ziegfeld's *Follies*. The girl spoke embarrassingly loudly with a working class accent that she failed to disguise as she bragged about her family's recent stock exploits.

Tapping the young woman on the shoulder, Helena launched into a diatribe before the ignorant offender even had a chance to turn around. Her eyes piercing and voice full of derision, she asserted, "Mademoiselle, if Guerlain had known when he launched *Shalimar* in 1925 that his perfume would be so abused, he would have never brought it to market!"

Much to Helena's surprise, the accused remained recalcitrant and even attempted to match the doyenne's disdain by her own actions. Rising from her chair, the offender turned around to face her accuser. After glaring at the "ignorant" middle-aged woman, she retorted tartly as she rolled her eyes, "*Shalimar* embodies the spirit of the decade." Then, turning away from Helena to face her own table, the girl snapped her fingers for more champagne. Grabbing the magnum out of the waiter's hands, she poured herself another glass and deliberately let it spill over. She loudly exclaimed as she held up the glass to toast those at her table and rebuff her accuser, "We live in the most decadent decade of the century. We bathe ourselves in champagne and dance until dawn, why shouldn't we bathe ourselves in the most expensive perfume, as well?"

While her table cheered her, the rest of the dining room put down their cutlery and intently watched the scene unfold. The Captain looked around uneasily, hoping he wouldn't have to intervene in what was becoming increasingly an uncomfortable situation. Sighing heavily, he thought that the most difficult part of his job was not steering the ship but rather keeping his passengers happy.

Outraged at the young woman's insolence, Helena would not sit down before she had in turn humiliated her. The doyenne walked around the table in order to face the offender who rudely ignored her.

Helena glowered as she said in a commanding voice, "Do you know who I am?"

The girl quipped, "I not only do not know, but I also don't care." Then she produced a bottle of *Shalimar* from her handbag and started to pour it over herself. Ignoring the pleas of a woman sitting near her, the girl continued to verbally assault her attacker and drain the contents of the bottle.

While Helena stared at her in horror, she exclaimed triumphantly, "Even though I bathe myself in *Shalimar*, I wouldn't waste a drop on the likes of you!"

Before she had a chance to empty the bottle completely, Helena snatched it from her. Tension filled the room as she peered down disdainfully at the reprobate girl.

As the girl got up to demand the return of her perfume, forcefully, Helena ordered her to sit down. Then she announced in a voice befitting the stage, "Mademoiselle, *I* am Helena Rubinstein and *you* are an utter embarrassment."

The young woman gasped at the revelation. Her face turned ashen and then bright red. There were chuckles in pockets of the room from those who had recognized Helena earlier as well as looks of mortification from the people closest to the girl. They didn't want their reputations sullied by the association.

After all, the fifty-eight year old Helena Rubinstein was the self-proclaimed, "World's Greatest Beauty Specialist." Her bank balance and international following at the very least ranked her among the top in the industry. Of course, the girl had heard of her. In fact, when she learned that Helena would be on board, she even had imagined herself hobnobbing with the celebrity businesswoman. She thought she would make a great model for one of Helena's lines. Now as she realized the magnitude of her fallout, she wanted to crawl away and hide. But since Helena stood in front of her blocking her escape route, hurling abuse at her, all she could do was listen.

Peering down at the young woman like she would an errant servant, Helena forced the girl to look up at her. As Helena ranted, initially the girl froze like a deer caught in a car's headlights, her eyes widened, staring blankly ahead. Then she reflexively sputtered out apologies.

But once provoked, Helena Rubinstein was relentless. Pointing her finger dramatically, she mercilessly commanded the offender, "Go back to your quarters and bathe immediately and whatever you do, don't put on any more of that hateful fragrance!" The grand dame of cosmetics only softened her stance when she saw that the young woman trembling before her, desperately fighting off tears, was so upset she couldn't move. Instinctively, the doyenne's arms reached out to the humiliated, wretched creature whose demeanor now reflected remorse in ignominious defeat. Making the grand, courtly gesture like a sovereign munificently bestowing a pardon, Helena announced, her distinctive, dramatic voice just loud enough for the entire room to hear, "Tomorrow come and see me at my suite, and I will teach you how to make the most of what you have."

Helena was quite impressed by the girl's subsequent actions. Collecting herself, she took a deep breath and looked Helena straight in the eyes. Then, as she steadied herself, she extended her hand as an equal to the grand dame of beauty and replied in a low, calm voice, "I look forward to it, Madame."

Her confidence renewed with that gesture, a bit of the girl's fighting spirit returned. Before departing, she cheekily quipped, "Perhaps you too should look forward to our next meeting. I think you might learn something from me yet." Then she quickly retreated from the dining room before Helena had a chance to disagree.

Davenport Pogue, Helena's financial advisor, led the captain's table in applause as Helena returned to her table. The beauty specialist thought they appreciated what she had done, when in fact, with the exception of Davenport, the others were just happy to resume eating their second course.

"Captain, do tell me, who was that insolent girl I just impetuously invited to my suite?" inquired Helena as she settled down to her dinner. "I'm afraid I didn't bother to get her name."

The Captain replied between mouthfuls, "Something Kohler. I think her first name is Lydia."

"She has a bad accent and no manners, but I admire her spirit. Few people ever have stood up to me," said Helena. After expertly tasting her red wine, the World's Greatest's Beauty Specialist stated, "She recovered quite nicely just before she left."

After taking a sip of wine, John Thompson said, "You know, with the right training, if she was a man, she'd make a darned good litigator."

"Why shouldn't she, even as a woman?" retorted Helena. "I could use a good lawyer that I could trust – who wasn't afraid to tell me the truth," the cosmetics queen said more to herself than anyone at the table.

"Well, the girl doesn't have to work if she doesn't want to. Her father's done well in the market," replied Captain Rostron.

"How's that?" inquired Helena and the Thompsons at the same time.

The Captain explained, "He used to sell dry goods in Brooklyn. I think he came over from Germany as a lad and then gradually built up a business from the lower Eastside."

"He's a Jew, then?" condescendingly sniffed Prince Mikhail Stravinsky, who was at the table sitting between Catherine and her mother.

"And what if he is?" retorted Helena.

"Some of the most creative and talented people are Jewish," chimed in Davenport as he reached over to hold Helena's hand.

The Prince asserted, "They're also a menace to society. Just look at what they've done to Germany."

"With all due respect, Mikhail, Germany's ills largely are a result of the last war she waged and the French reparations," said John Thompson. As the Prince shook his head vehemently, the banker took advantage of the fact the nobleman's mouth was full by shifting the conversation to assert, "In any case, as long as the American market continues to boom, the Weimar Republic should be able to make the payments and eventually prosper again."

Tension continued to build at the table. Looking around his guests, Captain Rostron feared he'd have another scene if someone didn't say something soon to change the subject completely. Helena Rubinstein and Max Warburg and his wife clearly were furious. He sensed Helena was about to verbally assault the Prince for his anti-Semitic comments.

Trying to be diplomatic, Captain Rostron said, "Speaking of the market, Lydia Kohler's father started buying stocks in the early twenties and hasn't had to go into a dry goods store for some time now as a result of his earnings."

Continuing to do his part, John Thompson asserted, "I can't believe how many ordinary people have made overnight fortunes through stocks."

"The market's simply breaking down the class barriers. *Berengaria* has more millionaires on board on this trip than any other Cunard liner to date and most of them generated their money through the market," exclaimed Captain Rostron.

Davenport was about to correct the Captain but thought better of it after looking around the table. *Titanic* still had that record, but he knew several of those in his company would not like to be reminded of the fact.

It was Captain Rostron who led the *Carpathia* across the glacial field to rescue Gertrude Bayer Thompson's mother and brother and retrieve the body of her father and so many of the other *Titanic* passengers. Whenever curious passengers approached Rostron to ask about the *Titanic* – an all too frequent experience – his eyes became distant and a wan expression crossed his face. Then, he would excuse himself as soon as possible. Davenport thought it was the same reaction he had seen displayed by the survivors who had seen the worst fighting during the last war. Those who looked death in the face rarely wanted to talk about the experience. There was nothing glorious about it.

So, instead of mentioning *Titanic*, Davenport asked about the online brokerage facilities.

The Captain proudly responded, "*Berengaria* is pleased to carry the first online brokerage facilities of any liner." Then with a chuckle he said, "I always know when the brokerage is open because the lounges and·Promenade decks are empty during those hours. I'm sure several of my officers live better than I do because of their stock investments.

"I'm a banker and I can assure you, everyone is crazy about the market!" said John Thompson.

"I have never invested," replied Helena flatly. Then, after looking around the dining room, she said, "If they're here because of market profits, perhaps it's time I put my money to work for me."

As Helena got up from the table, she said, "Anyone *game* for bridge tonight? I'll play for stock tips."

"I'm in. But Madame Rubenstein, please understand I can only give advice that is in the public domain," replied John Thompson.

Waving her hand in dismissal, Helena said as she turned to go, "You can join me if you like John, because I like you, but I'll go with the prolls. They're doing something right in order to be getting into *our* dining room."

Then she turned back and asked, "Captain? Are you in?"

The Captain replied as he shook his head, "I'll stick to doing what I do best – steering the ship."

"I'll drink to that!" stated John Thompson and Davenport concurrently.

Catherine looked inquiringly at her mother, "Could I stay up and play bridge with Helena?"

Gertrude replied, "But you don't like bridge darling."

"I'd like to find out a little about the market since everyone seems to be involved," said Catherine.

Her mother informed her, "I hardly think the people with whom she will be associating tonight are socially appropriate, darling. Besides, your father handles these things just fine for us."

Catherine looked up inquiringly at her father. His reply was a direct, "No."

While Catherine looked around the room and reflected on the evening, she knew snobbery was the one thing that united the group at the captain's table. The elite would do anything to keep the have-nots out of their ranks. Prince Mikhail and her parents embraced the Jewish Helena Rubinstein just to shun new wealth such as Lydia Kohler's. She accepted it as the way her parents had been raised and the way they had brought her up. She had no doubt it would be that way for the children that she would have one day and those they in turn would produce. Although she enjoyed periodically behaving outrageously with her friends, it never occurred to the privileged daughter of John Thompson to really question the status quo – even to contemplate doing so would have been unimaginable.

A few minutes later, as the ship's orchestra started playing *Siboney* from the new hit *Havanna*; any thoughts of class barriers and the stock market already had vanished from Catherine's mind. As she listened to the music, she wanted to dance. She tapped her foot and nodded her head to the beat.

Catherine's movement did not go unnoticed. Sitting across the room, at a table composed entirely of desirable bachelors who preferred their own relaxed company to the generally stuffy conversation of the Old Guard that tended to dominate the Captain's table most nights, a tall, attractive, regal looking man in formal attire watched her with great interest. As their eyes met, he raised his glass to her. The daughter of John Thompson intrigued him. As he continued to gaze into her azure eyes, she felt a sensation she had never known before. She blushed from embarrassment and quickly looked away. He reveled in her youthful response. Putting down his glass, he got up and walked towards the Thompsons. All the while, his eyes remained locked on hers. As he approached them, Catherine held her breath.

The young man kissed Gertrude's hand and then Catherine's. After bowing deeply to John, he introduced himself and asked Catherine's father if he could have the pleasure of her company on the dance floor. Smiling at his wife, John readily agreed.

Very few fathers would have refused *this* young man. He stood in line to inherit a financial empire that spanned the globe. His name was Morgan – Junius Morgan. He, and his brother Henry, had been reared to rule the legacy his grandfather J.P. Morgan, had built over the last century and his father, Jack had expanded.

As Catherine danced in the arms of Junius Morgan, she envisioned her wildest dreams coming true.

That night, she sent a victory cable to Josie. She had always wanted to be the first of the girls to get married and had been determined to make it a celebrated match. Having been slightly miffed when Cholly Knickerbocker dubbed her friend Debutante of the Year instead of her, Catherine felt her new success, a more lasting achievement. Before the ship docked, the daughter of Gertrude Thompson had secured the match. With the promise of the exalted social and financial position as the future Mrs. Junius Morgan, a triumphant Catherine no longer felt the need to compete with her friends; she just looked forward to having them in her wedding party and helping her plan her big event. Along with the victory cable, she sent a message to Josie asking her to be the maid of honor and requesting that Geraldine and Rebecca be bridesmaids.

* * *

CHAPTER V

Catherine and Junius' wedding ceremony and reception was held at one of the sprawling Morgan estates in upstate New York. The bride had so much to do in preparation for the wedding, that she hardly had time to see her friends before the ceremony.

Because of the overflow of overnight guests attending the wedding, Josie and her parents, Henry Jay, the Whitney Straights, and the Ashleys as well as a few others stayed with the Rockefellers at their family estate in Pocantico Hills.

On the day of the Morgan-Thompson wedding, Josie overslept. Nocturnal by nature, she had no trouble staying up until dawn talking with Geraldine and J. D. Rockefeller, but as always, a terrible time waking up in the morning.

Although the actual ceremony wasn't taking place until late in the afternoon, Jack Morgan hosted a pre-wedding luncheon in honor of the bride and groom. By the time Josie got downstairs, everyone already had left for the estate. Despite repeated attempts to get her up by both her mother and Geraldine, Josie couldn't be stirred. Exasperated, they had finally left without her.

Josie jumped into her burgundy Bugati convertible and drove like mad to make up for lost time. As the sun broke through the morning mist, she thought the countryside was simply breathtaking. Everywhere she saw evidence of the fall foliage at its height. Like a painter's palate, the bright red, orange and yellow hues when mixed together, created the most beautiful scene that changed with each passing moment. Determined not to forget the

Fall of 1929, Josie momentarily slowed her car down to take in the natural splendor. Then, as she basked in the sun, she pushed down the accelerator as far as it would go. The speed gave her a thrill. She was going so fast that she missed the turn to the Morgan estate without realizing it. Turning back a quarter of an hour later, she had to admit she wasn't sure where she was.

Just as Josie was coming out of a rather tight curve that she thought she took rather marvelously, she heard a loud pop like a gunshot. Almost before she knew what was happening, she lost control of her Bugati as it swerved from one side of the road to the other. Finally regaining control, as she slowed down, she could feel that something still was not right. She heard a repeated thumping noise and felt the Bugati heaving to one side. Her stomach muscles tightened as she sensed she had a real problem.

As soon as she could, Josie pulled over to the side of the road to check it out. After walking around her vehicle to access the damage, she stopped in front of her front left tire. It was completely flat. She guessed she had gone over some sharp object when the car was out of control. Regardless of how it happened, the damage looked irreparable. Realizing there was no way she'd be able to drive under these circumstances Josie looked around the area for possible help. Immediately she could tell she was in trouble on that front too. Not a building or person was in sight. She was in the middle of a mountain range where tranquility reigned. While she usually would find a view like the one before her rather splendid, on this particular occasion, it merely irked her.

The debutante had no idea where she was or even what road she was on. Realizing the next vehicle to appear or person, for that matter might not come this way for hours; she walked over to her trunk and took out the tools she needed. She knew what she had to do; she just didn't feel like doing it. It had been some time since she was last in this situation and the first time she faced it alone. Finding the equipment under her suitcase in the trunk, Josie went to work on the problem. Oil and dust covered her hands and got on her face as she worked on the tire. As she finally yanked it off the rim, her light dress ripped and she fell down.

Before she had the chance to get up, Josie heard someone laughing. She had been so engrossed with trying to change her tire that she hadn't realized help had arrived. Startled and annoyed, as she tried to get up hurriedly, she slipped and fell back down again instead. She felt her face flush from embarrassment, which only made her more mortified. Her mishaps were rewarded with more chuckles. Irritated, as much by her predicament as by the bemused response of her would be rescuer, she angrily demanded to know: "Did you come to help or laugh?"

While the young man walked around from the other side of her car and placed his two strong arms around her to pick her up and turn her around, he replied with laughter in his voice, "I hope to do a little of both."

When she heard his voice, she became ecstatic. She recognized *that* voice – *his* voice – anywhere as a welcome sound. As the autumn wind gently blew on a country back road in the middle of a mountain pass, Josie was re-united with her barman.

Quickly turning around, her eyes met his. His blue eyes twinkled with delight. Clearly he had enjoyed watching her flounder. She tried to hit him for it. As she leaned towards him to do so, he moved back. Much to his amusement, she lost her balance and fell forward as a result.

Goading her, the fresh-faced agile young man teased, "Is that the best you can do?"

Taking the bait, Josie got up immediately and went after him. As she chased him, he grinned and laughed. Repeatedly, he'd let her get very close, only to turn around and then take off again. Finally, just when she thought she had him, he unexpectedly stopped short and picked her up.

The barman swept her up in his arms with the words, "We have unfinished business."

Josie's heart beat faster in anticipation. She wanted him but was still angry about making a fool out of herself and the fact that his amusement was at her expense, so she fought her own desire and instead, kicked and screamed, "Put me down!"

When she saw he was approaching her car, she stopped kicking.

The barman gently set her down inside the driver's seat. Then he leaned on the steering wheel and bent over her. As she looked up intently at him, he gazed fondly down at her. In the afternoon sunlight, his golden hair glowed and she thought this lithe, fit young man whose simple attire merely accentuated his natural good looks, could have attracted the lust of the gods. In any case, he appealed to her. For a very long minute they remained locked in each other's gaze, while all around them the crickets and other wild creatures produced a natural symphony of sounds. Josie held her breath as she waited for him to make a move.

But the barman wanted proof of her feelings before he did anything.

As Josie leaned expectantly towards him, she closed her eyes and her lips instinctively moved towards his. Then she waited for his lips to touch hers. She opened her eyes as soon as she heard him laughing at her. She desperately wished she could undo what she had done. But it was too late; she felt her face getting flushed again.

Furious that she had let him make such a fool out of her, she got out of the car and slammed the door. As she stormed away to hide the tears of anger and humiliation that formed in her eyes, he immediately came after her. Flabbergasted, she pointed back at her convertible and practically shouted, "I have a problem!"

Feeling confident by her reaction, he replied, "I think I know how to fix it." Then, as his eyes sparkled radiantly and a smile beamed across his face, he pulled her towards him and their lips finally touched. While the gentle breeze blew, they completed the kiss they started the last time they had met. Josie no longer felt stupid. She was thrilled.

While the minutes ticked away, he leaned against the outside of her car, holding her. With his strong arms wrapped around her and her head buried in his broad chest, Josie felt completely content. She loved his simple soft white cotton shirt and his scent. As he kissed her and ran his fingers through her silky, dark hair, Josie wanted the moment to last forever.

Unfortunately, time interrupted.

After glancing at his watch, the barman said as he collected himself, "I completely lost track of time. I'm afraid I've got to go. I'm hideously late." As he straightened up he said, "Do you need any help?"

Although disappointed their encounter would end so soon, she replied quickly, "I'll be all right." She didn't want him to know how she really felt – how much she desperately wanted to get to know him better.

As she expected, he inquired, "Are you sure?"

Playing cool, she said, "Yeah. I've taught three different men how to change their flat tires. I think I can do my own."

When he turned to leave, he flashed *that* smile of his that she found irresistible. Then he said with conviction as he looked at her fondly, "You're a most unusual girl."

For another long moment, they gazed at each other again. Not wanting the magic moment to end, Josie stopped him as he prepared to go. Touching his sleeve, she said as she looked up at him imploringly, "I don't even know your name? Will I see you again?"

His eyes sparkled as he said, "There's a distinct possibly. You gave me your card." Then he slowly started walking away.

Josie wanted to stop him, but there was nothing she could to do to bring him back. She didn't want to throw herself at him.

Boys had always chased *her*. She had never met anyone before who she wanted who was so cool towards her. When Josie stood next to her car watching him go, she felt utterly helpless until he turned around. She smiled in anticipation.

But much to her chagrin, all he said in reference to her calling card was: "I think I still have it."

Josie was incredibly disappointed. Her dismay turned to anger as she thought what a complete fool he'd made of her. As he continued on his way, she angrily shouted out, "If you don't, it doesn't matter to me. I was just trying to give you an opportunity – you looked like you could use it."

Turning back once more, he smiled smugly as his eyes danced with amusement, "Much appreciated. But I do okay on my own."

"I don't need you either!" she snippily replied.

Tears swelled in Josie's eyes. As they streamed down her face, she swiftly put the spare tire on the rim. Then she jumped into her Bugati and turned her attention to getting to the Morgan estate. It was two thirty. She had missed brunch but needed to get there for the ceremony. She knew after messing around with the tire she looked like a wreck and would need to bathe and change before hand. Hastily, Josie shoved her key into the ignition and turned. Nothing happened. She tried again and had the same response. The Bugati just wouldn't start.

Thinking quickly, Josie knew she was just about out of options. Scanning the area, she sighed with relief as she saw the barman in the distance. He was almost out of sight. Running after him as fast as she could, she yelled, "Stop! Wait!"

"I thought you didn't need me," the barman teasingly said to Josie when she caught up with him.

Frowning, she said, "I don't. But my car won't start."

"Guess it's a good thing I didn't take off," quipped the barman. He explained that despite her assurances, he really hadn't wanted to leave her stranded so he had moved his car a bit down the road and then returned to wait and watch from a short distance to make sure the proud girl could in fact change her tire before entirely leaving the scene.

The couple quickly walked back to the Bugati. Then the barman took Josie's keys and attempted to start her car. Failing to do so, he looked it over and started laughing.

"What's so funny?" she demanded to know.

He said grinning, "You!"

Exasperated, Josie practically shouted, "This is no time for jokes. Just tell me what's wrong with my car!"

Tossing the keys back to her he said smirking, "You're out of gas."

Josie couldn't believe it. She had never run out of gas before. She had to look for herself to be sure. Once again she felt extremely embarrassed.

Taking Josie's hand, the barman said, "C'mon. I'll give you a lift to town."

Fretting as she looked at her watch again, Josie said with concern, "I'm *so* late. I have to be at a wedding in less than an hour and I'm not even dressed!"

He sighed, thinking of the time, then asked calmly, "Where's the wedding?" He explained, "I'm awfully late as well. But if it's not too far out of my way, I'll take you there."

"It's at the Morgan estate," she stated nervously, figuring he wouldn't have the time to go that far out of his way.

He said with disbelief, "You're going to Junius Morgan's wedding?"

She explained, "I'm the maid of honor."

"Then we better hurry," replied the barman who challenged her to race him to her car.

Quickly, Josie and the barman picked up her bags and bridesmaid dress from the Bugati and set out for his vehicle that he had parked a little ways off the main road. As they approached the barman's car, Josie could see another reason why he hadn't parked it next her hers. Looking at the heap, she gasped, "You're going to take me in this?"

Not one to put up with spoiled brats, he retorted, "Would you rather walk?"

"Does it actually run?" she asked, her voice a mixture of doubt and distain.

Fondly tapping the car as he opened the passenger door for her, the barman said, "I put this beauty together a couple of years ago from salvage pieces."

She said flatly, "I can tell."

While they headed towards the Morgan estate, they hardly spoke to each other because the jalopy made so much noise. Josie had never ridden in such a hunk of junk. It clearly looked and sounded like a vehicle that had been put together by bits and pieces of several cars. In fact, it had the body of a Pierce Arrow and Cadillac doors. The barman was proud to inform Josie that his car had a Ford's engine and back end. If she wasn't so late already, Josie would have been embarrassed to be seen riding in the contraption. As it was, she alternatively silently prayed for and cursed at the form of transportation offered. When they finally arrived at the baronial gates of the Morgan estate, the flivver sputtered to a complete stop. Just as the barman restarted the engine, the Gateman stopped them.

"Sir, I believe you have the wrong address," stated the Gateman with condescension as he stared at the claptrap vehicle and its passengers as he would an irritating pest in the moment just before he would squash it.

Josie said sheepishly, "I'll get out here."

"Are you staff?" inquired the Gateman.

She stated quite clearly, "I'm the maid of honor."

Clearly without listening to the shabby couple, he stated quite emphatically as he pointed dismissively, "Servant's entrance is a half a mile down the road, Miss."

"I am in the wedding party!" exclaimed Josie indignantly as she handed the invitation to the Gateman. As the astonished man stared at her, she explained, "I've had car trouble."

"I see," said the Gateman as he gave their car a long, icy look before opening the heavy wrought iron doors in order to allow Josie and the barman through.

The grand ½ mile drive that led from the gates to the main residence was lined with luxury cars whose chauffeurs eyed the barman's slow moving, sputtering car with disdain. Josie was so concerned about the time she hardly paid any attention to either the drivers or the estate's lovely Frederick Law Olmstead designed lawn and gardens.

As they finally approached the ivy covered main house that resembled a residence hall at Princeton, Josie said, "I can get out here."

"Are you sure you want to?" asked the barman eager to embarrass her further.

She said in a half-hearted attempt to make an excuse, "I thought you were running late as well."

He replied grinning, "I am. But I'm really not going out of my way."

Josie was so busy thinking about everything she needed to do before the wedding and how she'd explain her tardiness that she hadn't heard a word he said. While they drove up to the front of the magnificent stone house, she jumped out of the car before it stopped and landed right in Jack Morgan's arms. Jack had come out when he heard there was a most unusual arrival. Josie was so harried she thanked the barman for his assistance and greeted Jack at the same time. Flustered, she ran inside the fusty, fifty-six room mansion, leaving Jack, the barman and the Morgan's butler to sort out her bags as a number of well dressed, stunned guests stared.

The ceremony was scheduled to take place in thirty-five minutes and Josie still needed to bathe and change. While Rebecca continued to fuss over the bride, Geraldine came into the ornately furnished, forest green bedroom that was assigned to the maid of honor to help speed her up.

Eighteen minutes later, while the harpists played Franz Lizst's "Liebestraum," guests were seated, and Josie emerged dressed in a floral printed, pink satin gown with tulle flounces and a coiffed but still wet Marcel wave that was hidden by a wide-brimmed horsehair hat. Gently she kissed Catherine on both cheeks, careful not to smudge lipstick on her wan friend. In response to her apologies, the bride insisted that everyone was just relieved the maid of honor had arrived safely. When the afternoon had progressed with no sign of her, they had become seriously concerned. After the girls hugged, Josie told the bride that she looked radiant.

To accentuate her height and slim figure, Catherine wore a simple, long, satin and chiffon dress embroidered with pearls and orange blossoms sewn together with gold thread that matched the color of her hair. The fabric as well as her rectangular-shaped twenty-foot train came from Italy. The bride had been told that the material used in the train once had been part of a Medici daughter's trousseau. Regardless of its origin, the ensemble suited her. For jewelry, Catherine donned a double strand of perfect pearls and a clasped pearl bracelet with diamonds from Harry Winston. The groom had given her both items two weeks before the wedding. Her matching pearl drop earrings had belonged to her mother and were most striking against her Eton cropped hair. Catherine's veil had been a present from Henry Jay. She had proof that it had belonged to Napoleon's wife, the Empress Josephine. By the time Josie pulled the veil down over her tall friend's pencil thin eyebrows and aristocratic nose, she thought the regally dressed, statuesque Catherine certainly looked like a queen.

The wedding ceremony took place in the grounds of the estate overlooking the rose garden and the hills beyond. Jack Morgan erected an intricately carved, elevated, white gazebo to serve as the altar for the nuptials. Ten thousand red and white roses decorated the structure and the garland lined aisle. Josie knew Catherine had wanted the perfect wedding. Despite the short notice, every last detail seemed to have been ideally planned and executed. As she gazed at the setting and view and took in the intoxicatingly sweet aroma from the plethora of flowers, the maid of honor thought her friend had pulled it off.

But as the pianist began playing "The Bridal Chorus," Catherine nearly had a fit when she saw the flower girls tossing rose petals from their baskets at each other instead of saving them to line her march down the aisle. Josie stopped the children just before Catherine screamed at them for "trying to ruin her wedding." Then the maid of honor slowly started walking down the long path from the stone manor towards the gazebo. She knew all eyes would be on the bridal party as they walked down the aisle. Based upon experience, she expected some guests to scrutinize them closely, looking deliberately for something to gossip about later. Josie worried most about tripping because she felt her left shoe strap coming loose. She forced herself not to think either about the guests or the Yantorney T-strap evening shoe and just to concentrate on walking straight ahead. She was so focused on the task at hand that she didn't notice anything except the aisle and the altar in the distance.

When Josie finally made it to the front and turned to stand on the bride's side, she was stunned.

Standing across from her was the barman. He was Junius Morgan's best man!

* * *

CHAPTER VI

The barman's eyes sparkled with delight as he nodded his head knowingly. She was sure he was laughing at her. As he flashed *that* smile at her, Josie wanted to kill him.

Throughout the ceremony, she felt his eyes on her and she was even more anxious than she had been as she walked up the aisle. He made her feel incredibly insecure. For the first time in her life, Josie wondered if she was attractive and more importantly, if he found her so. She fretted that she was more interested in him than he was in her. As she blushed, she felt embarrassed.

Dressed in an immaculately fitted morning coat, with his wavy blonde hair smoothed down and center parted, the best man looked very different from the commonly outfitted, scruffy barman of their previous encounters. Although she had been attracted to him even before, as Josie now studied him, thus attired, he easily could have passed as one of the Harvard men who ushered the debutantes to their coming out parties. But what Josie found most appealing about the best man was his presence.

Few people in the world possessed an electrifying energy that made them universally attractive. His eyes sparkled with *that energy* that was as magnetic as his smile and charm. Josie sensed these attributes were powerful weapons that could convince just about anyone to do just about anything for him. Because she found him attractive, she knew she should be wary of him. But instead, she couldn't stop herself from surreptitiously looking at him. Although not the most handsome man she had ever seen, he was without a doubt the most attractive.

While they walked down the aisle together to the "Wedding March," Josie knew she wasn't alone in thinking so. The gazes and whispers of several of the female attendees revealed their private feelings. While wedding guests usually focused on the bride and groom, Josie knew she and the best man attracted a lot of attention as well. When they reached the end of the aisle, they joined Catherine and Junius in the receiving line.

Kissing her hand, the best man said with a mischievous smile, "Once again, it has been a pleasure, Miss Baxter-Browne."

Holding her hand longer than necessary, he said with a devilish smile, "Do I make you nervous? You have very cold hands."

Recovering quickly, Josie replied, "I can also get cold feet."

Laughing, he said, "I'll keep that in mind for future reference."

As they congratulated the bride and groom, Junius admitted as he patted his best man on the back, "I was worried about you, Blakesley." Then as he glanced at his friend and Josie, he joked, "I should have known you'd not only pull through, but pick up the maid of honor as well."

Catherine looked at Josie and said, "I think you've found your match."

Two hours later, Josie still didn't know if Blakesley was his first or last name and how this barman came to be Junius' best man. Famished from not eating anything all day, what she did know was that she looked forward to the six course wedding feast. Her mouth watered as she glanced at the menu.

The dinner included: pan seared fois gras, a tossed salad of arugula, endives and Roquefort cheese, watercress soup, sturgeon and beluga caviar, and half a dozen different kinds of oysters. As their fish course, guests were offered a choice of turbot in a champagne sauce, wild salmon, or lobster tails. The meat course options that accompanied their dauphinoise potatoes and creamed spinach, included: roasted pheasant, duck l'orange and Chateaubriand. Despite Prohibition, servers topped up guests' glasses with special wines for each course. Between courses, sorbets refreshed guests and cleaned their palates.

Before the traditional wedding cake, Josie learned that the Morgans planned to provide each table with an assortment of twelve imported cheeses followed by dessert plates with miniature apple and pear tarts, chocolate-covered strawberries and crème brulee.

Despite her best efforts not to stuff herself quickly, by the third course, she felt extremely full. From her seat at the bridesmaids' table, she had a good view of the groomsmen's table. Periodically she couldn't help herself from glancing at the barman. When he caught her looking at him, she blushed. Her heart beat faster as he got up and winked at her. She was sure he planned to come over to talk to her. But instead, he walked over to a small podium that had just been erected.

* * *

As the best man stood up in front of the assembled group that included everyone in the East Coast social register as well as a number of international notables, the wedding party and guests fell silent in anticipation of what he was about to say. Clearly, as he smiled warmly at the audience, he seemed at ease with the situation and the group. Before he started, he acknowledged Helena Rubinstein who moved closer and nodded towards a group of recent college graduates who shouted out, "Bottoms up Blakesley!"

While he addressed the five hundred guests, Josie thought the relaxed best man spoke with confidence. When he began, she noticed his magnetic eyes and smile had laughter in them. Judging from his body language and poise she sensed he'd deliver a comical speech as had become the rage in their set. After clearing his throat and deliberately waiting a moment longer in order to have all the guests' and staff's attention, he stated, "Today, Junius has taken more than one leap of faith. Looking at Catherine, I am sure everyone here understands why he wanted to join her at the altar. However, when I'm finished with this speech, I'm not too sure if he will still think he should have taken a chance with me as his best man!"

Like a seasoned speaker, Blakesley waited for the laughter to die down before he continued. Then he explained, "I've known Junius since we attended college together. In fact, I've gotten to know him better than I'd like to admit. What I will say is we were roommates at Princeton, where Junius introduced me to the finer things in life, spent a summer in Europe together, and took a year traveling around the world after graduation."

While the best man looked at his friend fondly, he said, "We've done many crazy things, most of which both of us would like to forget, but a few worth mentioning from our year of traveling."

The best man continued while the groom shook his head and rolled his eyes in recollection. "After we found out how to read a map when not quite sober, we took part in the Northern Expedition in China. Although I hasten to add Junius spent more time in Shanghai at the Long Bar and in the French Quarter than in plotting military strategy with the native troops."

As Junius laughed, Blakesley continued. "In Africa, we went on an ill-fated safari where we became the prey and then recouped luxuriously from the experience after Junius convinced the local ex-pat community we were in fact members of the esteemed Oppenheimer family. I need hardly say we high-tailed it the day some real Oppenheimers turned up." While Junius colored from embarrassment, Jack Morgan patted the laughing Oliver Oppenheimer, who sat at his table and with whom he had done a number of deals including an investment in the Oppenheimer family company, DeBeers.

After pausing to take a sip of water, the best man said, "Tahiti was absolutely fabulous and I'll leave it at that! In Fiji, we wore

sulus and drank kava on the beach until Junius had this strange desire to seek adventure by visiting some outer islands inhabited by
cannibals. Mercifully after looking us over, the islanders decided
we wouldn't taste good."

The best man paused for effect before he said, "Sadly, our tour
of the Middle East was cut short. I had dreams of Lawrence of
Arabia and Bedouin bazaars, but we only got as far as Morocco because Junius stole a harem, that needless to say we freed upon closer inspection. Chased by Berbers, our funds depleted, we worked
our way back to Europe as deckhands on a yacht owned by an aged
Contessa who did her best during the voyage to add Junius to her
collection of novelties."

Looking around the room at his audience, the best man said,
"Given the circumstances, can you blame him for joining the
House of Morgan as soon as we reached land?"

While the laughter quieted down, the best man paused to
take a sip of water before winding up his speech. As he put
down his glass, he stated: "Through all these experiences, what
I admire most about Junius certainly is not his great mind – because those of you who know him, know he doesn't have one.
Nor his amazing good looks that I'd attribute more to his wallet, but rather, in all seriousness, his fierce loyalty to his family and friends and the esteemed bank that the Morgans' have
founded."

While guests laughed and clapped, the best man finished with
a flourish. Pouring a glass of champagne in preparation, he said
as his eyes sparkled, "As Junius' friend, I welcome you, Catherine,
into this most elite family, with the hope that you will make my
dear friend extremely happy and continue to build the empire
that is Morgan!" Then to great applause, the best man proposed a
toast to: "Junius and Catherine!"

Having finished the toast, Blakesley sat down, as the guests continued to laugh.

"That was more of a roast than a toast!" replied Jack Morgan between chuckles.

Rising to the occasion, Junius got up to thank his best man in kind. Tall, aristocratic, and ever the deserving pedigreed son of Jack Morgan, Junius was clearly amused by Blakesley's humor and in schoolboy fashion, determined to give his friend his due. After setting his glass down, Junius began, "I would like to thank Charles for that fine speech which was clearly composed by someone with charm, wit, and a keen understanding – three qualities my best man has never displayed in the years we've been friends."

Knowing his audience was having a great time at the wedding party's expense, Junius paused to let the laughter die down before continuing, " If Charles had charm, he'd be the one getting married." As Junius said this, he looked adoringly at Catherine. Then addressing his guests, he winked at his father as he said, "With wit, obviously he wouldn't have any investments with the House of Morgan. And if he had a keen understanding, he never would have remained friends with me." Raising his glass, Junius said, "Here's to you old chap, the most charming, witty, perceptive friend a man could ever ask for – To Charles Blakesley."

Jack Morgan shouted, "Here Here!"

Then the roomful of guests responded together in toasting Junius' best man. Shocked by the apparent long-standing relationship between Junius and Charles, for a second time that day, Josie stared in disbelief as the rest of the packed room reverberated from giggles and chuckles. She felt relief that everyone else was too preoccupied with the speeches to notice her obvious bewilderment as she came to terms with her own actions and behavior and this new knowledge.

After thinking things through, Josie walked over to Charles to confront him. She had to wait for the group of female admirers gathered to complement him on his speech to finish before she had the opportunity she sought. Finally, after the dozen or so, mostly young, attractive women who had swarmed around him at his table, returned to her seats, Josie marched up to him.

Before she had the chance to accuse him, he said smugly, as he offered her a chair, "So did you come to tell me how much you enjoyed what I had to say?"

Ignoring the gesture and his question, she said incensed, "You lied to me!"

Grinning contagiously, he replied, "Do you know how beautiful you look when you're angry?"

Infuriated by his attempt to charm her when he knew she was annoyed, she shot back, "Charles Blakesley! You're not any more amusing now than you were during the toast!"

With mock dignity he uttered, "Well, at least we agree I can't be any worse!"

Unable to remain antagonistic for long in the face of such catchy humor coming from a man she found increasingly irresistible, she laughed despite herself.

Taking her hand in his, he said flashing *that* smile of his, "Shall we go somewhere where we can talk?"

While the guests prepared for the next course, the couple walked out of the noisy, crowded ballroom through the hallway to a sitting room that was filled with curios from around the world and heavy, ornately carved, dark pieces of furniture that suggested the place hadn't been touched since the Victorian Age.

After surveying the room for the most optimal sitting arrangement, Charles led Josie to a massive, black walnut sofa with claw feet and dyed green, horsehair upholstery that had a particularly faded, aged look. He told his companion that he wouldn't have been surprised if the piece pre-dated J.P. Morgan himself! After politely waiting for her to sit down first, he chose to sit uncomfortably close to her. Much to his pleasure, he could feel her breath lighten and see her face flush ever so slightly as his magnetic eyes bore down on hers.

To regain composure, she moved a bit farther away from him. Then, with indignation, she claimed, "You led me to believe that you were just some bartender at Texas Guinan's!"

Charles shook his head as he laughed at his companion. "You never asked what I did. You just assumed that because I was behind the bar, I worked there."

"A logical assumption," she insisted.

"Not entirely."

Not one to give up easily, she demanded to know, "Why else would you have been there?"

While they sat facing each other on opposite ends of the sofa, he said calmly but firmly, as if he was litigating a very basic case, "Like you, I was having problems getting served. Unlike you, I chose to do something about it. I had a fine bottle of champagne waiting at my table and needed glasses. I went behind the bar to get some."

She exclaimed, "You took advantage of my ignorance then and continued to deliberately mislead me today when my car broke down."

He chuckled, "You mean, when you ran out of gas."

She warned him, "Don't try to wind me up!"

"Do you mean I'm succeeding?" he replied smirking.

Piqued, she shouted, "I don't see how nice boys like J.D. and Junius can possibly be friends with the likes of you!"

"I've helped them out of some difficult situations," he stated seriously.

"Softening, Josie replied as she moved closer to him, "Like you helped me the night of the raid."

"In a manner of speaking."

"Oh?"

He acknowledged, "Yes." But quickly claimed: "It really doesn't matter."

Josie begged, "Oh, come on, tell me." Not getting anywhere, she pleaded, "You can't just mention something and then leave a person hanging! It's unconscionable!"

He replied, his voice serious, "Defiling someone's reputation is unconscionable. Leaving a person to die when you can help is unconscionable. *This* is not unconscionable."

Not giving up, she pushed, "Can't I at least ask for hints?"

"You can – but I won't tell," he replied honesty.

Probing, she asked, "And why's that?"

"Discretion is the better part of valor."

"I suppose I really should thank you for your discretion," said Josie slightly disappointed but at the same time impressed by his chivalrous code.

Not thinking his gentlemanly conduct was anything other than normal, he replied slightly surprised by her response, "Oh?"

She explained, "For not telling anyone what I was doing at Texas Guinan's."

He said, "You did nothing wrong."

By the tone of his voice, Josie could tell he genuinely meant what he said. She was delighted that he felt that way. She just wished others did as well. As she thought about it, she said glumly, "Not everyone would approve of my presence and behavior there."

Charles nodded in agreement as he said, "That's the problem with our society. There's nothing wrong with me slumming." As he gave her a meaningful look, he said smiling, "So I don't see why you shouldn't either!"

Josie quipped, "Is that an offer, Mr. Blakesley?"

He replied, "You can take it for what it is." As he gazed at her, Josie smiled. She looked forward to getting to know him better.

The best man told Josie that while Junius had been ready to settle down to a proper job as soon as they returned from their travels, he had spent the last several years continuing to seek adventure and enjoy life around the world. She thought she could never tire of his tales as he described mountain climbing in Bolivia, swimming in the Aegean Sea, and hunting for lost treasure in ancient archeological digs. Her only concern about this modern day Robinson Crusoe, who took random jobs along the way to support his travels, was that he might not be the kind ever ready to settle down. Despite this fear, the more they talked, the more Josie realized she really liked Junius' best man. Unlike many of the boys she knew, Charles Blakesley wasn't an elitist and he didn't patronize her by treating her differently just because she was a girl. Frank with his thoughts, he seemed just as interested in her opinions.

Josie and Charles sat in the sitting room chatting for two hours and forty minutes before they realized how long it had been. Knowing their absence would raise eyebrows they agreed it would be best to return to the party. But before they actually made it back to the reception area, they spent another hour and a half talking in a hallway. By the time they finally strolled into the reception room, the couple had traded childhood stories and told each other secrets "they had never shared with anyone else before."

While Charles asked Josie to join him at the groomsmen's table, which by this point had just as many bridesmaids and other female guests as men, he made it clear that he admired her passion and outlook on life.

Offering her the chair next to his, he said with conviction, "I just wish more girls were like you."

She thanked him both for the seat and the complement but protested because she really didn't think she was that unusual. As they nibbled on the desserts, Charles begged to differ. After debating the issue for some length of time, Josie finally tired of trying to convince him to concede the point. Shrugging, she said, "In any case, things are changing for the better." She explained, "I was in a ladies' brokerage recently and saw women making their own money just like men." Vivaciously she said, "From what I saw, through market investments, women are beginning to measurably impact their quality of life." Charles looked at her with great interest as she whispered, "Did you know Mrs. Whitney-Straight plays the market?"

"The grand dame of New York society?" replied a shocked Charles.

Josie claimed, "She's doing immensely well, too!"

He admitted, "I would have never guessed."

"My dear Charles, " said Josie confidentially, "The difference between men and women is that when men are successful, they tell the whole world, while successful women, quietly gloat as men drone on about achieving much less."

"Men have such fragile egos, one wonders why women bother!" said Geraldine as she walked past Josie and Charles.

The best man replied, "It's called innate attraction."

"In some cases," retorted Geraldine as she took a long look at Josie. Then, as she tapped Charles on the shoulder, she said, "But others have evolved."

"Regardless," said Josie, "By investing, women can influence every major public company. I read that female shareholders own 37% of US Steel and a lot of GM stock too!" Excited, she asked Charles, "Did you know over 50% of Pennsylvania Railroad's stock is owned by women?"

"So that's why they call it the Petticoat Line!" replied Charles chuckling.

She asserted, "But one day they won't snicker. Women are making inroads around the world in every profession – from car racing to medicine to high finance." She became animated, her passion clear. While Josie told Charles about her article on the ladies' brokerage, she could tell her companion seemed as interested in her views and impressed with her as she was with him. Unfortunately, she had become so consumed by the conversation, she didn't even notice when her mother walked over to their table and positioned herself right behind her daughter. Josie had no idea how long

Claire had been listening, but she certainly felt the hard pinch her mother gave her and the often repeated, weary look of disappointment, followed by the warning, "You sound just like Geraldine!"

The young flapper rolled her eyes. But before she muttered something she would have regretted, once again, Charles saved her.

Taking Josie's hand in his, he said, "With all due respect, Mrs. Baxter-Browne, I think the liberalization of women will only better society and make for happier relationships."

"You're very unusual, Mr. Blakesley. Perhaps you owe your understanding of women to your mother?" replied Claire Baxter-Browne with a smile.

Frowning, Charles replied, "Unfortunately, I don't know my mother."

"I'm sorry," replied Josie and her mother at the same time.

Not wanting their pity, quickly he said, "That's okay. It's been a long time." Then softening, he explained, "She died when I was really young. I have a few pictures of her – she was a beautiful woman – full of adventure and life I'm told."

"And your father?" inquired Claire.

Josie said, "It must have been really hard on him."

Looking away, Charles said, "Actually, he was killed a few months before I was born." Then as he turned back to the women, he explained, "My mother's brother and his wife, who weren't able to have children of their own raised me as their son." Smiling as he remembered his idyllic childhood, he said, "I couldn't ask for better parents."

"You're very lucky," replied Claire.

The best man said, "So I am regularly told."

"Where did you grow up?" inquired Claire, warming to the attractive, young man.

Proudly he said, "Ada, Oklahoma, M'am."

"So you're a Midwesterner, then?" replied Claire obviously surprised and a bit disappointed that the seemingly sophisticated young man who roomed with Junius at Princeton and traveled around the world came from a place she could only imagine as a backwater.

"That must have been a very nice place!" suggested Josie diplomatically.

He replied, "It certainly was." Clearly not in the least bit embarrassed by his background, he asserted, "The air is clean and fresh and the land so expansive, you can ride for miles just taking it all in." As he looked fondly at Josie he said, "Sometimes I think that's why the people from there are so friendly – there's plenty of room to breathe."

"How very fascinating, I'm sure," replied an unimpressed Claire as she nodded to Mrs. Whitney Straight who was heading in her direction. Then out of politeness she said, "Perhaps you can tell us about it sometime."

"Over dinner, Mother?" suggested Josie eagerly.

Giving her daughter a displeased look, Claire said, "Clearly Josie would enjoy your company, so of course, her father and I would like to know more about you." Due to Josie's persistent urging, Claire inquired, "Are you free next week, Mr. Blakesley?"

Ignoring Claire's reluctance, Charles replied without any hesitation, "It would be my pleasure, Mrs. Baxter-Browne."

For the rest of the reception, despite Claire's frowns, Charles and Josie danced to every song Benny Goodman and his orchestra played. They were so focused on each other that they were completely oblivious to their surroundings. A few times they didn't even realize the music had stopped. Their behavior did not go unnoticed by others.

When the band struck up the hit song, "Runnin Wild," Junius walked up to J.D. and said, "Looks like I lost my best man!"

"I wouldn't be so sure yet," replied J.D. "Fancy a wager?" Although J.D. generally didn't bet, in this instance, he had his reasons.

After the reception ended, as the couple sat outside in the gazebo, Charles told Josie a little more about his childhood. His eyes brightened and he became animated as he described the home in which he grew up. As sophisticated and urbane as four years at Princeton and his world travels had made him, it was clear Charles Blakesley remained grounded by the land where he spent his formative years.

The best man and the maid of honor stayed up all night talking about history and politics, philosophy and business, and dancing to the love songs in their heads.

The next morning, after the traditional wedding breakfast, Charles offered to take Josie to pick up some gasoline and get her Bugati. They held hands as they walked towards his car.

When Charles opened the passenger door of a dark blue Morgan convertible instead of his wreck, Josie said, "What are you doing?"

He said coolly, "Opening the door for you."

"But this isn't your car," she exclaimed.

"Trust me."

She replied skeptically, "I don't know what the custom is in Oklahoma, but here, we don't take other people's vehicles."

Charles insisted, "Just get in."

As he started the engine, Josie said, "Whose car is this? It's beautiful – what is it – a Morgan?"

He answered, "Yep."

She said, "It's wonderful but you know I really don't mind riding in your car *that* much. I'm not with you for your car."

Confidently he replied, "I know."

Charles was making good progress on the road now. Josie noticed the Morgan took corners as well as her Bugati – maybe even better. It was a fun car to drive.

"So whose car is it?" she persisted.

"Mine," replied Charles with a smile.

"But what about…"

Charles interrupted Josie to explain. "This is my car and so is the other one. My Aunt and Uncle gave me the Morgan as a graduation present. I put the clunker together this summer for fun. Actually, it was a bet. An old family friend who worked his way up the hard way didn't think a college boy could build anything with his hands. I had to prove him wrong. I have to admit, though, sometimes I just like taking it out for a drive to see people's reactions."

Getting the distinct sense that Charles' family was considered well off in Oklahoma, she said, "I suppose you have another car in Ada as well."

He replied, "Yeah, I guess you could say that."

Sensing evasiveness, she probed, "So what kind of cars do you have?"

He asked, "Do really want to know?"

He laughed when she retorted, "Would I have asked otherwise?"

He replied, "I have a boat tail speedster that I used at college and a bashed up L29 front wheel drive Cord that I found out the hard way was bad on ice." Flashing *that* smile at Josie he said, "My quarter horse is far more reliable."

"I like horses," replied the city girl smiling as she conjured images of Charles riding like a cowboy on the range.

His eyes sparkled as she asked about life on the range. Relenting to her inquiries, he said, "I shouldn't tell you this, but they're a good way to pick up girls."

The smile disappearing from her face, Josie said, "I wouldn't think that's a problem you have."

She was glad she could see her Bugati just ahead as he replied, "It hasn't been in the past." But before Josie had a chance to get too mad at him and herself for falling for him, as he pulled over next to her car, he looked deeply into her enormous brown eyes and said, "But I've never found anyone before meeting you who *really* interested me."

Feeling like an emotional roller coaster, as Josie got out his car and walked over to hers, she sulkily said, "Maybe you better not come to dinner; I don't want to disappoint you!"

In response, Charles pulled Josie back towards him and said, "You're going to have to come up with a better excuse than that if you want to get rid of me."

As Josie looked at Charles she said, "Unlikely."

"Until then," he promised. Before seeing her off, the young man from Oklahoma took the dark haired debutante into his arms and kissed her with such feeling that long after he had left she felt her body still quivering with desire.

* * *

New York's most eligible bachelor had had every intention of attending the Morgan-Thompson nuptials. When circumstances and fate conspired against him, James didn't need Evelyn Maker's powers to divine the outcome. He knew what he had to do. As much as the playboy loved to party, money came first. While Junius and Catherine and much of New York's establishment celebrated, James stayed in Boston for the entire week waiting for his great uncle Thomas Peabody DeVere, to die. The young scion had grown up as the man's only living relative. He wanted to ensure he received the appropriate compensation for this fact.

Descended from the first pilgrims on one side and one of the first Virginia families on the other, every branch of the DeVere family for the first 200 years had managed to amass more than its predecessors. Most male members of the family seemed gifted with financial acumen. Health and happiness proved far more elusive for the tribe.

Mercurial and dictatorial, Thomas Peabody DeVere had been a stern and demanding taskmaster who expected as much from others as he did himself. Through drive and diligence, he significantly increased his own wealth and the DeVere family holdings but at a cost to those around him. His valet hypothesized that his workaholic employer had wanted to die the richest man in the world. Much of his life Thomas DeVere's goals reflected that pursuit.

James counted on the fact Thomas' only child; Nathaniel Thomas "Nat," DeVere, had died in a sudden accident over twenty years before. After Nat's untimely death, a curse descended upon the DeVeres. An unusually high number of children were still born, several DeVere women died in labor, and Thomas' wife went insane, expiring in a fire she started herself. Disease, accidents, and war weeded out the men. Lightening struck down Ellison DeVere while he played golf. Another, while hunting, shot himself. Seven more returned from World War I in coffins after an entire branch was lost in a train derailment when their private car overturned. James' parents and the only other DeVere uncle along with the Uncle's wife and two children perished when the Lusitania sank. The men's bodies were so mangled it took dental records to identify them. The women and children were never found.

When he was young, James' alcoholic playboy father, in a rare display of responsibility, had made him visit his great uncle Thomas regularly since his boy had become the heir apparent. Although his uncle's dark, cavernous Gothic mansion was an uninviting place for a child, to say the least, James was more than happy to comply because the old man rewarded him with bountiful presents and money for whatever he wanted. Perhaps in an attempt to ameliorate the wrongs he had done many years before to his own son, Thomas over reacted by spoiling James. Regardless of the reason, Thomas was the best uncle a child could possibly hope to have if material goods were the measure of happiness.

After James' father perished when the Germans sank the Lusitania, which according to Thomas was his only distinction, the elder DeVere became his grand nephew's legal guardian and taught the boy every business secret he knew from his vast years of experience. In work as in life, Thomas had been a very tough bird. Initially he was delighted to see the same business acumen and callousness mirrored in his ward. But as the boy grew up and his mentor aged, Thomas had mellowed.

As he approached the winter of his own life, Thomas hoped his young heir would soften as he had. But much to his distress, the elder DeVere found time and success only made James more ruthless and arrogant. Regardless, by 1928, the mentor unwittingly opened Pandora's Box and the protégé made it clear he had outgrown his master. Through cajolery and the complicity of Thomas' accountant and lawyer, James convinced his uncle to make him acting president of the companies. The old man lived to regret the decision. James had just turned twenty-eight and in accordance with the guidelines of his trust fund, came into his own money. With wealth and power, his attitude towards his uncle immediately changed. He no longer had any practical use for his adviser and made that very clear. Although his nephew was a clever businessman, Thomas felt hurt that despite his tutelage, James not only showed no interest in his mentor's financial views, but also acted as if he had little concern for his uncle's emotional and physical well-being.

When he complained, peers scoffed at him. It didn't help that Thomas had ruthlessly screwed so many of these very same people in business. Furthermore, most of the Old Guard had horror stories of similarly bred young men who had no interest in furthering the family coffers. Like James' wastrel father, there were plenty of Ivy Leaguers even from James' year who lived like dew droppers and leeches, diminishing the family trusts by their lavish lifestyles, serial marriages, and costly divorces. Few could see any fault with James' interest in wealth and power particularly given his great Uncle's track record.

Lonely and frustrated, but without the will or a desirable alternative to launch a takeover to wrest the holdings from his nephew, all the old man could do was call James repeatedly. Pre-occupied with his own life and bored with his uncle's ramblings about deals long dead with people now six feet under that he had heard about many times before, he dismissed Thomas as an irritatingly needy, slightly senile, grumpy old man. Despite his pleas to see or even just talk with the heir apparent, at James' request, more times than not, Bentley informed Thomas his master was "not available."

In the spring of 1929, after a fatalistic medical prognosis, Thomas, who was not quite as out of it as he sometimes appeared, thought seriously about his life as well as the kind of legacy he wished to perpetuate. He yearned for a worthy heir not only to continue to increase the family's holdings, but also to serve as a leader and model for the less fortunate. Like most DeVeres, the curmudgeon had no problem holding up the banner of compassion while nursing grudges and vowing revenge. After many restless nights and extensive research, the wily old businessman finally decided to use his will to make amends and punish his ungrateful kin. Thomas radically changed the document at his nephew's expense.

With Thomas in bed, gravely ill, James finally felt compelled to make an appearance. It was neither love nor compassion particularly that led him to his old mentor. It was the urgent message from the family accountant and a confirmation from a lawyer that resulted in James' newfound interest. For years Thomas' financial advisors had been browbeaten and verbally abused by the brilliant but irascible man. Because Thomas was such an important client, they cowered before him, hiding their resentment. With James, they saw an opportunity for revenge and more importantly to make more money.

Informed by his uncle's advisors that the new will left him only token items that belonged to his grandfather and the family holdings and money that couldn't be stripped from him, James acted as soon as the shock of the news wore off. He hoped this was just another ploy by his uncle to get his attention or that his sources were wrong. Nevertheless, the more James thought about what the crooked lawyer and accountant had told him, the more he realized in all probability Thomas truly had expunged him from his most recent will.

The advisors informed James that his uncle planned to pass on the remaining stock in the family's iron and steel companies and other concerns as well as the bulk of Thomas' vast personal fortune to a worthy individual named in a sealed trust document the advisors hadn't even seen.

When challenged, the old man had informed his advisors that he had gone to great lengths to do this legally. When they told him they were surprised he didn't involve their services in his efforts, the old man replied chuckling, "I wanted to be effective."

Tact had never been Thomas' forte. It would cost him dearly.

Unaware that James was tipped off, as the smell of dead leaves filled the New England Autumn air, Thomas rested peacefully in the belief his final wishes soon would be executed. He had expressly informed his staff and advisors not to inform his nephew of his prognosis. James' sudden appearance came as a most unwelcome surprise.

When his nephew was announced, Thomas refused to see him. Displaying the famed DeVere temper, like a thunder bolt the young businessman gave the staff an unforgettable verbal jolt before striding up the elliptical, rosewood staircase, his ominous sure steps sounding, thundering echoes of doom, straight into the heart of his uncle's Circassion walnut decorated bedroom.

But once he faced his dying mentor, James' demeanor softened. He knew how to play his audience. To disarm the weakened old man, he began with an apology. But in this case, acting was almost unnecessary since James simply spoke thinking of the elusive money he wanted to inherit and as he actually faced the old man on his deathbed, even he felt pity for the condemned. Deferentially standing by the foot of the bed, as he peered down sympathetically at his gravely sick uncle, James said sounding contrite, "I suppose it serves me right that you don't want to see me. I haven't been much of a nephew these last few years, let alone a friend." Reaching for his uncle's hand, he continued emotionally, "For this I am truly sorry. No excuse is good enough." And at that moment, New York's most eligible bachelor actually meant what he said.

Patting the young man's hand to assure him, Thomas was forgiving. "What matters is you're here now."

Then the mind games began.

For several days, James did his best to ingratiate himself with the dying man. After reading excerpts of *Oedipus Rex* to his uncle and other classics and talking about their family history, Thomas' life and the numerous shared memories, James finally broached the subject he had been waiting to discuss.

Drawing on all the emotions he knew would affect his uncle, James began, "Haven't you ever made a mistake that you desperately wished to change?" As Thomas shifted uneasily, he pressed, "I beg you to give me a second chance."

James was putting on a great show. He knew all the buttons to push and when to do so. He could tell he had touched Thomas. So he continued speaking in that vein. With feeling he said, "Please don't give up on me, I want to learn from you like I used to." As his uncle looked up at him with peeked interest, James asserted, "Although financially we both know I've done the DeVere name proud, I've made a number of mistakes you wouldn't have." Honestly, he admitted, "Certainly I've been hard on people and I've been inattentive to you."

Growing tired, Thomas yawned. Not wanting to lose his audience, his nephew, reached out for the elderly man's hand and said with conviction, looking straight into his uncle's startled eyes, "I want to change." James could tell he was making progress with his uncle based upon the man's response when he claimed he cherished the past few days that they had spent together. He brought up fond memories of James' first investment under his uncle's tutelage, first property purchase, and first painting. He thought he had almost cinched the deal when he told the old man, "Please be my teacher again." But then he blew it with one reference – one comparison, – a gamble that could have sealed the deal but that he should have never made.

Glibly, James claimed, "I want you to help me – to treat me like your son – like I was Nat."

Immediately, the sickly sallow complexion of his uncle's face turned crimson red and his body started shaking. "Don't you dare talk about him!" replied Thomas fiercely, as he lunged at his nephew, making clear his disgust with the unworthy comparison before he collapsed from the pain – both from the memory of his beloved dead son and from his own precarious physical state.

Undeterred, James pleaded as he tried to get his mentor back under control, "Can't you see, through me, you can do what you wanted to do for him?" Before the words even were fully out of his mouth, James knew he had made a terrible mistake by pushing the issue. But it was too late.

Slumped back down on the bed, his head propped up by a down pillow, Thomas laughed bitterly. He saw through the veneer completely. He understood why James had come. He said his tone as cold as it had been when he was first reunited with his prodigal nephew, "They told you I was dying, didn't they."

James shook his head no.

His anger energizing him, Thomas sat back up in bed, and gruffly barked, "Don't lie to me! It's insulting! I may be a dying man, but I haven't lost my mind!"

Losing ground quickly, James tried to salvage what he could. In an attempt to calm down the old man, he quietly said, "I wasn't trying to insult you, Uncle Thomas. I just didn't want to hurt you."

Briefly energized by his anger, the countless hurtful memories flashed back of James' impudence, and Thomas replied hotly, "Then you should have thought of returning some of my calls or even considered coming out here once in a while." Never one to be steam rolled, he then demanded to know: "Who told you?"

Stalling for time, James said innocently, "I don't know how else to explain this. I just sensed it. I felt I needed to see you. I don't know why. I just woke up and knew I had to come."

Seeing through the ruse Thomas shouted, "Don't lie to me!" Relentlessly, he demanded again, "Who told you?"

Knowing his nephew almost as well as himself, he roughly pressed, "Was it the worthless accountant or lawyer?"

In James' silence, Thomas got his answer. Satisfied, the old man asked, his voice raspy from the confrontation, "What do you really want to tell me?"

Grudgingly he respected the old codger for not being taken in by him, but ever a game player, instead of acknowledging the fact, James replied instead, "I thought I should update you on the companies." Reacting to his uncle's yawn, he shifted his weight and strategy at the same time. Humbly, he claimed, "I also want your advice."

"Really," replied Thomas skeptically. He muttered bitterly, "That would be a first." Then, amused at what he might hear, he urged his nephew to continue.

As James pulled up an eighteenth century Spanish leather chair next to his uncle's bed, he claimed, "I want to know what your vision is for the future. How should we position our assets? What industries do you see as the future earners? What advice can you give me?"

Looking at James intently to glean his real feelings, Thomas said, "Do you really want to ensure the success of the companies?"

"Of course," replied James pleased as he thought the old man was warming to him again.

The dying man asserted, "Then you will abide by my last wishes."

James pressed, his heart beating faster as he inquired, "They are, uncle?"

Quietly but firmly Thomas stated, "I have dictated them in my will."

Still angling one last time for a change of heart, James pressed, "Can't you share them now so if I have questions I can ask you while you are capable of answering?"

Not interested in doing so, Thomas replied as he lay back down in his bed, his eyes suddenly tired of the discussion, "We've talked a long time. Leave me alone. Let me rest."

"But I need your help." James pleaded for once, feeling like the little lost boy he had been when he first learned of his parents' untimely death and had turned up with his houseman to his uncle's imposing edifice – not knowing what would await him but knowing that his immediate family, however limited and irresponsible, was gone forever.

Unmoved, Thomas replied resignedly, as he looked away, "You're beyond that, my boy."

"You *do* trust me then?" asked James looking intently at his uncle as he continued to try to save himself. Like a caught criminal, James desperately wished he could undue his wrongs or be given a second chance.

"I trust you always will do what you perceive is in your best interest," said Thomas sadly.

James clenched his jaw as his uncle requested, "Now let me rest in peace."

As he got up, James said callously, "You better not die tonight."

"Would it be inconvenient for you?" whispered the old man wryly.

"Isn't that obvious?" muttered the disinherited heir, who had already started scheming his next move.

"Sleep well, my boy," said Thomas as he pulled his sheets up to his chin and closed his eyes.

James grumbled, "Not likely." He knew from experience based upon the conversation, he wasn't going to get the old man to change the will again by playing nice. It really made him furious as he realized he had wasted his time kissing up to his uncle the last few days. New York's most eligible bachelor didn't go home that night. In fact, he didn't even go to sleep. He spent the night pacing back and forth in the mansion's elegant library, trying to figure out what to do.

As a young boy, James had enjoyed the room that had a vaulted ceiling made of fine timber from South America that held over 2,500 volumes and a massive marble fireplace that once graced a Renaissance palace. But this evening, James hardly paid any attention to his surroundings. Quietly murmuring to himself, he walked like a zombie, his brain exhausted from the mind games, his eyes dead. Occasionally, when his temper got the best of him, he threw books at the wall, smashed glasses and anything within reach. For the first time in months he didn't think about a woman or have any desire to sleep with one. Rarely one for regrets, for once he cursed himself for not paying a little lip service to the old goat. That night, he vowed henceforth to be more careful and never again to risk losing what he most valued.

Unfortunately, this pledge didn't make his current predicament any easier. Finally, as dawn broke, while sitting at his uncle's grand desk, his head in his hands, he came up with a plan. He knew it wasn't optimal, in fact he downright disliked the task at hand – but when it came to money and power, James Ellison

DeVere was a survivor and would let nothing stand in his way to what he wanted.

In the next few days, James got rid of his uncle's staff and dug in doggedly. As soon as the last servant was gone, he began hurling abuses at the bedridden man, berating him for being a bad uncle and dishonoring the family by distrusting his nephew, Thomas' only living relation.

Unrelenting and perceptive to the end, despite James's verbal attacks, Thomas refused to change his will again or sign anything his nephew gave him. As time passed, James fumed. He knew he was running out of options. Worst of all, he knew the old man understood this too.

While the sallow-faced tycoon prepared for the inevitable, a sense of peace filled Thomas. He believed that although he would not be able to see things through himself, and in many ways he felt he wasn't worthy given what he had done in his lifetime, through his will he believed the DeVere name would be restored to a level unknown since Nat died.

For the second time in his life, Thomas was seriously wrong.

While his uncle lay on his deathbed, James called in the accountant and lawyer. He arranged a meeting in his uncle's faux Ashler walled home office, where years before Thomas, in a piqued state, had rashly disowned his only child, Nat, months before the young man's untimely death. There, under the fleur-de-lis patterned ceiling, James made a proposition. Over a million dollars exchanged hands before a copy of the latest will was torn up. For James to become the main beneficiary of the entire estate as dictated in Thomas' previous last testament, three more million passed hands and the deed to a house in the South of France.

As the conspirators sat in chairs that once belonged to the Grand Inquisitor of Spain, only a few yards away from the dying man's ebony desk, the lawyer tried to rationalize his actions. He muttered, "The old man was losing it when he drafted that document."

James laughed sardonically. Pouring the men drinks from a bottle of vintage Ruinart, he said morosely, "You don't have to pretend with me. The bastard's my uncle. I know you hate him." As he handed the men their glasses and proposed a toast, he said with foreboding, "Just keep this in mind, if you ever double cross me, I'll make you wish you were still working for him."

Then James went back up to his uncle's bedroom to wait for the end.

Day after day, he watched as the semi-conscious, shriveled up old man prepared to die. Thomas lay almost immobile, his face filled with the look of death. But now that his nephew wanted him to pass away, he stubbornly refused to go to the next life. The flicker of life burned weakly, but obdurately. The day after Junius and Catherine's wedding, James lost patience. To hurry the old man along into the next world, he tore off the blankets covering his uncle and opened all the windows in his bedroom, letting in the damp, cool evening air. Finally, as dawn broke, the tough old bird's heart finally gave out.

Boston society interrupted news of James' vigil as a testimony to his great love and devotion. The *Boston Globe* dismissed rumors of foul play by former servants as specious gossip expected from the discharged and instead reported that James let the staff go because he wanted to spend the last cherished moments taking care of his dear uncle himself. Despite the difficulty of his upbringing, the paper depicted the young heir as personifying the type of model that Thomas had hoped he would have been.

Remaining in the city until just after the reading of the will, James took full advantage of this impression. A debutante and a very young widow privately helped the heir get over his grief. James found his sexual encounters with the stunning widow particularly satisfying. He even was late to his uncle's burial because he convinced her to join him in the sacristy before putting the casket below in the cemetery that adjoined the church.

The minister and mourners who waited a full forty minutes outside by the gravesite on this rainy afternoon, interpreted the heir's tardiness and flushed face as yet more proof of how this deeply caring young man was so much affected by his great uncle's passing. Even James' failure to visit the old man in the last decade although he had been in Boston for parties numerous times, was interpreted as proof that he was occupied by family interests – both business and in searching for the right mate for the continuation of the dynasty. Many a Boston girl pinned her hopes and dreams on the playboy businessman selecting her to be the next Mrs. Ellison DeVere. But James' interest was back in New York.

Papers in hand, James smiled smugly as Bentley, who had taken the train up to attend the funeral of the man who had retained him to work for the DeVere family so many years before, opened the car door for his young master. James was in a great spirits. He had enriched himself conservatively by over $80 million dollars and had secured the controlling stock of his family's companies.

Pre-occupied with business plans and exhausted from his sexual exploits, James dozed off as Bentley got behind the wheel of his master's roadster. When his deceased uncle's valet walked up to the driver's side of his model J Duesenberg and handed Bentley a little safe, James was soundly asleep.

The old valet, parted with the words, "I must pass this on to you for safe keeping and eventual restitution of the family."

Bentley's journey had just begun but it would take him some time before he fully appreciated this. The valet died several months days later and was buried a few plots away from the master he had served his entire life. Hoping to find a few clues to help him with the contents of the little steel box, Bentley attended the funeral.

But whatever secrets Thomas' valet had known, he took to his grave. James' houseman was left with a lock of hair and a sealed document to be opened only by the family of Madeline DeVere. Shaking his head, Bentley put the safe aside. Given possible recriminations, the houseman really didn't want to get involved. He also knew he had other more pressing matters.

* * *

CHAPTER VII

A week after the Morgan-Thompson wedding, a relaxed James Ellison DeVere lounged on the corner of Henry Sturgis Morgan's ornately carved, black oak desk looking at the coffered ceiling. Most people would have felt intimidated by the grand office that had wood painted walls to resemble marble and an Egyptian sarcophagus on display. But James was not like many people. He felt almost as comfortable as Henry Morgan in the hushed, tomblike environment. James hardly even noticed the eerily accurate portraits of the banking clan's dead progenitors that stared down at the occupants from the hallowed walls as if silently passing judgment on each deal discussed.

He laughed when his friend told him that the cleaners refused to work alone in the room late at night because of the portrait of Henry's grandfather, J.P. Morgan. From every angle and direction, it appeared as if the great banker's piercing eyes looked straight at the room's occupants. Working in pairs, the apprehensive janitors carried amulets and charms to help protect them against the supernatural spirit of the deceased pictured whom they feared might do them harm as they cleaned.

Accustomed to grand old piles with haunted legends like his late Uncle Thomas' place in Boston, not much spooked James. He had been to the office many times before and even had become quite drunk there late at night with his friends without a single visit or sign of any nighttime specters.

As James and his old prep school chum Henry chatted about business and politics, an ebullient Jack Morgan burst into his son's office with the wedding pictures that the photographer had just developed and promptly delivered. Beaming, the noted banker uncharacteristically displayed paternal pride as he thumbed through them, putting his favorites aside on the large, carved and gilded wood table with a Verde antique marble top where his son had spread out various business documents of mutual interest to James and the Morgans.

Pointing to the pictures on the table, the elder Morgan practically shouted, "Take a look at these, they're quite good – he's actually managed to catch the spirit of the moment!"

When Henry reached over to take the album, Jack noticed James and extended his hand warmly as he said, "Good to see you again. Didn't know you were in town."

As James glanced over Henry's shoulder to see the pictures, he replied, "Just returned from Boston, sir. I had to settle my uncle's estate."

"Thomas Peabody DeVere?" replied Jack. "My condolences. As I recall, he was quite an operator! We did a few deals together years ago." Jack chuckled as he reminisced. "We made out particularly well in the Far East."

"He was quite a fighter up to the end," said James as he narrowed his eyes thinking of how long the old man took to die. Then he said politely, "I'm just sorry I wasn't able to attend Junius' wedding."

The elder Morgan smiled in reply as he said, "It was a great party!" Then as Jack winked at James he said, "We had lots of lovely ladies there."

When Jack described the ceremony and reception like the proud father he was, James did his best to pretend he was interested. Finally passing the book to James, Jack said, "See for yourself.

The photos do a far better job of explaining the event than I ever could." While he turned to leave his son's office, the elder Morgan said to Henry, "Do come by when you're finished. We have a few mundane matters to discuss."

"Oh?" said Henry.

The older Morgan explained, "To fund or not to fund."

Henry cocked his eyebrow, "The railroad deal in China or the loan to Russia?"

Jack Morgan said, "*Those* are *your projects*. I'd like your take on Germany."

Henry guessed, "They're running behind on payments again?"

"The government is nearly bankrupt," replied Jack, his tone serious.

Henry quipped, "What else is new, father?"

"You might do something worthy of the Morgan name," replied Jack his eyes twinkling.

Henry said, "Unlikely, sir."

"I'll see you in my office in an hour." Nodding to James, Jack said, "Come by later this week. There are some people I'd like you to meet." As he turned to go, he said, "I think you'll find them quite interesting."

"Thank you, sir," said James delighted. It wasn't often that the elder Morgan gave a young man the time of day let alone invited him to a meeting. He knew it was a great opportunity. Usually he dealt with one of the more junior partners or relied on Junius or Henry to pass on tips.

After Jack left the room, Henry said to James, "My father likes you. He thinks you're tough."

James smiled at the thought. The esteemed banker had no idea just how tough he really was. Then he turned back to the photos. There were quite a few pictures of attractive girls that the bachelor feasted his eyes on. He enjoyed himself until he came across a photo of Geraldine. Pointing to the picture, he said barely disguising his contempt, "Who's the fat cow?"

"Not a close friend of Junius', I can assure you," said Henry laughing.

Then James pointed to Charles. "I don't think I've ever seen him before."

"Blakesley?" replied Henry quite surprised. "Capital man. Surely you've met!"

James said, "I always remember the significant."

"Then I guess you don't know him," replied Henry. "Charles was in Junius' year at Princeton. He's one of the brightest and most decent chaps I know. A real good sport all round."

"Where's he from?" inquired James skeptically.

"Somewhere in the Midwest – Oklahoma I think," replied Henry.

Scoffing, James said, "No wonder he left!"

"Actually, he belongs in the right set." Henry went on to explain to his friend, "Charles' family came from out East. They bought their land from the railroad years ago."

Clearly unimpressed, James replied, "So the Blakesleys were settlers who picked up the land nobody wanted!" He sneered, "Where did they make their real money – whoring and gambling?"

Shaking his head at his friend, Henry said, "Trust me, what matters is when it comes to cattle and farmland, Charles' family practically owns half the state. Junius went out there to visit one summer and came back mightily impressed."

James, who instinctively did not like the young man, said, "I heard the ranchers and farmers have been having it pretty hard lately."

Henry shook his head yes. Then he explained, "That's one reason Charles stopped traveling and decided to come back to the States." James smiled as his friend asserted, "His family certainly has been hurt by a combination of depressed prices and serious costs of investments in new farm equipment over the last few years." But the playboy businessman's smile vanished as Henry said, "Still, Charles' family is among the very small group of major players in Oklahoma."

While James continued to look with interest at the picture of Junius' best man, Henry admitted, "They've still got a little portfolio at our bank." Leaning closer to his friend, Henry said confidentially, "Between us, I'm thinking of letting him in a few deals."

"Are you sure you can trust him?" said James. Then, as he pointed to Charles' photo, he suggested, "There's something shifty about his eyes. I don't know about him. He looks like the kind that could get mixed up with the wrong sort."

Henry laughed. "Charles shifty? Not a chance. I've seen him dance with old ladies just to make them smile."

"Maybe he has a thing for older women," suggested James.

"Not this guy! He has eyes for only one woman." Turning the page, Henry pointed to a shot of Charles and Josie dancing cheek to cheek. He asserted, "She's the luckiest girl I know."

For a moment, James just stared at the photo. Then as he moved the album closer to him to make sure his eyes weren't deceiving him, James said lingering over the photo, "It looks to me like he's the lucky one."

Henry said, "Josie and Charles really hit it off. I'll be shocked if they aren't engaged by Christmas."

"Well, she's certainly beautiful," replied James dejectedly as he lifted a photo of 1929's most celebrated debutante and one of her beau and tucked them into his pocket. He didn't know what he was going to do with them but he had a feeling they would be useful. With the revelation that this young man from Oklahoma seriously was dating a girl James wanted, his instinctive dislike for Charles Blakesley grew intense while his interest in Josie increased significantly. Competitive by nature and always thrilled by the chase, after New York's most desirable bachelor recovered from the unexpected news, he looked forward to seducing Josie away from Charles.

Unaware of James' true motives, Henry said, "I'll introduce you." Then as he thought about it, he said. "You know if she wasn't already taken, she'd definitely be your type."

James shrugged indifferently as he closed the album and resumed the business discussions. While he had every intention of pursuing 1929's most celebrated debutante and making her, his, he had no interest in letting anyone know just how keen he really was.

Fifteen minutes later, Henry and James walked over to consult Charles MacVeagh, a savvy, young investment banker at Morgan's. They stopped in the main hallway and stared with disbelief as they witnessed Joseph Kennedy walk into the building. Kennedy strode right past the guard in the vestibule as if he owned the place.

"Where does he think he's going?" exclaimed James clearly shocked.

"Not where he thinks he is!" replied Henry coolly.

While Joseph headed towards the second doorway, a doorman came forward just in time to block his path. The doorman, who was very large, towered over Kennedy. He stared down at the intruder like he would a vagrant. No one pushed his or her way into the House of Morgan. Kennedy's behavior was deserving of contempt and the doorman knew it. He acted accordingly.

Glaring at the man, Joe said arrogantly, "Mr. Kennedy to see Mr. Morgan."

Not budging an inch, the doorman replied stone faced, "Do you have an appointment?"

Thinking fast, Joe said, "Tell Jack, Joe is back from California. It's very important."

When the doorman didn't move, Joe thundered, "Hurry up and give him the message if you don't want to lose your job!"

Still not moving, the doorman replied, "Mr. Kennedy, as I'm sure you are aware no one comes to the House of Morgan without an appointment."

Undeterred, the brash man barked, "I don't care what other people do. I'm Joseph P. Kennedy and you can consider that reason enough."

The scene developing between the doorman and Joe Kennedy attracted attention inside. Secretaries and junior associates clustered to watch the unfolding events. As the news of the distraction spread through the bank, more employees, gawking and straining their ears, congregated by the doorway. After finally getting Joe to agree to wait in the vestibule, the doorman walked past the gathered employees, through partner row and into the inner sanctum that was Jack's office. The bank was as silent as a tomb as all waited. Staff from every level, leaned forward to watch as the doorman whispered to Jack's secretary, who after finishing a note approached her boss. After a minute, they saw Jack nod. Joe could see Jack's reaction as well. He smiled triumphantly. Then, he picked up a newspaper that lay nearby, confident that he would soon be called inside. What he didn't see was the expression on the doorman's face. As the doorman headed out of the area, Joe was so engrossed in an article on the French Bourse he failed to notice Jack's secretary close the door to her boss' office. Employees didn't miss the cue. Most went back to work.

After sometime, Joe put the paper down and looked at his watch. Clearly getting a bit irritated, he motioned to the nearest employee to find out how much longer he was expected to wait. The junior associate went up to Jack's secretary. After a brief conversation, the associate walked back to his own office. Then the secretary rang a bell which summoned two errand boys who walked slowly back to the doorman and handed him two notes. After glancing at the notes, the doorman self-assuredly strode up to Joe Kennedy who had stood confidently upright during the previous proceedings. By this point, the office buzzed with interest again.

Taking Joe firmly by the arm, the doorman said roughly, "This way out, sir."

Joe was indignant. Fending the doorman off, he exclaimed, "What!"

"Mr. Morgan will not see you." The doorman made sure he said this loudly enough for all the clerks and secretaries to hear.

Joe's face and ears immediately turned bright red from anger and embarrassment. But as the slight sunk in, he clenched his jaw and his eyes hardened. The humiliated man managed to hold his head high as he left the building disgraced, by vowing he would seek revenge on the House of Morgan. No one ever had crossed Joe Kennedy without suffering.

While Joe was ushered out, employees clapped and the doorman smiled because he now had a personal note of thanks from Jack Morgan himself.

When the applause died down, James said to Henry, "Can you believe that uppity Irish Catholic swine? He knows the rules. We don't like Jews, we don't tolerate Catholics and we don't like him."

"I can't believe what he just did. He's so brash. It's utterly distasteful. Everyone makes an appointment with father before coming here," replied Henry clearly stunned by the man's action and disturbed by the unnecessary confrontation that resulted. After stopping by Charles MacVeagh's desk, he suggested James return with him to his office.

"I say, let's have a drink to upholding the rules of the establishment," suggested Henry as he walked over to the sarcophagus and lifted the top to retrieve a bottle of champagne and several Baccarat crystal glasses.

After ringing for a container of ice to sufficiently chill the bottle, Henry and James resumed their earlier business discussions. Twenty minutes later, when they had finished going through the papers and various angles of the deal, Henry felt the champagne had been sufficiently chilled. He called in Michael Mansfield, another former prep school chum and Morgan employee, to join them. After passing out the glasses to his friends as well as to himself, he said, "Cheers!"

Before taking a sip, James offered a toast, "To the domination of Wall Street by the entitled – To us WASPs." While James downed his champagne, he said, "Wonder what old Kennedy wanted."

"Does it matter?" replied Henry not even wanting to think about the awkward situation.

After taking several sips of his drink, Michael asserted, "I can't imagine Joe Kennedy or any Irish Catholic ever could have any substantial impact on our business or Wall Street for that matter."

James muttered, "Kennedy? What kind of name is Kennedy anyway?"

The men laughed.

After Henry topped up their glasses, Michael asserted, "The man's a two-bit bootlegger who's manipulated a few stocks. Mark my words; he won't be in any history books.

By nightfall, all of Wall Street was celebrating another great day in the market and gossiping about Joe Kennedy's public humiliation at 23 Wall Street. Joe Kennedy was already calculating his next move; even if it took a long time, he planned on leveling the playing field.

* * *

Charles was so concerned about making a good impression on the Baxter-Brownes that he arrived fifteen minutes early for dinner. To kill time, he walked across the street to Central Park. Nervously, he paced along the big path. He knew he really liked Josie because he had never been so concerned about a girl's feelings let alone her family's.

The good-looking young man had never had a problem attracting eligible girls' and effortlessly winning over their parents' approval. He experienced difficulty only when he would inform the parties that he was more interested in traveling than in settling down.

Certainly Charles had not expected to get into a serious relationship anytime soon, but despite his resolve, he felt differently about Josie than he had about any girl he had ever met. Although it had been her striking looks that caught his attention, during their first encounter, initially he had found her quite obnoxious. He almost wrote her off as just another spoiled socialite like so many others in her set. Having now spent hours upon hours meeting up at parties, walking around the park, driving in the countryside, and just talking on the phone, as much as he was drawn to her beauty, it was her intelligence and spirit that captivated him.

This evening, as Charles looped back to head towards the Beaux-Arts style mansion designed by McKim, Mead, and White, at the corner of East 78th Street and 5th Avenue, the young man from the Midwest couldn't help but feel a bit intimidated by the impressive, stark limestone façade as he hoped for the best. But before he got the chance, before he had even left the park, he was hit over the head by a heavy, sharp object. The impact was so hard that he fell forward and collapsed without a fight.

Hit from behind, Charles didn't have the opportunity to see his attacker. The last thing he remembered hearing was a gruff voice that muttered, "I did time because of you!"

He moaned as he felt someone kick him in the ribs and then blacked out.

When Charles regained consciousness, he found himself lying in a heap of withered leaves, his clothes scruffy, soiled. Blood dripped down his face and onto his once crisp, white shirt. He ached all over. As he fumbled to find a handkerchief to wipe the blood, he realized his wallet was missing. But he was too weak and in too much pain to care.

Darkness had long since descended, scattering the few who had remained from the park. Dazed, Charles slowly made his way alone to the Baxter-Brownes. He felt very light-headed from the loss of blood. His body was so bruised that he had trouble putting one foot in front of the other. Twice he collapsed in the distance between the park and the Baxter-Brownes' home.

Lying on the street mumbling, he didn't care that he now looked like a bum, the cold cement felt good against his bruised body. But somehow, after a few minutes, Charles managed to get back up and stagger towards his goal. It took all the energy left in his body just to reach for the knocker. He summoned the strength to bang it several times against the imposing door bearing the insignia of the Duke of Vendome. There he waited for what he thought seemed like an excruciatingly long period, clinging to the knocker for support. When it finally opened, he fell forward, fainting in the arms of a very formal, alarmed butler. He heard Josie shriek; he saw a vision of her gliding down the marble staircase into the foyer in a light green silver sequined evening dress, a flurry of pastel glitter, the scent of her perfume – the sweet smell of rosewater and then darkness.

When he woke up, he heard Josie screaming urgently for her father, for anyone, to call the doctor. His limp but heavy body ached with every step that Dexter, the Baxter-Brownes' butler, took as he slowly carried the wounded young man up the grand staircase at Claire's instruction. Charles' eyes stared blankly at the beautiful art deco Tiffany glass sunroof above the staircase that due to his state, seemed to spin around in an elliptical fashion. He could hear servants murmuring, bustling around as Claire coolly, efficiently issued orders for boiled water, disinfectant, bandages. Dizzy, his vision a bit blurry, his thoughts jumbled, Charles finally realized Josie was next to him. It pained him to see her ashen face, her large soft dark eyes wide with fear, peering at him as he rested in Dexter's steady hands, walking by his side, clinging to his hand, quietly murmuring prayers as he groaned, all the way up the stairs, down the hall and through a hand painted archway to the right. He felt a little more comfortable when Dexter finally placed him on a bed in the Cathay room.

While they waited for the doctor, Claire and a few of the more experienced servants administered to his superficial wounds as Josie stroked his hair and offered comforting words. At the sound of the arrival of the doctor, the ladies of the house temporarily left the injured in the servants care in order to brief the physician.

Wincing with pain, Charles wished he could black out again as he listened to a few of the more superstitious hypothesizing on his predicament and the future of his relationship with Josie, while others envisioned the worst possible prognosis. Too weak to respond, he felt helpless, infuriated, but mostly concerned as they gossiped about him as if he couldn't understand a word they were saying.

Despite his pain, Charles almost found it funny, when Mary, a large middle-aged servant that smelled of garlic, pompously asserted as she examined the blow to his head, that without a doubt he'd be left with brain damage. His humor failed him however, when Suzie, a homely girl who helped in the kitchen, claimed confidently that even if Miss Josephine's friend wasn't left with ugly facial scars from the gash over his eyebrow, she had overheard Miss Claire telling her friends that she didn't think the relationship was serious. The patient's mood worsened to the point that he no longer held back when the servant stated that after the seemingly endless stream of suitors who had arrived in fancy sports cars and limousines to the house, *she* thought that any boy who turned up courting on foot was out of his league. Lunging out of bed, despite his pain, his look leering as he towered over her, Charles told her in no uncertain terms and all others present that given *her* personality, no matter what *she* looked like, *he* would never date *her*!

After immediately silencing the gossip and speculation and sending this most vocal critic flying from the room in a fit of tears through his successful outburst, an exhausted Charles slumped back in the bed. Although generally a decent fellow, when provoked Charles Blakesley made it quite clear he was no pushover. Several minutes later, the remaining sheepish staff were as relieved as the cantankerous patient when at long last the doctor came into the room. The injured victim was not prepared for the lengthy preparatory cleaning necessary before the physician could sew up the ghastly gash with twelve stitches. But he was happy when the doctor left him with painkillers. As Albert, Claire and Josie walked the doctor to the doorway, Charles overheard the physician say, "He's suffered a concussion, a broken rib and some nasty bruises." Then, he heard the medical man say, as he looked at Josie, "No long conversations and certainly don't ask him anything that might upset him tonight."

Despite the doctor's orders, Charles was thrilled when Josie raced back up the marble stairs to rejoin him as soon as the physician had left. As the drugs kicked in, the young man from the Midwest took in the showcase bedroom designed to encapsulate all the romantic imagery of the East. With its wall panels and upholstered furniture made of fine yellow Chinese silk, delicate colored chinoiserie screens and secretariat, Ming dynasty porcelain vases and Chinnery oil paintings of pretty Chinese boat girls, he thought it reminiscent of the Imperial court of the Emperor Kang-shi. He just wished he was sleeping there under other circumstances.

Smiling weakly, Charles mumbled miserably as he looked at his lovely surroundings and thought about his condition and what the servants had been saying, "Guess I made some impression."

Soon however he felt secure when in response Josie kissed his forehead and told him, as she pointed to one of the panels on the wall depicting the wooing of a Chinese maiden by a famous 14th century poet, that his prospects were much better than Master Lui's had been, and his love story was legendary. As Charles drifted off to sleep, Josie recited the saga.

* * *

Josie sat with Charles holding his hand well into the night, administering water and pain killers when he woke up periodically. Around dawn, when she finally got tired, she decided to lie down next to him. Instinctively, he reached out for her. She woke up the next morning in his arms. It felt so right that she didn't want to move. But she knew her parents wouldn't approve if they found her like this. Still, Josie found it difficult to leave her love alone in the antique mahogany bed whose yellow silk canopy with tassels stemmed from a rosette in the ceiling that enveloped the furniture cozily like a fanciful tent from the time of Kubla Khan. Only the sound of her mother's approaching footsteps propelled her up and out. As she dashed out of the chinoiserie filled guest bedroom, Charles moaned and then rolled over.

Several days later, as the Baxter-Brownes sat around a Jacobean gate-legged table in their intimate Breakfast room, Charles came down to join them. He still lacked color in his face and winced from the pain, but he was in good spirits considering what had happened.

Glancing up from the morning paper, Albert inquired, "How are you feeling?"

Embarrassed, Charles' cheeks colored slightly as he replied, "Much better, sir. Thank you for taking care of me." He explained the peculiar circumstances. "I think I was robbed because I'm missing my wallet."

"That's terrible!" exclaimed Claire aghast. Horrified that such an occurrence could happen so close to her home in an area where she frequently strolled, she asserted, "You really should report this to the police!"

Realizing that despite their guest's polite nod in agreement, the young man clearly looked unconvinced that the action would accomplish anything, Albert offered, "We're just happy you're with us now."

Thinking he was well enough to discuss the events, Josie asked the question she had wanted to know the night before. She inquired, "What exactly happened?"

Trying to make light of the situation as best as he could, his sardonic humor evident, Charles explained. "I got here a little early and made the mistake of strolling into Central Park while I was waiting."

'Next time, just come right in," replied Albert chuckling. Ignoring his wife's frown, he said winking, "I'd rather have an extra drink before dinner than no dinner at all."

Coloring as he thought of the inconvenience and spectacle he had created, Charles quickly stammered, "I'm just so sorry."

"Don't be," replied Claire, ever the proper hostess. Thinking of the scandal that could have been created had the situation been worse, she quickly said, "We're just grateful you're going to be all right."

"Do you have any idea who attacked you?" asked the more practical Albert.

Charles lamely offered, "Someone who wanted my wallet, I guess."

Later, he told Josie about what he remembered hearing just before he blacked out. He shivered as his mind replayed that menacing gruff voice. The young man had never dealt with shady people before. His only encounter was with the thug at Texas Guinan's. Shivers ran through his body as he realized he'd have to be extra careful in the future and watch out for Josie as well. If the thug recognized him, he wouldn't forget her face.

* * *

After lunch, Josie gave their houseguest a tour of the residence. Built as a wedding present from Albert to Claire and modeled on a French nobleman's eighteenth century hotel, the perfectly symmetrical twenty-four-room rococo style mansion with striking hand painted ceilings had been hailed as one of the finest examples of Beaux Arts architecture in America. The tour guide admitted her parents wouldn't be able to afford to buy the land, let alone build the same house today because of the skyrocketing cost of property, construction, and taxes in the city. In fact, she acknowledged the majority of the most valuable pieces in the house, like the property itself, had been bequeathed by her family's successful progenitors. Much to his relief, the more time Charles spent with Josie, the more convinced he became that although the Baxter-Brownes were very wealthy, they did not have nearly the amount of money he would have expected given the type of mansion they lived in. Although he had no doubt Josie's family had more liquidity than his, since land made up the bulk of the Blakesleys' net worth, in terms of raw assets, he felt his family's holdings put him in the "eligible bachelor" category.

Josie laughed when her down to earth companion informed her that what he liked most about her parent's place was that despite its grandeur, it felt homey inside.

She then told him that she most appreciated it was well heated in the winter, kept cool in the summer and always smelled of fresh flowers and good food. He laughed when she said that despite milk and cookies and the best college food available anywhere, four years at Mount Holyoke still had made her appreciate the Baxter-Browne's cook.

Charles noted that seven spacious, public rooms dominated the first floor of the 15,000 square foot limestone and marble mansion. The thirty-foot by sixty-foot marble entrance hall with bas-relief friezes depicting scenes from the courtship and marriage of Hercules to Hebe was at the center of the mansion and contained the grand staircase that led to the second floor. The center hall, with powder rooms on either side of the main entranceway, was flanked by the formal Louis XV style drawing room, red ballroom and a conservatory with a Tiffany-tiled art deco wall fountain, on one side, and Albert's study, the library and dining room on the other. Her ease in showing off the highlights of the home didn't escape him; he was sure she had been giving the tours since she was a child.

The smaller ground floor rooms that included the breakfast room, butler's pantry and small salon, were hidden behind the entrance hall. While each of the larger rooms was designed with distinct historical styles, Charles thought the smaller family rooms reflected an eclectic mixture of stylistic influences that made them cozy. Although he was awestruck by the exquisite array of artwork from ancient Greece and interested in the modern flower paintings by Georgia O'Keefe, he also was quite taken by the two portraits of Josie that John Singer Sargent had painted of her. He chuckled as she tried to rush him past the one of her at age eight holding a basket of calla lilies as she stood next to her seated mother.

Josie smiled knowingly when Charles told her that out of everything in the house, what the young man from Oklahoma was most impressed with was the Baxter-Brownes' antique furniture. When he pointed at a pair of George II chairs in the Ballroom as his favorites, she admitted her mother had commissioned one of them to match the other as well as a number of other reproductions she wanted but couldn't find anywhere. Josie made him feel a little better when she informed him that he wasn't the first guest who found the high quality replicas that came from Paul Sormani's Paris shop indistinguishable from the originals. Ever cognoscente that Easterners considered Midwesterners, much as Europeans considered Americans as backward, country cousins, lacking sophisticated taste, Charles felt embarrassed by not knowing the difference and insecure that he wouldn't measure up. He thought, even if the Baxter-Brownes were not among the ranks of the super rich in New York, there was no doubt they were very much a part of the establishment – the rarefied, sophisticated, aged money that lived, breathed, and celebrated a certain defined taste that was passed on from one generation to the next but couldn't be bought.

With these thoughts, although he tried to hide it, a mild depression came over Charles as Josie continued to show him around her family's New York residence. When Josie asked if he was okay, he let her believe he was just weak from his injuries. Still, despite his gloom, he couldn't help but be struck by the second floor of the house. In addition to the Cathay room where Charles stayed, Josie showed him the seven other bedroom suites with connecting bathrooms and a chintz patterned, family sitting room. He marveled at the extent of detailing throughout the upstairs. Each bedroom had its own decorative motif that was carried out completely to the most trivial of the furnishings, fixtures and woodwork. While Josie's parents' bedroom was decorated in the rococo style of Louis XIV, other rooms she showed Charles featured the Neoclassical Empire style, Louis XV, and Art Nouveau fashion.

Diplomatically, Charles claimed Josie's Marie Antoinette inspired bedroom suite was his favorite. She believed he truly was awed by her mother's pale-blue room sized closet with built in wood paneled wardrobes. The closet room was so large and high that it required a circular staircase originally designed for a private library to lead to a walkway that provided access to the upper level of drawers. As Josie described how she used to play dress up waltzing around the closet room in her mother's favorite gowns, the immense room took on a special meaning for Charles. But by the end of the lengthy tour, he was so exhausted he needed to go back to rest in his bed. After his respite, Charles challenged Josie to a game of chess.

While the young couple cheerfully faced off, New York's most eligible bachelor plotted his next move.

* * *

CHAPTER VIII

Vinnie Graves knew his place; he walked up to the back door of the red brick Georgian style double townhouse. The goon had spent most of his life skulking around back alleys and hiding out from the law. He was born on the South side of Chicago and had killed his first man by the age of fourteen. He stabbed the victim a total of fourteen times. He told the judge he gave the guy one jab for each year of his own rotten life. Al Capone's boys picked him up the day he got out of jail. When things got too hot for Vinnie in the Windy City, he was set up in New York in 1926. There, he worked exclusively for the king of easy money, Arnold Rothstein. He did the jobs for Rothstein that the underworld czar's own boys wouldn't touch and he enjoyed doing them. Even by gangland standards, Vinnie got perverse pleasure out of human suffering to a noteworthy degree.

A month after Rothstein's fatal shooting, an entire family in Jersey City was found diced up. Vinnie saved the husband, who had been a rat, for last, so he could watch his four children suffer excruciatingly as they slowly were sliced up first. When the police entered, they doubled back sickened by the blood-splattered sight. Limbs lay everywhere. The lifeless body of the informant's wife lay propped up against a wall. Vinnie left an ax in the middle of the pregnant woman's stomach. The thug got paid handsomely for the murders – some said out fear, he'd do the same to anyone who didn't reward him. But afterwards, no one wanted to hire him. The word on the street was he was a little too cool and good at what he did. Vinnie started working odd jobs where he could. He was on the job the night Texas Guinan's got busted. As soon as he broke out of the slammer, the thug had been looking for revenge. Now it was payback time.

Vinnie looked at his watch, rubbed his nose, spit and then knocked hard on the door. There was no answer. Impatient, he knocked again. It was cold outside and he wanted his dough. Walking around to the front of the red brick townhouse, he picked the door lock and strode inside the sixteen-foot wide entrance hall. It was beautifully decorated, but Vinnie who was focused on his objective didn't notice. Quickly he moved like a burglar towards the graceful mahogany staircase with spiral balusters and the most unusual, recessed curve handrail detailing, instinctively knowing it led to the wealth he sought. But he wouldn't get far.

Vinnie froze when he heard a very curt, condescending British voice demand to know, "What are you doing here?"

Not expecting anyone home, the underworld goon initially was caught off guard by the snooty accuser.

He quickly recovered as he turned around to face the uniformed adversary who challenged him. Vinnie informed the houseman in a cock-sure voice, "I'm here to see Mr. DeVere."

"Do you have an appointment?" inquired Bentley as he looked at the thug with utter disbelief.

Not believing in doing business with anyone other than the man who employed him, the goon pressed, "Just tell him Graves is here to see him – to get paid."

"Very well. You can wait in here," said Bentley as he motioned to the cloakroom in the front hall. After ushering Vinnie inside the room, the houseman closed the door and locked it. Bentley didn't want to take any chances. The pockmarked thug certainly looked and acted like a thief.

"Don't you call no police now or I'll kill you!" threatened Vinnie from his cloakroom cell as he regained his confident, surly demeanor. As he pounded his fist against the wall, he thundered, "I'm here on legitimate business!"

Bentley quickly walked up the stairs to James' office. He knocked but didn't wait for an answer.

As the houseman strode into the Cordovan leather covered room, James' looked up from his Kingwood veneered desk with annoyance. He demanded, "What do you want?"

"There's a goon downstairs who says he has business with you, sir," explained the houseman.

To Bentley's surprise, James replied coolly, "What's his name?"

"Graves, sir," replied the houseman. "I've locked him in the cloakroom. Should I telephone the police?"

James said carefully, "Not just yet. I'll see him. But if I'm not satisfied, I'll ask for brandy and that will be your cue to send for them."

Bentley inquired, "Shall I bring him up here, sir?"

Resuming his work, James replied without looking up, "That'll do."

James peered up at Vinnie as he entered the room. He dismissed Bentley with the reminder, "I'll ring for you when I require a top up."

James thought the thug looked even more menacing than he remembered. He was pleased with what he saw. Sipping his brandy, he said, "Well?"

"I came for the scratch," stated the goon pointedly.

Never one to part with money easily, the businessman asked, "Were you successful?"

Vinnie replied as he chewed on tobacco, "I did what I was told. You won't be having any problems with them union boys anymore."

"Excellent," replied James. While he continued peering over the documents on his desk, he inquired, "And the other problem?"

"I roughed him up good. Shook 'em up real bad. I don't think he made it to any dinner party." As proof, Vinnie took out a brown leather wallet from his pocket and handed it over to James.

James looked inside. He smiled. The wallet belonged to one Charles Edward Blakesley. There was a picture of the owner with an older couple, his address, some identification and slips of paper inside. Flipping the photo at Vinnie, James said coolly, "I gather he doesn't look like this right now."

"The last I saw of him, he was covered in blood." Vinnie smiled contently as he remembered what he had done.

The thug was extremely pleased that he was getting paid to beat up a guy he wanted to hit anyway for being responsible for his arrest at Texas Guinan's. It was the first time Vinnie had been locked up since he was fourteen. Since that first arrest, he had always stayed one step ahead of the cops. The goon hated the young twit, Blakesley, for the inconvenience. Vinnie wanted to make him pay and pay dearly. But he didn't let James know this.

The thug had stayed ahead of the game this long by keeping his feelings to himself. He could tell DeVere was a double-crossing snake and a powerful and rich one at that. Vinnie knew he had to watch his back with the businessman, he had seen plenty of men like him before. There were a lot of old boys in his business; that had been knocked off because of these sorts of relationships. Rich men had a way of keeping their dirty laundry hidden, usually by getting rid of the people who tied them to it. So Vinnie stayed silent, playing dumb, as he smiled to himself.

Opening up the billfold, James said, "I see you helped yourself to the contents." He threatened, "I should deduct it from your pay."

"Hey, I don't think so," replied Vinnie vehemently. He reasoned, "It ain't your money, either."

James stated unemotionally, "I paid you for the job."

"I did the job," countered the thug. "I gave you the wallet like we agreed." Getting upset, at the thought of making less than he had already expected, he raised his voice as he made the claim, "You never said nothing about no money."

As Vinnie glared at him, James smiled smugly and claimed, "It was expected you'd hand it over as you found it."

Stunned, the goon claimed, "We never agreed to that." Furious, he wanted to spit on the Persian carpet that covered the floor of the room to show exactly what he thought of the idea. But knowing he really needed the money, all he did was narrow his eyes at the businessman as he swore under his breath.

James smiled, not missing a thing. He knew these sorts of operators. They always skimmed. He expected it. But he knew it was important to make sure the goon remembered who was in charge and that he wasn't a fool. Rubbing the point in, James arrogantly said, "I'll deduct $100 from your pay. Consider the rest a reward from me."

Vinnie contemplated rushing his erstwhile employer, but he could tell the guy wasn't easily rattled. There wasn't a trace of anxiousness in James' voice. Even more importantly, he noted that throughout the meeting, the businessman had kept his right hand on the trigger of a small but very powerful revolver. Given the distance, the thug knew he couldn't miss his mark.

As the goon backed off, James laughed. Condescendingly he said, "*Attaboy*, just back down." Continuing to address Vinnie like he would a dog, he said, "Now sit and don't challenge me again."

James wasn't at all surprised by the turn of events. Content with the goon's performance so far, as he continued to keep his gun trained on the thug, with his other hand the businessman took out a plain envelope that contained money. As he tossed it over, he said, "This should do."

Vinnie took the money out and counted it slowly to make sure it was all there. Satisfied, he got up and turned to go. James perceptively noted that the goon bent his head subserviently low. He had learned his place.

The businessman didn't bother to get up to see Vinnie out, but he kept the gun handy just in case the goon suddenly tried something stupid.

Turning back to his work, James said, "If I want your services again, how can I reach you?"

"Just let the word out you're looking for Graves," replied the thug.

Peering up from his work, James queried, "Graves?"

As James looked at him with some interest, the goon said with a sick smile, "The name's Vinnie Graves, but they just call me Graves because I like burying people."

"I'll keep that in mind," replied the cunning businessman as he continued going through documents on his desk. As he frowned at what he was reading, he said, "I may very well need your assistance again in the future, Mr. Graves."

When Graves emerged from James' study, Bentley stood ready to escort him to the backdoor. The houseman wondered what had transpired. Eyeing the thug, he knew it couldn't be pleasant. He had overheard snippets of their conversation. Bentley thought he'd phone his sources at the DeVere steel works to find out what was going on.

Thugs never had been in the townhouse before.

* * *

Given Charles' state, the Baxter-Brownes insisted he stayed with them to recover fully. Much to Charles and Josie's delight, they were left largely to their own devices since Claire needed to supervise repairs on their country home and Albert, when he wasn't working, was much more relaxed than his wife. The young couple took advantage of the situation by flirting and chatting well into the night.

Charles spent several weeks convalescing at the Baxter-Brownes' before Claire returned. He had been well enough to go home for some time, but Josie had used his injury as an excuse for them to be together longer. Knowing they were pushing their luck and sure of their mutual feelings, Charles didn't want to upset her parents by overstaying his welcome. To celebrate his full recovery, the Baxter-Brownes planned a special dinner.

For once, Josie actually spent hours getting ready. After failing miserably to improve her looks through her own efforts, in frustration, she asked Suzie, who knew from years of practice, how to help. While her parents' had their customary drink before dinner, Josie changed into an evening gown that she had been waiting to wear for a special occasion. The ivory-gold crepe designer dress had four godet inserts in the skirt, and gauzy scarves that draped her frame, making her look like a Hollywood siren. To complete the look, Suzie brought out her eyes with Helena Rubinstein's latest eyeliner and highlighted her cheekbones with a shade that complemented the rich, red lipstick she wore.

Much to Josie's surprise, Charles also made an extra effort to look his best. He not only smoothed down his hair but he also wore a dinner jacket that belonged to Albert. Much to Josie's delight, her former patient, although slightly bigger than her father, fit almost perfectly into the clothes. Just after they had finished dressing, in their respective suites, Dexter informed them dinner would be served. As the couple took the elevator downstairs, Josie teasingly told Charles, as they laughed about how they met at Texas', that if he wanted to bartend a party for her family she could arrange a room for him in the third floor servant's quarters. Always one to appreciate humor, he retorted in kind, that he'd consider the offer if she let him send her down to the basement in the dumb waiter so she could get training in the kitchen or laundry area.

As they got out of the elevator, Josie and Charles immediately smelled the savory aroma of braised lamb coming up from the kitchen. Josie knew the cook had been working on their dinner all day. Both felt famished as they walked into the rococo-style dining room with a trompe l'oeil sky ceiling and finely carved and gilded over-mantle mirrors. Josie smiled when she heard Charles' stomach rumbling.

After Claire, Albert, Josie and Charles sat down at the Heppelwhite table in their matching chairs, the family said grace. Then, they discussed the latest news. While Josie was most interested in the cosmopolitan Ethiopian Emperor Haile Selassie's efforts to modernize his country, Charles informed them he had been intrigued by Edwin Hubble's scientific paper that the *New York Herald* had reported confirmed that the universe was in fact expanding. Claire was most concerned about the recent rise in crime in the city and what the Mayor was doing about it. While Albert calmed his wife down by saying he believed all the deaths were mob related or fell into the lowest strata of society, he made it clear to his daughter that it was important never to invite trouble of any kind.

Thinking of Charles' mugging, Claire once again recommended that the recovered victim file a complaint with the police.

Although clearly unconvinced, Charles diplomatically said, "I guess it can't hurt."

"But without a good look at the perpetrator, it probably won't help much," said Albert defending the boy. Pouring a glass of champagne to accompany their smoked salmon starter, he suggested, "Shall we drink to better times?"

Josie, Charles and Claire raised their glasses in the toast. As he put his glass down, after taking several sips of the fine champagne, Charles said, "It's very unusual. What is it?"

"A '74 Irroy," said Albert, as he took another sip. "Most people think Veuve Cliquot, Roederer Cristal and Moet are the best champagnes, but I prefer Laurent Perrier and Irroy." As he finished his glass, Albert said almost to himself, "Yes, I have a special fondness for Irroy."

Charles replied, "I've never had it before, but it's simply superb."

"By all means have some more," said Albert topping up Charles' glass and his own. He explained as he urged Charles, "I have several cases in my wine cellar."

Looking at Josie slyly, Charles said as he thought of Texas Guinan's which was still closed, "It's good to know there's one decent place left in New York where you can get served a drink without being disappointed or busted." He then addressed Albert and inquired, "How do you manage to keep your collection hidden?"

"After our main course, I'll show you," volunteered Albert. As he smelled the delicious lamb being prepared, he had a feeling they would all eat so much of it that they would need to pause before cheese and dessert.

An hour and a half later, Charles and Albert were engrossed in a discussion about whether red burgundy merited the high esteem with which it was widely regarded. When Charles said he thought 1911 was a particularly good year for burgundy, Josie was delighted to see her father reach out to him to warmly pat him on the back and say with a chuckle, "I can see we're going to get along very well."

A few minutes later, Josie watched her father and Charles as they excused themselves from the table and headed towards the cellar. As they walked away, she listened carefully in order to overhear fragments of their conversation.

Finally, she became aware that her mother was talking to her when she heard her exclaim, "Josephine Clarissa Baxter-Browne!" As Josie stared at her, an exasperated Claire asked, "Have you heard a word of what I said?"

In response, Josie looked up from her plate. She had been so engrossed eavesdropping on the men's conversation that she truly didn't realize Claire was still in the room let alone attempting to communicate with her.

Josie smiled sheepishly and shook her head yes and then no as Claire sighed and said, "You *really* like that boy."

She answered, her voice reflecting a dreamy quality, "I've never liked anyone like this before."

"That's what scares me," said Claire flatly. Her voice was firm as she looked meaningfully at her daughter. She commanded Josie to remember, "As a woman, you always must think with your head, not just with your heart."

Concerned about what her mother was intimating, Josie hesitantly inquired, "What are you trying to say?"

"I don't want to see you get hurt," stated Claire emphatically. "Or sell yourself short."

Smiling as she thought of what Charles had said in his sleep the previous night, Josie said assuredly as she leaned back in her chair, "Don't worry."

Not entirely convinced that her daughter should settle for a cowboy from the Midwest who arrived at their house for his first dinner beaten up, when there were so many more suitable bachelors, Claire replied cautiously, "Well, we'll see."

Ignoring both her mother's tone and suggestions, Josie got up from the table and walked over to the floor to ceiling window. As she gazed outside at 5th Avenue and Central Park, she whispered under her breath so softly that she thought only she could hear her vow, "He doesn't know it yet, but he's the man I'm going to marry."

"Well, you just make sure he asks first before you give him any ideas," retorted an irritated Claire coolly as she got up in a huff and walked past her daughter before ringing for a servant to bring out the next course.

Taking a deep breath before speaking, Josie sighed heavily. Then as she turned around to face her mother, she rolled her eyes and lashed out from annoyance at her mother's reaction and from her own embarrassment. She hadn't meant for her mother to hear what she said. As her mother stared at her unhappily, Josie muttered, "I'm not stupid!"

"Then don't behave like you are!" replied Claire clearly frustrated. As she dug into the cheese course, she began pleading, "You're so young..."

"By my age, you were married!" exclaimed Josie not giving her mother a chance to complete her train of thought.

"To a man my parents considered *eminently* suitable," retorted Claire pointedly.

"I thought you liked him!" charged Josie crossly as she thought about how perfectly Charles had behaved and how well he seemed to get along with all of them.

Clenching her jaw, Claire acknowledged grudgingly, "He's a nice boy." Then, she said damningly, "He's fine – as a friend – even as an escort."

Josie didn't bother to hide her anger as she demanded that her mother tell her what she thought was wrong with Charles.

Knowing her nonconformist daughter wouldn't like what she was about to say, Claire replied as diplomatically as she could, "I just think you shouldn't limit yourself so quickly."

Ringing for the staff to bring in another tray of cheeses, she claimed, "You hardly know him. You should be open-minded." Josie could see her mother's face had had begun to flush red, as it often did when she became really upset. But despite her agitated state, Claire continued stressing, "There are so many available young men!"

As Josie stared at her mother in stony silence, finally Claire stated what she really had in mind. "Think of your friend Catherine – what a *wonderful* life she has with Junius." Looking at her daughter meaningfully, she tried to say persuasively, "You know Henry is still single!"

The mere suggestion infuriated Josie. She tried to control her temper as she thought first about the slight to her love and then that once again she was falling short of family expectations. It seemed so unfair to her that the boy she loved was getting short shrift just because her provincially minded, snobbish mother, who seemed so tolerant on other issues – even very modern, was terribly narrow minded on this topic.

Exasperated, Josie practically screamed back at Claire, "Why can't you accept, I am not interested in marrying for social reasons or money. I am in love and that's all that matters to me!"

Calmly Claire replied, her blue eyes cold, totally devoid of emotion, "You can fall in love with a rich man as well as a poor one." In frustration she said, "You're so naive. You don't understand."

Josie shouted angrily, "I'm not chattel to be bartered."

Shaking her head in disapproval, from experience Claire explained, "Difficulties in life can kill love." As she looked directly into her daughter's eyes for the greatest affect, she asserted almost mournfully, "Why do you always have to make things so difficult?" Hushing her daughter before she could protest, Claire insisted, "I only want to ensure your long-term happiness."

Refusing to accept her mother's jaundiced view, Josie claimed, "No matter what, my love for Charles makes every moment worth it."

"And I just don't want to see you hurt," replied the upset mother. "Love isn't always a good thing." Frowning, she insisted, "It can be very painful. You're so headstrong and stubborn. I just hope and pray your romantic idea of love doesn't ruin your life."

Claire feared her daughter liked this boy too much. She knew they had made a terrible mistake letting him stay at their home so long. He just wasn't the sort of young man she had expected or wanted as a future son-in-law. As charming as he was, even if he had come from an East coast family that they knew or was an European aristocrat, she had expected her daughter to marry a career-oriented boy who had settled into a proper job with great prospects soon after university, not some impulsive, adventure-seeker. Claire just hoped and prayed her daughter came to her senses before it was too late.

* * *

While the women had been bickering, Albert and Charles had been so engrossed in their discussion of wine; they had remained in the cellar for over an hour. When Albert finally stuck his head inside the dining room, feigning a smile, Claire said, "Don't worry darling, just go on." She knew from experience her husband wanted to show off his revolving bar in the library and, after her discussion with her daughter, she wasn't in the mood to play the charming hostess to Charles Blakesley.

Moments later, Josie's exuberant father excitedly told Charles as he ushered him into the ornately carved walnut paneled library, "You're going to love this!"

After walking over to the west wall bookcase, Albert said as he pressed the small button behind a book entitled: *The Temperance Guide To Living*, "I've had zealous supporters of Prohibition here and they've never suspected."

Charles thought it was one of the best-stocked private bars he'd ever seen – both before Prohibition and since.

Albert inquired as he reached for a bottle, "You did say you like claret, didn't you?"

Charles replied, "Absolutely. It's a great drink and it's been a brilliant decade for it, too."

While he poured the drinks, Albert inquired, "Have you been buying claret?"

Charles acknowledged, "A bit." As Albert handed him a glass of the drink, he explained, "My uncle has quite a good cellar. He bought twenty six cases last year because he said it was supposed to be a superb year." The young man speculated, "From what I've heard about this year's harvest, my guess is he's collecting '29 in bulk now, too."

At Albert's suggestion, the men sat down in front of the Italian Baroque marble fireplace with an oversized gilded mirror to enjoy their drinks and room's painted ceiling that depicted the crowning of knowledge. After they had taken a few sips, Albert asked Charles what he had on his mind. Josie's father had become especially fond of Charles. In many ways he found the boy to be like the son he never had. Their political views and tastes were quite similar; instinctively he could tell the young man truly loved his daughter. But knowing how his wife felt on the matter, and as a responsible father, he felt he needed to make sure before things went any farther that Charles had a future that would lead to financial security for his daughter.

Given his past, Charles did his best to alleviate the Baxter-Brownes' doubts. He promised, despite his love for traveling and climbing mountains, he would settle down and start to do more investing on Wall Street. Delighted that his potential son-in-law showed an interest in his field, Albert volunteered to open doors and help the young man in any way he could. While Charles made it clear he appreciated the gesture and looked forward to discussing the market and various stocks and investments with the banker, he stated emphatically that he hoped to make money through his own efforts. Albert appreciated the idealistic boy's work ethic although he knew his wife would have preferred for their daughter a richer, more secure husband from the East Coast establishment they were so much a part of.

After graduating from Harvard, Albert himself had chosen to join a boutique organization that he grew into a prosperous business instead of joining a major bank. Given his position, he felt confident that he'd be able to help the couple in their first few years if necessary. After finishing several glasses of claret, both men thought the conversation went better than either had expected. Josie, who had popped out of the dining room ostensibly for a breath of fresh air after the heated conversation with her mother, was pleased to catch the conclusion of the conversation.

From the hallway she overheard Charles say, as he got up to extend his hand to her father, "I hope I'll be invited back again."

Her father's words, delivered with a warm smile, weren't lost on her. "I'll leave that choice up to Josie." Then, as he took Charles' hand and shook it after patting him on the back, he replied, "But you're definitely welcome to join me again for a drink."

Relieved, Josie rushed back to the dining in better humor just before the men walked through the pair of double paneled pocket doors that separated the library from the rococo style dining room.

Several hours later, after the elder Baxter-Brownes retired for the evening, Josie and Charles walked over to the formal drawing room. For several moments, they stood in the doorway, listening. Finally, after she heard her father snoring, Josie closed the door.

Charles couldn't believe how loud he was; they even could hear him all the way downstairs. Then he teased, "How about your mother?"

Josie retorted gamely, "She doesn't snore."

As he moved closer to Josie and pulled her towards him, Charles asked, "So how can you tell she's asleep?"

"I can't." She looked up at him meaningfully, explaining, "But I know she won't come down again which is the important thing."

Provocatively playing with her hair, he pressed, "And the servants?"

"Tucked in," she acknowledged, as she looked at his slightly unbuttoned his shirt.

Pleased, he said smiling *that* smile at her as his energized, sparkling eyes met hers, "You mean we're the only ones still awake?"

"Uh-huh," said Josie as Charles pulled her in front of him so he could reach over and play with her hair and kiss her neck.

Josie's heart was starting to beat very quickly, but she tried to appear unaffected. As he continued to touch her, she whispered, "Mr. Blakesley, perhaps I had better ask your intentions."

As he picked her up and carried her over to the red silk neo-classical Louis XV sofa in the middle of the room, he said grinning as his eyes undressed her, "I plan to seduce you."

* * *

The following night, as the crescent moon shone over Manhattan, Josie, Geraldine and Rebecca walked into Evelyn Maker's Carnegie Hall suite. Despite the late hour, eager clients waiting for the answers to their prayers packed the plush waiting room. Although a few were speculators looking for windfalls, the majority came to solve personal and family matters or out of romantic interest. An hour and forty-five minutes passed before the clairvoyant's secretary informed the fashionably clad flappers they were next.

"I can't believe I'm here!" muttered an irritated Geraldine as she paced back and forth.

Rebecca replied, not even trying to disguise her delight, "You lost the bet!"

"And I'm sure even the great seer herself wouldn't have predicted that," retorted the surly Geraldine.

Josie said, "Unless we ask her, we'll never know."

"Even if we do, I wouldn't count on it," snorted Geraldine as she rolled her eyes.

"So then what will you ask?" inquired a curious Rebecca.

Geraldine muttered, "Obviously something I won't rely on."

"With that attitude, you won't learn anything," asserted Evelyn who stood in the doorway staring at the girls.

"How long have you been listening to us?" gasped Rebecca, totally caught off guard by the sudden appearance of the renowned fortune teller.

"Longer than she's been standing there," retorted Geraldine before Evelyn had the opportunity to reply. Turning to her friends,

Geraldine speculated, "I bet she eavesdrops on all her clients." Then striding up to Evelyn, Geraldine said, "Pretty clever operation. Tell me do you spy on all your clients from the waiting room or in your office?" As she snooped around Geraldine asked, "What kind of little devices do you use?"

"I have *special* powers," asserted Evelyn in a stern, commanding voice.

"We all do," retorted Geraldine skeptically as she continued to look for evidence.

Evelyn replied in a huff, "I have a very busy schedule. Miss Ashley, if you are not serious, I don't need to waste my time."

Josie thought the four-eyed fortuneteller that dressed severely in black looked more like a spinster librarian or worse, an apparition from a horror movie than a world famous guru. While Josie shivered, she noticed Evelyn's appearance didn't intimidate Geraldine in the least. In fact, Geraldine seemed rather intrigued.

Picking up one of the many copies of Evelyn's newsletter in the waiting room, Geraldine said, "So how many subscribers do you have?" As she looked at the price of the publication, she gasped, "You get close to a buck for the impersonal celestial chart reading?

"For the information given, it's a bargain!" declared Evelyn emphatically.

Geraldine shook her head. "I suppose in your profession it's the easiest way you can expand your market. As a businesswoman, I applaud you." Taking a good look around she asserted, "My guess is you're pretty good at figuring out what people want to hear."

Motioning for Geraldine to sit down at the consultation table, Evelyn challenged her, as she took place in the chair opposite, "See for yourself."

As Evelyn stared at Geraldine, the room fell silent. Josie and Rebecca huddled around the two to watch the proceedings intently.

Taking Geraldine's hands in her own, the seer held them as she closed her eyes. Dramatically she exclaimed she needed to *feel* the *energy*. Then she studied Geraldine's hands very carefully. After several moments, Evelyn claimed, "You have a strong energy force running through you." As she rubbed Geraldine's hands she deduced, "You like to work with your hands. You sculpt and you're a good painter." After she analyzed the cards Geraldine picked, she asserted, "I see you don't like men very much."

Unimpressed, Geraldine replied, "Tell me something I don't know."

While the clairvoyant drew up a chart for Geraldine, she informed her client, "You will live to a ripe old age and your life will always be easy."

Geraldine got up seemingly unconvinced. "I'll give you this – you make a person feel better by telling them what they want to hear."

Evelyn smiled. "Not much goes past you, Miss Ashley." As she motioned for Josie, she said still addressing Geraldine, "But I reckon I could teach you a thing or two."

"I don't doubt it," said Geraldine. Then as she walked past the seer, she whispered in her ear, "But then, I'm not a huckster."

"Josie, you're next," exclaimed Rebecca excitedly as she pushed her friend towards Evelyn.

Hesitantly, Josie muttered, "I don't know if I want to do this."

"Why not?" inquired a surprised Geraldine. As she rolled her eyes she said, "Even I was pushed into it." Glancing at Evelyn, she said smiling coyly, "And after meeting Miss Maker, I think I might enjoy further discussions."

"I told you you'd think the consultation was worth it!" said Rebecca enthusiastically.

Josie smiled knowingly as Geraldine laughed.

Catching on that she was missing something, Rebecca asked, "What's so funny?"

"I don't want to go into it right now," replied Geraldine. Then as he patted her friend on the back she said, "I'll give you this, I am glad we came."

"I knew I was right!" exclaimed a still clueless Rebecca. Then as she motioned to Josie she said, "C'mon. It's your turn!"

While Josie looked at her friends and the seer, she said warily, "No offense, but this creeps me out. I had a bad experience with an Ouija board. It took me weeks before I slept normally after that. I don't want to be told anything that might spook me."

Disarmingly, Evelyn promised, "I never tell anyone bad things unless they ask."

Reluctantly, Josie offered her hands to the seer.

As she looked at them, the clairvoyant said, "Would you prefer financial advice instead?"

"Thanks, but…"

Geraldine interrupted Josie to say, "We already got your stock tips by reading your newsletter and the *Wall Street Journal* while we were waiting."

The astrologist offered, "I could personalize it."

"Josie's set. She has a trust," replied Rebecca. Then she explained, "We came out of romantic interest."

Josie's blush made it obvious this was indeed the real reason for their appointments.

Evelyn began, "You have been much desired by men."

"That's obvious," said Geraldine unimpressed.

"Shush," said an irritated Evelyn. "I need silence."

"Let her concentrate, Geraldine," nagged Rebecca.

After some time, the seer said, "I see two great loves in your life."

"Two?" replied Josie surprised.

Slowly the seer said, "They are related."

"What is she going to do? Marry a relative?" jibed Geraldine sarcastically.

After taking some time, the clairvoyant seriously asserted, "No. But there are definitely two strong men – at least two."

"Have I met them?" inquired Josie. Then as she looked at the clairvoyant with great anticipation in her eyes; she beseeched her for the information that she really wanted to know. As Josie held her breath, she asked, "Have I met the man I will marry?"

Without hesitation, Evelyn replied, "Yes."

As Josie implored her to continue, the seer said, "Your husband is extremely handsome and comes from a good family."

Thinking of Charles, Josie smiled and then asked, "Will I have children?"

The astrologist predicted, "I see a big wedding – in New York - and a pregnancy in the future."

Josie queried her voice full of interest, "I'm afraid to ask, but can you tell me my husband's name?"

The debutante's face fell as Evelyn snapped, "I don't give names." In part to placate the sweet girl, the seer offered, "But I do see a long courtship."

Josie jumped up excited. But before the seer could call upon her next customer, Josie sat back down and asked, "Anything else?"

Evelyn's eyes narrowed as she peered at the cards the debutante had chosen. Slowly, she nodded her head no.

"Nothing you can say or nothing you want to say?" inquired Josie suddenly concerned.

"It's been a very long day, girls. I'm spent – exhausted. I must end the session," replied Evelyn wearily.

"But you haven't done me yet, and it was my idea to come!" pleaded Rebecca.

"I'm sorry, Miss Stanley. But I need to rest. I'd rather give you back your money than risk giving you inaccurate information because I'm tired. If you like, you can re-schedule with my secretary. I'll give you an hour session for the price of a half hour one."

On the way out, Geraldine discovered she was missing her scarf. She told her friends to leave without her because she had thought she had left it in Evelyn's office and claimed she was not sure how long it would take for her to retrieve it. Going back upstairs, she stormed up to the seer and demanded an explanation. Looking the clairvoyant straight in the eyes she said firmly, "The truth. Tell me. You think something bad is gonna happen to my friends."

Warily, Evelyn said, "I'm tired, Miss Ashley. The session is over."

But Geraldine wasn't easily dismissed. Forcefully, she pressed, "Don't lie to me."

Evelyn scoffed, "I thought you didn't believe in my powers?"

"I don't," admitted the artist. "But you're definitely keeping something from them. You had a bad vibe or you know something."

The clairvoyant said, "You're very prescient. I am tired and I could be wrong. Regardless, if you're really a good friend, you'll look after them. Bad things sometimes happen to good people – no one is ever totally assured a perfect future. Even with all my powers, I will suffer and pass away."

Geraldine exclaimed, "That's a rather morbid thought!"

"Yes it is," stated the seer. "But it has been divined!" The clairvoyant proclaimed with a flourish, "I will die in 1932."

"How do you know?" asked Geraldine.

"I just do," replied Evelyn curtly. Then she stated with conviction as she looked meaningfully at Geraldine, "Of course between now and then, I intend to make the most of my life."

While Geraldine and Evelyn looked at each other, the clairvoyant declared, "Perhaps you could help me enjoy my last days?"

As Geraldine's heart pounded, the seer came up to her and touched her hand as she looked deeply into her eyes.

Evelyn asked, "Would you like to paint me?"

"You do realize I'm only doing nudes now," replied the artist meaningfully.

In response, Evelyn took off her glasses and the clips in her hair. As she unbuttoned the top few buttons of her blouse, she inquired, "Well? What do you think?"

Geraldine asked in response, "Do you like Southampton?"

"I've been to a number of parties there," acknowledged the seer.

The artist said, "I'll be having one next weekend to close up the house for the winter." As she gazed into Evelyn's eyes, she touched the older woman's hand and explained, "It should be a *very intimate* gathering."

"I look forward to it," replied Evelyn warmly as she ushered her new friend out into the blackened darkness.

But once outside, the clairvoyant left the artist alone to find her own way as the dark clouds covering the crescent moon cast sinister shadows on this September night.

* * *

CHAPTER IX

A week later, while James talked business with Henry Morgan at his friend's grandfather's old office at the Morgan Library on Madison Avenue, Josie, Geraldine, Rebecca and Charles gathered together in Geraldine's Southampton studio.

The smell of the fresh wood burning and crisp, dry leaves filled the air as a giant fire blazed in the artist's massive stone fireplace that had been imported from a French convent. The flames danced on the stark white walls and over the numerous canvases and portraits in various states of completion.

Josie and Charles held hands as they reclined on the bright red divan. Rebecca rested in an overstuffed chair and Geraldine stretched out on a silk blue cushioned chaise lounge that was positioned in such a way as to allow her to watch her friends and enjoy the view outside at the same time. Through the oversized floor to ceiling windows on the south wall of her studio, Geraldine could see the blackened sea and the starlit night sky.

"I wonder what secrets the stars hold," pondered Geraldine.

Charles replied, "It's an age-old question."

"But one that I'm sure Evelyn Maker will be more than happy to elaborate for you personally," said Rebecca.

"I can't believe you've invited her over!" exclaimed Josie. "When is she coming?"

Geraldine replied her voice full of anticipation, "Tomorrow morning after all of you leave. She's staying until Monday."

"And if it wasn't for me, you would have never met!" said Rebecca. "We had to force you to go for a consultation. You thought it was total rubbish and now listen to you. You're completely converted!"

"Obsessed is probably a more accurate description," said Josie as she smiled at Rebecca.

After putting several chocolate truffles on her plate and pouring another glass of Sauternes, Geraldine said, "My dears, you are rather jumping to conclusions."

"Oh really?" said Rebecca. "How's that?"

Geraldine replied, "It is true I am very interested in Miss Maker and I do have a newfound interest in the study of the stars, but..."

"Yes?" Rebecca asked.

Popping a truffle in her mouth, Geraldine explained, "Although I hope to gain her respect and friendship, my interest is also physical."

"You're not actually going to sleep with Evelyn?" gasped Josie, choking as a sip of her champagne went down the wrong way.

Geraldine envisioned the scene, "I'll paint her first." As she put down her Sauternes after taking another long sip, she pointed towards Josie and Charles and said smiling, "In fact, I'll position her on the divan right where you and Charles are sitting now so she can gaze into the stars and emptiness of the ocean. It could be quite a soul searching moment."

Josie grimaced as Charles looked down at the divan uneasily.

"But she's so, so old and harsh looking!" exclaimed Rebecca. "She must be over fifty!"

"I think she's quite attractive," replied Geraldine. "She's different and I like that."

Rebecca said, "Well, you've certainly never been conventional in your choices."

"Who's to say what's beautiful or right anyway?" inquired Geraldine. "Taste is very personal."

"And as long as you're happy, we're happy for you," replied Josie as she squeezed Charles hand.

"Thanks Josie," said Geraldine. "I knew you'd understand." As she fingered another truffle, the artist explained, "Evelyn intrigues me. I respect her as a businesswoman who understands the human mind exceptionally well. Jokes aside, she's managed to flourish financially in a man's world and hustle the best of them."

"Here Here," said Charles. "That's not an easy task even for a man!"

"So you still don't buy into her celestial powers?" asked Rebecca confused.

Geraldine asserted, "My gut tells me she has incredible intuition and a keen understanding of human nature and desires."

"She's like a snake oil salesman," said Charles.

"But she has much more class," replied Josie. "Believe me her family pedigree is without question."

"I think you'd make a good couple," asserted Charles.

"Geri, you're really acting like a man," replied Rebecca wide-eyed, as she thought about everything Geraldine had said.

As Charles got up and looked around the room, he said, "You know if you were a man, your paintings would be some of the hottest sellers on the market."

Pointing to a very realistic portrait of Josie that Geraldine had done a year ago he said, "Is there any way I could buy this from you?"

"If she agrees to sit for another one I think we could agree on a price," said Geraldine. "But it's one of my favorites, so it'll cost you."

"I wish I had someone wanting to buy a picture of me!" declared Rebecca. As she slumped back down in a chair she said glumly, "At any price."

"Your time will come," asserted Geraldine. "Just be patient."

"Argh!" exclaimed Rebecca. "It seems I've been waiting all my life!"

"Stop waiting!" advised Geraldine. "Desperation is never appealing."

"I used to be worried that I'd never find someone I really cared for," admitted Josie as she moved closer to Charles. "But if you stay strong and you don't settle for someone other than the person for whom you are absolutely in love with – I believe you will end up with your soul mate. Eventually it'll work out. You just have to believe in yourself."

"And just not be too picky," suggested Charles.

Josie gasped, "Charles!"

Under pressure he quickly restated. "Don't be too judgmental. Sometimes the right person isn't what you expect."

"That's true," said Geraldine. "I never would have thought I'd be attracted to someone older than I am."

"And I thought Charles was just a barman!" said Josie.

"But he wasn't," replied Rebecca.

"But I fell for him even when I thought he was," explained Josie.

"Really?" questioned a doubting Geraldine. "I always thought of you as quintessentially high maintenance."

"She can be," replied Charles knowingly despite Josie's protests. Then as he bent over to kiss his love, he said, "Of course, I love her just the way she is."

As Josie and Charles kissed, Geraldine looked at Rebecca. She could tell something was wrong.

Noticing Rebecca was staring out at the sky. Geraldine said, "Becca, fess up. I may not have Evelyn's powers, but even I can tell you're keeping something from us. There's someone you really like."

"No. Not particularly," replied Rebecca quickly. "I just hope there's someone out there."

Coming up behind her, Geraldine said, "Oh come on. We've all known each other since our nannies preferred gossiping to pushing our prams in Central Park! You're definitely hiding something."

Josie said, as she put her arms around her friend, "Becca, you know you can trust us."

In response, Rebecca rolled her eyes and moved away. "Sure Josie. Just like in the 5th grade when I told you I liked Edwin Baruch and you promised you wouldn't tell anyone and then you blurted it out to Catherine and she told the world."

"I never knew you liked Edwin," said Geraldine shocked as much by the revelation as the length of time she had gone without knowing it. As she thought about the guy in question she said gasping, "Isn't he the one who went mad at Choate?"

"I know who you're talking about! I ran into him once with the Morgans!" said Charles laughing. "Junius told me he wore safari clothes everywhere and after Choate, he was expelled from Andover because they couldn't get him to wear the uniform!"

Rebecca blushed with embarrassment. "I liked him before he thought he was in Africa hunting animals."

"Well, at least you didn't have a crush on Alvin 'Shipwreck' Kelly," claimed Geraldine not above poking fun out of her own misadventures.

"You had a crush on the guy who sat on a flagpole for 23 days?" gasped Rebecca.

Downing her Sauternes, Geraldine replied proudly when she finished downing the hatch, "23 days and 7 hours to be exact and yes."

"You really do have bizarre taste!" exclaimed Rebecca.

"So dish the dirt, Josie – before you met me, who did you find irresistible?" prodded Charles.

Josie retorted, "You think I find you irresistible?"

"Yes!" exclaimed Geraldine, Rebecca, and Charles at the same time.

Not giving her friend a chance to answer or worm out of the embarrassing question, Geraldine blurted, "Josie went to see every Valentino film."

Getting into the action, Rebecca explained to Charles, "She made us go with her because she didn't want to be seen attending the cinema alone."

"Oh and you really had to be convinced, Becca!" replied Josie annoyed. Accusingly she muttered, "You were as eager as I was to see his movies!"

Rebecca exclaimed, "But I didn't go into mourning after he died!"

"I only wore black for one day – or two," said Josie defensively as Charles and Geraldine laughed. As she frowned she asserted, "Thanks. You know with friends like you two…"

Charles quipped, "I could find out a lot."

'Just wait 'til we spend time with your friends," warned Josie.

Charles replied, "You think I'd make that mistake?"

Rebecca inquired pointedly, "Who are your best *single* friends?"

"Mostly boys I wouldn't fix up with any girl I liked," admitted Charles as Rebecca's face fell. Thinking about them he said, "Wait a minute. What do you think of J. D. Rockefeller?"

Rebecca's blush spoke for itself.

"You're pretty, petite, Protestant, and your background's good – you're just J. D.'s type!" said Charles. "And he isn't seeing anyone right now either."

"But would he be serious?" inquired Josie.

Charles replied confidently, "You know J.D.! For the right girl? Absolutely!"

"Then it's all settled," said Geraldine. "Just don't you dare pick some pastel pink for the bridesmaid dresses, Rebecca, or I'll kill you before your wedding!"

"But I thought you looked particularly *sweet* in the flowing floral ensemble Catherine chose for you to wear at hers," replied Josie rubbing it in.

Geraldine said, "Oh, shut up!"

"At least it wasn't as prissy as the dress she chose to wear at the brunch before leaving for the honeymoon," rejoined Rebecca cattily.

"You know Junius and Catherine have been gone a long time." said Josie. "They should be coming back soon."

"And just think," said Rebecca romantically as she looked out the window, "They're looking at the same stars tonight as we are."

"It's an amazing thought," remarked Charles.

As Charles and Josie looked at each other starry-eyed, Geraldine said rolling her eyes, "I think we should leave these two alone."

After giving the couple hugs she said, "See you in the morning!"

Looking at his watch, Charles said, "You mean in a few hours."

"Knowing her," Geraldine said pointing to Josie, "After lunch."

Even before Geraldine and Rebecca left the studio, Charles and Josie had started kissing. As the girls walked outside to head towards the main house, they caught a glimpse of their silhouettes through the windowpane. For a moment, they just paused under the starry sky to enjoy the view. Geraldine was so taken by what she saw, that despite Rebecca's protests, she snuck back inside the studio to grab her sketchbook to capture the moment. She called the piece: *The Perfect Kiss.*

Before she went to bed, as Geraldine looked admiringly at her sketch, she thought Josie and Charles seemed so right for each other. The artist was thrilled for her friend and hoped the relationship would last. Too exhausted to give it any more thought, she curled up on the far left side of her oversized poster bed, dropped her weary head onto her favorite down pillow and drifted off immediately.

Unfortunately, the artist's night was disturbed by unsettling dreams.

* * *

CHAPTER X

The sunlight streamed resplendently into the room through the French doors as the last embers burned in the fireplace. Both warmed the cool autumn morning. But as Bentley served breakfast, he could tell his master was in a particularly petulant mood. James seemed to be looking for a reason to blow up at someone – anyone. The tense staff tiptoed around, attempting to fulfill their household duties without attracting any attention. While the houseman brought James the morning papers, he thought, no wonder Cook decided to take this opportune time to shop for groceries. Any moment now, Bentley knew only too well from experience, his master would explode.

Bentley could see there were dark circles around James' eyes as he stared at the paper without actually reading it. He wondered whether it was a woman or a long night of partying that contributed to the appearance. In either case, the houseman sensed he would suffer unduly as a result.

To avoid the certain unpleasantries, the servant attempted to fulfill his duties as quickly as possible without conversation. Just as he was nearly out the door of the breakfast room, James bellowed. "Where do you think you're going?"

The houseman demurely stated, "To the loo, sir."

James barked, "I haven't dismissed you!"

Knowing by the tone in his master's voice that James was going to pick a fight anyway, Bentley couldn't resist the opportunity to retort, "You usually don't."

"Take this away this minute!" said James as he pointed to his breakfast. Shoving it at his houseman he screamed, "It's terrible!" Then he demanded, "Where's Cook?"

"Shopping."

"What the hell do I pay you people for, anyway?" said James as he stormed away.

Picking up the plates quickly, Bentley cleared the table and ran off to relieve himself in the staff bathroom. As he washed up, he couldn't help overhearing a conversation through the vent.

"Don't give me crap!" bellowed an irate James. "I don't care who's been asking questions. Rectify it! And the next time you phone me, it better be to tell me we no longer have an investigation, there are no more unions in the plants, and you've got this bull shit girl case wrapped up!" There was a pause, then "Do what you have to do – just get it done!"

Bentley heard James slam the phone down. Then he heard a moan and, "What a fucking headache. Useless piece of shit!"

The houseman was surprised by what he heard. Business had never before impacted the hedonistic playboy's lifestyle.

An hour later, Vinnie Graves turned up at the servants' entrance. James sat sequestered with him for the rest of the morning. Bentley couldn't hear a word that was said, but he could only imagine it had something to do with the steel plants. As the houseman ushered Vinnie Graves out, the goon was in good spirits. He even flashed a tooth-gapped smile for a moment. Bentley thought it resembled the sick smile of a mass murderer just after a particularly satisfying kill. The look alone convinced the houseman he really didn't want to know anymore than he already suspected.

For the second time this morning, Bentley rushed through his duties, attempting to not get involved. And once again, his efforts were futile.

Taking his time walking out, Graves paused in front of family portraits and fingered a few of the antiques. "Pretty swish place he's got here."

"It's not bad, sir."

"Not bad, eh?" replied Graves mocking Bentley's accent. "It's nothing like the slammer!" Then, as he addressed the houseman, the goon straightened his jacket and thrust his chin up in an effort to mimic the rich in a way he had seen in the movies. As he cockily walked, he said to the houseman, "Maybe someday I can get a place like this and hire a guy like you to fix it up for me, eh?" Jabbing Bentley in the arm, he proposed, "Wanna work for me?"

"I'm sure that would be interesting sir," replied Bentley attempting to be diplomatic as he thought that hard as it was to believe, a worse employer than James existed.

"Interesting? I dunno 'bout that," said the thug looking around. "But I'll tell you, we'd sure get us some good stuff to put in here if it was my pad." As he waved his arm disapprovingly, pointing out offensive pieces, he muttered, "None of this museum shit. It's like a mausoleum!"

His voice devoid of emotion, Bentley said, "I'll take your word. I gather you know a bit about those sorts of places."

Swaggering around, the goon countered, "Why you think they call me Graves?"

The houseman inquired, "Is that what your name is, sir?"

"To you, it's *Mr.* Graves," replied Graves putting on airs.

"Yes, of course, *Mr.* Graves, *sir,*" said Bentley sarcastically as he opened the door to try to give Graves the hint to leave. As he motioned to the street, the houseman said, "I'm sure you have a great deal to do today, *Mr.* Graves."

"I got work," replied Graves as he waved a couple big white envelopes that Bentley guessed were filled with money that James had given the thug. "But," said Graves, flashing his sick smile for a second time, at Bentley, "I'll be back – real soon."

"If you say so, sir," replied the servant. He almost smirked as he said, "I'm sure the entire staff will look forward to your return as much as I do."

As he walked out the door, Graves reached over to a plate of food Bentley had prepared to bring to James. The goon dug right into the middle of the dish and scooped up the stuffed pigeon with his hands.

Bentley glared at Graves horrified. The thug's hands were very dirty. Bentley thought he saw dried blood under the fingernails but wasn't entirely sure if his own imagination wasn't running wild.

Disgusted at what he saw, Bentley stated, his exasperation clear, "Why don't you just finish it?"

Graves was so busy gobbling the food he didn't take time to respond. After wolfing down most of the meal, the goon tossed the remainder onto the plate and licked his fingers. He wiped his mouth with his sleeve and strutted out.

Turning around one last time, Graves said to the houseman, "Next time I come, get me some good food."

Returning to the kitchen, Bentley said to Cook, "Don't ask."

Replenishing the plate, she said, "Better hurry. He's already rung twice from upstairs."

Bentley brought the food up to James just in time to meet him at the door of the study. As James pushed the houseman out of his way, he exclaimed roughly, "You stupid fool! Get out of my way. I'm late."

Bentley just managed to move back in time to save the plate from being knocked out of his hand by James. As his master left, the houseman muttered, "Guess I'll just eat it myself."

James jumped out of a cab fifteen minutes later on 5th Avenue. He darted across the street to enter the Heckscher Building. A

burly Irishman who looked like a thug but claimed to be a doorman approached him. "Name, sir?"

"James Ellison DeVere to see Mr. Goldman."

Garrett Goldman was the one person on Wall Street who James
mingled with even though he thought he was Jewish and tacky.
James would have been mortified if anyone of his set knew he was
a friend.

Whenever the young businessman had a doubt about the market, he always visited Garrett Goldman. In fact, the only time he
went out of his way to see the Wall Street wizard was when he wanted financial advice.

As James stood at an angle, careful not to be seen from outside
the building, the doorman checked his list. A few minutes later, he
waved the playboy businessman into a discreet, but lavishly decorated elevator. When James got off at the eighteenth floor,

Garrett Goldman's twenty-person staff was so busy no one
paid any attention to his arrival. With heavy trading, the staff was
stretched thin. James could see Garrett was operating at full capac-
ity, using the trader's famous worldwide network. Wires and calls
came in at the same time from Minneapolis to Amsterdam to Len-
ingrad and Lima. James was so engrossed in the atmosphere that
he didn't even notice when Garrett came out to greet him.

"I hear Kennedy received a warm reception from Jack Morgan," said the obese man, huffing between words because he was
so out of breath from moving around the office so quickly.

"I was there," replied James nonchalantly. He was pleased for
once to have heard the information before his mentor.

While he peered over documents a secretary handed him, Garrett burst James' bubble. He explained, "He's thinking of getting
out of the market, you know."

"Oh really?" replied James surprised and chastened. It always
amazed him how often Garrett managed to know everything that

was going on before anyone else did. Sometimes he thought the Wall Street joke that Garrett knew what operators planned to do even before they decided it themselves was actually true.

Garrett went on to say, "Kennedy thinks there are too many little guys playing the game."

James asked, "And your take?"

Garrett explained, "After Morgan kicked him out, he got a shoe shine and the shoe shine boy told him what to invest – now he thinks if the shoe shine boy knows what to play, the market's no place for him."

"I can see his point," replied James.

Motioning for James to follow him into his office, Garrett said, "There's a lot going on."

While they sat in Garrett's office, overlooking 5th Avenue, Garrett offered James a cigar. It was the largest one James had ever seen. "Where'd you get this?" he inquired.

"I have them rolled for me in Cuba and sent up specially," replied the impressive man who was called the Bear of Wall Street. Handing a box to James he generously offered, "Take a few back with you. You won't find them anywhere else."

"Thanks, G.G.," replied James deliberately invoking the abbreviation Garrett preferred his friends to use.

"No big deal," stated the pleased man shrugging. "I owe you anyway."

"How's that?" inquired James, who secretly delighted in having an I.O.U. that he could now claim.

"That girl you sent up to see me last week was the Cat's Pajamas." said Garrett as he took a particularly long puff. "We had a good time together at my place in Great Neck."

"Glad she was of service," said James as he tried to remember which girl Garrett was talking about. Both Garrett and James went through so many women the playboy found it difficult to single any of them out afterwards.

As Garrett leaned back in his chair fingering his cigar, he said, "I think I'll take her down to Florida on my next trip." James knew the investor had helped perpetrate the spurious Florida land boom that had left thousands of unsuspecting suckers with nothing but worthless paper and flooded swampland.

James smiled as he thought of the idiot investors. Then he inquired, "You going soon?"

"Depends on the market," replied Garrett as he lit his cigar and James'.

"So what do you think?" prodded James as he attempted yet again to get Garrett to focus on the issue. Much as he liked the cigars, a read on the market was after all the reason he visited Garrett and supplied him with women.

Garrett laughed. "I think it's time for me to make some real money."

James prodded, "Go on." As Garrett smiled, the playboy said, "Morgan, Raskob, Riordan and your close buddy, Cutten, all see the market rise continuing indefinitely."

"Is that so?" remarked Garrett, taking another puff. "You know I had the pleasure of screwing Cutten on wheat back in Chicago years ago. Call it intuition but I think I'll make the right call again. If Cutten doesn't, it'll be an added bonus."

James laughed in response. The feud between Garrett Goldman and Arthur Cutten, the renowned commodity speculator and Wall Street bull, was legendary even by the financial district's standards.

"So other than instinct, what's your basis," pressed the student.

Leaning forward from his chair, the round-faced trader looked like a Buddhist sage, as he seriously stated, "Never under-estimate gut instinct. Instinct is the most important fundamental tool in the market." Like a teacher, he lectured, "Whatever you do – remember this – no matter what – *never* go against your instinct."

James responded, "Unless you have hard evidence."

"You're learning!" exclaimed Garrett excitedly. Then as he continued to smoke, he explained, "I just returned from the Midwest."

"My condolences," said James quickly.

Garrett replied smiling, "There were a few decent farmers' daughters whose acquaintances I made."

"Bet you got very familiar," said James, a wicked smile on his face.

As he slapped his hands on his desk, Garrett shouted gleefully, "Skipped the wedding and went right to the honeymoon!" Then after he stopped reminiscing, Garrett lowering his voice, and quietly admitted, "I also did a substantial amount of checking out the brokerages there."

"Oh," said James perking up immediately.

His mentor stated between luxurious puffs on his cigar, "Confirmed my suspicions."

James pressed, "Which are?"

Garret said as he extinguished his cigar, "Regarding AOT."

"The premise that you can buy Any Old Thing and make money on it?" inquired James. As he looked at his mentor, he said glumly, "It's been working unbelievably well for the last few years. Everyone's been making money in the market – from teachers and preachers to busboys – even housewives!" exclaimed James with obvious frustration. "It annoys me to no end to see them succeeding. Even my mill and factory workers have been buying stocks. They've been getting ornery as a result – thinking their wages should be higher for real work since the market makes it so easy."

"Having a few business problems are we?" inquired an amused Garrett.

James replied tersely, "I've got things under control."

"Regardless," said Garrett, "What you described may not be the case much longer. All over the Midwest and here in New York, your housewives, busboys, teachers and all the rest that have been used to buying any old stock and making money are in for some rough times. As we've discussed, soon the tide will turn – very soon. Already the decliners are outpacing the advancers in New York, Chicago and around the world." Passing out supporting documents to his eager pupil, he explained, "I've had my boys checking into this. I saw it in the Midwest and I see it happening here in New York now. Most investors are going to get screwed. They'll panic and lose – everything."

James could see the excitement in Garrett's eyes as he said, "Mark my words, the little people are going to lose it all. They have no savings and they've been buying everything on credit - their houses, their motorcars, their dishwashers, radios, even clothes – all purchased with borrowed money to be paid over time on installment plans. Their wages go towards bills and buying stock on margin. When the bubble bursts, there'll be hell to pay!" He promised James, "Your workers will be begging you for jobs regardless of the pay." Gleefully, he forecasted, "It'll get real ugly all over, but it will be a great opportunity for those of us with the intelligence and the means to take advantage."

James smiled with delight as he asked, "When?"

"Soon," said Garrett as he got up from his desk to light another cigar. "I felt it in 1906 just before the San Francisco quake and again before the market collapse in 1919. Now my gut tells me once again it's a good time to be a bear."

James asked, "Were you *ever* anything else?"

"Yeah," said Garrett as he offered James another cigar. "I figured World War I was the one good time to be a bull." As he lit his pupil's cigar, he said sarcastically, "It was *my patriotic duty*."

James said between puffs, "And it made you millions."

"And then some," acknowledged the smug trader. As he fingered his cigar, Garrett said, "Now it's time to swing back the other way."

"And when it does, I'd like to be right here with you," said James. "Working side by side – helping you out."

"I'll let you know," said Garrett noncommittally. "Certainly I can't think of a man who'd gloat over a market correction more than me, except you."

To help change the noncommittal reply into a confirmed yes, James took a picture of a girl out of his wallet with a phone number and address, as he said, "I almost forgot. Are you busy tonight?"

"It depends upon who's asking," said Garrett with a smile. "If it's my wife, I'm definitely occupied!"

Handing over the photo, James said, "Peggy Mitchell - petite girl with a great pair of legs and a nice ass. She likes a good time. She was a Ziegfeld girl. Now she's auditioning for a bigger part. She takes directions well."

After looking at his watch and the address, Garrett got into the elevator with James and said, "You going uptown?"

The playboy nodded yes.

The trader offered, "I'll give you a lift on my way to meet Peggy."

James quickly got into the back seat of Garrett's canary yellow Rolls Royce. Even though it was dark outside, he didn't want to take the chance that someone would recognize him as he got into the flashy colored vehicle. James was shocked to find the interior just as gaudy as the exterior. He slouched in the back. Much to his chagrin, the Great Bear of Wall Street took an excessively long time to give his chauffeur directions.

James was ready to get out of the motorcar just as they finally set off. Settling into the backseat, Garrett loosened his tie and popped a bottle of champagne. After a hectic day in the office, he was ready for a night on the town. With his wife back on the booze and his two young sons, whom he adored, visiting his parents, he was ready for an evening of fun. James was just looking forward to a nap before heading out himself. He had big plans for the evening.

As they whizzed away, Garrett said to James, "Remember what I told you. The smart people are quietly getting out – Kennedy, Baruch, Bouvier, Lord Ashley - a number of people."

"Thanks. I'll keep that in mind," replied James registering everything his mentor told him.

As Garrett dropped James off in front of his townhouse he said, "By the way, don't forget to send Bouvier a card."

"Why's that?' inquired James.

"His wife just had a baby over the summer."

James asked, "Boy or girl?"

"Beautiful baby girl," replied the trader who loved children. As he lit another cigar, he said, "I think they named her Jacqueline."

"You don't miss a thing!" exclaimed James.

Garrett stated, "You never know when you'll need a favor and who can help."

"A baby?" said James doubtfully.

"One day, this little girl might grow up to be somebody important." Garrett said, "Trust me. I feel it in my gut."

As James got out of the Rolls, he said, "I better let you go meet the most important girl in your life for tonight."

"So you have a little more time to try to charm Miss Baxter-Browne?" replied Garrett not missing a beat.

James' jaw dropped.

"Don't worry, your interest isn't common knowledge," said Garrett as he closed the door and rolled down the window. "But it might interest you to know…"

"Yes?" said James as he heartbeat faster.

"It's not worth going to the Horseman's Ball tonight."

"Why not?" demanded James.

Laughing, Garrett said, "She won't be there."

Once again, James was awed by Garrett Goldman's knowledge. Trying to recover, he sputtered out loud, "How do you know?"

"You know I never divulge my sources," replied Garrett slyly. "But if you still want to see her, I'd try her godfather's townhouse. She's planning to be there most of the evening."

* * *

After Garrett Goldman dropped him off, James had a wonderful nap. He loved dozing in the early evening. It enabled him to party all night. His friends and female acquaintances were always astonished at how little sleep he needed and how much energy he had. James' vigorous bedtime behavior was renown in his circle. None suspected the secret to his nocturnal agility and alacrity.

The playboy took great pride in giving the impression he only rested for two to four hours each day. The truth, as Bentley could attest, was a rather different story. James' usual routine was to nap between four and eight in the evening and then sleep from five in the morning until the last possible moment. His houseman usually began attempting to rouse him around ten thirty or eleven except in the rare occurrences when he had an earlier business appointment. James generally avoided morning meetings at all costs. But no matter what time Bentley had been summoned to wake him, the task was always an onerous one. James just hated getting up – any time – and he made sure whoever woke him was punished accordingly. Because none of his staff could any longer take the abuses James hurled at them when he was roused, Bentley doubled as both his valet and houseman. Often, to save Cook, he also served James his meals when he ate at home.

This evening, after his nap, James felt particularly randy. Sitting in an overstuffed leather chair in a silk dressing gown, he took a leisurely puff on one of Garrett Goldman's fine cigars as he contemplated what he wanted to wear to Henry Jay's party. It would be a memorable night, he thought. He wanted to look particularly dashing.

As he extinguished his cigar, James rang for Bentley. By the time the houseman appeared, James knew exactly what he wanted to wear. Designed out of the most expensive wool and tailored made to fit him perfectly, the playboy chose his favorite tails with the finest gray, silk waistcoat. It was the last outfit made by the late British tailor, Edmund Tates. Tates suffered a debilitating stroke just after putting the finishing touches on the white tie ensemble and died a week later when his heart gave out. Having accompanied James to several of the fittings, Bentley was convinced James' fits contributed to the tailor's collapse and untimely death. Characteristically, his master's only concern when he learned of the man's passing was his own clothes.

Demanding the widow open up the shop the day her husband was buried, James tore up the place until he found his tails. Then, adding insult to injury, he refused to compensate her. Lying, he claimed he had paid in advance. On the way out, Bentley slipped the grieving widow some of his own money. James complained the whole way back to his hotel because he felt he himself had been inconvenienced by the poor man's death. That night, over a brandy, Bentley noticed his master's mood improved dramatically when his companion, an old Etonian, said how upset he was about the tailor's passing because the tradesman had had such a unique style. Having not found an apprentice worthy, he informed James, Tates had died with his secrets.

The playboy had been further delighted to learn that although the tailor's English clients included not only those of the best breeding but also an assorted sundry of Englishmen with dubious reputations whose only redeeming quality was an ability to pay for his services, as far as his friend knew, James was the only American on the tailor's roster. Xenophobic, Tates disliked all foreigners. His only reason for taking on James was that the dapper young man had the best physique the tailor had ever seen. Vain about his work, Tates knew the American with an affected transatlantic accent that could almost pass for British, could wear his clothes like no other client. The tailor considered the bachelor his muse.

As he looked smugly in the mirror before heading out the door to Henry Jay's latest party, James smiled with satisfaction by the knowledge that no one in his set would ever have a wardrobe exactly like his.

A half an hour later, James strolled into the old codger's townhouse. Debonair, exuding confidence, the handsome young man made *quite* the entrance. As he nonchalantly walked into the ballroom, women turned to look at him. Completely forgetting their dates by their side, they gawked and made inane excuses to leave their partners in order to strut in front of the desirable bachelor in the hope of catching his attention. As James sipped a glass of his favorite champagne, Veuve Clicquot, he held court. Surrounded by girls, desperately trying to engage him in conversation, he made minimal efforts, not bothering to disguise the fact that he continued to look around the room.

Spotting J. D. Rockefeller arriving with Rebecca Stanley, James made his excuses in order to join his friend and J.D.'s attractive date. Henry was handing J. D. a cigar as James approached them. Inebriated, Rebecca swayed as she giggled like a schoolgirl. James could see the pretty, petite brunette only remained standing because J.D. gripped her firmly by wrapping his right arm around her slender waist.

"I really needed this," said an exasperated J.D. as the host lit his cigar.

"I want to try!" shouted Rebecca as she reached for the cigar.

"I thought you wanted to see your friends," replied J.D. irritated as he moved the cigar out of her range.

Ever the good host, Henry tried to ease the increasingly tense situation by motioning to James.

"Good to see you, old boy," said James addressing his friends.

Henry laughed. "Are you to referring to J. D. or myself?"

"Anyone with a sense of humor," replied James smiling as he accepted Henry's offer of a cigar.

"That rules him out!" said Rebecca as she attempted to point towards J.D.

Extinguishing his cigar, J.D. said crossly, "I think I better escort you home."

"But you promised you'd take me to a good party!" pleaded Rebecca.

"I'm honored," said Henry as he bowed to J.D. and James. Then, motioning to the grand staircase, he said to the group, "Shall we?"

As they headed upstairs, Henry whispered to J.D., "Josie and Geraldine are upstairs. You can leave Rebecca with them and they'll straighten her out."

J.D. nodded relieved. Since Charles and Josie had set them up, he had become quite fond of Rebecca but had been extremely taxed by her behavior this evening. As a teetotaler, his date's inebriation and loose behavior under the influence was a complete turn-off.

By the time they reached the private party upstairs, J.D. wasn't the only one in a bad mood. As James walked through the double parlor, the first person he saw, directly in front of him was Charles Blakesley, pouring Geraldine a glass of champagne. James narrowed his eyes as he stood opposite the man who stood between him and the object of his affection.

James tried to get his feelings under control as Geraldine proposed a toast. "To the one woman we both love."

"To Josie!" exclaimed Charles enthusiastically.

While Charles and Geraldine clinked their glasses together, J.D. approached Geraldine and explained what had happened with Rebecca. Taking just one sip, Geraldine immediately put down her glass and went over to her friend, whom J.D. with the help of James, had propped up between several pillows on a sofa.

As Geraldine attended to Rebecca's needs, J.D. motioned for James to join him, so he could make introductions. As he put his arms around each of his friends, J.D. exclaimed, in a cheerier mood, "I can't believe you've never met!" Looking at Charles and then at James, he continued, "I guess at least this means I'm the lucky one who gets to introduce you two. James Ellison DeVere, I'd like you to meet my college friend, Charles Edward Blakesley. Charles Blakesley, James Ellison DeVere, one of the cleverest men I know."

Catching a glimpse of Josie who was bending over Rebecca, James smiled more broadly as he extended his hand warmly towards Charles. He thought a friendship with the unsuspecting Charles could work to his advantage. He wasn't going to make the mistake Warren Bates made with Randolph Churchill and get into a pissing contest.

As they shook hands, James said as his eyes continued to follow Josie, "I'm sure we have a great deal in common."

Raising his glass to James, Charles said, "Here's to finding out." After taking a sip, he said, "It's the best."

Still watching Josie, James said under his breath, "Certainly is." Then, turning his attention to Charles, he inquired, "What are you drinking?"

"Sauternes," replied Charles. "May I pour you some?"

"Which one?" asked James.

Charles handed him the bottle as he replied, "Chateau d'Yquem. It goes down well with the ladies."

"Dessert wine always does," declared James as he chose instead to pour himself a glass of vintage Roederer Cristal.

"Shall we rejoin the ladies?" asked Charles thinking of Josie.

J.D. replied flatly, "I've had just about enough of one for one evening."

"What happened to Rebecca?" inquired Charles concerned.

J.D. muttered, "The Horseman's Ball was positively tedious."

"Josie and I heard it wasn't worth attending, so we came here straight away instead," explained Charles.

"I wish I had known that," said J.D. As he finished his glass of water, he said glumly, "Still, it would have been out of the question since Rebecca's mother organized it."

"Another good reason to skip the ball," quipped Henry. As he proceeded to top up the boys' glasses, he said, "On the rare occasions I find myself at a Stanley dinner party, I always have a few stiff drinks first."

"So does Mr. Stanley," replied James. Then, as he leaned closer to Henry, J.D. and Charles, he lowered his voice to say confidentially, "I've heard that Stanley doesn't leave his club before he's totally smashed. Every night, the doorman has to usher him back home."

Henry asserted, "Certainly if you had to put up with Mrs. Stanley every day, you might prefer inebriation too."

"But Mrs. Stanley is a lovely looking lady," said Charles attempting to be polite.

"A nag is a nag no matter what she looks like," responded Henry knowingly.

J.D. said, "She's certainly the most opinionated woman I've ever met."

"Guess Stanley's just not man enough to know how to keep her mouth shut," asserted James as he puffed on a cigar. As he fingered it, he said, "I know a very effective way." Then, looking at J.D. as he complemented his friend's taste, he said, "Rebecca and her mother look quite similar. They're both very pretty."

From experience, J.D. asserted, "Becca's a lot sweeter than her mother."

"And naïve," said Henry as he motioned to where the girls were gathered around her.

"She certainly behaved terribly tonight," replied J.D. "I was quite embarrassed."

Charles said, "I've never seen her drink before."

"I don't think she is used to it," acknowledged J.D. "I guess I made her nervous."

"Will you take her out again?" asked Charles, hoping the best for Rebecca who he thought was very sweet.

J.D.'s hesitation left little doubt.

Agreeing with his friend's sentiments, James said coolly, "Inebriated ladies cease to be ladies."

"You think men behave any better?" responded Josie joining the group. She had a tired look on her face and was in no mood for chauvinism after having taken care of her friend.

"*Gentlemen* know how to handle alcohol!" retorted James as he raised his glass to Josie and took another sip.

"I've known a number of *gentlemen* who failed to hold down their liquor at least once in their life," quipped Josie tartly.

"I guess you're just spending time with the wrong men," declared James as he luxuriously exhaled his cigar smoke in her direction.

In response, Josie walked over to Charles, put her arm around him and sat down in his lap. Now it was her turn to face James with a triumphant smile.

James quickly recovered. "I meant no offense, of course, to Mr. Blakesley." Smiling smugly as he thought about how *he* would handle Josie, he replied after exhaling another puff of cigar smoke, "I have all the faith that your views can be reformed."

Josie laughed as Charles said, "That's unlikely."

Never one to waste his time, James decided he should take his leave since he believed nothing positive would be achieved by his staying. Graciously, he extended his hand to Charles. Then, as he kissed Josie's hand, deliberately he snubbed her by continuing to address her boyfriend as he spoke about her. "Well done, old chap. She's most beautiful but clearly a handful." He wore a satisfied grin on his face when he saw Josie coloring in response. He knew if he couldn't be with her, winding her up was the next best thing. He thought she wouldn't forget him. Furthermore, her anger and mixed emotions about him would make the challenge all the more enjoyable.

As James turned to go, J.D. said, "I'll join you." Turning to Charles, Josie and Henry, he asked, "You don't mind, do you?"

"Not at all," replied Charles and Josie at the same time.

"Happy hunting," shouted Henry as J.D. and James headed out of the room.

After J.D. and James left, Josie and Charles started laughing. Finally catching their breath, Josie said, "He's unbelievable!"

"Who?" inquired Geraldine as she rejoined her friends. "Did I miss something?"

"Nothing interesting," replied Josie.

"I don't believe you," said Geraldine. "Henry's parties are always great fun."

"I bet you would have scowled if you had been a part of our last conversation," predicted Josie.

Geraldine inquired, "What happened?"

"James Ellison DeVere," replied Henry.

"Say no more," said Geraldine. "That man gives men a bad reputation."

"Oh?" inquired Charles.

"James is damned good looking. I always thought he was considered quite the desirable bachelor," interjected Henry.

"He is," said Geraldine grumpily. "There have been a number of women I liked that have slept with him instead!"

Charles and Henry laughed as Josie said, "I can't understand why. I'd prefer you to him any day."

"Thanks," replied Geraldine flatly. "I'd be flattered except I have a feeling you'd choose anyone over him right now."

"What did you say?" inquired a distracted Josie who had missed what Geraldine said because she was engrossed with kissing Charles.

"She asked when you two will be getting married," said Henry winking at Geraldine.

"After he asks me," replied Josie without taking her eyes off Charles.

"And after she says yes," quipped Charles as he pulled Josie back on his lap and put his arms around her. As he hugged her, he said, "I just want to make my Josie happy."

While she gazed at the loving couple, Geraldine said with a deep sigh, "I think we'll be attending another wedding soon."

Putting his arm around her, Henry said, "Shall we leave them alone?"

"As if they'd actually notice?" replied Geraldine laughing.

Henry asked, "Fancy a dance, Miss Ashley?"

"Why not, Mr. Jay?" As she took his arm, Geraldine said, "After all, Rebecca's sound asleep, and you've got Bix Beiderdecke downstairs."

"I'll have a servant watch over her just in case," replied the thoughtful host.

Geraldine said, "Don't bother. There's nothing left in her stomach anyway." Then as she tapped Henry on the shoulder, she suggested, "You may want to have your bathroom cleaned extremely well, though."

Henry rolled his eyes as he said, "It won't be the first time."

Then, as Henry offered his arm to Geraldine, they glanced once more at the loving couple before they walked downstairs to mingle with the guests and dance the rest of the night away with New York's "A" list crowd and a number of visiting Hollywood stars.

As they headed for the dance floor, Geraldine smirked as she saw J.D. and James join Douglas Fairbanks and Charlie Chaplin in order to chat up a group of girls who surrounded them.

Henry, who also had noticed the group, whispered, "They're not quality."

"I don't think its quality they're looking for at this time of the night," replied Geraldine.

While Henry and Geraldine danced the Black Bottom downstairs, upstairs, Josie and Charles whispered sweets words of affection and made their own music.

* * *

CHAPTER XI

Several hours later, as they walked out of Henry Jay's townhouse, Charles and Josie held hands as Charles whispered sweet words of affection in Josie's ear. Josie giggled with delight. As they turned onto 5th Avenue, Charles suddenly grabbed Josie and pulled her out into the middle of the street. Putting his index finger on her lips before she could protest, he said, "Trust me."

Gaslights dimly lit the empty street as Charles stood in front of his beloved and proclaimed his undying love for the entire world to hear or at least all of New York. Then, in the middle of Fifth Avenue, he French kissed her.

As they started walking down the middle of the street, still holding hands, Charles suddenly stopped again.

Josie looked at Charles inquiringly.

Motioning to an entrance to Central Park, Charles said, "I've got to show you something."

"But it's *so* late and *so* dark," replied Josie cautiously.

Persuasively Charles said, "Don't worry. I'll take care of you." As he kissed her on the lips again, he promised, "Always."

"Okay," replied Josie hesitantly. "I trust you."

Charles put his arm around Josie to re-assure her as they walked inside the park. They strolled along a path inside the park, then, took another, doubled back and finally walked on a third that twisted all around until they could no longer even tell they were in the city. Josie wasn't sure how long had they been walking, but it seemed like quite some time. Just after they passed the dairy and before they came to the lake, Charles finally stopped.

Climbing up a magnificent rock with a commanding view of the lake, Charles motioned to Josie as he said, "This is it."

Josie looked up confused.

Charles said as he gestured, "Come on up."

Taking off her shoes and lifting up her dress so she wouldn't trip, Josie slowly made the ascent with the helping hand of Charles. When she reached the summit, Charles said, "Isn't it lovely?"

Josie could hear the soft whispering sound of the wind and a few night owls. As she stood next to him at the top of the rock, she took a deep breath. She could smell the fresh scent of the wood and the dew-laden grass. The lovers sat down to enjoy the view of the moonlit lake and the trees. Charles put his arms around her as Josie leaned on him. She relaxed and sighed happily, "It's so peaceful. It is a wonderful spot."

Putting her head on his shoulder as he stroked her hair, Josie asked, "Do you come here often?"

"I've been here only once before." He explained, "But I knew even then this is where I wanted to take you."

"It's lovely," said Josie, her voice purring as she cuddled her love.

Charles gently squeezed Josie's hand in response. Then, as he took her other hand in his, he reached into his pocket and produced a little ring made of grass. As Josie smiled, he explained. "The night we met at Texas Guinan's, I came here. I ran all the way from the speakeasy and didn't stop until I got to this spot. I climbed all the way up this rock and knew it would be a special place for me. I spent the rest of the night here, just sitting, like we're doing now." As he looked at her meaningfully, he said, "No matter what else I tried to think about, my mind wandered back to you – your face, our meeting - the banter. I couldn't get you off my mind. And afterwards, as dawn broke, as I sat up here, I wanted to do something for you. So when I climbed down, I made you this from the grass below the rock."

Tears came to her eyes as Josie put the ring on her finger. She was so happy she emotionally blurted out, "Thank you so much."

"I'm glad you like it," replied Charles. "I know some people would laugh but it comes from the heart."

Kissing him on the lips, Josie said touched, "I'll wear it with pride, because it came from you – from your heart straight to mine."

Taking her hand in his, Charles said, "Then, does that mean that if I asked you…"

"Yes!" Josie sputtered pre-emptively finishing his sentence.

"But you don't even know what I'm going to ask you yet!" exclaimed Charles.

Josie looked down at him full of expectation with inquiring eyes as she whispered, "You know I wouldn't deny you anything."

"Then I better ask you," replied Charles as he bent down on one knee, and said earnestly, "My darling, dearest love would you consider…"

Her heart pounding in anticipation, she blurted out, "Yes?"

Smirking, Charles said, "I can't pass up this opportunity. Please forgive me. But it may never come again."

Josie looked at him eagerly as she practically exclaimed, "Go on!"

Slowly he said as he looked at her with sparkling eyes, "Miss Josephine Baxter-Browne, would you consider doing me the honor of…"

She practically gasped, "Yes!"

"Would you kiss me?" stated Charles with mock seriousness.

Totally caught off guard, Josie exclaimed, "Would I kiss you?"

"On the lips?" he replied with a smile.

Shocked and dismayed, Josie said dejectedly, "Is that all you wanted?" She had been expecting him to pop the question and had been disappointed already on a number of occasions.

His eyes sparkling mischievously like a naughty boy after pulling off a trick, he said, "Will you?"

Fuming, she shouted, "NO!"

He countered, "But less than a minute ago, you said you wouldn't deny me anything and now you're already refusing a kiss. It's as if we're already married!"

"Damn you and you're jokes! Why don't you just go away and stop torturing me!" said Josie crossly as she got up and started to go down the rock. Turning back for a moment, she shouted, "You have some nerve! You dragged me all the way here, in the dark – in the dead of the night – near a place where you've been attacked before – just to kiss me! You're a complete nutter and a fool!"

"He asked rhetorically, "Who's the greater fool? The fool or the fool who follows him?"

Not in any mood for his jokes, she stated emphatically as she continued her descent, "I'm going back home." She stopped and turned to look at him momentarily just to say, "As far as I'm concerned, you can stay out here on your rock all night – thinking about it yourself!"

Having gotten the reaction he wanted, he tried to stop her. When his pleas for her to just wait a minute failed, he quickly made the descent. As he caught up with her he said, "I think you should stay with me."

She demanded, "Give me one good reason."

Unable to pass up the opportunity although he knew it would enrage her, the prankster said, "I haven't received my kiss, yet."

Turning away, Josie exclaimed, "And you're not getting one now!"

Before she had the chance to take another step, Charles grabbed her and hungrily started kissing her. At first Josie tried to fight him off, but her passion overcame her and within minutes they lovingly embraced each other on the top of the rock. As they kissed and held each other, they lost track of time and everything else except each other. Finally, when they stopped kissing, he said, "I actually brought you here tonight, because I wanted a memorable place to give you *this*."

Josie waited warily in anticipation as Charles took a Tiffany box out of his jacket. When he opened it up she stood back stunned. A beautiful diamond twinkled under the moonlit sky. It was a simple but perfectly shaped stone set elegantly in a delicate, antique platinum band. Although the stone wasn't overly large, she thought it was the most beautiful engagement ring. For the first time in her life, Josie was speechless.

She beamed as Charles took the ring out of the box and placed it gently on her finger. Then as his lips delicately touched her hand with a kiss, he addressed her lovingly as "My love."

As they embraced, Josie said, "I will."

Stopping momentarily between kisses, Charles said as he smirked again, "But I still haven't asked you!"

Pointing to the ring, Josie replied, "You don't have to."

While Charles kissed her neck and nibbled on her ear, he whispered, "Do you know how much I love you?"

She replied, "Not as much as I love you."

"I want to be with you for the rest of my life and through eternity," he stated earnestly, his love clear from his voice and expression.

She retorted, "Then I guess now you better ask me to marry you."

In response, he stopped kissing her. Standing straight and tall in front of her, seriously he said as the moon beamed down upon them, "Josie, will you?"

Even though she smiled knowingly, she demanded to know: "Will I what?"

He kneeled down on the soft, dewy grass and took her right hand in his. After kissing her hand tenderly, he said, his voice strong, but full of emotion, "Will you be my wife?"

As Josie looked Charles straight in the eyes she replied, her voice giving way to her feelings, "I thought you'd never ask."

Flashing *that* smile of his, he reiterated, "But will you?"

Without the slightest hesitation, she replied, "Yes, oh yes!" Then she kissed him fully on the lips and they held each other closely under the starlit sky until the sun rose from the east and the sounds of daylight invaded their sanctuary of love.

While Charles walked Josie home that morning, Josie said, "You know something?"

He replied, "No. What?"

"Much as I like the engagement ring and all, I have an admission," she said honestly.

"What's that?" he asked.

Looking at him coyly, she replied, "Do you really want to know?"

"Only if you want to tell me," he stated truthfully.

She pleaded, "Promise you won't get mad?"

"No," replied Charles with a smile. "But I'll try not to."

She said, "I like the grass ring better."

"Why's that?" said Charles laughing.

"I'm crazy," replied Josie.

"That's obvious. You wouldn't be with me otherwise. I'm a nutter, remember?" he said jokingly. "But why else?"

While she stroked his arm lovingly, she said, "You made it."

Once again, Charles kissed Josie in the middle of the street. Then he inquired, his voice full of laughter, "Should I take the other one back?"

Rolling her eyes, she retorted, "What do you think?"

"I could put it back in its box." Grinning contagiously, he said, "If you really don't want it."

"It's a beautiful ring," she said as she gazed admiringly at it.

He explained, "It was my mother's."

"I'm sorry," said Josie, stroking his arm again.

"Don't be. I wanted you to have it," replied Charles emotionally. After tenderly kissing his fiancée, he said, "I'm sure she would have wanted it as well."

Now it was Josie's turn to embrace him. As they kissed near the side of Josie's parent's townhouse, Bentley walked by. He paused for a moment to gaze at the beautiful, loving couple. He had just finished his early morning errands and was rushing back to rouse James but couldn't stop himself from staring at Josie and Charles. For a second, the very reserved, proper Bentley, disregarded all his training and enjoyed the view. He'd never forget what he saw. He had traveled the world over in the service of the privileged, and in his time, he had seen quite a few couples kissing, but there was something different about this strikingly attractive couple so obviously in love. When he got a better look at Charles, he felt there was something familiar about him, like family.

Bentley wasn't the only one who spotted Charles and Josie. As he looked out his bedroom window, Albert Baxter-Browne recognized his daughter immediately and became extremely agitated as he realized that she hadn't come home the night before.

It took quite an effort for Josie to separate herself from Charles. Each time she tried to drag herself away and walk up the front stairs of her parent's townhouse, she couldn't help but stop and gaze just one more time into her lover's eyes. And each time they looked at each other, they fell into each other's arms and started kissing again. Aware only of each other, they were oblivious to the morning sun that now streamed brightly down upon them as well as the bustling traffic. Finally, Charles stepped back. Kissing Josie tenderly on the hand that now was adorned with his engagement ring, he said, "I guess I better let you go."

Looking him fully in the eyes, she replied her voice extremely serious, "Don't you ever let me go!"

Charles kissed Josie in response. Then as he peered into her eyes again, he took her arms in his and became serious.

Emotionally he said, "There is nothing I wouldn't do for you. No matter what it cost me financially or emotionally. I love you – even more than myself. I love you unconditionally."

While Charles said this, tears came to Josie's eyes and she embraced her lover as she said burying her face in his shoulder, "I love you too, Charles Blakesley – more than you know." Then she kissed him on both cheeks, on the nose and then fully on the lips before wiping the moisture from her eyes.

As they finally let go of each other, he slowly took the ring off her finger. As she looked at him forlornly, he explained, "I better take this back until I ask your father's permission for your hand." He made it clear, "I want us to do everything right."

Kissing him again fully on the lips, Josie said finally smiling again, "Then I guess you'll be coming to dinner tonight."

He admitted, "I was planning on it even if I hadn't proposed."

While Josie shook her head and laughed, he said, "You don't mean to tell me you wouldn't have wanted me to come to dinner tonight if I hadn't asked you to marry me today, do you?"

"You want to bet?"

He replied, "Whatever makes you happy, darling. Besides, I'm just happy you said yes."

"That makes two of us," said Josie as she kissed Charles one more time before finally heading towards her front door.

Beaming with joy, Josie waltzed inside, not even noticing that the front door opened without her pushing it in. Softly humming Gershwin's *Rhapsody in Blue,* she happily twirled around in the front hall until she heard the door slam behind her.

Albert Baxter-Browne stood gravely in front of her. His expression made it clear he demanded an explanation.

Josie bit her lip as she tried to think of what to say. Since she always had a good relationship with her father, she finally decided to tell him the truth. Josie knew he would be extremely disappointed with anything else. Asking him to sit down in his study, she poured out details of the entire evening, omitting only Rebecca's inebriation. Josie was relieved when her father congratulated her and agreed to keep it a secret between them until the evening when Charles officially asked for her hand. Finished and finally exhausted, Josie went to bed at eleven in the morning.

* * *

Ten minutes after Josie went to bed James woke up with a mild hangover. The girl he bedded the night before was shaking him. Instinctively, he rolled over after throwing a pillow at her. This did not result in the desired effect. Finally, he turned around to glare at her. His eyes piercing, he demanded to know, "What the hell's the matter?"

She explained, "You took all the covers."

James bellowed. "You woke me up because you're cold!"

"Yes?" came the mousy reply.

Putting a pillow over his eyes, James shouted, "Get another god-damn blanket from the linen closet! Or better yet – just get up."

"But..."

"Go!" he yelled roughly. "Now!"

The girl started crying. His head ached more from the whiny sound. Furious, James got up and put his clothes on. Stunned, the girl sat up in bed horrified, watching him.

Then, as he headed toward the bedroom door, she panicked. Getting up to run after him, she asked in a quivering voice, "Where are you going?"

She was still whimpering after he left.

Expecting to get a little more rest, James headed back to his own townhouse. As he turned the corner of 5th Avenue onto 65th Street, he walked right into J.D. Based upon his friend's attire, James thought J.D. might not have been home the night before either. After patting each other on the back, they decided to go to the Metropolitan Club for breakfast.

While they ate, James asked J.D. what he planned to do about Rebecca. Secretly he was thrilled when his friend informed him he had decided not to pursue the brunette. James' mouth salivated as he looked forward to bedding the girl and her attractive mother. Just as they were almost finished with their breakfast, J.D. spotted Charles and invited him to join them. Charles was glad he had managed to change before he ran into James and J.D.

Josie's fiancé had been on his way to his brokerage house to invest more capital in his account. James smiled as he thought of Garrett Goldman's prediction that the market was over-valued and headed for a serious correction.

"Are you heavily playing the market?" he asked seemingly innocently.

"Increasingly so," replied Charles. "And you?"

"I have been known to dabble in stocks when I think they will go up or *down*," said James with emphasis. "But mainly I just focus on my family's concerns."

J.D. explained, "James' family owns one of the largest steel operations in the country."

"Actually, we're mostly just on the East Coast," insisted James in a rare moment of modesty.

"Have you been affected by union actions much?" inquired Charles. "I've heard there were some real problems in North Carolina."

J.D. joked, "Aren't there always?"

"I'm not overly concerned. I hire the best people," said James as he thought of Graves. He claimed, "I'd lose more sleep today over the valuations of stocks than any union."

"But you just can't lose money in stocks over the long run," asserted Charles. "I've been pretty cautious about my investments up to now and been rewarded with lower returns than a lot of housewives." J.D. nodded as Charles said, "The run up in last few years have been remarkable. I'm beginning to think the market is following a new paradigm. The valuations of old are meaningless. Earnings don't matter – it's all future potential."

"Kind of like digging for oil," replied J.D.

Clearly a contrarian, James said, "And how many people have lost everything speculating on what turned out to be dry wells?"

"Not one Rockefeller," responded J.D. as he shook his head in agreement.

"But a lot of little guys have been screwed by Standard Oil," asserted James as he asked for another cup of coffee. Raising his glass to J.D., James said, "I think we should drink to the financial empires our families have built on the stupidity of all the little guys!" Turning to Charles, he said, "What does your family do again?"

Charles stately proudly, "What the country eats, we provide – we're the breadbasket of America."

"So you're farmers," sniffed James.

Correcting the snob, Charles stated, "Actually we not only grow the food, but we've invested in some processing plants as well and have a cattle ranch. Altogether we've got a pretty sizable operation."

"I'm sure you do, *back* in Oklahoma," replied James leaving Charles not quite sure whether he was trying to insult him or merely stating a fact.

The men remained civil as they discussed whether the government should provide farm subsidies. But as the political conversation turned to social issues and back to strikebreakers, J.D. felt obliged to step in.

Putting his arm around James as he smiled at Charles, the affable Rockefeller said, "You have to forgive Charles. He has rather left-leaning tendencies. He sympathizes with the little guys and wants to better their lives – be they black, white, yellow, red – even women!"

"Well, I wish you luck in your endeavors anyway," responded James as he offered to put the bill on his tab. "Although I do recommend you minimize your stock holdings."

Charles inquired, "And why's that?"

"Aside from logic?" replied James condescendingly. "Gut instinct." After giving his membership number and name to the waiter, James said as he looked at Charles, "Of course, I'd be more than happy to take your money."

Getting up impetuously, Charles said, "Are you proposing a wager?"

"Careful Charles," cautioned J.D., "James never loses."

While Charles extended his hand to James, he said as he thought of Josie, "There's always a first time."

"Perhaps." Shaking Charles hand, James replied with a smug smile. "But it won't be with you, my friend."

As the men went their separate ways, James thought Charles represented everything that was anathema to him. Due to his liberal views, he considered Charles Blakesley weak and spineless.

More than anything, James hated liberals, especially those like Charles who were educated and somewhat privileged. He considered them class traitors. From his experience, most also were hypocrites; they didn't mind the benefits of wealth that had been accumulated through shitty means by their forebears. In James' view, they had the luxury to be progressive and benevolent to the less fortunate of the world. Little did the idiots realize that if the have-nots were given all the opportunities these liberals espoused, the liberals would find themselves have-nots with no power, abused by the same people they had helped.

While he had no use for liberals, James intrinsically distrusted and despised the masses. Aside from use as cheap labor and to do his dirty work, he wished they were dead. He believed only through ruthlessness could his class remain in control. There were no half measures. The minute the powerful showed any sign of weakness, even if it came in the guise of charity, it was the beginning of their downfall.

Whenever he went through his factories, James sensed his loathing for the workers was mutual. He knew what they thought of him and what they would do if given the chance. He was determined not to fall prey. James considered himself to be a part of an elite business aristocracy that had to be preserved at all costs for the sake of his future heirs.

But at this point, as far as James was concerned, the Charles Blakesleys of the world with their noble ideas were a greater threat to society and his future heirs than the masses themselves since the masses didn't have the power to ameliorate their condition.

James vowed there was nothing he wouldn't do to ensure Josie didn't end up with Charles Blakesley.

* * *

After leaving James and J.D., Charles walked to the financial district. He found Wall Street vibrantly alive with the vibe that comes from making money. Everywhere Charles witnessed first-hand signs of new wealth. The street was packed with expensive cars and brokers flush with cash. People rushed around, in hopes of not missing out in the biggest bull market. Charles paused as he walked past the curb exchange where the particularly frenetic activity sent penny stocks spirally upwards to a limitless price. Standing at the side, as a witness to this intoxicating scene, he couldn't help but get caught up in the spell.

It was a cloudless autumn day. Although September was known traditionally as the most volatile month for the market, the Princeton educated boy from Oklahoma saw no signs of the tremors to come. As far as he could tell, the sun seemed to smile equally down at the denizens of Wall Street and the lesser players who supported them. For the first time in his life, Charles was filled with a deep desire to make money and lots of it. After all, he thought, now he had Josie's future to think about as well as his own.

Before meeting his love, Charles had planned to spend the minimum amount of time working in the city in order to make just enough money to fund subsequent trips. He hoped to further explore the wilds of Africa and the tombs in Egypt. He even toyed with the idea of joining an expedition to the Amazon or supporting some romantic doomed democratic movement before seriously contemplating what he really wanted to do with his life.

Ever since Princeton, Charles had been restless, spurning his uncle's overtures to return home to help run the family concerns. Now, keeping his love in the manner in which she was accustomed became paramount. He didn't want to have to ask his family for money, especially since their reserves were tighter now, so he dug into his small trust and used the family's portfolio to play the market more aggressively in the near term, as he figured out what kind of profession suited him.

Noticing his shoes looked dull, Charles stopped momentarily to have them shined by a young immigrant who said he loved America. Alfredo informed him that since he had come to this *wonderful* country from Italy, eighteen months ago, he already had made several thousand dollars in the market through client tips. Every day, he poured all his money aside from basic living expenses into stocks. Feeling confident, Charles left the industrious boy a generous tip and headed over to his own brokerage house.

When Charles walked in, he was overcome by the same energy he felt on the streets. As runners raced to keep apace with the buy and sell orders, the friendly sound of the ticker clicked constantly in the background, bringing happiness to those who eagerly grabbed at the numbers as they were spit out so they could see how much they had just increased their wealth. As Charles scanned the room it seemed all around him fortunes were being made.

He heard an old codger chuckle as he looked up from the ticker. Over the last three years, Mr. Hedly-Dent informed him he had taken sizable family investments and quadrupled them through his stock picking. Now, at the age of seventy-five, Mr. Hedly-Dent announced to anyone who would listen, playing the market was far too much fun to ever consider retiring.

Tapping Charles on the shoulder he confided, "I spent fifty years of my life married to a big woman with bad breath whom my parents picked out for me. I slaved day and night, not only to get away from her, but also to provide well for my growing family. Now no one has to work like that anymore. I sit here all day, not only to get away from the wife, but also to make easy money. My sons do the same thing at their brokerages."

Taking Charles aside, he said, "Young man, you too can get rich through your investments."

After picking some stocks based upon the tips and advice he had gathered from friends, Charles handed them over for processing as well as his letters of credit from the House of Morgan.

As Charles watched while the paper work was completed, he was surprised given the relatively large amount involved that the clerk seemed so nonchalant.

Reading his mind, he was informed, "Several years ago, your portfolio would have been considered sizable, but today, it's rather commonplace." Then reaching over to shake Charles' hand, he said as he checked the name at the top of the file, "Nonetheless, we're glad to have you increase your investments with us, Mr. Blakesley."

Satisfied with his choices, Charles turned to go. He stopped abruptly when a runner came by shouting, "Miss Maker just bought another 10,000 shares of U.S. Steel."

"Evelyn Maker?" inquired Charles.

The clerk nodded yes and explained, "She's a client."

Putting in another order for more shares of U.S. Steel, Charles said, "If it's good enough for the Seer of Wall Street, it's definitely good enough for me." To the cheers of the other investors, the young man said, "Besides, being a bull is good for America."

That afternoon, Charles made just over $12,000 on his investments. As he walked out of the brokerage, he smiled as he noted the date and time. It was the last day in September 1929. As he put his hat on, Charles felt instinctively, October would prove to be a great month for investing as well.

* * *

While Charles significantly increased his stock holdings, Josie sat in her parent's sitting room, describing the wedding gown she had in mind to her mother, Rebecca, and Geraldine. Although it was the middle of the afternoon, as they lounged on the sofas and in the chairs, the girls wore long, triple strands of pearls over the latest fashion rage, silk pajamas.

Josie explained as she twirled her long strand of pearls, "I really want a simple dress."

"But elegant, my dear," asserted Claire, who had very reluctantly come to accept her daughter's choice as a husband. "You must be elegant."

"Aren't I always when *you* dress me!" retorted Josie clearly miffed by her mother's efforts to control all of the wedding plans.

Before Claire could respond, Mary, the Baxter-Browne's maid, interrupted to inform her that Mrs. Whitney-Straight was on the phone waiting to speak with her.

As Claire left the room, Geraldine joked, "I think you'd look perfectly divine in some lacy bouffant dress dripping with sequins – it would be almost as good as that pink outfit you used to wear every single day with the matching bow and socks."

"I was ten when I dressed like that!" exclaimed Josie. "Remember what you wore?"

"It wasn't pink," Geraldine said rolling her eyes.

Josie asserted, "But it had lots of frills!"

"And it was really big!" chimed in Rebecca laughing as she remembered.

Glowering, Geraldine claimed, "Everything I have ever worn has been big!"

"Well, I just can't believe you are getting married!" said Rebecca excitedly as she changed the subject.

"I don't know why you're so surprised," retorted Geraldine. She reminded the airy Rebecca, "She's been gaga about him since she picked him up behind that bar. It was *so* predictable."

"Don't be so damn blasé about it! Josie is the first of us girls to get married!" replied Rebecca practically shouting.

"Actually Catherine was," said the pedantic Geraldine. "Speaking of whom, has anyone heard from her?"

"I got a postcard from her from Italy. They're coming back on the *Berengaria* since it's where they met – isn't it romantic?" replied Josie. "The ship is supposed to dock in New York on the 30th."

Rebecca sighed blissfully at the thought. Then as she looked at Josie, she said, "I still can hardly believe you're really getting married!" as she jumped up and gave Josie hug. "I, for one, am truly happy for you and Charles!"

"Thanks Becca," said Josie. "I really love him and I'm glad you and Geri like him, too. Your support means a great deal to me."

"So when are you telling everyone?" inquired Geraldine.

Josie explained, "We're having my godfather over for dinner tonight to break the news." Rolling her eyes, she went on to say, "But you know my mother! Everything has to be absolutely perfect!" Clearly exasperated, she claimed, "She's been working on the announcement cards for ages! At the rate she's going, it won't be out in the papers until sometime next year!"

Rebecca asked, "Have you set a date yet?"

"Unfortunately, we're thinking about a year from this summer – in late June. At least the weather is beautiful then," replied a wistful Josie.

Nodding in approval, Rebecca said, "My mother always says proper weddings take a year to plan."

"But I just want to be with him," said Josie as she got up and wandered over to the window. As she wanly looked outside, she claimed, "It's torture having to be apart."

"So do away with convention and live the life you want to lead," suggested Geraldine levelheadedly.

"Your mother would have an absolute fit," exclaimed Rebecca.

"That's true," said Josie, smiling at the thought. "But more importantly, Charles wants to wait. He doesn't want to get married until he can take care of me *properly*."

"That's *so* noble," stated Rebecca impressed.

"No Becca. That's just *normal*," corrected Geraldine. "Most men work and even some women do."

"Well, we all know you plan to!" shouted Rebecca.

"Plan?" exclaimed Geraldine with disbelief. "What do you mean plan? I do already. I sketch three days a week and sculpt another two to three days."

Rebecca protested, "But you're with us most of the time!"

"When I'm not with you, I'm sculpting!" replied Geraldine scowling.

"Humph!" snorted Rebecca. "That's not saying much. When was the last time you sculpted anything, anyway?"

"As a matter of fact, Mrs. Whitney-Straight has just commissioned me to do a sculpture of her," replied Geraldine proudly. "She wants it to be a very *big* piece."

"What is it – her bust?" retorted Rebecca laughing.

"No," stated the artist emphatically. Her expression and tone serious, she stated, "In honor of her stock market killings, it's a piece I'm titling: *The Lady Bull*."

Josie asked, "How does she want it done?"

"In bronze," said the artist. Proudly, she claimed, "It'll be a great piece – it's for her library or her private study. I don't think she's decided yet."

Josie looked at Geraldine skeptically, thinking of the Elsie de Wolfe decorated house. Then glancing at Rebecca who also seemed confused, she said, "I just can't imagine it fitting in either place."

"Actually Geri, I'm having problems visualizing this too. What is it going to look like? A big black bull with massive horns?" asked Rebecca.

Frowning, Geraldine explained, "The Lady Bull is Mrs. Whitney-Straight riding astride a gigantic male bull that is impressive in every way."

"Does the bull look anything like her husband?" inquired Josie with a smirk.

"It's a piece for the library not the bedroom!" shouted Geraldine. "You know I want to get paid for this!"

"Then I suggest you have someone else do the sculpture for you!" quipped Rebecca between giggles.

Geraldine threatened, "You won't be laughing when you see what I do to you!"

"I wouldn't make the mistake of paying you anything either!" retorted Rebecca as she made faces at her friend.

After a few minutes of bantering, Josie said, "Jokes aside, I look forward to seeing whatever materializes." As she poured her friends tea and offered each of them sandwiches and scones she continued, "I really like your idea, Geri. When did this happen?"

Geraldine replied, "The other night at Henry's."

"Are you sure she wasn't drunk?" said Rebecca between bites. Then as she wiped her lips with a napkin, she said, "You know, in the light of day, she might not remember."

"She wouldn't be the only one," retorted Geraldine as she narrowed her eyes at Rebecca who clearly didn't recollect a thing about that evening. Fighting off the urge to bring up J.D. Rockefeller, Geraldine changed the subject instead. Turning to Josie she inquired, "Have you given any thought to where you and Charles want to live?"

Josie said, "You know, we haven't discussed it yet. But as long as I'm with Charles, I don't care."

"And wherever Josie wants to be is fine with me," stated her fiancé as he walked through the sitting room doorway.

Charles warmly kissed Geraldine and Rebecca on both cheeks before coming over to Josie and giving her a long, passionate kiss on the lips. Then, as he settled down on the settee next to her, he said, "I hope you don't mind my intruding, but I want to spend every minute I can with my fiancée."

"I think it's marvelous!" responded Rebecca enthusiastically.

Geraldine remarked, "If you don't feel this way now, you probably shouldn't get married."

"I'm glad you approve," said Charles addressing the girls as he looked lovingly at Josie.

Geraldine responded, "I didn't say that exactly." Then, as she looked at the loving couple, she said more softly, "But it doesn't matter. I do happen to think you're right for each other but the important thing is how you both feel." Not wanting to be a third wheel, Geraldine nodded her head at Rebecca and said, "C'mon Becca. Let's leave these two alone."

"Don't go." Stopping them, Charles said as he got up. "I just dropped in to tell Josie we should be able to move up the wedding." As Josie beamed, he exclaimed, "I'm making a killing in the market!" Taking Josie by the hand as he looked into her radiant eyes, he said meaningfully, "We're going to have the best!"

Before he could say more, Josie interrupted him to tell him she didn't care how much they had as long as she was with him.

"That's a good thing," muttered Geraldine under her breath. When Rebecca who overheard her murmuring asked her to elaborate, Geraldine said, "From what I've heard recently, the market may not be the best place to start investing."

"What do you know?" whispered Rebecca crossly as she tried to get Geraldine to hush up. She didn't want her casting any gloom over the lovers.

"Obviously more than you do," replied Geraldine as she motioned to Rebecca to get up.

As Josie started kissing Charles, her girlfriends quietly crept out of the room, shutting the door after themselves.

Despite her sarcastic front, Geraldine was so moved by the love that Charles and Josie had for each other, she had tears in her eyes. She tried to hide her emotions, but to no avail.

Looking at Geraldine, Rebecca said seriously, "That's what I want – that kind of love."

"Don't we all," replied Geraldine as she put her arm around Rebecca and they got into a cab to go see the latest Cecil B. De Mille film.

It was nearly a half an hour before Josie and Charles realized they had been left alone. After kissing, they had dozed off in each other's arms. Now, as the radiant sun slowly set, it cast a soft, golden glow that filled the room and the lovers once again embraced. Their bodies remained entwined for several magical moments. Finally, as the sun descended slowly from the sky, the spell was broken and they spoke.

"So what did you buy?" inquired Josie.

Gazing into her eyes, he said, "Our future."

Josie asked, "Which stocks hold the key?"

"We're in all the major companies." Taking a list out of his pocket, he read off the names to her. "General Motors, Ford, Bethlehem Steel, Standard Oil, RCA, Anaconda Copper, New York Central and lots of U.S. Steel." He explained, "Mostly we're in fundamentally sound companies with good returns. But I also invested in a number of high growth companies that we can play for quick profits."

Kissing her on the forehead, Charles said excitedly, "We're going to make lots of money!" Showing her several pieces of the ticker, he explained, "Today alone we made over $12,000."

Jumping up and kissing him, she exclaimed, "That's wonderful darling – you're so smart!"

Excited at what he had been witnessing, he continued to speak like a recent convert. Optimistic, his voice full of enthusiasm, his eyes sparkled with life. "It's a new economy! None of the old rules apply. The money our families took generations to make can be quadrupled overnight just by buying the right stocks!"

Initially Josie was caught up with Charles' excitement, but the longer he spoke about the market, the more she felt concerned in her gut that it seemed all too easy. Thinking how new he was to investing, she suggested, "Maybe you should talk to my father or Henry or even the Morgans and see what they think. Daddy was talking to Bernie Baruch just last week about this. I think I overheard him say to someone Mr. Baruch cashed out."

Charles inquired, "What did your father say?"

"Not to worry," said Josie shrugging.

"See." Kissing her again, he said considerately, "I'll discuss my investments with your father if you like, but I know what I'm doing. It's a new market – totally different than everything your father, Henry, Bernie, and even the Morgans have known. In some ways, they're not equipped to take advantage of it like I am and all the other young men who don't have all their experience and baggage from the way the market operated in the past."

She restated apprehensively, "You mean the way it has always operated."

While Josie continued to convey some misgivings, he said reassuringly, "Trust me. I love you."

Josie said with all her heart, "I love you, too."

He asked, "But do you trust me?"

Looking him in the eyes, Josie said with love, "I believe in you." Then she kissed him on the lips and said, "I'll check your stocks out when I go to the exchange with Winston Churchill. Just leave me the list so I can remember which ones you have. Winston said it'll probably just be another typical day at the Exchange, but now that I know you're invested…"

Charles interrupted her to say, "*We're* invested. I want you to understand everything I do financially is for us and I want you to know about it and be as involved as you like, because I love you," said Charles as he held her close. "That's why I wanted to tell you what I did today."

"I appreciate that," said Josie as she lovingly kissed Charles.

As Charles played with her hair, he said tenderly, "You know I love and respect you for your brain as well as your body."

"That's one reason I love you," said Josie as she played with his smoothed down hair until it became wavy again. Then as he swept her up into his arms, they lost track of time.

When they heard the grandfather clock strike seven o'clock, Charles jumped up from the settee and exclaimed, "I better go home and change before dinner."

After taking Josie into his arms again and kissing her rapturously, Charles said, "I'll be back in twenty minutes."

"Promise?" said Josie as she started kissing him again.

Taking her into his arms, he said, "A promise is a promise. Besides, every minute away from you is purgatory for me."

While they held each again, the minutes passed quickly. Finally pulling herself away from Charles she said looking at the rococo

Louis XV mantle piece clock, "Now you have less than twelve minutes to go home, change and get back in time for drinks."

Pulling her back down on the settee, Charles said, "Let's make it an even ten."

* * *

CHAPTER XII

The market suffered what was explained as a "technical correction," not long after Charles had gleefully told Josie he had doubled his investments. After assessing the damage, he was relieved that his portfolio only declined slightly, because General Motors had risen three points and RCA had gained ten. But as he studied the chart he had made for the month of September, it was clear to him that the market indeed had become more volatile since the last index peak on September 3rd. Although some of his stocks had increased since then, the overall market had been much weaker. Between the Labor Day holiday and the end of the month, he found that the 240 leading issues on the New York Stock Exchange had lost $2,814,255,346 in value. While he, like many others on Wall Street believed in the fundamental soundness of the market, he realized after this setback, that he needed to double his efforts in order to make the kind of money he sought.

As they strolled around Central Park together Charles told Josie he needed to spend significantly more time working. He heard of many people making a killing even when the market suffered an occasional sell off because of tips and their early analysis of national and international news. One man in his brokerage sent his driver to the *New York Times*' printing facility every morning at dawn to get the paper before anyone else. That same man had made close to $145,000 the same day that investors were slammed.

The young man made it clear that several other investors who did well today because of tips from friends with connections. Had

Charles been more cordial with these investors, he believed he would have been privy to the information as well. The customer room at his brokerage was just like any other club. He had explained to Josie, that if you were known and liked, you were accepted and given a hand up. The young man who once scaled mountains now was just as determined to make it into the financial elite. He knew he needed to make a lot of money quickly because as a wedding present for his bride he wanted to buy her a country home.

Although Josie was slightly depressed that Charles clearly would be pre-occupied with his investments, she was pleased he was taking such an interest in their financial future.

Kissing him on the lips, Josie whispered that she'd let him off the hook, "This time."

Later, the couple decided to go to the movies ostensibly to watch the acclaimed film *Broadway Melody*, but really because they knew there they could continue kissing uninterrupted at "the petting palace" as their set called cinemas. Much to her horror, as they started making out, Josie was tapped on the shoulder. Turning around, she was relieved to see Geraldine and Rebecca.

After Charles and Josie joined her friends, Geri pointed to another couple that publicly displayed their interest in each other. Geraldine explained, "They just walked in a few minutes ago, so I had a good look."

As Rebecca giggled, Josie squinted. At the same time, Charles practically screamed, "It's your parents!"

At the end of the matinee, Charles and Josie walked down to her parents. Claire blushed when her daughter said, "We were sitting right behind you."

Albert wasn't so embarrassed. In response to Josie's revelation, he reached over and gave his wife a passionate kiss.

Josie had never seen her parents so forward and in public no less. She thought they had loosened up considerably since she and

Charles had become engaged. It was almost as if they were remembering what they had been like. Then she wondered if she had just been oblivious all these years. As Charles and Josie walked to the Baxter-Brownes' townhouse, Josie knew it didn't matter. She was just glad her parents got along so well after all these years. It made her feel confident that her relationship with Charles would always be filled with passion and love.

Charles had every intention of going home early that night to review some companies' prospectuses and prepare for the morning market opening. But as he sat with Josie, he lost his resolve to leave. It was three-thirty in the morning before he finally dragged himself away from her. He knew he would be tired but he set his alarm for seven in the morning anyway. He needed to start the day early to go through all the papers and have breakfast with an old college friend who now served as a specialist on the floor of the New York Stock Exchange.

When Charles woke up the next morning, he felt sick to his stomach. He wasn't sure if it was because he had slept so little or he was coming down with a virus. But he forced himself out of bed and into the shower anyway.

An hour later when he sat with his friend, Charles had a very bad feeling in the pit of his stomach.

* * *

Garrett Goldman phoned James early that morning. Still groggy from the previous night, James immediately woke up when the bear said, "Get your ass over here."

The phone went dead before James could reply. Garrett had five other people on hold and two secretaries working like mad to connect him to sources around the globe. London had come through as he hung up on James.

When James walked into Garrett's offices, he found the bear in a manic state racing around his subordinates. He was in his element in the midst of what could only be described by a sane person as mayhem. Garrett was so energized and animated by the market's plunge James thought the large man almost looked attractive.

The young businessman was sure he was a lunatic as he watched Garrett bark orders at different traders as he held phones to each ear while continuing to ask questions and jot down notes and sell orders that he thrust in his underlings' faces as he was still writing them. One of Garrett's secretaries informed James her boss could hold simultaneous conversations – to be exact – five or six at a time. She claimed, "And on top of that, he still manages to catch totally unrelated mistakes the boys and I make."

Garrett didn't like screw-ups, but he realized no one was on his level. He tolerated minor mistakes from his employees as long as they gave him their complete loyalty and willingly worked as hard as he did.

As James phoned his contacts at the House of Morgan and the New York Stock Exchange, Garrett spoke with a reporter who called to inquire whether he thought the market was collapsing. Not having time to explain his views, Garrett barked, "Read my goddamn book." Switching lines, Garrett conversed with the Chicago Board of Trade and the L.A. Stock Exchange concurrently.

Neither James nor Garrett took any time to eat or drink. Pumped up with adrenaline, they thrived on nervous energy and made millions trading during the day.

So focused on the immediate activity, during trading hours the men didn't have the time to gage whether there would be follow-through selling on the following day. So as the trading day drew to a close, Garrett took his profits and closed out every one of his positions. As he had done for some time now, James followed the bear's lead.

After the market closed, the men sat down in Garrett's private office to analyze the situation.

"I can't believe he fucked the market!' shouted James.

The trader asked, "Who? Babson?"

James said, "Yeah, the Profit of Doom! He's been predicting the demise of the Bull Market pretty much since it started. Nobody ever took him seriously before. He's a fucking joker. I just don't understand why the market tumbled now because he gave one fucking speech."

"It may be a fluke." Looking through his notes, Garrett mused, "But even if it is, it's an indication the market is deeply unstable. For us to get the downward momentum we did today and the panic selling, there are clearly a lot of weak fundamentals."

Trying to take into account the big picture, James said, "From what I can tell, the market's been irrational for some time. There has been no reason for the kinds of valuations we've seen for the past couple years and yet stocks have continued to spiral upwards. Of course, there's also no reason for this type of depreciation exactly at this moment." James wondered aloud. "They've stayed up this long, defying every traditional law of economics. I just don't understand why stocks should suddenly depreciate now?" Looking at Garrett, he said, "I don't buy the Babson factor."

Garrett smiled knowingly.

James pushed him: "Tell."

Garrett cryptically replied, "I got another message from London."

"Yeah?"

The trader predicted, "There's going to be trouble – big trouble and I think it's going to affect the market over here."

As James tried to finagle Garrett to explain, the bear looked away. He wasn't about to let his apprentice in on everything he knew. Handing over notes to James for him to review, he said, "First things first. Let's concentrate on tomorrow. What's your read?"

Looking through the documents, James reasoned, "The market closed on the downside with heavy volume." The student suggested, "So it should open down."

"Good logic," stated his mentor nodding his head in approval.

Sensing there might be something he hadn't gotten, James said, "But?"

The Bear of Wall Street replied, "Babson is a joker. You're right about that. Overnight, most investors will mull over what they know and have heard. Brokers will do their best tomorrow to calm clients down and keep their money in the market."

"And the papers?"

"Journalists have to give fair coverage." Garrett explained smiling, "We should get a very positive rebuttal from that Yale professor Fisher."

James said smiling knowingly, "He's a major bull."

"Uh huh," replied Garrett nodding his head and pointing his finger for emphasis like a college professor. "The public prefers hearing good news to bad."

James chimed in, "And everyone likes Fisher."

"He's highly respected. He should calm things down." Garrett stated as he lit a cigar, "My bet is the market will stage a recovery."

James smiled. "That's why we closed our positions out."

"You're learning," said Garrett after exhaling.

"And you've got a date with a gorgeous blonde," replied James.

The trader asked, "What's her name?"

The playboy businessman said smirking, "Whatever you want to call her."

As Garrett chuckled, James handed him a number and went to get some food. Suddenly he felt starved.

While James was celebrating his market profits with the very eager although very married Lily Vanderhorn, Charles was slumped in a chair peering over his stock positions. It didn't take much analysis for him to figure out where he stood. His portfolio had taken a beating. As he commiserated with fellow investors at his brokerage, he tried to figure out what to do. He had considered selling out as his stocks had plummeted, but he reasoned it was a small panic that should pass. Unable to face his fiancée, he phoned to tell her he had been unwell all day and wanted to go straight to bed. It was true in more than one way.

After breakfast, just before the market opened, Charles had emptied his entire stomach in the bathroom. Either in reaction to the events or because of queasiness from the lack of sleep, he threw up again just after the market closed. As he made his way home, he barely felt like he had the energy to climb into bed. His spirits improved significantly when he got home to find Josie on his bed. She had brought crackers and other tidbits to make him feel better.

His charming fiancée had convinced his doorman to let her in. Under the doormat, she found the spare key to Charles' Frank Lloyd Wright inspired apartment. Before he arrived, Josie enjoyed looking at the numerous eclectic pieces her fiancé had collected from his travels. Had he been in better spirits, she would have asked him to tell her more about each of the pieces. As it was, she just took Charles' temperature and gently tucked him into his simple Arts and Craft style bed and comforted him as best as she could. He had a fever of 102 and was trembling. Wrapping him up warmly with multiple patchwork quilts, she lay down beside him and forbade him from going to the brokerage in the morning.

Figuring Charles not only was sick but also had suffered losses and felt bad about them, she tried to console him by informing him that her father said most people he knew were down and expecting the market would recover in the morning.

As Josie tried to get her fiancé to sleep, they kept talking. Even though Charles was ill, they enjoyed each other's company so much that they effortlessly went from discussing one subject to another.

Despite Charles' protests that he didn't want Josie to risk catching what he had, she insisted on staying with him. Kissing him good night for the tenth time as she held him, she explained, "I told my parents I was sleeping over at Geraldine's."

Smiling weakly, he joked, "And you told Geraldine…"

"That I was making wild, passionate love to you," she said giggling.

"If only I wasn't sick right now…" replied Charles teasing.

Josie claimed, "If you weren't, I wouldn't be here."

"I think I am going to be sick every night." Charles joked. "You're going to have to stay over Geraldine's pretty frequently from now on."

She laughed in response as she buried her head in his chest to smell his wonderful scent. But before she could get too comfortable, he started to tickle her.

Josie squirmed and threatened, "Mr. Blakesley, I think you are well enough to be on your own!"

Despite Charles' illness, the young couple had a wonderful time being together as the full moon illuminated the pine covered room with exposed beams and an arched ceiling. By morning Charles' fever subsided and the market rebounded – recovering almost all of the previous days' losses. Celebrating, Josie and Charles had a picnic in Central Park.

The more time Charles and Josie spent together, the harder Charles worked. In the next couple of days he doubled his efforts to make money. Renewing old contacts and making fast friends on Wall Street on every social level because he believed you never knew who would prove most helpful, he started realizing significant gains in his stocks despite the volatile market. His efforts paid off and attracted attention. Much to his surprise, Charles received several unsolicited job offers. Among others, the Morgans expressed interest in him, but understood he felt uncomfortable working for friends.

Charlie Mitchell, the President of National City, also asked the promising young man to join his firm just before he left for a month-long European vacation. Like Charles, he was bullish. Charles respected Mitchell immensely for the successful operation the man had built from almost nothing. National City, which now had the largest number of brokerages in the nation, was an incredible network with great opportunities. But Charles didn't think the firm was right for him. The bank had a reputation of focusing on small investors and pushing its own stock on clients regardless of the quality of the paper.

Just when he thought that he would remain a private investor for the time being, Charles met a banker who would impact his life tremendously.

The encounter took place before the market opened, over breakfast at Delmonico's. Charles sat with Mr. Hedley-Dent. Their table was covered with the morning papers, company prospectuses, government reports, and Charles' notes. As he explained to his older friend why he felt gold would rise today while RCA should be sold, a well dressed, intelligent looking businessman approached him.

Leaning over their table, the businessman stated, "I couldn't help but overhear what you've been saying. Do you mind if I ask you if you're with a bank?"

Initially Charles answered routinely not thinking much of the encounter, "I invest privately, sir."

But as he talked to the businessman, he was struck by the man's warm smile and even more by his magnetism.

While they discussed further Charles' investments and the market in general, the businessman clearly was pleased with what he heard. Before leaving he inquired, "Would you like to join my firm?"

Mr. Hedley-Dent, who recognized who this man was and was aware of his stellar reputation, gave his young friend a kick under the table. He didn't want Charles to dismiss this opportunity without further investigation.

At his older friend's prodding, Charles responded to the businessman's question by saying, "It all depends what you're suggesting. I'd like to continue to grow my own portfolio."

The man assured him, "That wouldn't be a problem."

As Mr. Hedley-Dent smiled with approval, the businessman handed Charles his card with the words, "When you have time, stop by. Have a look around and we can talk further."

His name was E. F. Hutton and Charles had a feeling his life was about to change.

*   *   *

In no time, Charles was pleased that he had decided to join E.F. Hutton's firm. Hired as an associate because he was interested in getting a handle on all aspects of the entire business, he was given the chance to spend his first two years rotating among different departments. In order to continue advancing his stock portfolio, Charles decided to start his training in the brokerage end of the business.

The office operated like a tight ship with a hard working crew. Charles immediately bonded with another young broker, W.E. "Hut" Hutton-Miller, who also heavily had invested his trust fund despite his own reservations about the future of the great bull market. Like many brokers, Hut knew the greatest economic boom in the history of the country couldn't last forever, but since it had defied the doomsday augurs for so long and had no reason to end exactly at this point, he continued to pour his money into stocks.

Even though Josie was seeing increasingly less of him, for her part, she was delighted with Charles' newfound happiness. She also was extremely proud that he was making such progress with their finances despite the recent volatility.

As the days passed in October, the market jitters continued. The problem in London that Garrett Goldman learned about before it broke seemed largely to blame. In a brazen attempt to take control over the British steel industry, financier Clarence Hatry committed a major fraud that led to the collapse of his empire and ruin of countless investors. The repercussions seriously impacted both sides of the Atlantic. The Baxter-Brownes, Ashleys, Whitney-Straights, and others in their circle knew a number of privileged British subjects adversely affected by the Hatry Affair. Josie was particularly saddened to learn that the sister of her friend, Joy Kenward-Edgar, was amongst those financially ruined with no recourse.

But not everyone suffered as a result. Getting the confirmation from his family's British steel sources not long after Garrett gave him the tip, James capitalized on the news. Not as privileged as either James or Garrett on the matter, Charles and Hut worked diligently to keep their portfolios as well as their clients from losing substantially. By working together, they did marginally well.

When he left the office at the end of the second week in October, Charles felt optimistic about his future. He also looked forward to this weekend very much. It was Josie's birthday. Hut agreed to cover for him on Monday so he could take the day off.

With the Baxter-Browne's permission and Rebecca and Geraldine's help, Charles planned a birthday surprise that Josie would never forget.

* * *

When Charles asked Josie what she wanted for her birthday, she had replied, "To be with you." Subsequent attempts to glean what else she wanted proved futile. When he consulted her friends and parents, they too had difficulty coming up with anything extraordinary.

Charles was determined to do something unique.

The morning of her birthday, Josie awoke to a room decorated with flowers. The sweet aroma was most intoxicating. Four giant bouquets of pink roses had been placed around her room on five-foot antique candelabras. Orchid garlands draped her canopied bed and mirrors. She wasn't sure how it had been done without her realizing, because clearly a great deal of laborious work had been necessary to create the effect.

For a while, Josie just stayed in bed soaking in the fragrance and enjoying the floral paradise. Then, as she walked over to her bureau, she noticed a beautiful long stemmed red rose in the most delicate Baccarat vase. The fine crystal shimmered like a thousand diamonds as rays of sunlight streamed through her full-length bedroom windows. She had never seen anything so lovely.

Josie was so captivated by the scene she didn't hear the knocks on her door. Finally, her mother gave up trying to be polite and just walked in. Kissing Josie on the cheek, Claire said, "Happy birthday, darling."

The birthday girl asked, "Who did this mother?" As she hugged her mother thanking her for bringing her into the world, she exclaimed, "It's breathtaking!"

A telling smile on her face, Claire replied, "Your fiancé and a few helpers." She handed her daughter a small package that rested upon three large wrapped boxes that she had previously put down on a side table when she had come into Josie's room. She said, explaining to her daughter, "The top three are from your father and me and the other one was delivered earlier this morning."

Opening them up immediately, Josie was ecstatic that her parents had given her a stunning diamond necklace and matching earrings from Cartier and several new Madame Vionnet dresses. She immediately put on one of the outfits – a white Grecian-styled crepe day dress. It was one of the most beautiful dresses she had ever seen. Josie delighted in the ensemble and the way it looked on her.

Turning her attention to the final box, Josie looked for a card but couldn't find one. With a knowing smile Claire advised, "Just open it."

The paper was so beautiful that Josie took her time to carefully unwrap it. She nearly gasped as the contents were revealed. Inside was an elegant black sequined Lesage embroidered gown. The attached envelope read: *To be worn tonight.*

Josie's heart pounded as she opened the envelope. Written in calligraphy on rice paper, the note inside stated:

At six o'clock
At this dock
You should be
Waiting for me
As the sun sets
The fun begins
All my love – Charles Blakesley

Josie couldn't believe Charles had gone to so much trouble and spent so much money on her. She had no idea what was to come.

Despite what he had indicated in the note, Josie didn't have to wait for Charles that evening. He was at the dock a full half an hour before she arrived making sure everything was arranged as he had planned. When she got there, he greeted her in formal attire. Stepping on to Henry Jay's yacht, the *Silver Moon*, he explained the old codger had agreed to let them use the boat for a romantic dinner while cruising along the Hudson. Josie and Charles watched the sun set as a quartet played musical medleys for their enjoyment. Feeling confident that the prohibition agents wouldn't disturb them, Charles broke out the champagne. A six-course dinner and dancing under the stars followed. As the night gave way to dawn, Josie said as they cuddled on the deck, "Shouldn't we be heading back?"

"Do you really want to?" inquired Charles.

As Josie shook her head no and then yes because she knew her parents would have a fit if she stayed out all night with her fiancé, Charles said, "Don't worry. It's taken care of."

Content, Josie fell asleep in Charles arms. When she woke up, it already was late afternoon and she was in one of the yacht's staterooms. Confused, Josie jumped out of bed. She noticed she had on a pair of pajamas. She didn't remember getting into them the previous night. In fact, as she thought about it, she didn't remember much. But what she did, she thought was wonderful.

Josie ran up the stairs to the main deck to find out what had happened. Before she got there, much to her surprise, her godfather stopped her.

"Did you sleep well?" he inquired.

Speechless, she nodded yes.

"In case you're wondering, I'm the chaperone," replied Henry with a twinkle in his eye. Overwhelmed, Josie stared at him as he said, "Charles, the servants, and I had quite a time getting you to bed last night."

Before she could ask any more questions, Charles appeared. After kissing her on the lips, he picked her up and carried her to the deck. Explaining he said, "We can't miss our first sunset at sea!" As he held her, he said, "Isn't it absolutely the best?"

"Yes, but where exactly are we?" inquired Josie very confused.

"Almost there," Charles said pointing to a dot in the horizon.

Josie inquired, "Is that Manhattan?"

"It's an island," replied Charles cryptically as he flashed his incredible smile.

"Which one?" asked Josie thinking that it felt awfully warm.

"Bermuda," answered Henry Jay as he joined them. As he handed them glasses of champagne he said, "You know we're lucky. They often get hurricanes this time of the year, but in honor of your birthday, Josie, the gods have been merciful and we shouldn't have any problems on this trip."

After disembarking, Josie and Charles wandered around the capital city of Hamilton. Josie found it a most charming place. As she kissed her fiancé in the park, she admitted, "This is the best birthday I could ever imagine."

An hour later, as they walked up a winding road to reach the top of the hill where Charles had rented a house for the rest of the weekend, Josie stopped to admire the view. She thought it was one of the most romantic spots in the world. When he reached over to kiss her, she knew Charles thought so as well. Then, as they looked up at the residence and its magnificent grounds, Josie told him she was impressed with how idyllic it all was. Charles informed her that a nineteenth century privateer had built it, picking the spot so he could see his ships from his bedroom window. Josie could very well understand why someone would want to be situated in this location so they could enjoy the panoramic view as long as possible.

As they approached their house, they could hear local music. It sounded like it was coming their way. Josie wondered if there were any local festivities going on that evening.

"Just a birthday," replied Charles under his breath as they walked into the dark house.

"What?" asked Josie only half catching what he had said. But before she could ask anything else, she was greeted with noisemakers and the words, "Surprise!"

As the lights were turned on, Josie saw not only her godfather, but also her parents and Rebecca and Geraldine. As they sang happy birthday to her, Claire brought out an incredible homemade chocolate cake with lots of candles for good luck. Josie blew out all of them in one go without any help. Later, the group enjoyed a traditional dinner and native entertainment.

It was the second night Josie ate, drank, and danced well into the night and hardly remembered going to bed. But this time, she woke up in a room with Geraldine and Rebecca as bedmates.

The next morning they went to services at St. Peter's Church in St. George and explored the various islands. After seeing everything they could see and playing a few mean games of doubles tennis against the Baxter-Brownes, Charles and Josie relaxed on the beach as Rebecca, Geraldine and Henry went sailing.

Although Henry said he couldn't spend enough time on the sea, Josie thought his real reason for exploring the area by boat was to meet up with some bootlegging smugglers. He had a longstanding arrangement with the men. Josie guessed Henry needed to replenish his recently depleted stock in time for the winter social season.

On Monday, Geraldine sketched natives as Rebecca and Josie went shopping with Claire. Josie's mother was delighted to buy sets of fine English china and woolen fabrics at hugely reduced prices to those she would have paid in England. Claire even purchased items for her daughter's upcoming wedding. Feeling her parents had enough British goods, Geraldine picked up some of the native art. After lunch, Albert and Charles took a clipper plane off the island to get back to New York so he could work on Tuesday. Henry remained to bring back his hooch and the girls – a prospect he didn't mind in the least.

Josie had such a wonderful weekend that she had a hard time letting Charles leave. She knew she couldn't have been more imaginative herself than Charles' had been in planning the romantic birthday celebration. She thought he had organized the most enchanting weekend she ever had experienced, down to every last detail. She also loved the presents he had given her. Each one showed great consideration on his part. Without any hints from her, he had taken the time to figure out her taste and to get her items that she really wanted as opposed to things he'd like or thought she should want to have. She loved her fiancé all the more that he invited those who meant the most to her to share the weekend with them. As she kissed him goodbye, she let him know how touched she was by what he had done.

As Josie and her mother walked back to the house to prepare for their return, she grew concerned as she thought how much the birthday bash had cost Charles. It became clear to Josie that her fiancé had spent a small fortune. Claire told her that he had refused to let her parents and Rebecca and Geraldine pay for anything other than the plane tickets that flew them to the island in time for the surprise.

Despite his exhaustion, when Charles returned to New York, he went straight to work. He knew he had to catch up to do before the market opened on Tuesday. After extravagantly spending on Josie's birthday, he indeed was under pressure to make up the expenditure in investments to keep their wedding date on target. Thinking of the weekend and how it had pleased her, he knew it was worth it. Charles believed money was to be enjoyed. He thought it also felt good to spend what he himself had earned. To him, it made the giving all the more meaningful.

Charles wasn't the only one with an agenda when he returned to the city. Josie had over sixty-five invitations and ten letters to peruse. For the better part of the morning on the day they returned, Josie and her mother sat in Claire's study reading the mail. As the socialite was about to take a break, she picked up a message from Winston Churchill. He reminded her that he planned to go to the Stock Exchange on the following Thursday, October 24th. He wrote her presence and humor was more than welcome if she still wanted to join him in the visitor's gallery.

* * *

While Josie and Charles were celebrating her birthday, James had concentrated on business. New York's most eligible bachelor hated visiting his factories and mills. He only made the trip when it was absolutely necessary.

Thirty minutes before he arrived in Pittsburgh, he knew he was getting close. The sun had been shining brightly in a cloudless blue sky. But as his car neared the destination, the air became heavy with smoke and grime. In the factory town itself, the pollution was so bad, regardless of the time and season, it was always overcast. James had been presented at various times with purifiers for the mills that might have helped, but he didn't want to waste his money on them.

As Bentley pulled the Rolls Royce in front of the main building, James told him to circle around slowly a couple of times. Although he normally walked around the area, he didn't feel like breathing the bad air today. He also felt confident that from the car he could ascertain the conditions. The exteriors of the factories and housing complexes were maintained although as gray and depressing as the sky. Satisfied, he instructed his driver to take him to the shops.

James descended from the car to inspect the company run grocery store and clothing outlets. He was satisfied with the merchandise and prices. Every item was marked up considerably. Since the factory stores were the only places the workers could buy items, James made sure he took advantage of the monopoly.

Stopping at the school as well, James presented the teacher with lollypops for the children. P.R. accomplished, the industrialist turned his attention to the real reason for his visit. He wanted to go through the books, meet with the salesmen and the supervisors and ensure that they were exploiting the workers to the maximum extent. Although he knew his factories were some of the most cost-effective, profit-oriented ones in the country, he always wanted to improve efficiency even more. The businessman noticed a trend that he used to his benefit. After each visit to his factory, for approximately one month, the quality and quantity improved, as did the bottom line.

James purposely did not alert anyone to his impending visit. He preferred to review the operation without giving his underlings the benefit of planning. He was delighted to see his workers scramble on all levels as they spotted him. The accountant, senior supervisor, his secretary, the clerks and their underlings behaved like dominoes falling on top of each other – all flustered by his arrival. This morning, the secretary spilled coffee on the accountant, the accountant dropped the books on the supervisor, and the supervisor hit his clerk in the face when he spun around.

James made the most of their discomfiture. He also managed to reduce both the accountant's salary and the supervisor's because in their panic they admitted their failings. At the end of the meetings, the men were pleased just to remain employed. He regarded all workers — cheats, who would try to get away with as much as they thought they could. So he made it his policy to minimize the damage by never letting them feel their jobs were safe. His network of spies and thugs throughout the operations helped reinforce the insecurity on all levels.

The cunning businessman was about to leave when he noticed a sales manager ushering around a tall, blonde, good-looking gentleman. The industrialist businessman thought this guest looked vaguely familiar. After staring at the Teutonic-featured man for some time, James finally placed him. He had seen him several nights before in New York at the Brooke Club. As James walked towards him, he thought, if only he could remember with whom the young man had been sitting.

Not wasting time as he watched the guest furiously taking notes, James strode up to him. Ignoring his sales manager, he said assertively addressing the visitor, "I don't think we met." Sticking out his hand he introduced himself. "I own this place." Pointedly, he asked, "And you are?"

Caught off guard, the man replied coloring from embarrassment. "I am pleased to meet you, sir." As he extended his hand, he said, "My name is William Messerschmitt." He produced a card as he explained, "I just bought the manufacturing license for the Eastern Aircraft Corporation."

Frowning, James said, "That's on Long Island, isn't it."

"Yes. Pawtucket." The man offered, "I'd love to show you around some time if you're interested." As he spoke, James detected a slight German accent.

As they talked, James figured out who Willy was. He had heard the young German was one of the best aviation specialists around. Motioning to the aviator to follow him to his office, James said cordially, "What brings you here?"

The German stated, "I understand you have aluminum plants as well as steel."

"And mining and other interests," replied James.

"Very good," stated Willy to himself. Then, addressing James, he said, "I hope we might be able to do some business together. I will need supplies to build my latest design, the M-18. You were highly recommended to me by friends." James listened intently as the man explained, "I will be dealing in volume."

Interested in what he had heard so far, James said, "Please continue."

In response, Willy pulled out some papers that he handed to James with the words, "You understand the project is *confidential.*"

James smiled. He sensed this could be an exceedingly profitable contract. After offering Willy a chair he closed the door.

As it shut, Bentley, who had come inside to see if his master was ready to depart yet, heard James say, "I'm sure we can work something out."

After several hours, the men emerged. They were extremely cordial. Clearly it had been a fruitful discussion. James, who had never done business with Germans before, sensed he would find this collaboration extremely rewarding.

* * *

While James and Willy discussed business, Josie and Charles enjoyed a quiet weekend with her parents in their townhouse. They spent time compiling wedding lists and making other arrangements. Claire and Albert jokingly warned the couple that they were running out of time to change their mind about getting married. Once they retained the caterers and florists, it would be a mere matter of days before their engagement would hit the gossip columns.

Putting his arm around Josie, Charles said, "I don't think that's a problem."

The couple did have a different issue. They still weren't sure where they wanted to go on their honeymoon. Henry Jay offered his yacht for as long they wanted and Charles' Aunt and Uncle promised to pay the bill since the Baxter-Brownes were taking care of the wedding and reception. Josie and Charles wanted to do something different and go somewhere neither had ever been. He recommended Marrakech. Josie thought it was a grand idea. Then they realized it would be beastly hot in June. At four in the morning on Sunday night, they decided they probably wouldn't come up with a solution before dawn and should get some sleep.

Overtired from the lack of sleep, Charles was relieved that the market had a quiet day on the Monday. Both Charles and Hut personally did quite well despite the lack of activity. Tuesday night, Charles accompanied Josie and her parents as well as the Ashleys and the Stanleys to the ballet. Afterwards, the group had a late dinner. Because they had been up so late the last few nights, the lovers agreed to go to bed relatively early. But as always, unable to leave his love, the young man didn't get to his apartment until one thirty in the morning.

When Charles got up, he saw the sun shining brightly. He thought October 23rd would be a beautiful day. That morning, he especially enjoyed his walk to the office. The air was crisp and had the scent of the falling autumn leaves. But the market opened with uncertainty. He hoped the previous day's rally would be sustained. By noon, as sell orders came from every direction, he knew it would be a very bad day. The office became frantic as the volume increased on the downside. By the end of the trading day, it was clear billions of dollars had been erased. Charles was sure it must have been one of the heaviest trading days in the history of the Exchange. As a result, he as well as everyone else in the office continued working well into the night to process all the orders. When he finally left Wall Street at two in the morning, all around him, offices were still well lit and filled with employees desperately trying to get the day's work done before the morning.

Charles was so exhausted he didn't remember his journey home. He certainly didn't want to remember the day he had just experienced. Unable to get through to her fiancé at his broker-age because of the number of investors tying up the lines, Josie had continued calling him periodically all night at home. She was very worried about him because he usually kept in touch with her throughout the day.

Unable to sleep, Josie decided to try Charles one more time. It was four in the morning and she still had no idea where he was. The phone rang seven times before her drowsy fiancé finally managed to pick it up. Twenty minutes before, he had fallen asleep sprawled on top of his bed still wearing his suit. After assuring Josie he was okay but telling her how rough the day had been, Charles whispered he loved her and would try to see her tomorrow when she came to Wall Street with Winston. Then he hung up.

Before he went back to sleep, Charles forced himself to open his diary and write down everything he had to do before the market opened. He couldn't fit the whole list on the page marked October 24th. As he closed his book and collapsed back on top of his bed, Charles had a feeling it was going to be a hell of a day. October 24, 1929 would prove even worse than he imagined.

* * *

CHAPTER XIII

Exhausted from working through most of the previous night, Charles had to splash cold water on his face to wake up. Just before heading out the door, he grabbed a change of clothes. Due to the previous day's unprecedented heavy volume on the downside, he had been warned to expect an all-nighter. As he made his way through the financial district, he could see he wasn't the only one who expected trouble.

Well before the opening bell, crowds gathered outside the New York Stock Exchange and surrounded the brokerage houses. They gathered from all walks of life and every background. Yet, to Charles, they all looked the same. Their faces were grayish in color; their jaws' clenched, their mouths drawn. Their eyes looked dead. From the bricklayer to the lawyer, the crowd was united by common fear. In expectation, reporters, photographers, and policemen gathered as well.

Whereas customers usually were friendly, as he approached his office, Charles noticed the hoard surrounding the place looked tense. Tempers were short, tolerance nonexistent. Charles was harassed as he pushed through the group to get inside. The clients thought he was cutting the line, but he figured that it was probably better for them to think that than the truth. He knew he had been right when he saw Hut, who had made the mistake of announcing his position, angrily punched and shoved as he was verbally assaulted. The mob labeled him the enemy; he was a representative of those who were responsible for their financial distress.

Once inside, Charles was glad to learn that he would be working the phones most of the day. He didn't want to deal with the people he had just walked through.

* * *

Charles planned to sell out his own positions if the market weakened. As the opening bell sounded and tickers moved across America, he sighed in relief as his stocks maintained their prices and the market initially steadied.

For the first hour after the opening bell, business proceeded as usual. Charles tore up his sell orders and relaxed. All around him, investors did the same. No one wanted to sell out if there was more money to be made in the Great Bull Market.

Concerned clients who phoned from around the country calmed down. Taking advantage of the previous day's sell off, a few customers even issued buy orders. Charles yawned as he filled out the slips. With the brokerage packed with clients, the temperature of the place had risen. The warmth made him drowsy. A few minutes later, as Hut processed some of his orders, Charles yawned again and his stomach growled so loudly that his friend laughed and told him to get something to eat. The young broker knew he needed some sustenance to stay alert; he hadn't taken the time this morning to eat anything.

During a brief lull in calls, Charles left the brokerage to pick up some food.

When he returned ten minutes later, a harried looking Hut shouted, "Thank God you're back!"

In the brief period that Charles had gone for food, the market had dramatically changed. Their brokerage, like others over Wall Street, had become overwhelmed with calls from across America to "sell at the market." The young broker didn't have time to touch his breakfast. Hut thrust piles of paper at him as clients screamed at them and anyone else who would listen. All the phones in the brokerage rang continuously. As he handed heaps of orders to the

clerks to process, Charles was given back stacks of clients to call
with requests for more money to cover their margin accounts. The
lists got longer literally by the minute as the market plummeted
with no end in sight. Like a dam with a crack, they could not stem
the tide against such a deluge.

At first, the calls were brief and to the point. Clients gasped
but coughed up what was needed. They pleaded with him to just
make sure they weren't sold out because they didn't want to lose
their initial investments. As the market continued its plunge, covering the margin became increasingly difficult if not impossible.
Charles made hundreds of calls on behalf of the firm. By noon,
he had phoned some of the same people he had reached earlier.
Late in the afternoon, he had to make additional rounds. After
leveraging all their assets earlier, by the third call, most now were
tapped out.

Calling places like Boise, Idaho and Holdingford, Minnesota,
Charles began to realize just how widespread the market crisis was
becoming. He hated making these calls. So often, the people on
the other end of the telephone were just ordinary folks who had
no idea their stock purchases could result in them losing not only
their initial investments but also everything they had.

Fueled by the myth of becoming overnight millionaires
through a handful of stocks in companies they knew nothing
about, no one had explained to these novice investors what they
stood to lose in a down market. For years, movies, books, magazines, even the radio told them about people just like them
who had become rich quickly and effortlessly through any good
stock. Far from offering objective analysis, the professionals
who understood the market – the bankers, brokers, even ana-
lysts – encouraged the buying binge. America was sold the idea
that buying on margin was how the rich leveraged their assets
and how the middle class and poor could break into those elite
ranks. It was good for them and, it was great for the country's

economy. Now, as the great sell-off began, the innocence of a generation of optimists was shattered forever.

Call after call, Charles heard voices that belonged to a race of people who suddenly found themselves damned. In one terrible day, their dreams and aspirations callously were murdered in the stampede of panic that stormed through Wall Street and would shake the very foundations of the free world. Their voices haunted him – condemning him for the role he played.

As the day progressed, each call became more torturous. There were old men who sobbed because they no longer would have pensions. Families, who would lose their homes because they had borrowed against them to play the market, and who spent their children's college tuition, their wives' inheritances, even their future paychecks to buy stocks. Charles found the reactions of the damned differed markedly. Some cursed; others went silent on the phone as the reality of their situation sank in. A few actually begged him to have mercy on their plight.

The worst call Charles had to make was to a Midwestern housewife. It was the third time the woman had been called by the brokerage in the past forty-eight hours. Hysterical, she informed him she couldn't put up the money because she had spent the family's entire savings already on the previous margin calls.

The desperate woman pleaded with him over the phone, "What am I gonna tell my husband? He works three jobs to support us. We have four little ones and now we don't even have grocery money. Everything we got has to be paid for. Our house is mortgaged. Our furniture we bought on credit to be paid in installments and the car as well. Now what am I gonna tell them? Nobody knows I've been playing the market."

She sobbed, "Oh, God, what am I going to do?"

Slumping into a chair, Charles said sadly, "I wish there was something I could do. But I'm sorry. We're going to have to sell you out." He heard a single gunshot and then silence. He knew she was dead.

Dropping the phone in anguish, Charles covered his eyes with his hands and wept. He asked himself, how many more would die because of their faith in the Great Bull Market and lack of understanding the financial risk?

Charles even didn't care that he knew he was facing near ruination himself by not selling his stocks. All that mattered was that a wife and mother, was dead because he called to tell her she had just lost all her money. Disgusted, he felt he deserved to be punished along with the rest of America and for his own greed that had placed him into the market and the brokerage business in the first place.

As more margin call requests were tossed at him, Charles threw them down in frustration and pounded his fists against the wall. He could hear the clerks freaking out as the ticker fell behind to the point where no one knew what prices the stocks were trading at anymore. Next to him, Hut was on the phone screaming at the brokerage's boys on the Exchange floor. He couldn't understand a word they were saying because they were cracking up. He kept yelling, "Calm down! Just calm down!" To no avail, the young broker repeated the words until his voice grew hoarse and perspiration drenched his shirt.

All around Charles and Hut, people lost control. So disturbed by his market losses, a thick set gentleman went after a clerk with his cane. Another kept banging his head against the wall until friends finally overpowered him and led him to the medical clinic set up for these cases of market shock. Several men ran out of the brokerage screaming inaudible gibberish. At the worst point in the day, security had to usher out a man who threatened to kill everyone.

* * *

Winston picked Josie up in front of her house at ten thirty in the morning. Because of the crowds in the financial district, their driver was unable to drop them off in front of the Exchange.

Noting the concern on Josie's face, Winston said, "Don't worry. Americans always over-react."

Even outside the Exchange, Winston and Josie could hear the rumbling roar of the traders. The grand windows in the stone building seemed to shake from all the activity.

At any moment, Josie half expected a man to throw himself through the glass.

As Josie smiled weakly, the former Chancellor of the Exchequer escorted her inside with a brave face. She knew he was invested heavily in the American market as well.

While they were taken up to the Member's Gallery by William Crawford the superintendent of the Exchange, Josie whispered to Winston, "I guess if things were really bad, they wouldn't have let us enter the Exchange."

But when she looked down on the activity, Josie realized it really was *that* bad.

The stench of nervous perspiration permeated the air. On the floor, belligerent traders besieged specialists. To thrust their orders forward, they aggressively shoved each other. Although these were useless gestures given the overwhelming demand to sell positions, the floor traders persisted in a frenzied state of panic.

Tempers flared as they pushed against each other, grabbing and tearing shirts, discarding their jackets and ripping off their glasses that got squashed along with their wads of sell orders under the feet of the panicking mob. Several went berserk. A specialist who couldn't handle the pressure anymore grabbed the nearest trader and started choking him. Another trader nabbed an unsuspecting runner by the hair and wouldn't let go until the boy broke away after losing clumps of hair. Scalped, he retreated to the medical clinic that unfortunately couldn't re-grow or replace the missing strands.

The boys, who worked the phones that connected the posts to their brokerage houses, screamed incoherencies. Some smashed the phones. They were beyond explaining the situation to their brokerage counterparts who called with even more sell orders.

No one understood what anyone else was saying, but it didn't matter in the least because everyone could see that there was an avalanche of sellers with no end in sight.

Clasping a paper with the stocks that Charles had purchased, Josie watched in horror as each one on the list declined precipitously along with the rest of the market. She held the list so tightly that her nails dug deeply into her skin and her fingers turned white. If her grip was firm enough, subconsciously she felt the items she held might make it through the panic.

Josie could tell Winston wasn't faring much better. Even his favorite stock, Simmon & Company steeply declined. As Josie squeezed Winston's hand reassuringly, he said with sardonic humor, "That's what you get for buying a stock based upon a good advertisement."

Feeling sick to her stomach from what she had witnessed, Josie walked downstairs for some air. On her way, she bumped into some of Stock Exchange members. Curious as to what they planned to do about the situation, she followed them to what she found out was an undisclosed meeting organized to decide whether to keep the Exchange open for trading or not.

Peering through the doorway, Josie saw a group of the most powerful men in the world assembled. Obsessively, they lit cigarette after cigarette. Repetitiously they dropped them after only one or two puffs only to light up another again and again and again. While they did this, their eyes stared blankly ahead like the fish on display blocks away at the Fulton Market.

Several hours later, after a representative from the House of Morgan came through, Josie heard the members agree to keep the Exchange open for the moment. Relieved, Josie returned to the gallery, where Winston busily jotted down notes for an article on the correction. With his stocks tanking, he knew he'd need to support his family through other means.

When Josie stared down at the floor of the Exchange, she saw the atmosphere was even direr than moments before. There was less trading taking place, just lots of men running around wildly gesturing, waving, shouting loudly.

In a most horrible moment that spread like a plague contagiously across the Exchange floor, groups of stocks could not find any buyers at any price. It was like a reverse auction with specialists reducing their bids by tens of points until they pleaded, "Does anyone want to buy any of this stock? Do I hear a price – any price?"

As the babbling gibberish subsided, a deafening silence answered.

Gasping, Josie said to Winston in horror, "They're worthless!"

Clearly affected, a grim Winston wiped the perspiration from his brow. Then displaying the calmness and resolution that would be his trademark in the most terrible of times to come, he dryly remarked, "Now that's a sight to remember."

At that moment, they were informed the gallery had been closed.

Josie imagined the closing of the Exchange would soon follow and with it, unimaginable havoc. While she walked through the crowds gathered outside, she saw the look of those who know there is no hope, only failure. In despair over their losses, many no longer had the will to fight. Shattered, robbed of the fantasies that made their lives, even when most miserable, worth living, Josie thought, the financially ruined resembled hunted creatures at the exact moment they recognized they were finished.

Desperately feeling the need to pray, Josie went to Trinity Church. She saw people of all faiths and backgrounds gathered in union at this place of worship, begging the All Merciful for salvation. Many prayed out loud. Men, who never cried even in front of their families, publicly shed tears. Finally finding a spot to kneel in one of the packed pews, Josie bent down to pray for the numerous investors suffering and particularly for Charles. She wanted to visit him at the brokerage, but she knew she shouldn't distract him since she was certain he was swamped. Feeling more confident after her prayer, Josie rejoined the waiting Winston to set out to find their driver in order to return uptown.

Casting a long look at the scene, Josie thought it was a most dreadful day. She had no idea how much worse it could get.

* * *

Charles forced himself to continue making the hated margin calls. Although he had made so many already, each miserable call still affected him. He seemed unable to remain detached from the job. An hour before the close of the trading day, Charles finally got a break when he was asked to run to the Exchange with a message for Richard Whitney.

While he made his way through the crowds, the young broker felt like a zombie. He wasn't the only one. Much to his surprise, he had no problem picking his way through the mob. Like Josie, Charles noticed the fight was gone from the people. He thought all that remained in the wake of the Crash was a vanquished army of beaten down men and women who like him, no longer cared. It was as if they were doomed prisoners waiting for the sentencing that they knew would directly lead to the executioner. Immobile, they stood around in anticipation of the inevitable news, knowing it would condemn them and they could do nothing about it. None seemed to have the energy or desire to leave. Morbidly fascinated by their own damnation as well as those around them, they remained rooted in the same place, as if stopped by time.

Without a future, all that these former investors had left was the chance to experience the very real, horrible present. Few wanted to hear about anyone else's misery, but this didn't stop some of the unfortunate from mumbling anyway. Occasionally victims commiserated with each other about their misfortunes. The terrible losses united the strangers with nothing else in common.

Before walking into the Exchange, Charles took a last look at this pitiful sight. Then he summoned the energy to demand a meeting with the Acting Head of the Exchange.

As Richard Whitney read the note, a big smile came across his face. It was the first smile Charles had seen all day. The significance was not lost on him. Sensing a momentous event, the young broker decided to stay at the Exchange to see what transpired. A few minutes later, Charles watched the Acting Head of the Exchange purposely walk across the floor to Post Two. Loudly, the towering man inquired at what price U.S. Steel, the bell weather of the Exchange, had just sold. Repeating the price so everyone in the Exchange could hear it, he then said in his patrician voice, "Very well then, on behalf of J. P. Morgan and Company, and as Acting Head of the New York Stock Exchange, I shall take 100,000 shares at 205." The traders gasped as they heard the purchase price. To strengthen the market, Whitney bought shares substantially higher than both the bid and ask prices. Repeating the performance at half a dozen other posts, Whitney got cheers and pats on the back all round. Relieved at the organized buying support, Charles raced back to the brokerage with the news that prices finally would stabilize.

By the time the ticker finally finished tallying the day's quotes, it was well into the evening and over 248 minutes late. Working through the voluminous paperwork, Charles and Hut smiled as they read the ticker news update: "The 35 largest houses on Wall Street report...the worst has passed."

The boys hugged each other as they read the familiar, "Good Night," that always signaled the end of the ticker.

Ripping the paper to save those words, Hut said as he put it in his pocket, "I want to keep this so one day, years from now, I can tell my grandchildren that I worked on Wall Street on the worst day in its history and I survived it. This'll be the proof!"

Kissing the ticker, Hut continued enthusiastically, "It's a symbol of the resilience of the financial markets!"

Thinking of all the people who suffered, many of whom were sold out of the market at its worst points like the Midwestern housewife for whom there could no longer be any hope for recovery, Charles said, "This is a day I'd rather forget."

Charles rang Josie to let her know he was stuck at the office and probably would not see her for the next few days because of the backlog of paperwork. Although relieved by the organized buying support, he told her it had been a most difficult day. He said he loved her but, before she had the chance to tell him how much she cared, he had already hung up.

* * *

The market's late afternoon recovery made one person extremely unhappy. Convinced that the correction would be irreversible, James had sold a number of stocks short in the morning. He initially made substantial money doing so, but then lost ground on his gains just before the end of the day.

James cursed the organized buying support of the House of Morgan and the other leading banks. Still, as he analyzed the day's events, he was certain more turbulence was yet to come. He vowed to be ready to take full advantage of it. To do so, after the market close, he placed calls to his most influential contacts. The businessman spent time talking with Henry Morgan, Garrett Goldman, John Jacob Raskob, and Joseph Kennedy. James laughed as he thought how appalled Henry would have been if he knew he now listened as carefully to Garrett and Joseph as he did to the Morgan clan.

* * *

On the evening of October 24th, Evelyn Maker's office was so packed her secretary opened all the windows for circulation. The line of clients seeking the seer snaked down the hallway and into the street. As she peered into her waiting room, the fortune teller thought she had never seen such a desperate group. Realizing there was no way she could physically see all these people individually, she announced that she would hold group sessions. Even by doing this, she worked well into the night. There were many sighs of relief when the clairvoyant announced that there would be a market recovery.

* * *

Late Thursday night, while Evelyn held group sessions, the goon Vinnie Graves returned home to receive an unwelcome message. His wife wisely left the room when he got on the phone with his broker who had requested more money to cover his margin. The goon claimed he had never heard of such a thing.

He said, anger and disbelief in his voice, "Hey! Put it up yourself!"

"I don't have time for this." The line went dead after the broker muttered, "Fuck you."

The broker was found dead in his car the following week. He had been badly beaten before he was strangled.

Hoping to make up for his market losses, Vinnie decided it was time to start betting on horses again. One of the boys he knew had some information on a thoroughbred that was supposed to be the next Man O' War. His more practical wife suggested he give James a call.

* * *

Like most of the workers in the financial district, Hut and Charles worked most of Thursday night. When they walked outside to take a short break to get some food at 11:30 p.m., they saw the whole district illuminated. There were so many people working, it was as busy as a normal working day.

At dawn, the young men finally had finished the processing. Yawning, they used their clean shirts as pillows and curled up on the floor like several of their colleagues. Although quite a few employees had been sent to spend the night in hotels, Hut and Charles had so much work to do they hadn't thought it was worth the effort. They also knew they'd need all the rest they could get to prepare for tomorrow's trading day. Even minutes were precious. The twenty minutes it took to get to the hotel was time they could spend sleeping under their desks. Since both young men still were invested heavily, they were relieved when they realized they had survived another day. They also were optimistic the major banks' support would stabilize the market and provide them opportunities if they didn't sell out.

* * *

Early the next morning, Friday, October 25th, the sound of a telephone ringing jarred Evelyn awake. Exhausted, the groggy seer dropped the phone before she managed to say hello. She didn't bother to apologize when she realized her broker was on the other end of the line. Her jaw dropped and she put the phone down again when he informed her that she was in the red to the tune of several hundred thousand dollars. Now wide-awake from the news, the astrologist instructed him to sell her out.

Shocked and wondering if he misheard her, the broker said, "Would you like to have the bank cover you?"

She reiterated, "I thought I made it clear what I wanted to do."

"But Miss Maker, I heard you divined a recovery," muttered the confused broker.

Snorting, the clairvoyant replied, "Of course the market will rise today. That's why I want you to sell me out – completely."

Exhausted, the seer of Wall Street hung up as the broker drew up the paperwork. Once finished with her sell orders, he wisely unloaded his own positions as well.

* * *

A few hours after Evelyn Maker ordered her broker to sell her out, the sound of fire trucks and commotion awakened Winston Churchill. Getting out of his comfortable bed at the Savoy-Plaza, he went to his window to investigate the cause. Twelve floors below the notable Englishman, on the pavement of 5th Avenue, was the crushed remains of a speculator who had minutes before hurled his body outside his hotel window. He now lay dashed to pieces.

James was quite put off by the sight as he walked past the scene on his way to meet Willy Messerschmitt. Although he delighted in the prospect of more suicides and increased panic for that matter, the businessman didn't personally want to see the effects.

Over breakfast at the University Club, James was not surprised when Messerschmitt informed him that his company, Eastern Aircraft Corporation now was bankrupt. James was relieved the German did not try to borrow money. He always found it distasteful when desperate people came to him begging. Never one to throw good money after bad, the cunning businessman rarely proved helpful to anyone in need unless he believed there were substantial gains for him. He reasoned to do otherwise was pure charity and James was never charitable.

When Willy informed him that he had powerful backers in his homeland and was planning to return shortly to Germany via France on the *Ile de France*, James became very interested again.

Warmly Willy said, "I respect you – as a businessman and a man of principal."

"The feeling is mutual," replied the delighted American businessman.

Leaning closer to his friend, Willy confided, "I also believe that in the new Germany that is being formed – a strong Germany - overseas friends like you can prosper."

James claimed, "There's nothing I'd like more than to see Germany return to her former glory."

"We must re-arm and become greater than before," asserted Willy.

"As you wish," stated James without emotion.

Leaning closer to his confidante, Willy whispered, "Things are changing. You know what they are saying in my country? They say the Jews are to blame for everything! People are saying even your market failure here is a result of their influence." As James looked doubtfully as his new friend, Willy explained. "I just build planes; it's what I know. But even I can tell we are living in volatile times. The future is most uncertain and the unknown brings danger."

"Opportunity arises out of uncertainty for the brave and the smart," replied James coolly. Then, as he leaned closer to Willy he said what he really meant, "If your friends in Germany need my help and they have the finances, you know I would be more than happy to help build a stronger Fatherland."

With that sentence, James made it clear that if there was enough money involved, he didn't care about breaking the treaties that were enacted at the end of World War I to keep Germany from re-arming.

As the men shook hands cordially, Willy said, "You will hear. Things are happening as we speak." Before turning to go he promised, "I will be in touch."

Smiling broadly, James said, "I look forward to it."

* * *

Although it was too late for Willy Messerschmitt's Eastern Aircraft Corporation and a whole host of other unfortunate businesses and stockholders, as Evelyn Maker predicted, the market recovered somewhat on Friday.

Sightseers who toured Wall Street looking for signs of trouble were disappointed that there was so little activity. A few enterprising entrepreneurs did manage to sell scraps of Thursday's ticker to tourists who eagerly sought pieces as souvenirs. Vinnie Graves heard the guy behind the operation was a mobster from Jersey City.

During the shortened trading day on Saturday, stocks held up until near the close, when they started pulling back substantially. Although many of the little investors who Garrett Goldman referred to as "the minnows," had been wiped out Black Thursday, there were plenty of others who did not have the limitless resources of J. P. Morgan and Company that still were invested in the market and now faced additional margin calls on Saturday.

Charles and Hut worked all weekend processing the paperwork and reconciling the books. Missing him desperately, Josie decided to visit her fiancé at the office. Charles' co-workers greeted her warmly when she appeared with trays of homemade food. Josie was concerned about her fiancé. She could tell the stress as well as the lack of sleep affected him. Having forgotten his razor at home, he hadn't shaved in several days and had a deep, hacking cough. Josie made him take a short break from his work to take a walk with her.

After their stroll, Josie and Charles wandered into Trinity Church where she used a pew to cuddle up to him and remind him how much she loved him. Deliberately not bringing up the market, Josie thought it was important to boost his spirits. Charles was so down; Josie's unconditional love was just what he desperately needed. As he looked at his beautiful, caring, fiancée, he thought she was the most wonderful girl he had ever known. Leading her up to the altar in the church he told her that – ever so tenderly – in just those words.

Then, after kissing her, Charles said his voice serious, "Are you sure you still want to be my wife?"

In response, Josie threw her arms around him and passionately kissed him. Before she knew it, he was kissing not only her lips, but also her ears and neck. His scruffy three-day beard tickled her until she couldn't take it anymore. Later, as they walked outside the church, they teased each other as they had when their lives were more carefree.

As he held her, Charles teasingly whispered the lyrics from the popular song:

"I'm the sheik of Araby
Your love belongs to me.
At night when you're asleep,
Into your tent I'll creep."

After uttering the last line, he swept Josie into his arms.

Josie looked forward to the day she would be walking down the aisle to become Mrs. Charles Blakesley. Realizing the sun was setting and Charles still had a lot of work to do; Josie left him at the brokerage doors after several more passionate kisses. She promised she'd come back Monday if the market trouble continued. Then she joined Rebecca and Geraldine on an outing to see the new Cole Porter-Irving Berlin show, *Fifty Million Frenchmen*.

After Josie left, Charles resumed the nasty business of making margin calls. With so many still to make, no one in the office cared what the time was. For the fourth time in three days, he phoned Groucho Marx, Eddie Cantor, and Mrs. Whitney Straight. They were particularly hard calls to make because he respected all three of these notables for different reasons. He hated telling them he needed more money to support their positions. Groucho informed him that he would be forced to mortgage his house on Long Island to come up with the money. He had already borrowed against future earnings from the latest Marx brothers' film.

Breaking with company policy, Charles asked the comedian if the investments really were worth the risk.

Unable to fathom things could get worse, Groucho said, "I've lost so much on these stocks already, I can't sell them now and risk not getting the money back!"

After asking for a few hours to go through her books, Mrs. Whitney Straight was less confident. As promised she rang Charles back at the brokerage and asked him to sell her out. She didn't know if this ultimately would prove a wise decision. But she was certain she didn't want to risk all her capital.

Charles returned to Trinity Church that evening to ponder what to do with his own stocks. He was so exhausted he couldn't rationally think straight, let alone assess his own portfolio. In the sacred place, Charles tried to find solace. The idealistic investor fell asleep on his knees praying to the Almighty. Hours later, when he discussed the matter later with Hut, his friend recommended riding out the storm.

Confidently, Hut proclaimed, "My uncle and all the major players I know always say the big boys don't panic at the first sign of trouble."

That night, when he finally got the chance to properly fall asleep, Charles still wasn't sure if what he had witnessed was the first sign of trouble or the death knell of the Greatest Bull Market in the history of the world. And he sensed he was too tired even to try to figure it out.

* * *

Evelyn Maker awoke just before dawn on Monday morning. A chill ran through her as took off her sleeping mask and climbed out of bed. She had another bad feeling as she pulled the curtains back from the window.

The air stank with the scent of rotting, dead leaves; the sky was unusually dark.

Ringing for her chauffeur, the clairvoyant threw on a coat over her nightgown and rushed for the door. She sensed time was of the essence. Evelyn jumped into the back seat of her black Bentley and ordered her chauffeur to follow the black cloud. Fifteen minutes later, they found themselves on Wall Street. There, in front of the Stock Exchange, the great seer witnessed from the sidewalk, the descent of thousands of black birds. Starving, they screeched loudly as they scavenged for manna that didn't exist. An hour later, as the waiting clairvoyant watched, the dwindled flock resumed their journey, leaving hundreds behind.

Black carcasses fell from the sky, littering the sidewalks and street.

Evelyn shuddered as she ran back into her car for cover. Despite her nerves of steel, she screamed as they fell, like rocks, thumping against the windshield, hood, trunk – flying off the roof, scattering across the street and into gutters. Horrified, the fortune teller urged her driver to speed away from the macabre scene. The seer knew this only could only be an ominous sign.

In her journal entry, the clairvoyant referred to the day as Black Monday.

* * *

James jolted up early Monday morning, too. Or at least, it was early for him. Ringing for Bentley, the playboy businessman didn't even wait for the houseman to enter before he started dressing himself. He had a feeling it would be an extremely hectic day. When the servant entered, James requested a watch.

Bentley looked dumbstruck. "Sir?"

James hadn't worn a watch since he left school, but today he knew one would be critical. Realizing he might not even have a wristband anymore, James instinctively reached for Bentley's timepiece.

Unapologetic, he muttered, "I need to know the time."

As the houseman glared at him, James tossed a few coins at him and said, "Buy another one."

"It was a gift from the Royal Family for services rendered," exclaimed the irritated houseman.

Throwing more money at him, James callously said, "Then get a good one."

Before Bentley could respond, his master was off. Uncharacteristically, James raided the kitchen for food to take with him. He didn't have time to sit down for a proper breakfast, but he knew he would need the energy later. A quarter of an hour later, he was meeting with Garrett Goldman, preparing for the market opening. Like a racehorse anticipating the gun, adrenaline filled the young businessman.

The stock market opened with a bang. James eyes sparkled with excitement as he saw major movement on the downside. He didn't have to wait for a trend.

The market collapsed from the start.

While Garrett worked the phones, fielding calls from across the country and around the world, James barked orders. He was delighted he hadn't closed out his positions over the weekend. Today he was sure he would make a killing.

* * *

As the ticker sputtered under the sheer volume of the opening trades, Charles and Hut found themselves immediately under siege. Once again, investors jammed into the offices and lined the streets. The crowds grew even bigger than on Black Thursday. Although many investors had been wiped out over the past few days, they too turned out in order to watch those who previously had managed to scrape enough money together for their margin calls and, to witness the very wealthy suffer.

Telephone companies and cable and wire operators struggled under the strain to keep services working. Within the first half an hour of the Exchange's opening, the ticker lagged hopelessly behind, setting the tone for the day.

Very quickly, Charles and Hut discerned they were dealing with a different market than they had on Black Thursday. Whereas many of the shares sold previously had been in small denominations, today, large holdings were dumped wholesale.

Looking at Hut, after he confirmed with their specialist on the floor by phone, Charles said with concern, "The big boys are unloading their positions."

"But it doesn't make sense," replied Hut in disbelief. "The heads of the big banks promised to support the market. They said Friday the worst has passed."

Disenchanted, Charles reasoned, "Even organized support has its limits. How much do you think J. P. Morgan and the others want to drop before they decide to let the market find its own bottom?"

Just as Charles was about to dump his own highly depreciated holdings, an ecstatic messenger came running through the office with the news that Charlie Mitchell, the renown President of National City Bank, the largest brokerage in the country, just had been seen walking into J. P. Morgan's offices.

Once again, Charles and Hut sighed in relief. Charles ripped up his sell orders after he learned twenty minutes later Mitchell had left the offices with a broad smile on his face and offered positive words of encouragement to the crowd gathered outside. As the market temporarily took a breather, Charles and Hut doubled their efforts to keep their brokerage operating despite all the margin calls and sell orders still pouring in.

Job titles and responsibilities became meaningless as everyone in the organization rose to the occasion, to pitch in to do whatever was needed at the moment. When the boy writing the quotes on the board was overwhelmed, Hut went over and continued to do his job. Later, he took orders from clients and helped process them.

Charles was everywhere at once. Loosening his tie and rolling up his sleeves, he ran around doing the jobs of two or three men. Energized in the manic frenzy, he forgot his own problems and how tired he was. He just wanted to do his part, serving as an effective role model for the rest of the staff.

By the time the market closed, Charles got a standing ovation from the boys for his work. A few hours later as they processed the paperwork, he also got a call from Josie. Worried about the reports that the district was filled with desperate hordes ready to resort to violence at the least provocation, her mother forbade her from visiting her fiancé at his office. After a brief conversation filled with kisses and utterings of love – much to the amusement of his co-workers – the couple agreed it was best for Charles to go home and get a good night's sleep instead of stopping by to see Josie.

Charles didn't remember how he got home. He didn't even recall getting into bed. But he slept soundly until he started vividly dreaming about the market. In this nightmare, he was back at the brokerage where the phones rang non-stop. No matter what he did, they kept ringing. Charles woke up in a sweat, screaming.

A few hours later on Tuesday morning, October 29th, the market opened with a scream, too. It was the primal sound of a million souls facing sure financial annihilation.

* * *

CHAPTER XIV

James smirked as he watched the first quotes coming across the ticker in Garrett Goldman's lair. The numbers confirmed his strategy. Burned once by the organized support of the major banking concerns, James had been extremely wary of Mitchell's visit to the House of Morgan the previous afternoon. After making a number of calls, he had been pleased to learn from Henry earlier this morning that the bankers planned to let the market find its own bottom today. He had informed James that Charlie Mitchell had gone to his family's bank the previous day on personal business. James wondered what exactly was involved in the transaction. Although Henry, of course, would disclose nothing more and James knew enough not to press, he had the feeling Mitchell might even have found himself extended by the market's precipitous decline. After discussing the matter with Garrett, the men agreed the most likely reason for Mitchell's visit was to get the necessary cash to buy out the Corn Exchange that he had made overtures to acquire just before the Crash.

"It's a bad time to have offered stockholders cash," remarked Garrett gleefully as he thought of Charlie Mitchell, one of the Biggest Bulls on Wall Street, getting smacked.

"Isn't that how Hatry got caught?" inquired James.

"Uh-huh." Garrett smugly replied, "He's in jail now."

While James focused on the ticker, Garrett fielded calls for confirmation about the Corn Exchange and National City deal.

Garrett and James were elated as they relentlessly helped drive down the prices of stocks.

Although James very much wanted to take a drive through Wall Street to survey the damage, he knew he had to continue to keep an eye on developments until the market closed. The stakes were too high for him to risk getting caught short.

* * *

The *Berengaria* was making good time on its return voyage from Cherbourg to New York. Captain Rostron thought he might even arrive a day early. His passengers didn't care. They had become far more interested in their stock holdings than in the trip. Through the wires, they had learned of the devastation on Wall Street. Thursday had wiped out many of the smaller investors. But enough of the first class passengers had survived for the ship's brokerage to be packed early Monday morning in anticipation of the market's opening.

Noting the time, Junius Morgan kissed Catherine tenderly on the forehead before heading out of their honeymoon suite. Concerned that things could get pretty ugly if the market continued its downward spiral as the wire his brother sent him suggested, he forbade her from setting foot outside their magnificent suite until he returned. As she lay in the comfortable bed, Catherine didn't mind in the slightest. She arranged to have her hair and nails done and to get a massage while he was out.

Junius wasn't the only one racing towards the brokerage offices. Concerned about the emotional state of his passengers, Captain Rostron and two deputies strode quickly towards the trading facilities. Even before they reached the passageway leading to the room, they could hear the roar from outside. Investors jammed into *Berengaria*'s brokerage. The overflow of passengers backed up into the hallway.

The din of the thick crowd was so loud, there was no chance anyone could make order out of the situation. The brokers and clerks frantically worked as panicked investors bombarded them with sell orders.

Junius followed in the path of Captain Rostron and his deputies as they pushed their way towards the front of the room. It took twenty minutes for the men to do this. Pre-occupied with what was left of their stock holdings, no one in the room had any deference for the ship's captain. After a few words with the brokerage workers, Roston turned to go, leaving his deputies who Junius noted were well armed, next to the office boys. Junius squeezed his way over to the side where he spotted a small opening. As he leaned against a wall, he continued to watch the unfolding events. He kept his perch throughout the trading day, with one eye on the ticker and the other trained on the hysterical investors'.

While he surveyed the room, Junius noted one exception to the pandemonium – Helena Rubinstein. As the market plunged, Helena, who had heavily invested following the infamous poker game during her last voyage, calmly sat in a massive 15th century carved chair beside the ticker – intently watching each number as it was spit out. To Junius, she seemed regally enthroned. Her face was like some Oriental despot – inscrutable.

As usual, Davenport stood next to her. Clearly his nerves were not holding up as well as hers. Beads of sweat accumulated on his forehead almost as quickly as he shakily wiped them away with his monogrammed silk handkerchief. As she gazed intently at the numbers coming out, Helena seemed oblivious to him and to everyone else in the packed room.

All morning the *World's Greatest Beauty Expert* watched her stocks depreciate precipitously, but remained unflustered, devoid of emotion. Finally with an hour left in the trading day, she acted. Convinced there was no end in sight, the doyenne decided to cut her losses. Pushing through the rabble, the grand dame of cosmetics made her way to the order desk. As she came through, crazed men with glazed eyes who had been screaming sell orders to no avail, silently stepped aside. Rumors pertaining to her holdings had been widely circulated on board, but when she issued the actual sell orders, audible gasps were uttered over the room and into the hallway as the numbers were whispered back to those too far away to hear them.

Helena sold 50,000 shares of Westinghouse and a slew of equal allotments in ten other companies. The expansion of her empire into the world of finance incurred staggering losses. As the boys immediately processed her sell orders, Helena turned to go. Her fellow investors made a path so she could walk through the crammed room. Several bowed their heads at her with admiration. Men, who knew nothing of lipstick and beauty secrets, respected her for having the balls to invest like a man and act like one when she faced financial calamity. Many in the room having lost less were far less poised.

Many fortunes were wiped away that afternoon. More than a few men broke down, weeping openly, their eyes red and puffy. Several had to be restrained. Others unsuccessfully tried to throw themselves overboard. Rumors were rampant about alleged suicides. Catherine heard from her masseuse that a man had shot himself in the head. She never was sure if it was just a story or the truth. But when she accompanied Junius on a walk around the decks late that evening well after dinner, she noticed the ship's doctor looked intensely distraught. The following day she heard he had been heavily invested in the market as well. Catherine had no doubt that he would be taking a number of the sedatives he had dispensed as routine nightcaps to distressed passengers.

That night, the dining room was more like a funeral parlor. The musicians were asked not to play. Small groups congregated to eat in silence. Many plates were returned to the kitchen untouched.

Captain Rostron warned Junius that it would be no place to bring his sheltered bride. Masking the severity of the Crash from his young wife, Junius suggested a romantic dinner in their suite instead of the dining room.

For her part, Helena Rubinstein announced that she would spend the remainder of the voyage in her suite with Mungo, her favorite Dandie Dinmont. In truth, she worked intensely hard with Davenport developing a strategy.

* * *

Despite her mother's misgivings, Josie insisted on heading down to Wall Street Tuesday afternoon. Rebecca and Geraldine accompanied her. The girls felt secure in numbers. Convinced that they would be watching history in the making, Geraldine brought along her sketchbook. Josie was more interested in seeing Charles. Rebecca, who had snuck out of the house without her mother knowing, just hoped she wouldn't get caught.

Josie brought along a picnic basket full of sandwiches, imported strawberries and pims as well as a few other items she had made. She wanted to do whatever she could for Charles during this trying time.

Traffic was snarled long before they reached the financial district. There were plenty of sightseers, joy riders and a few panicked investors who found themselves outside the district desperately trying to get into the same narrow streets. On Broadway, the girls abandoned their vehicle and set out on foot. They were not prepared for what lay ahead.

Outside the Exchange, spilling into the main arteries, the zombie crowds milled around in shock. A particularly large crowd gathered outside a bank where the body of a former investor lay. Some whispered that he had jumped. Others claimed he had shot himself. Josie heard later that he had had a heart attack. As the police cordoned off the affected area, the curious hordes, perversely fascinated by the grim sight, crept closer to get a good look. Stunned, Geraldine dropped her sketchpad. Rebecca screamed and then hid her face in Josie's dress after seeing the body.

While she ushered her friends away from the scene, Geraldine momentarily paused in disgust as they witnessed a group of fashionable women in exquisite furs driving along the street. Ostentatiously out of place in their touring car and speaking unnecessarily loudly, they ordered their driver to honk as they condescendingly shouted at the crowds to get out of their way. Clearly, they had come down to the financial district to gawk at the misery.

"This is just fabulous." One gloated, "*They* won't be taking tables in our restaurants anymore."

"Or trying to get into the clubs," chirped another gleefully with a laugh.

Changing the conversation to the upcoming winter social season, the third inquired, "What are you wearing to the opera tomorrow night?"

"I haven't decided yet, but haven't you had enough of this already?" asked the fourth.

"Drive on," commanded the first. "Let's go celebrate!"

While the women giggled, Geraldine reached into Josie's picnic basket and pulled out an egg. Lobbing it as hard as she could, she hit the side of the car just next to the 3rd woman. The yellow yoke splattered against the motorcar and onto the woman's sable coat. As the society women screamed for a policeman, the girls ducked.

Quickly but calmly Josie and her friends walked away, pretending they had nothing to do with the incident. When they were out of earshot, Josie, who was smirking, said, "Guess I didn't boil it long enough."

Giving her a big hug, Geraldine exclaimed, "I've never been so glad you can't cook."

After wandering around Wall Street for a few hours, the girls made their way towards Charles' brokerage house. The streetlights were just coming up as the girls arrived. Outside, someone had parked a brand new Packard. They read the handwritten sign on the windshield. "$100 will buy this car – lost everything in the market." The sight made the girls even more depressed.

As they walked in, their hearts felt heavy, their legs tired. They could see that although the earlier crowds had dispersed from the brokerage, it was clear that the workers had a great deal to do before they could call it a night.

Not wanting to disturb her love, Josie left the picnic basket for him with one of the boys at the customers' desk. Attaching a note, she wrote, "Miss you." Then she headed home with her friends.

On the way back from their gloomy tour of Wall Street, the girls decided to stop for dinner. Just off Broadway, they wandered into the Hotel Pennsylvania where they took a table so they could listen to the evening's entertainment as they ate. The girls weren't alone, although they were the only ones ordering food. All around them were the glum faces of ruined speculators and bankrupt bankers drowning their sorrows in alcohol. Aside from the girls no one talked. They just stared blankly ahead or into their drinks. Rebecca felt uneasy and wanted to leave because the dark place reminded her of a funeral parlor.

The hotel had been booked solid with investors who wanted to be near the stock exchange and brokerage firm employees unable to commute home because of the unprecedented activity. Josie wondered how many of them would be able to pay their bills before they left.

When they heard that the President of United Cigar had just jumped to his death from an upper-story room after his stock depreciated from 113 to 4 during the day, Geraldine quipped, "Guess that's one tab they won't get!"

While Rebecca hushed her, a man got on the small stage to introduce the first song.

Looking at his chronically depressed audience, he said nervously, "My name's Jack Yellen. But that doesn't really matter. You probably have never heard of me." He paused before he explained, "I'm a lyricist." While his oblivious audience continued to stare into their drinks, he said uncomfortably, desperately trying to break the awkward silence, "Tonight, to introduce this song, I think you might as well think of me as a comedian – a really bad one."

Yellen paused for laughter but didn't get any from the depressed audience. After clearing his throat, he anxiously continued, "A few months ago to sum up my sentiments on the market, I wrote this song that I bring you tonight." Tensely he said, "It's entitled: *Happy Days Are Here Again!*"

Finally the musician got a response. Throughout the room, there were sarcastic bursts of laughter as Yellen bent over to the band to pep them up.

After glancing once more at the audience, Yellen whispered to the musicians, "Let's play it for the corpses!"

Yellen and the band were shocked when the "corpses" joined in on the refrain.

Leaning close to Josie, Geraldine whispered, "Guess the Crash hasn't robbed everyone of a sense of humor!"

* * *

Hours later, slumped in a chair, Charles thought he had nothing else left other than his sense of humor as he accessed the damage to his personal fortune.

He had been almost too afraid to calculate exactly how much worse off he now was. But Charles knew he had to do it. When he finished, he laughed cynically. It was the same sardonic laugh that filled the Pennsylvania Hotel as Yellen debuted, *Happy Days Are Here Again.*

"How bad is it?" inquired Hut who had just figured out that today alone he had lost over two and a half million. Tapping his dejected friend on the back, he exclaimed merrily, "You can't be worse off than me; I've lost 75% of my trust!"

In response Charles threw up the paper work that showed his staggering losses as high as he could. As he watched the documents hit the ceiling before falling straight down to the floor, he said laughing, "Actually my portfolio is close to 90% down!"

"That's terrible!" exclaimed Hut shocked. "I don't know what else I can say other than I'm so sorry."

Not wanting pity, he replied quickly, "Don't be." As Charles picked up his papers, he tried to put a good face on the despondent situation, "Unbelievably I'm actually up in two stocks?"

Interested, Hut asked incredulously, "What could possibly be up in this market – coffin makers?"

Charles smirked. "And Western Union."

Charles had not been the only one to own Western Union. James had bought the stock Friday and sold it just before the market closed on Tuesday. He figured, given the market collapse, many of investors would have to wire money to their brokers. James found his profits in the company extremely satisfying. It had been the only stock he had purchased instead of shorted. He had thought that with his purchase no one could criticize him as one of the short sellers that helped bring down the market.

* * *

While James celebrated, Charles slowly made his way home late that night. He embraced the cold night air. Somber, he looked up at the moon as it shone down brightly on Wall Street. The district was silent and empty but haunted. The young broker thought, after what had transpired the last few days, Wall Street seemed cursed. Not even a bum wanted to be there.

As Charles stood for a moment in front of the Stock Exchange, he thought it looked like a giant mausoleum. Leaning against a street lamp, he could hear the echo of the panicked steps running through the streets and the voices of the thousands of ruined speculators who would never come back. He saw their grim faces and his heart ached.

Like the flock of blackbirds that had temporarily descended on the district, so many of the investors had come in search of manna only to be left cruelly spent with much less. At that exact moment, Charles knew most definitely he was not cut out to be a broker.

Determined, he walked back home and went straight to bed. He planned to hand in his resignation whether the market recovered or not.

* * *

Covering *Berengaria*'s arrival into New York, journalists reported the ship of *former millionaires* practically limped into the harbor. For most disembarking, it was a most unwelcome landing. They had left Europe among the wealthy, caring only how well received they had been and the success of their last party. They arrived back in New York depressed and debt-laden. Several questioned whether they should spare the little cash they had left on taxis to their sprawling estates and deluxe apartments they no longer could afford.

When snapped by a photographer and asked how it felt to be the greatest loser on *Berengaria*, Helena Rubinstein had glared at the little male inquisitor and retorted, "That's what I get for asking for advice from men!"

After Davenport got her under control, Helena agreed to pose for a picture and provide a beauty tip. Smiling graciously, she said, "I will be coming out with a new line for these changed times. With my latest product, a woman in the '30's even on a limited budget will achieve more grace than money alone can buy."

After kissing Catherine delicately, Junius left his wife with the Morgan family's driver. While she headed to their town house in their Duesenberg, he jumped into another waiting car to go straight to 23 Wall Street. He knew his brother and father could use his help.

Catherine had no idea how little she would be seeing her husband in the next few months.

* * *

The day after Tuesday's market collapse, as Wall Street licked its wounds and tried to catch up on the mounds of paperwork, Josie brought Charles another care package, Geraldine spent the morning painting, and then accompanied Rebecca to the Metropolitan Museum of Art. Later, the girls took a dance class together and prepared for the evening activities. Due to stock losses, the hosts of the dinner party they were supposed to attend cancelled their event. So, instead, they had dinner at the Ashleys and then headed to their favorite haunts.

Although few patrons walked in to find out, none of the owners of any of the joints charged a cover *this* night. Around midnight, the debutantes ended up at the 21 Club. The atmosphere even in this speakeasy matched the mood of the Hotel Pennsylvania the night Jack Yellen debuted *Happy Days Are Here Again.* Inside, listless patrons drowned their sorrows in bottles of the cheapest, most lethal alcohol they could buy. Only a few asked for the best in the house on the grounds they had lost so much already, it didn't matter.

Depressed by what they saw, the girls were thinking of leaving when Geraldine spotted Izzy and Moe, at a table in a quiet corner. Grabbing her friends, she told them they needed to make a dash.

The girls didn't get far.

The agents laughed as Geraldine; clearly the most nervous of the group, shakily said to her friends, "Just act natural like me. Walk out like nothing's wrong!"

Izzy and Moe couldn't resist winding them up. With Moe egging him on, Izzy came up behind them and tapped Geraldine on the shoulder. When she turned around to face the prohibition agent, she yelped. She only calmed down after he told her they had taken the night off. The agents explained that they felt it would be unconscionable to bust the place when so many patrons had suffered such staggering losses in such a short space of time.

The girls were delighted when Izzy and Moe subsequently invited them to join their table. Geraldine, who respected the pair for their flair, offered to buy them a drink. It was then that she realized they really didn't break the law they enforced. Despite the dearth of alcoholic drinks, the girls were greatly entertained. For several hours, the pair regaled them with true accounts from their experiences. Josie laughed so hard her stomach muscles cramped.

At the end of the evening when the girls got up to go, Geraldine gave the men hugs. She left them with two more sketches and the words, "You two are the best!"

Rebecca, Josie, and Geraldine's spirits were high when they left the speakeasy. Josie led her friends in a rendition of the Mount Holyoke drinking song as they started walking home. Several blocks later, they were still singing when they got into a cab and pulled up in front of the Stanley's townhouse. Immediately, Rebecca knew something was wrong. Despite the late hour, all the lights were on in the house. Several policemen lounged on the steps outside. Jumping out of the car before the taxi driver had even stopped, the petite brunette ran up the stairs. A few minutes later, when Geraldine and Josie walked in, they saw a mostly covered body, being carried out. Even though the policemen tried to stop her, Rebecca insisted on looking. She had recognized the Church shoes. Sobbing, she covered her face and collapsed in her friends' arms after the men reluctantly pulled the sheet back for her to see the face.

The girls spent the night at the Stanley's. Josie and Geraldine took turns watching over Rebecca and her mother. Under the advice of a doctor, Mrs. Stanley had been given several tranquilizers.

Rebecca cried herself to sleep.

The next morning, Mrs. Stanley asked the girls to go home so she could talk with her daughter alone. Smiling weakly, Rebecca promised she'd phone her friends later.

While they walked home, Geraldine and Josie speculated on the cause of death. As far as they knew, Mr. Stanley didn't have any serious health problems.

That evening, as they sat with a very depressed Rebecca, things became clear. Unbeknownst to both Rebecca and her mother, Mr. Stanley had been losing money for some time in his business. He had leveraged all of their assets and even broke into his daughter's trust, bankrupting it to hide their financial problems. When this proved insufficient, Mr. Stanley forged his financial records to get loans in order to buy stocks on margin to make up for his losses. The calamitous decline in the market and repeated margin calls ruined what little he had left.

Humiliated and ruined, Mr. Stanley felt unable to face his wife and daughter for what he had done. He was determined to end his life. After giving his chauffeur time off, the failed businessman closed all the doors in the garage and locked himself in his favorite car, a black 1927 American Rolls Royce Phantom I that had been manufactured in Springfield, Massachusetts. Several hours later, the chauffeur found his remains.

Rebecca cried uncontrollably as she explained the sad situation. "We've lost everything! Daddy borrowed against our townhouse and place in the country. Mother checked with the bank and we have only $275 left in one account! She's selling all her jewelry, the cars, paintings, and our furniture and we're moving to Boston to live with my Great Aunt."

As Josie and Geraldine cried as well, they hugged their friend.

Briefly perking up, Geraldine asked, "Didn't your father have life insurance?"

'The policy doesn't cover suicides!" sobbed Rebecca.

Josie offered, "You know you can always live with me."

"Thanks, but I don't want to be a third wheel," replied Rebecca wiping her tears.

Geraldine suggested, "There's my place."

As Rebecca squeezed her friends' hands, she said, "I appreciate it. But mother says we're ruined – socially." She continued sobbing as she explained, "With what my father did I can't stay here. It's too embarrassing." Trying to be optimistic, she said smiling weakly, "Mother thinks we can start over in Boston and I know, as annoying as she can be, she needs me with her."

Geraldine and Josie reassured their friend that they didn't care what her father had done and that they would always be there for her. After they left Rebecca to make funeral arrangements with her mother, the girls tried to figure out what they could do for their friend. Clearly money was a major problem. Quietly, they started a fundraising effort. The girls were shocked and dismayed by the reaction they got.

Mr. Stanley's debts and death were sensational news. After reading about what happened in the New York newspapers, instead of showing sympathy for the family, many of the people, who knew the Stanleys well and even regularly attended Rebecca's mother's parties, claimed they had never been close. Others showed delight in their failure while some were so hurt by their own losses that they felt unable to give much, if anything.

After making over 250 calls, Josie and Geraldine had raised only $15,700. Most of the money came from one donor: Henry Jay. As they went through their lists, Josie saw only one more person left on the list. At one glance, she was ready to call it quits. She couldn't believe it would be worth her time. But thinking of Rebecca's desperate plight, she forced herself nonetheless pick up the phone and ask the operator to connect her to Plaza 5 – 8870.

Bentley picked up the phone.

Josie's sweet hesitant voice caught his attention. It wasn't at all like the women who usually called. He knew this girl was special. Before he even asked her name, he motioned to James who was walking past him. As he handed his master the phone as he said, "You want to take this call."

Frowning with irritation, Bentley's master said in his no-nonsense business tone, "James speaking."

"Oh, hello," said Josie slightly off guard by his quick, curt response.

"Yes?" he replied curtly to the airy sounding greeting.

The girl on the other end of the phone half whispered, "Do you have a moment?"

Now James thought her voice sounded familiar. He found it quite melodic and soft. To him, her voice was most appealing, but he still couldn't place it.

Hesitantly she said, "I have a favor to ask."

He definitely liked the sound of that. Whenever women needed something from him, James always made sure it was well worth his while.

Sweetly she explained, "It's regarding Rebecca Stanley. She's a dear friend of mine and as you may be aware her father's just passed on."

Delighted, James smiled smugly as he realized it was Josie who was calling.

Not even thinking of Rebecca, he said excitedly, "Yes. Yes of course." Then trying to sound sympathetic, he replied, "It's just so terrible. Poor girl!" Before Josie had the chance to go into details, he pointedly asked, "What exactly is it I can do for *you?*"

Josie immediately corrected him. "You mean for Rebecca and her mother."

As he fingered a long fountain pen that he had recently purchased and hadn't yet used, he said pleased, "Just tell me what I can do."

Before hanging up, James pledged $5,000 to help the Stanleys and he managed to get Josie to agree to come to his townhouse to pick up the check.

Patting Bentley on the back afterwards, James said jovially, "Take the rest of the day off and have some fun, old boy!"

Bentley dropped the tray he was carrying. James had never been so generous. He could tell his master really liked this girl. He knew he should have asked for her name, but he had the distinct feeling he'd soon have the chance.

* * *

Three days after the market collapse, Mr. Whitney Straight informed his wife they needed to talk. They had just finished dinner in their opulent 5th Avenue mansion. Slowly they made their way to their library.

It was an uncharacteristically uncomfortable moment for the couple. In forty-seven years of marriage, they had never had a disagreement.

Mr. Whitney Straight feared what he was about to tell his wife would cause the first disruption and a most unpleasant one at that. Mrs.Whitney Straight sat down on the 17th century embroidered sofa in order to face her husband who stood next to a stiff medieval chair from the private collection of an Italian Cardinal.

The room was so silent they could both hear the clock ticking back and forth.

He began, "My dear. We have a problem."

"Yes?"

"I'm afraid we've suffered significant losses."

"How significant?" Her eyes were piercing.

"Substantial."

Emotionlessly she said, "Out with it."

"We have to move out of here – sell our other places – cut down on staff." He swallowed hard before he whispered, "*Drastically* change our lifestyle."

Stoically she replied, "Give me the numbers."

But he couldn't. His answer was too painful to utter immediately. The clock continued to tick like a timer attached to a bomb, as the motionless couple stared at each other like wax figures frozen in time.

Finally, when the words came to his parched throat, William Whitney Straight averted his wife's penetrating gaze. Head bent, he admitted, "We've lost over twenty-three and a half million."

There was another horrible moment of silence. As he waited for the expected outburst from his usually calm wife, William Whitney Straight once again was aware of the clock's ticking. Defeated, he finally slumped into the medieval chair. From there he saw his wife get up. His eyes followed her as she slowly walked across the room, past the bronze statue of the *Lady Bull* that she had commissioned Geraldine to do, over to the roll top desk that had belonged to her mother. As he continued staring almost blankly, she unlocked a compartment and methodically went through the contents. After several minutes, she returned armed with her reading glasses and an accounting book clasped tightly in her hand.

Handing it over to her husband, Adele Whitney Straight said after some time, "It seems my gains over the last several years have covered a third of your losses. We should be able to just manage if we close up the place in Newport and significantly watch our spending."

As he looked at his wife in wonderment, she explained. "I did well buying on margin. Earlier this year, I took my profits and just re-invested my initial capital. Luckily, when the momentum changed, I bailed out before my previous gains were erased significantly."

Closing the book firmly and taking it away from him before he had a chance to go through it, she said, "From now on, I suggest we make our financial decisions *jointly*."

Mr. Whitney Straight took a deep breath knowing what his wife meant was henceforth he had damn well better consult her before he did anything. She would be writing the checks from now on. Relieved, but at the same time feeling his manliness insulted, he nodded his head and retreated to his study where he spent the rest of the day drinking.

William Whitney Straight wanted to tell his wife she was the smartest woman he had ever known. He should have thanked her for saving them. But all he could think of was what an ass he had been. He felt like a total failure.

Several hours later, Adele Whitney Straight found her husband snoring at his desk. Next to his glass lay an empty bottle of Macallan's 25. With some effort, their butler and his valet carried him up to his bedroom. For the first time in fourteen years, the grand dame of New York society climbed in next to her husband instead of sleeping in her own bedroom. She wanted him to wake up comforted and loved, feeling very much like a man who still was desired. As she fell asleep cuddling him, she felt warm. Despite his losses, he had been a good husband and she was still very much in love with him. But Adele Whitney Straight, more than ever, also was delighted to be in control of her *own* money.

* * *

The day after William Whitney Straight informed his wife about his losses, Charles phoned Josie to ask her to meet him outside her family's townhouse. He was so upset about his losses that he couldn't face her parents. He didn't even know if he could face her.

Charles slowly walked in the rain to meet his fiancée. Passing vehicles splashed him as they drove by. He didn't care. He had forgotten to take an umbrella so he already was wet. Pre-occupied with his losses, as he walked, Charles hardly even noticed that the rain had brought out the worst of the city's street odors – the smell of garbage and dog dirt. Two blocks before he reached his destination, the pelting rain diminished to drizzle before it stopped all together.

When he saw Josie running into the street, Charles couldn't get over how fresh and beautiful she looked. She was the vision of everything he had ever wanted. But it made him feel all the worse.

Given his losses, he felt he didn't deserve her. At that moment, he realized he couldn't marry her.

Josie's heart went out to Charles when she saw how bad he looked. Throwing her arms around him, she stroked his hair as she kissed him tenderly on the lips. He felt her warmth and love as they embraced. Between kisses she said, "I've missed you so much these last few days."

Returning her kisses, he said passionately as he thought this could be the last time he touched her, "I've missed you, too."

Black crows screeched and squirrels scurried away as they walked through Central Park. Wanting to cuddle her fiancé, when Josie spotted a park bench she suggested they sit down. The bench bordered a lake that looked black from the reflection of the dark clouds in the overcast sky. The water in the lake mirrored Charles' mood.

As he spoke about the last few days, he reminded Josie of the war veterans who became distant, their eyes veiled, when they spoke of the horrors of the last conflict. He was visibly shaken. Wearily he admitted, "I keep having nightmares about the market."

Realizing she made a mistake bringing up the Crash, Josie reached over to kiss him.

Filled with disgust for himself for his failings, Charles pushed her away.

When she refused to back off, he muttered, "You don't understand."

"Tell me. Please - so I can," replied Josie sweetly. More than anything, she wanted to help him through this difficult time. She thought he might be having a breakdown induced by stress and sleep deprivation.

Unable to look at her, he said emotionally as he turned away, "I've just about blown my entire trust as well as almost all the money in my family's portfolio."

"I'm sorry," she said as she took his hand in hers. As she held his arm, she softly said, "I know many people who have lost just about everything." While she continued stroking his arm, she told him, "But as long as we have each other, we'll get through this."

Charles smiled sadly. As he touched her face, he said, "You deserve a better man."

Josie looked at him with meaning as she took his hand in hers and said forcefully, "You're the only one I've ever wanted."

After swallowing hard, he said, "Josie, I'm a failure"

She exclaimed, "Don't say that!"

He sighed. Then he said, "Unfortunately, it's true." With an effort, he looked her in the eyes and explained, "Financially I'm ruined and because of my losses, my family's had to sell their processing plants. If livestock and crop prices don't improve soon, I don't know what they're going to do."

As she reached out to him, she said, "I'm so sorry, darling." Trying to be upbeat, she said optimistically, "Maybe the market will recover soon. I know I've heard people predicting a bounce."

Looking down, he said, "You don't understand." He explained, "No matter what happens to the market, it can't help me. I've cashed out what little I have left." As he looked at her meaningfully he said, "Besides, I hate Wall Street. I just can't do what I did before."

"I'm sure there are other jobs you can get," offered Josie.

Uneasily, he admitted, "I'm not even sure what I want to do anymore. I just feel like I'm living in a nightmare and it's not going to get any better."

"We'll come up with something," she said optimistically. She suggested, "You need to take some time." Her eyes full of caring, she insisted, "I don't care what you do, as long as I'm with you."

Slowly, he touched her cheek one more time with his hand. Then, he said full of sadness, "Josie, I can't marry you." He had to look away for a moment before continuing because he found the words so painful. After a minute, he swallowed hard and explained, "I no longer can give you the kind of life you deserve. Marriage would be unfair to you."

Josie stared at him in shock. She had been totally unprepared for this. At first she refused to believe what she was hearing. Then she realized just how serious he was about breaking off their engagement. She desperately tried to refute his claims that his losses made him unworthy.

A romantic, madly in love with her fiancé, Josie believed in passionate love, anything was possible and all obstacles surmountable. Trying to impress this upon Charles, she said emotionally as she looked into his eyes, "I don't care what you do or how much money you have! I just want to be with you! I would have married you if you were just a barman." Tears streaming down her face, she pleaded with him, "We can get through this together."

He tried to stop her as she reminded him of what they had shared and how unusual and precious their relationship was. Finally, she realized not matter what she said, she wasn't getting through to him. Frustrated, she got up and threw herself at him as he stood up as well. As she buried her face in his shirt, smelling his wonderful scent and feeling his protective, warm body, she sobbed.

Charles held her and stroked her hair. Upsetting her pained him more than he could take. After finally calming her down, he tried to make her understand how disillusioned he had become and how much deeper the problem was. After they sat back down on the bench, he tenderly explained, "Life without you is a death sentence. But not being able to provide for you will make you miserable, too. You can't see it now, but I can."

She tried to interrupt him to refute his statements, but he hushed her so he could continue explaining his feelings. Calmly he said, "I don't know what I want to do in life. It's just not fair for me to marry you without resources and a plan.

Forcefully she said, "We have a future together."

"Darling, what can I say to make you understand? If we got married now, I'd only end up ruining your life as well as mine!" Looking her in the eyes as he held her in front of him, he explained, "I love you too much to do that."

Josie shouted, "Well, if you want to break my heart, you can congratulate yourself now!" As she fought off the urge to cry again, her voice choked up as she said, "If you break off our engagement, I don't know if I ever will be happy again!"

Feeling terrible for upsetting her, he said, "I don't want to."

She pressed, "Then don't."

Sadly, he replied, "I have to. I'm lost and I can't take care of you – not like this."

"I'll wait for you," she offered.

As he got up to go, he said, "I can't expect you to."

Josie got up to stop him. Shaking him hard, Josie said almost hysterically, "NO! You're not going to do this to us! I won't let you! I don't care how depressed you are. I am not going to walk away from you or let you get away!"

"Damn it! Pull yourself together." Hitting him, she yelled as she sobbed and kept repeating herself as if by saying the same comforting things he'd change his mind. "We will work something out. You can take time exploring options. We can live at my parent's house after we are married. But you are the love of my life and I am not going to give up on you today or tomorrow or ever."

After calming her down, Charles replied quietly, almost as if he was trying to convince himself by the logic of his arguments. He began almost trancelike, "Sometimes the greatest love is one that lets someone go. You can't see it now, but I know the way I am. I could never satisfy you. I am no longer the same man you fell in love with. I don't know what I am but I know I can't marry you now and I know it would be unfair for me to expect you to wait until I can. I love you too much to do that."

Tears streaming down her face, Josie said softly, "You don't have to ask me to wait. My heart belongs to you." As she looked meaningfully into his eyes, she said, "It always will."

"I have never felt sadder in my life," said Charles as he reached out to hold Josie.

She replied, "Neither have I."

Josie and Charles fell asleep on the bench, arms around one another. An hour later, as the cold, evening wind picked up, ripping through the fallen leaves, he awoke, shivering. After kissing his still sleeping fiancée on the forehead, he noticed the moon beaming brightly above them. He thought, as if it were a sign, it illuminated the mound where he had proposed. All this time, Josie and Charles had been just yards away from that magical spot. As he thought about that evening and the many others he had enjoyed with Josie, he knew he didn't want to lose her. As selfish as he felt his holding on to her was, he wanted to believe somehow that he would find a way to get through this difficult period. After napping a little longer, Charles felt much better. He looked lovingly at Josie as she lay asleep in his arms. He thought she looked like an angel sent from God to save him.

Kissing her on the forehead, he whispered, "I'm sorry."

When she awoke, she said, "I had the most awful dream."

Smiling as he lovingly stroked her hair, he assured her, "That's all it was."

Her gentle, large brown eyes and voice imploring, she whispered, "Promise?"

"I *should* let you go." Charles said tenderly, "But I can't."

She vowed, "I won't let you!"

As he held her hands and looked into her eyes, he said, "I just pray I will prove worthy of your love and commitment."

In response, Josie kissed Charles and teasingly said, "We'll see on our wedding night!"

* * *

James Ellison DeVere's jovial demeanor was a stark and welcome contrast to Charles' melancholy state. This was not a co-incidence. Having heard of Charles' losses through the grapevine, he had deliberately planned to present himself to Josie to high-light their differences.

Josie had planned to stop by James' townhouse only long enough to pick up his check for Rebecca. He had given her the impression on the phone that he'd leave it with his houseman. She was quite surprised when James answered the door himself and felt obligated to come in when he invited her. As Josie sat on a circular sofa facing James who rested in a gilded chair in his Regency style sitting room, she was impressed with his refined taste. She also found his conversation a pleasant diversion. He was so attractive and wickedly funny that she couldn't help but laugh.

Josie had forgotten how much fun it was to be light-heart-ed. Life had gotten so terribly serious since the Crash. With Mr. Stanley's death and Charles' losses and what she had seen on Wall Street, she felt as if an oppressive pallor had descended over New York City. It was as if some dark curse lingered from one end of Manhattan to the other.

Years later she would read that the Crash had raped America of its innocence. But like so many other people during great times of change, Josie was unaware of what others felt. She only could vouch for her own experiences.

At parties she had attended recently, the pervasive gloom hung over everyone. Not a single family had been left untouched. Even those with strong finances had friends, acquaintances and some family members who had not been as lucky. All around the city, there still was a lot of drinking, but unlike the pre-crash days when everyone drank for fun, now they all drank out of misery.

Going through their social circle, James did cruel but funny impressions of their set. He deliberately left out Charles and Josie but decided to make fun of himself so he didn't seem like he a total shit. Then he took her on a tour of his art collection. He knew for a man his age, he had an impressive array of pieces. Josie told him her favorite was a striking 19th century statue of a young girl adorned with roses that graced his conservatory. As he admired the statue and then Josie, he smiled and then informed her it had been carved from stone taken from the same quarry Michelangelo had used. What he didn't tell her was he thought that the nude piece resembled her.

Josie and James talked for three hours without realizing it. Only the grandfather clock's dongs alerted them to the hour. They walked upstairs towards James' study where he had claimed he had left the check for Rebecca. He paused just outside the room, in the hallway to point to a large portrait of one of his De-Vere ancestors. As posed mockingly below it, he joked, "See the resemblance?"

As Josie laughed, he continued, "I always know when people are being polite when they say it's a lovely painting."

"It is well done," commented Josie. As she looked at it admiringly, she said, "Isn't it a Gainsborough?" That was another reason James had selected the painting to highlight.

"Well cited, my dear," replied James practically cooing. "And well done it is – but *lovely* it could never be. Look at her, she's a dog! Now admit it, if you were a man, you'd rather sleep with another man than with her."

As Josie laughed, he said, "I beg your pardon, Lady *Trollop* De-Vere could well be a man in drag! The chin, the broad shoulders, even that smile – it's all terribly masculine! These are my ancestors – what a frightening thought! And to think she's not even as ugly as she really looked. You know Gainsborough was always kind to his subjects since he wanted to get paid!"

"I have some rather unappealing-looking relatives as well," commiserated Josie as she thought of her overbearing Aunt Celia who had several warts on her face.

"That I find difficult to believe," asserted James as he sat down next to her.

Feeling slightly uncomfortable as he looked at her rather intensely, Josie mentioned she should be going. Backing off immediately, James got the check. As he handed it to her he said how awfully sorry he was about the Stanley's situation. Before she left, he forced himself to send his regards to Charles.

As she walked home, Josie thought about James. Despite his chauvinistic comments the night of her godfather's last party, she had found his company and light banter most enjoyable. She thought he was so terribly good looking and charming and his wit was simply outstanding. She knew she had had an excellent time with him when she arrived home and still had a big smile on her face.

* * *

Over dinner, Josie was buoyant. Claire and Albert assumed it was because of Charles. Their future son-in-law's spirits had not been so good since before the Crash. Eager to give the young couple time to be alone, after dinner, the older Baxter-Brownes excused themselves.

Josie and Charles adjourned to the library. With all the books and wood paneling, Josie always had thought the room the coziest in the house. As they sat together in one of the comfortable leather sofas, they enjoyed each others' company just as they had done before the Crash. While Charles read from a collection of John Donne's poetry, Josie felt warm and secure and that this was the way she wanted their lives to always be.

But as the evening progressed, Charles grew restless. Finally putting down the book, he said with difficulty as he looked at his love, "There's something I have to tell you."

With trepidation Josie implored him to, "Go on." Her hands went cold. She had a feeling she wasn't going to like what she was about to hear.

As her heart beat quickened, he paced around. After walking back and forth a few times, he stopped in front of the window. While he looked outside into the darkness, he stated, "I talked to my Uncle today."

Concerned, Josie asked, "Is he all right?"

When Charles walked back over to his fiancée, he said, "Basically, yes."

She inquired, "And your Aunt."

"Her health's fine." He turned around to face her as he explained, "They weren't phoning for that reason."

Josie stared at Charles with a look that demanded to know what he meant.

He explained, taking her hand in his as he looked into her worried eyes, "I've got to go back to Oklahoma. They need my help."

She immediately suggested, "I'll go with you."

He adamantly replied, "No." As he saw her crestfallen face, he explained more gently, "My family is going through some really tough times. I don't want to put you through them as well."

She pressed, "I don't care how hard it is out there, I'd rather be with you in any circumstance."

"Josie, you don't know what it's like." He explained, "I need to go out there and work really hard to salvage what I can for them. I can't be responsible for taking you out there when I know how bad it is and I won't have time to look after you the way I want to."

Worried he was about to try to break up again, she said warily, "What are you saying?"

She sighed with relief when he said, "I need to leave this week, but I should be back in a few months."

Although she was upset he was leaving and going so soon, she felt relieved he wasn't having doubts about their relationship again. Considerate by nature, she inquired, "Is there anything I can do to help?"

As he adoringly looked at Josie, full of love, he thought she was the most caring and supportive woman he ever had known. When he replied to her question, his eyes sparkled and he flashed that smile that she loved so much but had seen so rarely since the Crash. Moving closer to her, he said, "There is something you can do for me."

While Josie looked up at him expectantly, he pulled her towards him and said, "You can kiss me."

As they kissed, he promised, "I'll try to write or call every day."

Returning his kisses, she said, "I love you, Charles Blakesley."

"I love you, too," he said as they embraced.

While they embraced on the leather sofa he vowed, "I want us to start our life together the right way."

When Charles described to her how he hoped to revitalize his family's operations, for the first time since the Crash Josie noted he seemed excited. His eyes were full of life and he smiled easily again. She was happy that he was back to his old self. She just wished he wasn't going so far away or that she could go with him.

* * *

Garrett Goldman celebrated the demise of the Great Bull market with panache. Of course, he was flamboyant in every way. Having made millions shorting the stocks on the downside, by the end of November, the Bear felt the market had bottomed out for the year.

The day after Charles turned in his resignation to E. F. Hutton; Garrett advised James it was time to start buying for the short term.

* * *

Just before Mr. Stanley's funeral, Josie sat down with her parents to discuss what had happened in the market and to ask about their investments. She had been badly shaken up by Rebecca's father's suicide and what she had seen on Wall Street and read in the papers. Josie knew her father hardly had been home recently. When he had been around he was pre-occupied, alone in his study.

Ever trusting of her husband, Claire was sure he would continue to handle the finances effectively as he had in the past. Unlike Josie, the trip to Mrs. Whitney Straight's lady brokerage only convinced her that she had neither faculty nor interest in the world of finance. The market crash confirmed this belief that selecting the right stocks and bonds was far too confusing for her.

Josie's mother was glad she had married a man who enabled her to do what she enjoyed. As long as she had the resources available to do what she wanted, she didn't care about the details. However, she did realize her daughter came from a different generation and one that was now expected to know more about finances. So, as bored by the subject as she was, she encouraged the discussion of the market and the family's finances between her husband and daughter.

Much to Josie's relief, Albert informed them that the Baxter-Brownes were fine. He told both women, "There's no question we have taken some serious hits like everyone else, but we're in no danger of losing everything."

Josie sighed in relief as her mother said, "I told you so."

Albert then went on to admit that he served on the board of directors of several companies that were in trouble, but that the bank he headed was solid. He assured them, "Don't worry. Our organization hasn't been involved in the margin business at all." He explained, "There were times over the last few years when I thought of getting into it because the business was so lucrative, but I decided it was too risky. Now, obviously I'm relieved."

Josie inquired, "What is it exactly that your bank does, Daddy?"

Proudly he asserted, "We're primarily in the lending business. We finance companies, institutions, and smaller banks. In the past ten years, even during the little panic of '22, we've never suffered a major default."

When Josie asked whether he thought the recent Crash was worse than previous ones, Albert shook his head and explained, "No correction is ever exactly like any of the previous ones." He admitted, "There's no question we've had a panic." But he predicted that after everyone calmed down, the market would rebound. The banker assured Josie, "that President Hoover, the Chairman of the Federal Reserve, and the Presidents of all the big banks have expressed confidence that the economy fundamentally is sound for valid reasons."

Putting his arm around his daughter, Albert said confidently, "Even if it takes awhile, I want you to feel comfortable we're in a good position because of the businesses we fund."

Josie slept peacefully that night.

* * *

Rain relentlessly poured down the day Mr. Stanley was laid to rest. It was a cold, hard rain on a dismal November morning. The wind blew mercilessly ripping through the cemetery, ensuring even the mourners with the biggest umbrellas got soaked. Rebecca's mother muttered it was why so few people had come. Josie and Geraldine knew there were other reasons.

The girls shed more tears after the service as they bid farewell to Rebecca. Mrs. Stanley insisted that they needed to leave immediately for Boston. She claimed it was because she heard the city was supposed to be hit with a heavy snow storm that evening, but the girls sensed she just wanted to get out of New York as quickly as she could.

Rebecca hugged Josie and Geraldine as they briefly reminisced about happier times. As she embraced them, she said teary-eyed, "You're the best friends anyone could ever have!"

"Promise you'll write," said Josie.

"And call!" chimed in Geraldine.

"We're here to help you and be there for you as we know you'd be there for us - anytime," promised Josie.

Then they slipped Rebecca the checks as Mrs. Stanley who already was in an awaiting taxi, yelled at her daughter, "The meter's running!"

Astonished at her friends' thoughtfulness and financial accomplishment, Rebecca hugged them again before turning to go.

In total, Geraldine and Josie raised $15,700. Ten people contributed small amounts. In addition, Charles insisted in giving a couple hundred dollars that Josie knew he couldn't afford, but he gave nonetheless because he felt Rebecca needed the money even more than he did. Aside from Henry Jay and James' generous contributions, the Ashleys, Baxter-Brownes, J.D. Rockefeller, and Catherine had contributed substantially.

Catherine was unable to see Rebecca off. She had phoned Rebecca from Jekyll Island after she heard the news.

Only one week after their return to New York, Junius had sent his wife to the Morgan's estate on Jekyll Island for the winter season. He knew he'd be working hard the next couple months and wanted her relaxed and unaffected by his demanding schedule. Junius also was concerned about what the city would be like if the market continued declining. He still vividly remembered the morning in 1921 when a Bolshevik terrorist attempted to blow up his family's bank. Determined not to put his young bride in any disturbing situations let alone dangerous ones, he decided the family's private retreat was the perfect place for her to remain comfortably secluded.

Catherine had phoned Rebecca and sent the money without informing her husband. Based upon their discussions, she was certain he wouldn't have minded her sending the money but she was not sure if he would have approved if he knew she was keeping in touch with her old friend. It wasn't that he disliked Rebecca; he just was extremely cautious when it came to preserving the family name. Although extremely charitable in the great Morgan tradition, he didn't want his family's reputation tarnished by direct association with scandals and bankrupts.

After Junius heard numerous accounts related to Geraldine's infamous weekend Southampton parties with alleged fast friends and left wing artists from the Greenwich Village, he outright forbade his wife from having anything to do with her. Although Catherine initially was upset, she loved Junius so much and enjoyed being Mrs. Morgan even more that since her return from her honeymoon, she had ignored all correspondences from the avant-garde artist.

* * *

The day after Mr. Stanley's funeral, much to her surprise, after several patient rings, Mrs. Whitney Straight opened her front door to face a melancholy figure. There before her, stood Bigford, her old driver, waiting to be let in. He wore his old uniform and carried one large suitcase.

When she enquired what he was doing, he replied, "You always said I could have my job back if I ever wanted it again."

The grand dame explained, "But Bigford, haven't you heard? We've suffered tremendous losses. I don't think we can afford a chauffeur anymore."

"If I can have my old room back, I'm sure we can come to an agreement," said the servant.

As Mrs. Whitney Straight welcomed Bigford back into the household, he informed her he had lost everything through his margin accounts. In fact, he now owed his broker over $100,000.

* * *

Bentley noticed that in the days preceding the Crash and in its aftermath James worked significantly harder. Not one to think in complementary terms when it came to his master, even Bentley had to admit New York's most eligible bachelor had become focused and diligent by anyone's standards. The houseman had spoken with a number of men in his profession who also had seen remarkable changes in their employers. Whilst many of them were concerned about the longevity of their own jobs, Bentley had no fear that James had suffered a reversal in fortune that could jeopardize his position. He had gathered easily enough by what James had said and left around that his master had made a killing as the market plummeted. But as far as he could tell, James' recent success only made him hunger for an even bigger score.

James immersed himself with all the information he could gather. Daily, he collected every newspaper and worked the phones tirelessly to glean which direction the market now headed. Like a lot of operators, he really was not sure. As Bentley brought his master his dinner on a silver tray, he wondered if James actually would leave his study at all this day. He had been in there since 6 a.m., taking all his meals at his desk without even looking up as he ate. Earlier, James had slammed the door after ordering Bentley not to disturb him with any matter unless it pertained to business.

When Bentley made the mistake of informing James that Serena Beaumont, a most attractive woman, wanted to speak with him quite urgently, James became irate. Waving the papers in his hand, he shouted, "Not now!"

"But sir, she says it's very important."

"Not more so than what I am doing." Then he commanded Bentley, "OUT!"

As the butler closed the door, he heard James say crossly, "You take care of her."

Bentley muttered, "I don't think that's the kind of service she requires."

Overhearing him, James stormed, "Can't I have peace and quiet in my own home!" Then he continued peering over the papers on his desk.

At nine thirty, as a bleary-eyed James stared at the indicators, he questioned the bankers' assertions that the market was healthier from the shakeout. Agriculture products were trading at an all time low; he knew only too well from his own concerns that steel output was down and now he had just received a confirmation that automobiles weren't selling.

James sensed the country was headed towards a recession – perhaps even a major one.

* * *

CHAPTER XV

Herbert Hoover was convinced the stock market crash merely was "a temporary halt in the prosperity of a great people." The President believed the media made more of the Crash just as it initially sensationalized suicides like Mr. Stanley's that resulted from the financial disaster. He rejoiced in the government statistics that revealed that there hardly had been more suicides in the month following the Crash than during other periods – although he admitted, when pressed, that a number of those who ended their lives during this period did so because of their market losses.

As far as Hoover was concerned the market decline although devastating to investors, would not necessarily spell doom for the rest of the economy. It was merely one of the major influences on the state of the economy, but not indicative of the whole economy itself.

After conferring with Secretary of Treasury Andrew Mellon, the Fed chief and a number of Wall Street bankers, the President declared the Crash would prove insignificant over the long term. In his radio address to the nation that Josie, Charles, and Geraldine and much of the country heard, he reiterated his Inaugural promise that, "In no nation are the fruits of accomplishment more secure [than in America]." While Geraldine snickered, many saw hope in his words.

The President explained that he relied on the people to continue to work hard to keep America strong. Hoover truly believed unnecessary government involvement, especially handouts, would ensure the destruction of the cornerstones of the American work ethic: individuality and self-reliance. He also feared it would lead to insupportable debt. He hated big government and distrusted the bureaucracy that supported it even more. Based upon principal, he didn't want to contribute to these structures. He didn't feel the market jitters worrisome enough to abandon his beliefs.

Although he wouldn't stimulate the economy with government subsidies, the President willingly approached the private sector for help. His previous experiences, made him confident in "Main Street's willingness and ability to sort things out." In addition to his massive scaled humanitarian relief efforts in Europe that had been organized mostly through private organizations, following the Great Mississippi Flood in 1927, Hoover had successfully prevented a large scale health catastrophe largely through private organizations and the help of volunteers that readily contributed to the effort when he called upon them.

Within days of the Crash, the President appealed directly to the leading business leaders who were the largest sources of the nation's jobs. He figured as long as Americans were employed, they would have the means to continue to buy goods and need services that would in turn stimulate the economy. In order to try to convince them not to reduce benefits and jobs, he invited them to join his special task force and attend a special meeting at the White House regarding the economy in Washington, D.C.

James was delighted to receive an invitation from the Executive Office to discuss the country's problems. He knew it was an honor to be selected, particularly given his age. He didn't give a toss about Hoover's motives. He attended in order to hobnob with the exclusive group and more importantly, to be *seen* and *associated* with this powerful set.

The young businessman also looked forward to visiting the Commander in Chief's mansion. It was the first time he had been invited by a President to visit the historic landmark. Riding down to Washington D.C. with Charles Schwab in his personal railway car, James felt very good, indeed. He wore a blue, silk cravat and his favorite Tate suit. As the businessmen gathered at the White House, reporters huddled around them and bystanders gathered in anticipation. Spirits high, despite an overcast sky and oppressive heaviness in the air, he gallantly tipped his hat.

Addressing the crowd, James announced, "We're here for America!" The crowd cheered in response.

That was the high point of the day for the young businessman. He found the actual meeting quite dull. As far as he could tell, everyone had a personal agenda. Some wanted tariffs. Others were dead set against them. Several promoted a reduction of tax burdens as the cure-all. How this idea could be implemented drew vocal differences. All the briefings given during the meeting from the President's to each of the tycoon's clearly were done with their own objectives in mind.

Although James got a better handle on the overall affect of the Crash across America, he scoffed as he realized during the entire day, he hadn't heard one original thought. As he looked around the Green Room, he realized even the most high-powered forums with the most influential people fundamentally functioned the same way as ordinary meetings with common people. It was a disillusioning experience. But always one to make the most out of a situation, he spent the rest of his day figuring out how he could most benefit from those gathered. After singling out a particularly uninspired, gray-haired, stooped gentleman who just happened to own several mills the business man wanted, James made sure he filled his prey with such trepidation for the future, that he was able to make the acquisition for even less than he had imagined.

Smugly, James thought few in the room were his equals until he overheard the President and Mrs. Hoover whispering in Mandarin. He later learned that the couple had picked up the language in China when the President had worked for a private corporation as the firm's leading engineer. James felt less intimidated when he was informed that the Hoovers had had plenty of time to practice during the Boxer Rebellion when they had been trapped in Tianjin. Still, James thought that proficiency in that difficult language was quite an achievement.

After the President challenged his guests to a game that he had invented to keep fit in the White House, which was a combination of volleyball and tennis, more discussions were held. Hoover told the business luminaries that in order to ease unemployment and alleviate the burden on municipalities' aid services, he planned to authorize the Mexican Repatriation Program. James gasped when he heard that the Commander in Chief estimated that this forced migration would result in up to 500,000 Mexicans and even some Mexican Americans leaving the United States. Wanting to make the most out of this inside information, the cunning businessman quickly made excuses and left. He swiftly walked across Lafayette Square to the Cosmos Club where he phoned Garrett Goldman to see how they could optimize the situation before the announcement was made public.

Choosing not to ride back with Charles Schwab that night, James checked into the Hayes-Adam Hotel and phoned a friend. When he told her he was quite upset, the very prominent Senator's wife did her best to cheer him up in the one way he appreciated.

As soon as he got back to New York, the cunning businessman did exactly what he had promised the President he wouldn't do. He fired 10% of his entire workforce.

James Ellison DeVere had "no comment" for reporters.

* * *

Josie and Charles agreed to spend one last weekend together before he left for Oklahoma. Charles thought this was particularly important since subsequent conversations with his uncle and aunt led him to believe that he would have to spend at least six months out west. When his uncle Teddy called him to ask if he could go to Boston to withdraw the remaining money they had left in accounts at a Beacon Hill bank there before he flew home, Charles decided to take Josie with him. The lovers decided to spend the weekend together before his Monday meeting in New England. Josie hoped to stay with the Stanleys the night after Charles left. She told her parents they would stay with Rebecca in Boston the whole time. Although Josie hadn't been able to get a hold of Rebecca before she and Charles left New York, she figured her friend was a safe alibi. If she couldn't get a hold of the Stanleys, she knew her parents wouldn't be able to contact them either.

Instead of going directly to Boston, Charles rented a cozy farmhouse for them in the scenic Pioneer Valley. Although the lustrous fall colors had begun to fade, the couple still enjoyed their time together. They hiked and picnicked during the day and talked and read by the gigantic stone fireplace at night. Josie adored her fiancé's voice as he read her favorite poems while she snuggled up in his arms. She thought his voice had the most wonderful quality. It was so strongly masculine and yet sensitive at the same time. Despite his Midwestern origin and tendency towards twang during speech, when he recited favorite passages, his annunciation and speech naturally came off like the best trained Royal Shakespeare Theatre actor. The words came alive when he spoke and he knew instinctively just when to pause for dramatic effect.

As they lay wrapped together in each other's arms, Josie decided that despite her intention to wait until their wedding night, she wanted to make love to Charles this weekend before he left for Oklahoma. She reasoned that after all they were engaged and would marry, but since he had to go away for several months, she wanted him to have a memory to keep him warm at night and inspire him to work all the harder. As remote a possibility as it was, she also secretly that hoped maybe it would make him change his mind and stay with her.

Josie was nervous about the idea of losing her virginity. She knew she was tense and that would only make it hurt even more. So she decided to get drunk to loosen herself up. As soon as they got back from their afternoon hike, she poured herself a big glass of red wine.

Glancing at his watch, Charles said, "We're starting early tonight, aren't we?"

In response, she also poured him a strong drink.

Over dinner, Josie continued to down her alcohol. The room was spinning, but she still felt insecure. Taking the bottle away from her, Charles said, "Don't you think you've had enough?"

Getting some dessert wine, Josie asserted, "For what I am about to do – *definitely* not."

Josie was so inebriated that Charles had to carry her upstairs to the colonial style bedroom they shared because she couldn't walk straight. He tried to get her to go to sleep, but she was adamant that she wanted to "do it."

As she started to kiss a rather reluctant Charles, Josie suddenly felt queasy. She stumbled out of the four-poster bed and staggered across the room before just making it to the adjoining bathroom. On her way, she tripped over the iron fireplace poker that had slipped down from its upright position next to the brick hearth. She spent the rest of the night throwing up in the toilet bowl as Charles stood by her side encouraging her to get it all out of her system. Just when she thought she had emptied her stomach, she'd feel the urge to vomit again. As he supported her with one arm, with the other one he held her hair back so it didn't get in the way as she stooped over the latrine.

As she struggled to get it all up, Charles said, "That's good. And again." The caring lover stayed up all night gently kissing her, rinsing her mouth and just taking care of her.

The next morning when Josie awoke, she had a bad hangover and felt terribly embarrassed. Explanations were unnecessary.

Charles knew exactly why she had done what she did. It made him love her even more. He was just sorry she had to go to such lengths because she had been so nervous that it would hurt so much.

Kissing her on the forehead as she opened her eyes, Charles said reassuringly, "I love you so much. Even if we never make love, my heart will always be yours."

That night, with a hangover and absolutely no alcohol in her system to help, Josie and Charles did make love. Charles did his best to make the experience as painless and loving as was possible. Despite his best efforts, Josie tensed up. But his patience and their overpowering mutual love made the experience memorable for both of them. Afterwards, as they lay in bed holding each other, he said, "You are so beautiful to me – every part of you."

Josie and Charles fell asleep knowing their love was even greater.

The lovers spent the following day in bed, repeating the previous night's activities. Charles reasoned that since it was raining outside, it wasn't worth getting out of bed. Rephrasing his explanation, Josie claimed since *he* was in bed, it wasn't worth getting out. Knowing it would be their last full day and night together for a long time, they made the most of every minute of it. As he held her in his arms and she caressed his every part, Josie was full of love. She had never even imagined that a man could make her feel so satisfied. For his part, the weekend only made Charles more determined to be worthy of Josie's love.

The next morning, at dawn, the couple awoke. Embers still glowed in the fireplace, but otherwise, the room was exceptionally cold and dark on this overcast day. Outside the sky was a dismal expanse that summed up the month of November. Nestled closely under the cozy down comforter, Josie and Charles found it extremely difficult to get up.

Holding each other tightly as if by doing so they could change the outcome of what they had to do, they stayed in bed as long as they could. Finally knowing they could not procrastinate any longer, Charles very reluctantly got dressed.

As they set off, the wind picked up ripping the remaining leaves off the trees, leaving them bare and empty against the desolate land. Josie thought it was like the Crash, whose violent undertow now swept Charles far away from her.

For the entire two-hour drive to Boston, Josie kissed and touched Charles as he drove. More than once, he found it difficult to concentrate on the road. Patiently she waited for him in the bank's lobby as he negotiated with the loan officers. When he finally appeared after three hours, forlorn, she comforted him, offering her warm smile and unconditional love. She boosted his lagging spirits as he told her he had only secured half the money because so many people were trying to liquidate their accounts that the bank was incapable of fulfilling all the requests and had instead resorted to partial payments. Her thoughtfulness was not lost on him. As they drove the final stretch to the airfield from where he would be flying, he vowed if he had to be away more than a year, he'd send for her.

Much to Josie's chagrin, when they arrived at the airfield, she saw the propellers already turning on the mail plane. She choked back tears as she got out of the car. As she reached over to Charles who had gone to take his bags out of the trunk, she saw he had watery eyes too.

After putting his bags down next to the car in order to say goodbye, Charles pulled Josie close to him and kissed her tenderly. As they embraced, he said lovingly, "I can never love anyone more than I love you. You are the love of my life and will be the mother of my children." Peering deeply into her eyes, he told her with conviction, "No matter what happens, never doubt me."

Emotionally, Josie said, "I won't Charles." After passionately kissing him, she vowed, "I promise." Not wanting the moment to end, she sealed her vow with another long, passionate kiss that left her dizzy. Overwhelmed, she whispered breathily, "My love for you is eternal."

For a moment Charles thought he had made a mistake and should have agreed to let Josie come with him, but deep down he knew he was being responsible.

As they heard the pilot screaming it was time to go, Charles gave Josie a kiss she'd never forget.

Then, as she watched helplessly, he picked up his bags and ran towards the plane. When he reached it, he turned around to shout, "I love you Josephine Baxter-Browne!"

Charles stood by the door as long as he could. As he waved to her and blew kisses in her direction, he knew she was saying, "I love you," but her words were swept away by the wind and the sound of the plane.

While the gusty wind blew on this cold November afternoon, Josie sadly watched as the plane gained speed on the ground and then lifted off. It soared upwards, becoming a small dot on the horizon, before completely disappearing into the sky.

Tears streamed down her face as she looked for the plane long after it had gone. As Josie stood on the grassy airfield, she never felt so lonely before.

* * *

Shivering from the cold, Josie finally wiped her tears and got back into her Bugati. As she drove towards Boston, she decided to look for Rebecca. Taking out the address of Mrs. Stanley's Aunt from her handbag, Josie asked for directions and set off. The Aunt's house and grounds were stately but dilapidated. Clearly, this branch of the family had not flourished during the heady days of the roaring twenties.

As Josie got out of her car, two hungry looking dogs raced up to her. A hunch-backed Groundsman called them off just as she was about to jump back into her Bugati. Josie thought the man looked old enough to have been tending the gardens when the first inhabitants first set foot in the place.

After sending the dogs off, he slowly asked, "Look'in for Miss Becca?"

She said, "Yes. I'm a good friend of hers." Looking up at the house, she asked, "Is she in?"

He replied, his mouth full of chewing tobacco, "Can't say she is."

"She really isn't here or you can't say she is here?" asked Josie perceptively.

Taking a minute to digest the question as he chomped on the tobacco, the Groundsman finally said as he spit out the chewed up bits, "She ain't here."

Josie inquired, "Can I ask where she might be then?"

"Yeah. You can ask," he replied as he spit out more of the substance. Then as he looked at her, he said just as slowly, "But it won't help you none if you was coming to see her."

"Where is she?" inquired Josie.

He nodded his head towards the road before saying, "They left 'bout a week ago."

Josie asked, "Miss Rebecca and her mother?"

He grunted, "Uh-huh." As Josie tried to coax him into telling her everything he knew, he continued to chew on his tobacco. For some time, she wasn't sure if he was deliberately being difficult to discourage her questions or just naturally slow. She received her answer when he finally replied, "The Misses have gone to Europe I was told." Proudly, he smiled, showing several large gaps in his mouth and a few yellow stained teeth as he remembered, "I helped them put some of their trunks in the taxi."

Josie thanked the man and asked, "Is Rebecca's Aunt here now?"

"She is, but she don't like no company," he explained.

Although her patience had been tried, she sweetly said, "Could you please tell her Josephine Baxter-Browne is here and I'd like Rebecca's address?"

"Jes wait here," he said as he limped across the lawn and disappeared into the house.

He was so slow; Josie thought she probably could have driven half way home by the time he got across the lawn and into the house. Just when she was about to give up, he returned with the information. He informed her Rebecca was in London, staying at Claridge's. Then he told her that Rebecca's Aunt wasn't feeling up to any visitors.

As Josie drove off, she thought she saw a ghost of a woman peering through the sheer curtains in an upstairs bedroom window. The place gave her the creeps. She had heard Mrs. Stanley's spinster Aunt had gone crazy years ago when her fiancé stood her up at the altar. Josie was glad Rebecca wasn't staying in this decrepit crypt. She quickly drove away from the haunted place, now understanding only too well why her friend had not been in contact often with Geraldine. Josie hoped Rebecca would have a better time in Europe.

Relieved that she was not in such circumstances, Josie momentarily felt better. Deciding to drive straight home, she turned on the newly installed Motorola model 5T71 radio, a prototype that her father had been given as a present from the founders' for his financing, and pressed on the gas. She hoped to get back in time for dinner and with enough energy left to write a letter to Charles.

When she arrived she found a cable already waiting for her. Charles had sent it from Ohio where the plane made a refueling stop and had some mail to deliver. It read: *Love you.* Stop. *Miss You Already.* Stop. *Kisses From Across The Country.* Stop. It was signed, *Your C.B.*

Josie took the message up to her room and kept reading it over and over again. After writing him a long letter pledging her love for him and telling him the news about Rebecca and her mother moving to Europe, she fell slept. When Claire came in to turn off the lights in her daughter's room, she found the cable lying next to her and Josie's letter to Charles. As she moved the papers, Claire couldn't help but catch a bit of what her daughter had written. It began:

Today was the bleakest day in the bleakest month of the year. But when I got home to find your message, my heart soared once again and the world seemed a beautiful place.

* * *

Charles kept his promise by writing to Josie every day. On his way home, he wrote several times during the same day because of the time he had and the stopovers due to mechanical problems with the aircraft. His letters were full of expressions of love and devotion as well as vivid descriptions of his encounters along his journey and quite a bit of humor.

Josie saved every one of Charles' letters. She kept them in a box right under her *Bible* on the nightstand next to her bed. They were her most precious possessions because they came from him. When she couldn't sleep at night, she would get up and re-read his words and then look up at the stars and talk to them as if she were speaking directly to him. Then she would add to whatever letter she had been writing that day.

* * *

The $15,700 Josie and Geraldine collected should have lasted Rebecca and her mother quite a while given the fact $1,200 was the average salary of the American family at the time. But Mrs. Stanley had high hopes for her daughter and these expectations incurred notable expenses.

Living cloistered with her eccentric relative in a dilapidated house had been not only deeply depressing for the mother and daughter; it also was counter-productive. Mrs. Stanley realized almost immediately that Boston society and the rest of the East coast for that matter knew what had happened to the Stanleys. So, after taking their belongings up to her Aunt's place, Mrs. Stanley decided to travel to Europe to help find a suitable husband for Rebecca where her prospects might be less informed.

Pouring through Debrette's and the social columns, Rebecca's mother made a list of potential mates. Much to her daughter's chagrin, age and appearance were of no concern. Mrs. Stanley hoped to get Rebecca a title, but given their precarious financial situation, she was willing to settle for a brute with money. Still, she dreamed of the big catch. So Mrs. Stanley booked the first passage out of Boston for Europe. During the voyage, Rebecca and her mother spent as little time as possible in the smallest first class cabin on *The United States.*

The trip proved rather uneventful, as did the Paris season. In London, Rebecca attracted attention, but failed to get any marriage proposals except from a ninety-year old Lord who succumbed to pneumonia a week after he had fallen for Rebecca's obvious charms. When the *Times* printed his obituary, Mrs. Stanley was horrified to learn the man was hardly better off than they.

Depressed, the Stanleys hoped to have better luck in Italy. On their second day, they were introduced to Count Nasogrande.

The corpulent Count was extremely interested in the petite brunette. He saw her as a shorter version of a dark beauty named Josephine Baxter-Browne that he had fantasized about marrying. His interest increased when he found out the girls knew each other well. Assured they were in the same social circles, Nasogrande was convinced Rebecca would have the dowry he required. He didn't believe that anyone who had lost their wealth in the Crash could have traveled to Europe *first class.*

The courtship began in earnest.

* * *

Geraldine coped with the aftermath of the Crash by embracing her own version of abstract art. Deeply disillusioned by what she had witnessed and Rebecca's losses, she turned to her creative side to express herself. Most of her pieces were done out of anger, painted when she was deeply upset. Geraldine had no intention of selling them. She didn't even want anyone to see them. She just hoped they would help her work through this terribly difficult period. But as the days passed, the artist only became more disturbed. Refusing to go out, she hardly saw anyone, including Josie, who also wasn't in much of a mood for socializing since Charles had left. Shutting out all natural light and beauty by putting up black curtains over her gigantic studio French doors, the artist surrounded herself with the melancholy darkness she felt. Geraldine's paintings catalogued her slide into depression. Finally, one afternoon when she was angrily painting, the moody artist had an unexpected visitor who discovered the truth.

Unannounced, Evelyn Maker softly crept up behind Geraldine. She stood there analyzing the current painting and the others in the room before she chose to make her presence known. Finally, she cleared her throat.

Geraldine jumped back and then quickly turned to see who had invaded her sanctuary. She smiled when she saw Evelyn. Then she colored from embarrassment when she realized the fortune-teller had seen all her personal "strife" pieces.

"I think it's time we had a little chat," quipped Evelyn as she motioned for Geraldine to sit down on the divan.

Pulling up a chair to face the artist, Evelyn said more like a psychiatrist, "Would you like to explain your work?"

"Is it really that necessary?" replied Geraldine flatly.

The clairvoyant stated, "You tell me."

After unburdening her soul to Evelyn, the astrologist held the artist in her arms. Later, knowing how helping others often ameliorated one's own condition, she invited Geraldine to accompany her on her rounds. Unbeknownst to Geraldine, the savant had been quietly supporting several charities for orphans and one for abused women. The shelters promised to keep Evelyn's involvement secret in exchange for her money and support. Each week, the seer spent two nights counseling for free. In addition, she provided the groups with a percentage of the profits from her newsletters.

Geraldine was amazed at how much Evelyn's counseling made a difference. Taking her aside, she said clearly affected, "You are so talented and so good with people. You really do have a gift." A visionary as well as an artist, she muttered half under her breath, "I just wish you could reach more people."

"Unfortunately, there are only so many hours in the day," replied the level-headed clairvoyant.

Still thinking out loud, Geraldine said, "But you reach more people through your newsletter."

"Over 4,000 now," acknowledged the seer.

"You're so effective one-on-one. There are so many people who are suffering these days. You should really have a radio program!" exclaimed Geraldine excitedly.

Giving it some thought, Evelyn said, "I'll look into it."

The following week, Geraldine accompanied the seer again on her charity rounds. This time the artist brought a sketchpad. As they left she said, "Thank you."

"For what?" replied Evelyn.

"My anger's gone," explained the artist. She then asked, "Would you mind if I came along with you from now on?"

"I rather hoped you would," replied Evelyn.

The clairvoyant was delighted when Geraldine offered to bring extra paintbrushes, sketchpads and pencils for the group sessions.

Both knew from experience that art could be an effective form of therapy.

After several months, Geraldine had become quite attached to the groups. Wishing more people could know about the charities so they could offer hope and resources to those in the most need, the artist decided to do sketches of the children and women that she submitted to the papers.

On her list were not only the local New York papers, but also those published in Washington D.C. From what she had been reading recently, Geraldine thought Congress and the President truly were out of touch. She hoped the faces of those in plight might elicit less talk and more action on their part.

Working side by side with the individuals in need and telling their stories to the outside world, infused Geraldine with an energy she thought she had lost. During this period, she did what she would later consider some of her finest work.

* * *

At the end of his first full day back in Ada, Charles collapsed exhausted in a carved walnut chair in his family's expansive thirty-five-room, Frank Lloyd Wright designed, Prairie-style, home. He found much changed at the ranch as well as in the town since his last trip back.

When they picked him up from the airfield, Charles was shocked by how much his Aunt Anna and Uncle Teddy had aged. He soon would understand why and would see even more disturbing sights. Charles felt uneasy as the Blakesleys drove through the area in their luxurious Pierce Arrow cruiser. Instead of the waves and friendly smiles that he fondly remembered whenever they came to town, those they now passed stared blankly back while others openly looked upon them with jealousy and hate. He noticed although it was an ordinary weekday, there were significantly more people in town than normal. His uncle informed him that most were men who should have been working but no longer had jobs. Sitting around immobile or standing in groups of clusters, the idle had hungry looks in their eyes, reminding Charles of the packs of wild wolves that he'd occasionally hear howling in the dead of night. As a child he had been afraid they would come to him if he didn't leave a light on to frighten them away. The desperate men he saw today made feel him just as vulnerable.

Charles thought the whole town had an eerie quality like a ghost town with possessed spirits, frozen in time, which sought the chance to avenge their ill fate. Instinctively he sensed the inhabitants wanted to pick a fight with someone, anyone, just to be able to take out their anger and loss. He sensed the smallest event or even rumor could turn this group into a mob as dangerous as those that used to gather in the last century to hang suspected cattle rustlers and bank robbers. As the Blakesleys drove past the shuttered bank, Charles' Uncle explained that was exactly the scene the bank president had encountered the week he closed the insolvent institution while angry customers demanded their deposits back. While Charles' Aunt and Uncle forfeited a substantial amount of money as a result, many others in the area lost their entire savings and sought to punish the bank president personally. The executive barely escaped with his family in their car just before the mob plundered and torched their home. The place burnt completely to the ground before a fire truck arrived. Anna told Charles she believed a number of the town's fire brigade had been amongst the pillagers.

Back at the ranch, Charles found more desolation and defeat. Desperate, the old, faithful hands and household staff looked to him for salvation. Until his arrival, Anna and Teddy had hidden the full extent of their woes from him. But as Charles surveyed on horseback their dusty land that suffered from a drought, their depleted herd of cattle, and their credit-stretched accounts, he realized all the plans he made in New York were useless. Survival would be difficult at best.

Charles slept for an hour under a stained glass window in a chaise lounge in his Aunt's terracotta-colored sitting room. Then he walked outside to smell the air. After this trying day, he sought refuge in the one place in Oklahoma he always had. He got back on his tired horse and rode until he reached an old Indian burial. There, on this once most verdant, sacred ground, he sat down and momentarily was filled with a sense of peace. As Charles picked up a pen and some paper he had in his saddlebag so he could write to Josie, he could just make out the outline of the town against the red-orange horizon as the sun set in the distance. He tried to express his feelings so she could share his experiences. He ended the letter with the following words:

As the light fades and dusk settles over this ancient ground, my heart and mind are far from this land. I can see your face in the rising moon. It is beautiful and I feel warm and loved as I think of you. You are my soul. I love you more than you can know. Each and every day I live for you.

Forever your servant and love, Charles Blakesley

* * *

As the days progressed since Charles' departure, Josie lived for the mail delivery and his occasional phone calls. Given the expense of phoning as well as the fact that Charles was out working most of the day, he didn't ring his fiancée often. Her parents, friends, and even the staff always knew if there was a letter from him or not, judging by Josie's mood. Although Charles and Josie continued to write to each other every day, the mail delivery from Oklahoma was erratic. As a result, after waiting a week or more, in two days, Josie would receive six or seven letters at once. Josie felt like an emotional yo-yo. No matter how rational she tried to be, she couldn't control her emotions.

To make matters worse, as Charles threw himself wholeheart-edly into saving his family's operations, he had very little time and energy to write. Although he still managed to send a few lines every day, they resembled the shortest of journal entries more than the lengthy witty documents he had written in the beginning. After waiting over two weeks to hear from her fiancé, she knew she needed to do something to get her mind off *him*. But she didn't feel like doing anything.

Since the Crash, Josie had folded *Twenties Humor*. She under-stood times had changed. The satirical rag magazine that focused on poking fun of the lifestyles and trends of the well-heeled young rich now seemed not only superfluous, but even in bad taste. With advertising dollars down significantly and a number of the con-tributors and editors too financially strapped to write for a living let alone for fun, the publication was headed for a certain death any way when Josie pulled it. Depressed by its closing and at a loss of what to do, the engaged debutante searched for a calling. Other than writing to Charles and the occasional journal entry where she complained about her mother, she lost interest in pursuing that hobby as well. Tearing up what she wrote thinking it wasn't good enough even during times when there weren't as many hungry authors, Josie determined to find a new calling. But bored and lethargic, the less she did, the more she wanted to do nothing at all.

Even the social circuit seemed dull. With so many of her friends away and without Charles, the privileged set's events lost their appeal. She also felt guilty. Since she had a fiancé, she thought she shouldn't be partying without him and potentially sending out the wrong message to available bachelors. As a result, she hardly went out other than for the occasional stroll or horseback ride in Central Park and the odd movie with Geraldine.

Stubborn and sullen, the more her mother tried to engage her, the more Josie just wanted to be left alone both to her letters and to take long walks by herself during which she could fantasize about Charles' return. Albert was concerned about his daughter but he was so consumed with business these leaner days, he couldn't find the energy to argue with her. When he tried to reason with her, she just stomped off in a huff.

The grim faces of reality finally propelled Josie, just as they had forced Geraldine, out of her mild depression. Although she normally strolled in Central Park, one afternoon Josie decided to walk downtown. She wanted to stop in a few shops for cute gifts she could send Charles. What she saw shocked her.

Josie had heard that pundits claimed the Stock Market Crash of 1929, was purely an upper class affair – a phenomenon that fundamentally only affected a small percentage of the elite like Charles and the Stanleys, who had invested large amounts of their inheritances. Others had alleged that the "little guys," the small time speculators, who had been sold out, actually were the ones who were hurt most since the market and the economy soon would stage a healthy recovery. As Josie walked the streets, she could see without any doubt that the Crash was causing a chain reaction affecting every layer of society.

Across the city, stores that had flourished several weeks ago were closed up, their tenants on the street hawking what they could. Businessmen in tattered suits sold apples on every corner, while their wives and children offered what they had. Churches were filled with the homeless, seeking a warm place to sit during daylight hours. Beggars and vagrants of every age, ethnic group, and social class, accosted Josie as she wandered through Grand Central Station. A policeman stopped the un-mistakable debutante who wore an eye-catching mink coat and a triple strand of pearls to warn her not to consider going down to the subway unless she wanted to be mugged. Everywhere, the optimism of the 1920's had vanished; in its place, hopeless-ness.

Josie wrote to Charles that night:

My love,

I have no thoughts of Shakespeare or Dante tonight. My sentiment is not with Keats or Shelley. It is very much with the crisis right now facing our nation and perhaps much of the world if nothing changes. Something must be done to help these people. I for one, hope as you work for us in Oklahoma I can do something for the plight of those most destitute in New York.

Determined to help the less fortunate, Josie once again had a reason to live each day. Although she still looked forward to reading the mail and writing Charles, her days and nights were spent working constructively. Initially, Josie volunteered in a soup kitchen. There, she was shocked to find not only the destitute, but also a sizable number of quite well-dressed, unemployed workers. There were former secretaries and bankers, shop girls, and store-owners as well as mechanics, day laborers, and domestics, who no longer had any income to buy even basic staples. Not infrequently, she recognized familiar faces. Deftly she tried to preserve what dignity the supplicants had left. Always with a warm smile and a friendly, non-judgmental look, she offered hope and aid.

But as the weeks wore on and the numbers of needy grew, the charity started to run out of food before the end of each day. Horrified at having to turn away hungry families, Josie realized fundraising would be necessary. This was also one area where New York's most celebrated debutante knew she could be extremely effective. Although many of the prominent families had suffered in the recent months, she was certain there were still some people with money left to spend if enticed to do so.

Josie started the Thursday Club as a way to raise money for the soup kitchen she continued to serve in. The debutante organized weekly charity events at speakeasies, hotels, clubs, and family friends' private homes. She picked the day of the week that New York socialites would be in the city and not in their country residences and did not have other commitments already planned.

Josie set about enlisting all the right people to serve on her committees and solidly back the effort. She also managed to engage the support of the press.

Even before their first event, the Thursday Club already had raised in excess of five figures. As Josie socialized with her guests, she realized how much she had missed going out since Charles had left.

Josie beamed radiantly as she circulated in a stunning black tulle dress trimmed with a large spray of ostrich feathers. Responding to the numerous complements she received on her ensemble, the debutante proudly asserted that the dress had once belonged to her mother and she had donated the money she would have spent on a new ensemble to the needy. Josie rolled her eyes when she overheard some of the younger debutantes gossiping that Catherine, whose latest shopping spree had been noted in Cholly Knickerbocker's column, was encouraging all those she knew to flaunt their wealth in the face of the Depression as their patriotic duty.

The perfect hostess, Josie effortlessly glided from group to group, making each guest feel as if she were truly interested in what they had to say. Watching her movements, James thought Josie lit up the room. Her eyes sparkled with energy and enthusiasm. Her vibrancy captivated all those who mingled with her.

Confident that his timing was right, New York's most eligible bachelor downed his glass of champagne and prepared to make his move.

* * *

CHAPTER XVI

When he wanted to be, James Ellison DeVere was devastatingly charming. Cocky and self-assured, he strode up to Josie.

Reaching for her hand, he said smirking, "Darling, shall we?"

"I don't know quite what you mean," replied Josie caught off guard.

"Dance, of course," replied James feigning innocence. As he led her onto the parquet floor he said nonchalantly, "Whatever did you think I meant?"

"With you," said Josie flatly as she looked him straight in the eyes, "One never quite knows." Then, as she danced around him so he had to follow her, she continued coquetishly, "But one should be afraid to ask."

Pulling her closer, James said, "My dear, as long as you're with me, you have nothing to fear."

Calling him out, Josie said with a big smile, "Then I can count on you."

"For you? Anything is not too much to ask," he replied.

She asked, "Are you sure you mean that?"

After gallantly kissing her hand, he looked at her meaningfully and then stated, "It is my pleasure."

"Then, you'll respect the fact that as I have told you before, I am engaged to be married," she said.

He replied not missing a beat, "Ah, yes. I heard about Charles' unfortunate situation."

"Unfortunate?" exclaimed Josie with irritation. "There's nothing unfortunate about my agreeing to marry him!"

"Marriage is an institution women invented to torture men," retorted James as he twirled her around.

Spinning away from him she replied, "Perhaps you see it that way. But I assure you, Charles feels quite honored to have the privilege of my company."

Smirking, James couldn't resist saying as he reeled her back in towards him, "I fully appreciate the company of women. In fact, so much so, I don't see the need to make the mistake of marrying just one." His eyes sparkled as he said this knowing full well his comments rankled her.

Unamused, she retorted, "Perhaps you should move to the Middle East?"

"Why?" inquired James. "I have women here who would like to be accepted into my harem."

"Rest assured," she informed him, "I'm not one of them."

Pulling her close to him, James said seriously, "I've heard, some women are worth giving everything up for."

She replied tartly, "Let me know when you find one."

"Perhaps I have," said James with a telling smile.

Josie stated unemotionally, "I'll send her my condolences."

"You won't have far to go," replied James as he looked down at her meaningfully. As his eyes were locked on hers, Josie felt a sensation go through her body and she blushed.

As the dance finished, Josie tried to collect herself. Coolly, she said, "Be a sport, go look for your ideal woman and get me some punch while you're at it."

As James momentarily left Josie for the drinks, Geraldine saw her chance to intercede. Like a determined bulldog, she strode up to her friend, cutting through everyone in her path without as much as an excuse me. She shook her head with such vehemence there was no doubt as to her opinion on the matter.

As she finally reached her friend, Geraldine muttered, "I don't like it."

"I was just dancing with him." Josie replied defensively, "He's a good dancer. Surely, Charles wouldn't mind."

"It's not Charles I'm worried about," exclaimed Geraldine. "James Ellison DeVere's dangerous. He'd sleep with his own sister."

"I didn't know James had a sister," said Mrs. Whitney Straight seriously as she joined the group.

"He doesn't," replied Geraldine as she colored, realizing the grand dame had heard her vulgarity.

"I see," said Mrs. Whitney-Straight icily. The dowager was furious as she thought of how she had been flattered when she thought that the young scion had a crush on her.

Josie and Mrs. Whitney-Straight were so busy talking that they didn't notice how long James had been gone. However, the fact was not lost on Geraldine. With one eye on her friends, she trained the other on James. Although she couldn't hear his conversation, she could see he encouraged the fawning females. She carefully took note of his flirtations until a rude drunk jostled her after stepping on her feet.

While Geraldine wiped his wine off her dress and rubbed her bruised toes, she missed seeing James run his hand over Lily Vanderhorn's backside as he made arrangements to meet her at the Carlyle, after the party.

When Geraldine finally managed to refocus on the bachelor she scorned, much to her chagrin, she saw him sauntering back to Josie.

After handing Josie her drink, he made a half-hearted effort to give Geraldine and Mrs. Whitney-Straight his.

"Don't bother," said Geraldine clearly unimpressed.

James said, "You know I'd offer you my drink, but…"

"You already had a sip of it," replied Geraldine finishing his sentence.

He admitted, "Actually I haven't touched it."

Reaching immediately for the glass since she knew how much he liked champagne, Geraldine said quickly as she grabbed it from him. "In that case, I'll take it."

Smiling broadly Geraldine suggested, "Guess you'll just have to go get another one."

When James failed to move, Geraldine pressed, "Go on." Not bothering in the least to hide her feelings towards James, she asserted, "Mrs. Whitney Straight and I will be more than happy to stay with Josie while you chat up anyone at the punch bowl who eluded you last round."

Making it clear what he thought of the present company, James replied as he looked meaningfully at Josie, "Actually, as long as Josie agrees to speak with me, I have no interest in conversing with anyone else.

The tense moment was broken by the arrival of Evelyn Maker who was very keen to speak with Geraldine alone. Much to his relief, a few minutes later, Mrs. Whitney-Straight's husband joined them and asked his wife to dance. Once again, James and Josie were left together.

James made the most of the situation. Pulling her outside to the terrace so no one else would interrupt them, James offered his arm to Josie as they looked at the stars. There he disarmed her by professing his desire to unburden his soul to her. He began, "I'm not surprised Geri hates me."

Knowing exactly how to play the moment, James said, "I know she's your friend." As he looked at her seriously, he went on to claim, "I think it's wonderful she cares so much for you. That kind of friendship is special."

Josie agreed, "We've known each other since we were toddlers and have been through a great deal."

"Then I guess I shouldn't be surprised she's antagonistic to-wards me," replied James.

Josie frowned. "She doesn't know you."

James exclaimed, "Exactly!"

Then as he held both her hands in his and looked her straight in the eyes ever so earnestly, James claimed, "The truth is no one really knows me." With irresistible puppy-dog eyes, he said, "I'm actually very sensitive."

At first, Josie looked at him incredulously, but as James continued with a serious tone in his voice, she couldn't help but take note. Solemnly he broke down her skepticism with his well-practiced lines. Like an actor, his delivery was perfect. "I've created this image of myself as a defense mechanism – it's what I thought my father and Great Uncle wanted me to be." He alleged, "When I was young, I was such a disappointment to my Great Uncle who raised me, because I wasn't ruthless." Pausing for affect, he waited patiently for a certain sympathetic look from her before saying, "I really shouldn't bore you with this."

As he purposely broke off, Josie pleaded with him to, "Please go on."

James deliberately fidgeted uncomfortably, before he continued his story. His routine had produced the desired affect countless times before and as Josie leaned closer to him, encouragingly, he had the distinct feeling his act would work like magic again.

Slowly, James claimed, "I've never told anyone any of this before." As she took his hand in hers and urged him to continue, he said almost like a little boy, "It makes me so vulnerable. I don't even know why I'm telling you except you seem so understanding and different. I feel like I can trust you like." He broke off momentarily to look meaningfully at her while he asserted, "You know I've been hurt before – by those closest to me. So I try not to care too much about anyone."

When he stopped to see her reaction, she immediately urged him to continue. Reaching over to touch his sleeve, she said, "James, you know you can trust me. I want to know." Earnestly, she said, "Please let me be your friend. Confide in me. This can be our secret."

He said, "You won't tell anyone?"

"No. No one," she replied without thinking.

"Promise?"

Immediately she said, "Yes. I promise."

Gazing into her eyes, he said, "You know how much this means to me?" As she looked at him expectantly, he lied. "I've never confided in anyone before."

She reached for his hands and squeezed them as she said, "I am honored."

Once again he said, "Then, you promise never to tell anyone else."

She answered, "Of course. I won't tell a soul."

He pressed, "Not even Charles."

Josie grimaced and looked away.

He reminded her, "You promised not to tell anyone – that means not even him."

"Yes, I did," replied Josie softly. If she hadn't been looking down, he would have seen a frown on her face as she explained, "It's just, we don't keep anything between us. We never have."

Adamantly he pressed, "But you gave me your word!"

"Yes. Yes – I did and I always keep my word," said Josie still frowning.

Raising her head towards him, so he could look her straight in the eyes, James said, "Then, you promise."

Shaking her head slowly, but trying to justify her actions Josie replied, "Not that it matters, but I won't even tell Charles."

But nonetheless, she trembled as she said this. For the first time, she felt as if she had betrayed her love. She tried to reassure herself that whatever James was going to tell her had no impact on her fiancé and wouldn't even be of any interest to him. She tried desperately to rationalize her promise. But deep inside, she knew this was the first time she had ever kept anything from him before and she felt it was wrong.

James smiled triumphantly. Smirking he said, "You're so sweet, Josephine."

Getting an odd sense from the tone of his voice, she demanded to know, "What do you mean?"

"You've never kept any secrets from your beloved Charles, have you?" said James slyly.

"No," replied Josie thinking hard. "Never."

James chuckled, "Not until now you mean, darling."

Josie colored. Angry, she got up and slapped him on the face.

As she started to walk away she said, "Geri's right, you're an evil man."

James swore under his breath. She was so damned skittish. He would have to woo her ever so gently and curb his intrinsic nature. Then as he smiled wickedly as he thought it would make the conquest even more enjoyable.

He knew he had to physically detain her. Hurriedly, James put down his cigar and moved like a panther to block her from leaving.

Roughly pulling her face towards his, he said, "Now don't get all huffy, darling. I'm just playing with you." Realizing pretty quickly these comments weren't going to muster the desired affect, quickly he changed tactics.

Lighting a new cigar, he said as he motioned for her to sit down again, "Let me say this." He swallowed hard as he said, "I'm sorry." He continued, "Perhaps I didn't express myself correctly." Honestly, he admitted, "I shot off my mouth without thinking." As Josie stared at him trying to decide whether to give him another chance or not, he said decisively, "I didn't mean what I said."

Looking downcast he said, almost weepy eyed, "No one really likes me." He admitted, "Of course given the way I act, why would anyone?" As Josie politely disagreed with him, he claimed, "I don't even like myself most of the time."

Reaching out to her hand, he said, "Perhaps you can teach me how to show I care."

As she leaned closer to hear what he was saying, he knew he had her just where he wanted her to be.

The girl, who had saved a horse with a broken leg and took on numerous charity cases, felt sorry for the attractive bachelor who claimed he had been unloved as a child. After he "confided in her" and asked for her advice, they danced again. Then, he teased and joked with her. Although Josie knew that what he said was often mean, she couldn't help but laugh; he was so wickedly funny.

This was the first time since Charles had left that she had laughed effortlessly. She was having so much fun talking and dancing with James that for a few hours she didn't even think about her love. When she finally got tired, she agreed to allow James to escort her home. Before he left her at her door, she had promised to have dinner with him the following week. Happily, she accepted his offer as a male friend who could escort her in Charles' absence. Having been upfront with him about her relationship with Charles, Josie now felt comfortable and looked forward to helping James become nicer. That night she slept better than she had for months feeling confident she would change him into a better person while at the same time enjoy some harmless fun in the upcoming months. If she had been pressed, she also would have also had to admit, James was the best dancer she ever had partnered with as well as the best looking one.

* * *

Things had gone so well with Josie, New York's most eligible bachelor was an hour late in meeting Lily Vanderhorn. His attractive lover was just stomping out of the Carlyle Hotel when he caught up with her. Luckily for him, she didn't realize why he had been late until afterwards.

As they made love, Lily could tell James was pre-occupied. When they finished, he didn't even give her a kiss. Upset, she said, "You were different tonight."

"I don't think so," he robotically replied.

"I know so." She stressed, "A woman always knows these things."

"Perhaps you're coming up to that time of the month again," suggested James irritated.

"No." She said slowly as she gave him a long look, "Something has definitely changed between us."

Getting up to put on his clothes, James replied annoyed, "That's right. You've just become incredibly boring."

"It's another woman isn't it? You've fallen for someone else!" Lily shouted clearly upset. Then as she stared at James for some kind of rebuttal or confirmation, which she didn't get, she demanded, "Well, Who is it?"

"Darling, you know we've always been casual," he replied defensively.

"Don't 'darling me'," she said aggravated. Wanting to know her competition, she claimed, "At least you owe me this. Who is she?" She pressed, "Do I know her?"

Cagily, he claimed, "You know I've been seeing a number of people." Taking a dig at her, he snidely said, "Unlike you, I'm not married! I'm entitled to do what I want."

The mature woman who was used to arguing with men snapped back, "Don't be unpleasant and don't avoid the issue." As James yawned, she accused him. "You've changed. Your attitude. Our sex. Everything is different." Her mind going crazy with jealousy, she demanded to know, "What's her name?" Fantasizing the worst, she practically exclaimed, "Were you having sex with her before meeting me? Is that why you were so late?"

Trying to put an end to her questions, he emphatically said, "No!"

Her voice calm and quiet, she asked, "Then why were you late?"

"My dear, that is none of your goddamned business," said James as he turned to walk out the door.

"Wait," she pleaded, stepping in front of him to block his path. Her voice shaky, she said, "I know you have fallen for someone else. Make it easier on me. Just tell me who it is."

James smirked. "My dear, to begin, I never fell for you – you have just been a source of amusement." Not hiding his contempt, he stately in a matter of fact way, "Had you not been so eager to spread your legs, I would be with someone else right now."

Lily was furious. But she controlled herself for one reason. Up to this point she hadn't believed him entirely. She had no doubt he was seeing someone else. But she didn't think it could be serious. She didn't want it to be. Possessive of her lover, now she feared she was losing him. She could tell he was trying to hide something from her – to shield someone. His protective, almost fatherly attitude made her even more determined to find out the truth. As she looked at him, she thought there was something about his smile and the look in his eyes. Slowly backing away from him, she continued to stare, fascinated and horrified at the same time as she slowly understood.

It was his eyes that gave him away. Lily Vanderhorn had seen James look that way just once. Her mind raced, trying to place it. Finally she remembered. It had been earlier that evening when she saw him huddling in a corner speaking with Josie.

First Lily was filled with anger. Then she grieved and felt total emptiness. As she came to grips with what happened, she felt used and worthless. He had spurned her for a younger woman – but more importantly, a virginally pure girl who represented everything Lily could no longer be. Josie was not just some casual fling. She was someone James might actually marry.

Tears running down her face, Lily Vanderhorn threw a vase at her lover and screamed, "Damn you, James."

As he calmly put his hat on and picked up his walking stick before turning to go, he replied coolly, "Why? It's not as if I didn't warn you not to get too attached."

"You'll get bored with her, too!" shouted the hurt woman, as she muttered curses at him.

He left her with the remark, "Certainly not as quickly as I have with you."

Back in his boudoir at home, James prepared for bed. He was in a jolly mood despite the little unpleasant episode with Lily.

James couldn't get Josie off his mind. Pouring himself a nightcap, he went through the evening again. He asked himself, what was it exactly about her that was most appealing? Her looks, wit, and reputation certainly contributed, but there was something more. Despite her sophistication, he thought she really was quite innocent. As he savored his cognac, sitting in his dressing gown by the fire in his bedroom, he knew it was what he always came back to – her striking looks and youthful naïveté. As he finished his drink, he thought she definitely was his idea of the perfect woman. Like the 19th century marble statue he kept in his house, he wanted to possess her.

* * *

Across America, the Christmas of 1929 was celebrated quietly when at all. Countless children found Santa Claus had suffered in the market aftershocks. When given anything, a piece of fruit was the most common present left in stockings.

Josie wrote Charles that she had organized a special Christmas party to try to provide gifts to needy children in New York. Although her charity event was well attended, the paltry gift-giving disappointed her. Questioning several heads of charities who had also witnessed shortfalls, Josie came up with several possible explanations. Extravagance and charity had gone out of vogue with the

Crash. The resources of many of the wealthy continued to diminish at a frightening pace and those with endless resources felt uncomfortable flaunting it. Regardless of the reasons, if it hadn't been for her godfather, Josie wasn't sure how she would have pulled off her fete.

Henry Jay made up for the shortfall and even agreed to go to a shelter the day before the holiday dressed as Santa. Pretending to be his helper, Josie accompanied him dressed in a short, cute, red and white silk elf's costume. On her head, she angled a matching cap. A reporter who covered the event described her as the best looking elf he had ever seen. Josie was delighted that he and the photographer came to cover the story, but disturbed that they seemed more interested in presenting a fluff piece on "the secret life of a society girl," rather than focusing on the cause and those in need. Only the reporter's promise to encourage readers to make donations finally placated Josie.

As they traveled downtown to help the needy, Josie and Henry were struck by the despair they witnessed. Wherever they turned, there was more evidence of poverty now than a month before. Vacant-eyed, hungry, haunted figures stooped, their spirits broken, their children too weak to cry huddled together outside their shantytowns. While their haggard husbands, now unemployed with nowhere to go, no purpose, no way of earning a living, helplessly journeyed as if to work, only to painfully stand around looking aimlessly at the boarded up shops where they once had their manhood confirmed by steady salaries. Most didn't notice let alone care as Henry and Josie passed in their chauffer-driven navy blue Rolls Royce. But when they momentarily got stuck at an intersection, a particularly desperate, perhaps even raving mad lunatic, lunged at them.

Banging on the passenger windows, the vagrant screeched, "You're next!" As Josie gasped in horror, Henry shouted at his driver and then calmly instructed her to close her eyes, and turn away. Then, as he had done when she had gotten scared as a little girl, he held her tightly. Despite her godfather's paternal gesture, for several weeks, she kept reliving the moment, in nightmares. She kept waking up in a cold sweat. Just before dawn, she would scream as she envisioned the vagrant's sallow face pressed against the window, his gigantic blue eyes damning her for her class – for her luck.

Once they reached the shelter, the despondent quickly over-whelmed the do-gooders and the incident was not the only dis-turbing glitch in the day. Josie and Henry had found themselves scrambling for more presents.

Later that week, when Josie told James about the experience, he scoffed and said he thought the ranks were swelled with free-loaders who heard about the gift giving in advance. Realizing al-most as soon as the words were out of mouth that his comments were callous and whether true or not, would merely elicit contempt from Josie, he duly informed her that he too had held a Christmas event. As James described how he enjoyed giving because of the pleasure he received from cuddling children and watching them open their unexpected packages, he could tell he was on the right track to winning over the object of his affection. Josie effusively warmed to him because of his tales of generosity. She applauded him and readily agreed to see him every night that week after he told her he had given each one of the families of his workers a Christmas bonus and a present for each of the worker's children. When she asked him if he had dressed up as Santa, modestly he claimed it was the least he could do.

Contrary to what he had informed Josie, just before Christmas, James had laid off another 5% of his workforce. Although it wasn't imperative based upon his calculations, and at the very least he could have waited until after the holidays, he figured he could maintain production while cutting unnecessary costs and increase the mandatory hours of the remaining employees without problems this way. James wanted to ensure that 1930 would be a very merry, profitable year for him. Given the economic outlook he considered pro-active cost-cutting to be the best way to achieve his goal. Deploying Vinnie Graves to keep morale low and troublemakers quiet, he knew his workers would have anything but a Merry Christmas and Happy New Year. Of course, he didn't really care.

Josie awoke early on Christmas Eve, 1929. She always looked forward to the holiday, its celebrations rituals, the fabulous 5th Avenue window displays and decorations, the spirit of giving, and her own family traditions. Much to her delight, she awoke to frost on her bedroom windowpanes facing Central Park and little droplets of snow steadily coming down, covering the brownish brush and decorating the barren trees, turning the city into a winter wonderland. The debutante felt there was nothing more wonderful than a white Christmas in New York!

Like always, Josie had a great deal left to do this special morning and limited time. But tucked in her cozy bed, under the triple layer of Hungarian goose-down feather duvets, and warmed by a cheery, small fire in her marble fireplace, she decided to stay put just a little while longer. From her bed, she savored the sweet aroma of the holiday feast that wafted throughout the house. Several goose and pheasant that had been hunted the previous week by her godfather cooked as the staff laid a table with delicacies from around the world. As the morning progressed, homemade pastries and pies and the scent of cinnamon and eggnog also filled the air. Pressed for time and knowing to expect a twelve- course dinner that she'd remember the rest of the year, when Josie did finally get up, she grabbed just a small apple to eat before starting to work on her lengthy task list.

Beginning at dawn, the household staff had busied themselves preparing for the evening arrival of the family's guests, making the grand house festive. During the day, the servants lit scented candles, assembled the 500 piece Italian nativity scene and holiday village, put up the last decorations, the garlands on the staircase and mantles, mistletoe and wreathes, and treasured fragile family ornaments on the eighteen foot Douglas fir Christmas tree in the hall. While they worked, Josie wrapped presents and practiced playing holiday carols on the piano. Every year, the Baxter-Brownes held a Christmas Eve afternoon party for their staff, where they sang songs in the ballroom and had a buffet luncheon. The Baxter-Brownes' passed out bonuses and gifts to each member of their staff. Josie and her parents always took special care in picking thoughtful presents for those who made their lives so effortless. Despite the economic downturn, they made sure their servants wouldn't be disappointed.

It always was Josie's job to wrap the presents for the servants. Refusing to accept that her daughter was incapable of doing as good of a job as the girls at Tiffany's, Claire insisted Josie learn how to wrap properly. She made Josie re-do any gifts that she didn't think were presented beautifully enough. A naturally elegant wrapper, Josie's mother believed that the packaging reflected what the giver thought of the recipient. Much to Claire's annoyance, although she always purchased the gifts well in advance, her daughter, who hated wrapping and struggled to do a passable job, always waited until the last minute before finishing. This year, New York's most celebrated debutante finished seconds before the Christmas party started.

By 4:30 in the afternoon, the party ended as planned and the merry staff hurriedly cleared up and made the final preparations for the Baxter-Brownes' family dinner. This year, in addition to Henry Jay, who always spent his Christmases with them, the Whitney Straights, who had no children, and James were present.

At first, Josie had been wary of inviting over New York's most eligible bachelor. She knew it was one thing to allow him to serve as an escort while her fiancé was away, but quite another matter to have him spend this intimate family holiday with the Baxter-Brownes, especially when Charles couldn't be present. But when James told her that he had given his staff the day off and reminded her of his Uncle's passing, she felt obligated to invite him. Despite his feigned protestations, as he had expected, she insisted that he join her family. He knew he could count on the fact that she couldn't bear the thought of anyone spending the holiday alone.

As much as Josie wished her fiancé could have been with them, she would remember the Christmas of 1929 with fond memories. The Whitney Straights were always good fun, Henry, jocular, and her father more at ease when his dear friend was around. Amazed that James not only was the best dancer she had partnered with, but that also he sang well, Josie had a fantastic time singing, dancing, and playing games with the amusing bachelor. As much as she adored Henry and the Whitney Straights, she felt having someone young and attractive like herself at home that Christmas made the holiday much more enjoyable. After so much stress and seeing so much hardship, she really appreciated New York's most eligible bachelor's humor and light banter. Unlike her fiancé, what difficulties James faced, he was able to keep from her. In front of her, James deliberately appeared even when under pressure, without a care in the world.

Until Josie's mother intervened, the bachelor thought he was making good progress with the object of his affection. Delighted by his interest and finding him far more appealing than the "penniless pauper", as Claire now referred to her daughter's intended, without subtlety she did her best to 'encourage' Josie and James' relationship. A fuming Josie didn't bother to hide her anger. Much to her mother's horror, publicly, she made it clear that if Claire ever tried to 'push' them together, she'd never invite New York's most eligible bachelor back to the house!

For his part, James thought things went better than expected. He had a fabulous Christmas. So taken with New York's most celebrated debutante, he thought his time with her, in her loving home, made it the best holiday he had ever had. For once, his interest in another human being inhibited his own selfish nature. Even though he noted the beautiful Claire was more sophisticated and polished than her daughter, he had no interest in flirting with her, although he sensed she would have enjoyed it. James had never before been affected by a girl like this; it was almost as if he cared about her feelings more than his own. When he finally returned home Christmas Day, Bentley noted a difference. Knowing his boss exceptionally well and a good judge of character to boot, the houseman asked his master as he shaved his face, "Are you in love, sir?"

Clearly surprised by the question, but not reacting entirely against the notion, the playboy businessman half amused, half confused, half just curious, and for once not imperious or dismissive, queried, "Why do you ask?"

Pausing to think for a moment in order to articulate his views best, the houseman offered, "I can't explain it, sir, except there has been a change and knowing you, I can only think it must be a lady."

James snickered. Nonetheless, he spent most of the rest of the day and night drinking brandy and wondering if Bentley was right.

* * *

Despite having a grand time with James, what made Josie's Christmas most enjoyable was two loving calls from Charles and his special present which she waited until Christmas Day to open. Inside, the package he had sent to her, wrapped in a fine, red silk scarf, he had placed a most beautiful, delicate gold bracelet that he had commissioned a native artist to design for her. The bracelet was done with the highest quality gold that had been mined in Oklahoma years before and came in a rosewood box that he wrote had belonged to his father's family. The initials T.E.D. were intricately inlaid in satinwood into the design on the box. He wrote the soft, malleable metal was 24-karat. The clasp was intricately fashioned and extremely elegant. Josie thought it was the most graceful piece of jewelry she had ever seen. But more importantly, she appreciated that despite his troubles, he still managed to send her such special Christmas gifts. In his note he explained he sent the bracelet because one day many months before when they had been looking at jewelry just for fun, she told him she hardly had any bracelets she liked. It meant so much to her that he understood her taste and thoughtfully remembered what she needed.

Josie wrote to Charles that she wouldn't take the bracelet off until he returned. As she admiringly looked at it, she expected to keep it on even afterwards.

One thing perturbed the socialite during the holiday. After Henry left, her father became noticeably distracted. When confronted, he insisted everything was all right, his health and business was fine, just tougher than before. When pressed, Albert explained that more of the banks that had borrowed money from his organization now were in financial trouble. He admitted he wasn't sure if several even might go bankrupt. In addition, he had discovered one of his employees surreptitiously had played the market with his institution's money. To replace the funds the man lost in stocks, her father had been forced to take two and a half million dollars out the Baxter-Brownes' personal accounts. But he reassured both Claire and Josie not to worry unduly. Albert remained optimistic that the market would recover in the New Year and with it, the economy. He reminded his daughter and wife that just yesterday, in his weekly address to the nation, President Hoover had reiterated his belief that the economy fundamentally was sound.

For his part, Josie's godfather was determined to start the New Year the right way.

* * *

Henry Jay planned a big New Year's Eve party. His invitations were addressed to "*My fellow former millionaires.*" Henry called his New Years' Ball the Last Great Bash. It proved to be in more ways than one.

For one last night, revelers forgot what a miserable year 1929 had turned out to be. Once again, there was dancing and laughter throughout the celebrated mansion. Every room had been perfectly staged and lit by a Ziegfeld's *Follies* crew. Henry served the finest caviar and piped champagne through the marble fountain in his courtyard as well as several other fountains he had installed for the party in other rooms. James thought it was the grandest party he had ever attended. Josie just wished Charles could have been there to enjoy the Ottoman Empire themed-costumed ball. Colorful tents covered the Persian carpeted pathway leading up to Henry's home. Inside, twenty sword throwers, sixty belly dancers and the Arab influenced music and games entertained the hundreds of guests. Costumed servers offered Turkish and Arab delicacies, cigarettes, and water pipes. Dimly lit, tented rooms and gauzy curtains created an added sense of Eastern mystery to the mansion that Henry had decorated especially with original furnishings from some of the most opulent palaces in Istanbul.

While Henry came as a Sultan, Josie wore an exquisite red silk embroidered Moroccan- inspired costume by a former Ziegfield *Follies'* designer. She sexily draped the scarf Charles sent her around her face and hair. Geraldine informed everyone she was the Harem Guard while James dressed as an Arab Prince. As he fenced with J.D. Rockefeller, who came as a Sheik, he impressed Josie with his 17th century authentic, carved sword and other moves.

The following morning, as his guests slept soundly in their beds or in those belonging to the revelers with whom they left, Henry surveyed the morning after mess, and wanted out. Down and slightly hung over from his New Year's Eve bash, he tried to go for a walk. He hoped the fresh air would help. But outside, the heavy, gray sky just made him less happy. His mood black, arthritis exacerbated by the damp cold, life suddenly didn't seem fun anymore for the raconteur who had seen and done everything.

With no wife, no children, his godchild grown, and no more business deals or other objectives, he no longer saw a point. He couldn't even get excited about planning another fete – he had done so many already, he thought, what was there left to do and who of interest was there left to invite? Then, as he evaluated the last few parties, he thought of all those missing – the casualties of the Crash, and the victims of the Grim Reaper. For some time, he had stopped reading the obituary column because it never failed to include someone around his age that he had known. He thought gloomily, his once limitlessly expanding circle of social guests was getting smaller in terms of quality. This morning, he came to the realization that the youth he attracted to his parties couldn't make his joints ache less or his eyes see without aid.

Depressed, Henry returned to his home to hibernate in his library. But even with a magnifying glass, there was nothing that he wanted to read, nothing that gripped him. He tried calling the Baxter-Brownes, but they were all out. He showered, shaved, felt the cold, clean water splash on his face one last time, listened to his favorite Bessie Smith recording, drank two glasses of his best whiskey and leisurely smoked a cigar he had saved for a special occasion. With a steady hand, he wrote a final message then felt the cold, hard trigger of the Colt Revolver his father had given him so many years before. Seconds later, Henry Jay took a slow, deep breath and let it all end.

At eleven thirty in the morning, his valet found him slumped over his desk with a cigar in his mouth and the revolver at his side. On the floor, his 1930 social planner that held so many names and functions had one final entry:

I am and everything I stand for is an anachronism.

For weeks afterwards, his friends asked why. Some thought he had been depressed about his health and the aging process. He had given up playing tennis at the New York Racquet and Tennis Club that fall because of achy joints. A week before New Years, a doctor told him he'd have to give up cigars – to which he replied he'd rather die. Others speculated he had suffered irreversible losses from the Crash and couldn't face curbing his lifestyle. Albert, who was the executor of Henry's estate, knew these were not the real reasons.

Yet, even he thought, in a way, Henry was a victim of the Crash. Through his decadent lifestyle, the old codger represented all that was excessive and good in the roaring twenties. The spirit of the times had changed when the market sank. The coming down of the mighty Dow signaled an end to the age of debauchery. With many of his friends ruined, the streets filled with the helpless and no end in sight, life for Henry Jay, could never again be a long series of endless parties sipping champagne while dancing with pretty, flirty girls who came to his gatherings without a care in the world. For the debonair bon vivant, summer was gone and he had awoken to a winter that was dark, cold, and heartless.

In his will, Henry left his goddaughter, Josie, a few token sentimental pieces as keepsakes. His art collection, furnishings and voluminous library went to the Metropolitan Museum and New York Public Library respectively. Servants were well rewarded as well. However, the bulk of his estate went to form a charity to help the needy and support a number of good causes, including some of Josie's. Not thinking his goddaughter ever would need his money, Henry had changed his will to reflect the times three days before his demise.

The papers printed a lengthy obituary on the colorful socialite and philanthropist Henry Jay. They cited heart attack as the cause of death. Albert's generous payment to the coroner ensured the death certificate misnomer.

* * *

Josie took Henry's death very hard. She blamed herself for pushing him to visit the poor with her when she knew he found it disheartening. She also was sorry she hadn't spent more time with him. Although as usual he had joined the Baxter-Brownes for the Christmas holiday and they had attended his New Year's Ball, Josie felt she had been so pre-occupied since Charles had left, first with her morose state and then with her charity work, James, and holiday activities. She knew she had not been there for her godfather as she should have been. She hadn't noticed just how miserable he was. She wondered, did he really hide the extent of his desperation that well or was she merely so self-involved that she had been oblivious. Her letter to Charles reflected her agony.

Charles was saddened to learn of Henry Jay's death because he had respected and truly liked the old codger. He also was deeply concerned about Josie. He could tell from her letter that she was morbidly depressed. He felt terrible that he wasn't able to be there physically to comfort her. He tried to put his feelings on paper but knew as much as his heartfelt words could help somewhat, they were inadequate to fill the grief she now felt.

Charles stayed up all night writing and re-writing a response to Josie. Nothing he wrote expressed his emotions fully and provided the solace he knew she desperately needed. As the sun rose in the east, he finally sealed what he had written knowing it was more important to get a response out to her quickly. No matter how much time he spent, he could never get it perfectly right. Despite his fears, when Josie received his sympathetic note, she phoned Charles immediately to tell him it had helped.

* * *

The day after Josie received Charles' letter, on a crisp, cold clear morning, she got another piece of mail that lifted her spirits.

In a fine, pale blue, delicate envelop that had the scent of flowers, was a hand painted card from Rebecca. Josie was delighted to learn that her friend was enjoying her time in Europe. Although she hoped Rebecca could find someone better than the obese, chauvinistic Count Nasogrande whom she recalled from her European tours, she also knew her friend could do worse based upon the descriptions of her choices thus far.

Easy going, Rebecca found the Count's exaggerated mannerisms quite funny. The way he gestured grandly and spun tales of his prowess endeared him to her. For his part, he enjoyed playing the teacher. He found her like most Americans, lacking in European sophistication. To him, this was a bonus because he could train her as he wished so she would become his ideal wife. He dressed her to his taste and had her learn the intricacies of his household and his quirks so she would be able to manage everything, as he desired. She learned to cook his favorite Italian food and allowed him to spoon-feed her delectables he thought she should have. She never protested or complained and above all else, she didn't show him up.

Three months after they met, on the infamous day that the United States' Congress approved the Smoot-Hawley Tariff Act, that taxed imported items, Rebecca and Nasogrande were engaged. Although he still fantasized about Josie and frequently asked his fiancée about her friend, he was perfectly happy to marry Rebecca. In Nasogrande's ideal world, Rebecca, his wife, would worship him even though at some time in the future when her friend, Josie, visited them, he would seduce her. He could think of nothing more satisfying than in having children with both women. The existence of Charles Blakesley never interfered with this fantasy. As a great Italian lover in his own mind, Nasogrande was certain, if given another opportunity, he would blow away the pipsqueak American boy, as he was sure he must be if Josie controlled him as he envisioned. The Count couldn't believe any American girl would choose another man over him.

Rebecca was just thrilled to have found someone socially acceptable who satisfied her mother and enabled her not to worry anymore. She expected a man to take care of her. So, even though Nasogrande was arrogant and overly opinionated to the point of being controlling, she didn't mind because she didn't have to assume any role other than that of a traditional wife.

With Rebecca engaged, Mrs. Stanley returned to Boston to sell their remaining possessions for at least a portion of the dowry Nasogrande expected. She was extremely concerned that even after her Aunt contributed as much as she could, they still were short of the amount promised. She went to several banks for loans. Rejected by each one, she didn't know where to turn. She pawned what she could, but she remained short on the cash amount. Noticing James' picture in the paper, she remembered how generous he had been after his husband's death. Desperate, Mrs. Stanley called him.

James readily agreed to meet Rebecca's mother in New York. After taking a good look at her, he offered half the sum she wanted in exchange for two nights with her. Desperate, she agreed to do whatever he wanted. When he had had enough, he passed her on to Garrett Goldman for a third evening. Needing cash, Mrs. Stanley complied with little resistance.

Rebecca missed her mother terribly while she was away. She knew immediately something was wrong when Mrs. Stanley returned, but because her mother was so careful not to reveal the true reason, Rebecca remained oblivious. Handing over the money to Nasogrande, Mrs. Stanley requested they marry shortly because she claimed she was concerned that news of her daughter's close relationship with the Count would soil her reputation otherwise.

Looking forward to his wedding night, Nasogrande raised no objections.

The evening before his wedding day, a friend told the Count that one of the wealthiest debutantes of 1930, Woolworth heiress

Barbara Hutton, was coming to his area of Italy and was keen on securing a title. Thinking of what *her* money could do for him, the Count quickly cooled on his fiancée. Hastily putting off the wedding, Nasogrande looked for excuses to get out of his marriage to Rebecca. When he heard from a British international houseguest that the Stanleys were really broke, he had his excuse. Although he discarded Rebecca, Nasogrande found no need to return the money her mother had given him for the nuptials.

He informed Mrs. Stanley that *his* reputation had suffered by her trying to hoodwink him. He yelled as he threw their trunks out the windows in a tantrum, "You have insulted me! Taken me for a fool! Passing your worthless daughter onto to me as an American heiress – and ruining my good name by linking it with yours!" Waving his arms around madly as he shooed them away, he screamed, "Get out of my house!"

Rebecca was in tears as they drove away. Mrs. Stanley filed claims against Nasogrande with the local courts, but she soon learned that as a foreigner and a woman without means at that, her chances of recovering the money in an Italian judicial system where even the natives rarely won cases without graft, were less than zero.

Two months later, the Stanleys returned to Boston as second-class passengers on a second rate ship. If Mrs. Stanley's Aunt hadn't sold a diamond brooch, rumored to have belonged to Alexandra the last Czarina of Russia, they would have traveled steerage.

When Rebecca and her mother arrived back in the United States, they found themselves dejected as well as broke.

* * *

Just a few minutes before sunrise, the day after the Stanleys returned stateside, Josie stood shivering outside the gates leading to Henry Jay's New York townhouse. Tears streamed down her face as she thought about her godfather and all the wonderful things they had done together. She tried to prepare herself for the fact that in a few short hours, the wrecking ball would descend and there would be nothing left of his magnificent Richard Morris Hunt designed showcase but her memories. As she ran her fingers fondly across the lines of the ornate iron gate, the pained look on her face left no doubt as to her emotional state. Taking pity on her, a sympathetic guard let her in to take one last look at the place she had always loved.

Josie gasped when she looked at what was left and what they had done to the place. Gone were all the antiques – the furnishings and even the fittings. The walls were marked where pictures once hung, the molding carelessly bashed in places, fireplace mantles sold, removed. The hardwood floors with intricate marquetry, always polished twice a day during Henry's life, scraped, scratched, scuffed and worn – as if forgotten. The grand double circular staircase was the only ornamentation left. The air musty, Josie sneezed from the crumbling plaster and coating of dust covering what was left.

Choking on her words from emotion, she whispered, "Henry, I am glad you're not here to see this." She doubted this is what he had had in mind when he re-drafted his will, but there was nothing she could do but mourn his passing and the state of affairs.

Only a week before, the largest auction in the history of New York had been held within these once grand walls and everything that could be stripped from the place had been put under the auctioneer's gavel. She knew her godfather's intention had been to help as many of the unfortunate as he could with his estate. But she hardly thought that the demolition of his fabulous townhouse was what he had had in mind. Unfortunately, due to the charity boards' eagerness to liquidate all of Henry's assets, after auctioning off what remained of the non-museum quality pieces they sold his home to the highest bidder. Initially, several of the charities had considered using the expansive pile for themselves, taking over the choicest rooms. Squabbles broke out amongst those who wanted it as a rectory and others who saw it as more useful as the offices for a girl's school. But after reviewing the heating, utility and maintenance bills, none of the groups thought they could afford the property's upkeep even if they split the costs. So the groups decided to sell Henry's mansion and divide the proceeds.

Because of the dismal economy, for months Henry Jay's architectural masterpiece had remained on the market without any serious interest. The property wasn't helped by the rumor that the place where Henry died was haunted. Local boys started using the vacant premise for target practice, smashing the windows with rocks. Others defaced the walls, writing of their misery, love, or just their names for all to see. The homeless began staking out places around the empty mansion. Wind ripped through the broken windows, slamming doors; the dampness warped the floors, making the once grand edifice – cold, uninhabitable. Citing it as a magnet for troublemakers and undesirables, which would bring down the prestige and safety of the neighborhood, the grand dames of the Upper East side put pressure on the charities first to hire guards and eventually just to get rid of the eye sore.

When no one but those whom nobody wanted showed any interest in the building, the charity boards finally made a deal with a dubious property developer to demolish the place and split the land value upon sale. They rationalized their decision with the claim that they knew that one day the huge one block parcel would be worth millions; but for the foreseeable future, they couldn't even afford to keep paying the guards to watch it. Josie and her parents didn't believe this logic; they thought it was a cover-up, a dirty deal that had passed due to substantial money transfers to certain members of the board. Unfortunately, although they had their suspicions, they had no proof.

Josie wrote letters to the *New York Post* about the artistic merit and irreplaceable craftsmanship of the building – but to no avail. She tried to get her father to hire a lawyer to sue the boards for mismanagement, but he was certain that legally they had done nothing wrong and there was nothing in Henry's will to prevent the action by the charity boards.

When Josie pushed, reluctantly, Albert reminded his daughter that times were tough. There were so many were jobless, homeless, and increasingly even undernourished people. Preservation even during the boom had been a difficult task. Josie knew only too well of so many of the grand homes that once lined 5th Avenue that had been brought low by the wrecking ball in the 1920's. Even before the Crash, the institution of the "income tax", increased property taxes, the escalating cost of maintenance and household staff wages and the ease of apartment building life had made the mansions largely white elephants.

After the sale of Alice Vanderbilt's palatial mansion, her daughter, Gertrude Vanderbilt Whitney had only managed to save the front gate from the wrecking ball. Even this was accepted very reluctantly by the Conservancy Gardens. The Metropolitan Museum also took merely one magnificent brownstone fireplace from the many in Gertrude's uncle, William K. Vanderbilt's place. These properties were the exceptions. Countless others had been demolished without fanfare or any fragment remaining of what had been lost. Josie cried at the architectural and historical destruction.

The socialite had so many fabulous memories of parties and gay gatherings at these beautiful opulent palaces with their antique furnishings and fittings mostly from the homes of 18th century European aristocrats. She loved the history. She adored the beauty and the romance of the past. She could spend hours lounging, dancing, dreaming about those who had spent time living within the walls. She loved the stories about them, where each room came from, who had walked through the doors and corridors before, sat and slept under the ceilings, loved and lost, lived and won, died and gave birth among the walls. In addition, she knew few could mimic the detailed artistry of the past and fewer could even afford it if they wanted that fabulous look.

Josie couldn't understand how others could not see what was so obvious to her – the precious value in preservation, especially as so many of these buildings had already been demolished and replaced in her short lifetime. Despite the financial realities, she felt strongly that preserving culture and heritage were critical to making New York City the kind of place she happily called home. She feared if people like her didn't do something, the city would become an ugly, unplanned, modern place with no character, surrounded by a suburban ghetto of practically built, uninspired architecture that periodically would be knocked down only to be reconstructed in slightly updated, but similarly unattractive ways. She thought the charm of Europe largely came from the preservation and incorporation of the ancient buildings into the countryside and cityscape.

Josie never loved Henry's home more than now in the last hour of its existence. Walking through the silent, darkened, empty hallways, her footsteps loudly echoed on the distressed hardwood floors. In the ballroom, she paused. Slowly she ran her fingers along a solitary remaining Corinthian pillar, then a fragment of a royal red, silk drape. For a moment, she was lost in time. She heard the music playing again, the sound of the parties of the past, clinking glasses, Henry's chuckling laugh, the whiff of cigar smoke, the jingling noise of the crystal chandeliers vibrating from the dancing, the reckless abandon, the fragrant scent of expensive perfume, lightness, beauty, then silence again. The haunting spirits driven out by a cold gust of wind that ripped through the broken windows, sent shivers down her spine. But even in its emptiness, perhaps because of its barren emptiness and doomed state, the grandeur and elegance of the bare bones, the spaciousness and flow of the design, the years of life that the structure had born, it became clear to Josie and made her appreciate the architectural treasure even more.

Before closing the door to the past, 1929's most celebrated debutante lingered in her godfather's entrance hall. She thought how ironic it was that the sweeping double circular staircase's exquisite 200-year-old banister that had been spared from smelting for Napoleon's cannon now was to be felled for scrap metal. Although Josie knew there was nothing she could do for Henry's place, she vowed she would not let this happen to another home of this magnitude again.

One week after Henry Jay's derelict townhouse was razed, Josie accidentally found herself staring at the site from across the street. Evening had descended early; the moon brilliantly glowed on the ruins. Josie tried to come to terms with what was left. The cornerstones, a few pillars, and part of the imposing limestone doorway remained surrounded by rubble and the prominent gates. As terrible as it was to see, she found beauty in the illuminated fragmented remains. They seemed almost artistic, like the prints she had seen of Mateo Ricci's Versailles-styled Summer Palace in Peking that the allies had pillaged and burned in the middle of the last century. What remained was an artistic treasure. She ran home to get her camera to take a few photos to send them to Charles.

That night, as she wrote to her love, for the first time since she informed him of Henry's death, she was at last able to write about her godfather. She thought back to her godfather's funeral, the media circus and public interest after his death. Unlike Rebecca's father's passing, Henry Jay's had been a celebrated event. Everyone who was anyone had turned up for the funeral at St. Thomas'. Many, who had come early to get a seat found there was standing room left only. Josie had had heard later that Mrs. Whitney Straight and the Ashleys even had been kept outside the front of the church because of the overflow. James had ensured his place by taking the pre-caution of getting Claire's blessing to escort Josie to the funeral. For once, despite all his best efforts to cheer her up, he seemed unable to do anything that pleased her.

Quite a few monogrammed handkerchiefs had been used during Albert's touching eulogy. But along with Henry, the gathered had mourned the passing of his extravagant lifestyle. Few had doubted anyone would ever again throw a party quite like the flamboyant Henry regularly did.

For weeks, the papers had run stories about Henry's colorful personal life and spirit. The editors had known any salacious tidbit could be used to sell copies. Josie had been disgusted by the investigative reporting and had written an editorial chastising the yellow journalism the day her godfather was laid to rest. But it had been too late. Henry had become a public figure in the mind of the masses – one that they could vicariously live through, of keen interest and fair game to attack.

For their part, the charities who had inherited the bulk of the wealthy man's estate initially fed the media frenzy believing the public interest would lead to higher prices for his personal affects. Despite the Baxter-Brownes' protests, the boards had even opted to open his house first to the media and later the public for a tour of what was to be auctioned. The mob scene that had resulted necessitated doubling the police force on duty and nearly led to a riot.

New Yorkers of all stations had jumped at *their* chance to glimpse the private domain of the beautiful set. For the first time, they had found themselves on the other side of the imposing gate as invited guests. On the appointed day, despite sleet, over 12,000 had lined up before the doors even opened. They had come from all walks of life –the young, old, from doctors to teachers to parlor maids, but mostly the unemployed. Vinnie Graves had brought his whole crew. By evening, close to 50,000 had walked through, but unfortunately, there had been many more left waiting. Those remaining outside, many who had stood quietly, patiently all day, had turned violent when the guards, who wanted to go home after the long day, had shut the door in their faces. Destitute, desperate, eager for a Hollywood-like experience, they had raged with anger as they realized that they had been duped.

From the sanctity of her parents' home, Josie had heard the police sirens blaring as ward after ward rushed to the scene to get the mob under control. Despite her mother's protests, the curious girl had wanted to see first-hand what was happening. As the sirens continued, Josie had defied her mother, who outright forbade her from going. She had raced on foot, uptown, stopping near the scene only where police barricades physically separated a large group of tightly packed, curious, gawking upper east-siders from the masses. She had not needed to get any closer to watch what had unfolded.

Much as Josie had not wanted the rabble in her godfather's house, the police brutality that ensued had been more than she could bear. She had found herself parting with her class to sympathize with the underprivileged. She had shuddered as she watched innocent people, caught between the raging and the law, physically assaulted, angrily punched, kicked, beaten down, despite their pleas and protests. As she turned around in horror to galvanize the gathered group of others like herself who had come to see what was happening and to put pressure on the police to stop, she found herself quite alone on the street. Content that the law enforcers effectively were dispersing the protesters 'who didn't belong in their neighborhood,' many simply went home. They hadn't wanted to be witnesses to the carnage. They had preferred not to know!

Josie slowly walked away from the scene, mortified at the inhumane cruelty she had seen and the gross indifference. She had felt raw inside and tried to help a few of the wounded that had been left by the fleeing. To them she offered apologies and soft words of encouragement. She understood why so many had voiced their anger about the two-tiered system of justice and wanted revenge and in her dark, soulful eyes, they felt her compassion. That night, her eyes defiant, as Josie passionately discussed what happened with friends and family, she had refused to back down in her assertions that attitudes had to change. With the exception of Geraldine, no one had agreed with her.

A few weeks later, when Claire got wind through James that Josie had written a number of pieces making her political and social views known, she outright forbade her daughter from submitting them. Refusing to be cowed, 1929's most celebrated debutante once again defied her socially ambitious mother. Although she didn't know it, her mother was right that her activities would affect her reputation in ways she didn't fully understand. In fact, Josie's activism caught the attention of some very important people. Unfortunately, they were not the ones she had hoped to affect.

While failing to ignite the passion amongst her peers, her views were noted with wariness in Washington. Since the 1919-1920 'Red Scare,' J. Edgar Hoover, the Director of the Bureau of Investigation, had been watching out for socialist sympathizers and collecting data on them for a time when the information would become useful to him. By the fall of 1930, the pugnacious Director had quite a substantial secret file on socialite writer Josephine Baxter-Browne.

* * *

Like Josie, Charles was making his mark in the nation's capitol. Realizing that autumn, that the ranchers and farmers in his area would not survive the winter of 1930 without help, he took it upon himself to save not only the Blakesleys, but their neighbors as well. Fighting the Oklahoma culture of self-reliance, after winning his Uncle and Aunt over – which was no small fete, Charles organized his neighbors to lobby the government for aid. He traveled across the state on a petition drive, met with dozens of reporters to make sure the news got out that the state farmers and ranchers were hard working but truly faced extinction. Eventually, in frustration, he went all the way to Washington D.C., where he met with Congressmen and even a representative of President Hoover's, to "prevent the total ruination of the cattle industry and farmers of Oklahoma."

Bringing back Senators and representatives of the Administration to his home state, for a tour of the devastation, Charles took the politicians to the worst sites. After visiting the once flourishing, now abandoned towns, he made sure the officials saw the desolate countryside with its stunted, wilted crops, unfit for consumption and the starving animals. They reported emaciated horses, hogs, cattle, even the family dogs looked far too weak to walk let alone run. Abandoned homesteads that resembled tombstones served as empty reminders – testimonials to the broken lives that once dwelled within and believed in the American Dream. Not sparing them, Charles showed the politicians the worst of the survivors – the ones certainly who would not make it through the winter without aid.

But as Charles suspected, it was the sight of the children, many whose eyes popped out of their hollow, hungry faces that led to the appropriation of emergency funds. With loans for seed, fertilizer and feed, and a government agreement to purchase the culls that were the worst of the cattle, Charles wrote Josie that he was optimistic that there was hope for the cattlemen and farmers and that she could start planning their wedding again after the Spring planting in 1931.

* * *

While Charles was busy saving his family's ranch and his neighbors' land, James continued to lobby Washington for his own interests and further cut costs at his factories at the expense of his workers. He also consolidated his interests in the steel industry and branched out into a number of lucrative deals with the Morgan brothers. As James and Henry Morgan sat in the cunning businessman's office in Pittsburgh, going through the latest set of reports from around the country, James' delighted in the news that commodity prices for corn and wheat were continuing to slide and beef was at its lowest level since 1899. His mood quickly changed when his friend informed him that Charles had just managed to increase the government subsidy to the farm belt as a result.

James ranted to Henry that he advocated pure capitalism and social Darwinism. As far as he was concerned, if the ranchers and farmers weren't clever enough to manipulate prices on their own, there was no reason for the government to bail them out. Having done some research on the topic, the clever businessman pointed out to his banking friend that over the long term it was in the financial interest of the United States to let South America take over livestock and farming production since the climate and natural resources there provided more grazing opportunities and a longer growing season. As usual, patriotism and people's lives were less important to the businessman than his bottom line. James feared any agricultural subsidies eventually would mean higher taxes for his class and less tax breaks for his industry.

After Henry left, James stayed in Pittsburgh for several more days to work out how to best protect his interests. He looked forward to getting back to New York City but a call from a reliable government source that was on his payroll made him further delay his return. James cursed when he was informed that Congress would soon raise the income tax rate from 25% to a whopping 63% and implement a 13.75% tax on corporations. With the news that estate taxes were about to be doubled, James sighed with relief that his uncle had already passed away. To avoid the new "2 percent" tax on all bank checks, the wily businessman ordered his managers to start paying employees in cash. Nonetheless, he had the 2% tax amount deducted from their salaries as a convenience charge for the hard currency.

When he finally left Pittsburgh, road delays caused James' trip back to New York City to take substantially longer than he had expected. Sexually frustrated after finding nothing of interest in

Pittsburgh, and very irritated by the journey, he didn't bother stopping at home first. Instead, he ordered Bentley to drop him off at one of his most fertile hunting grounds. Scouring the famous tea-room for a bedroom date, he was surprised and delighted to spot two attractive socialites in the corner. He was thrilled to discover upon closer inspection that one was Josie. Much to his shock, her slightly plump but very pretty companion was none other than Geraldine Ashley! If he hadn't been so interested in 1929's most celebrated debutante and her friend hadn't made it unmistakably clear that she despised him, considering how good she now looked, he would have actually considered a fling.

Waiting for the opportune moment to intercept his prey, James asked to be seated in the meantime at a table where he could over-hear their conversation, but would remain unobserved by Josie and her companion. In no rush, he leisurely ordered a drink. As he listened to their conversation, he thought, it must have been love that had led to the transformation of the artist's looks.

* * *

Geraldine and Josie sat at the most desirable table in the Rotunda of the Pierre Hotel discussing their activism and charity work as they enjoyed their afternoon tea. The girls had been so pre-occupied with their own conversation they hadn't even once looked up from their table to notice the other diners.

Knowing Josie adored scones with clotted cream, the artist handed over her portion to her friend. Responding in kind, Josie offered Geraldine her cream cheese and smoked salmon sand-wiches. As they savored the food, the conversation turned to love. Josie shared Charles' latest letter with her friend, describing the life he looked forward to having with her once they were married. Geraldine thought it was the most moving love letter she ever had heard, aside from a 15th Century monk's last message to his wife. She told Josie after hearing his wife had been murdered the man had given himself to God. Nonetheless, everyday of his life, he wrote her a letter, as he had done whenever they had been apart during her lifetime. At the age of eighty-six, half blind and suffering from all sorts of diseases and ailments, he used what energy was left in his fading body to write his last letter of love to his beloved. The Folio had been bound with an introduction by another monk who claimed to have known the author and was so touched by his commitment to his deceased wife that he had preserved the evidence.

Geraldine had come across the letters in a Folio she found in the library of an Italian monastery just outside Venice several summers before. Threatened by rising floods, she had helped the prelate relocate the most precious collections. The Folio lay buried behind stacks of books and manuscripts in an uncatalogued section that had been forgotten for centuries. It wasn't valued as anything of significance since it failed to pertain to the Father, Son, or Holy Ghost. But to Geraldine, it was the most precious find.

Moved, Josie said, "Death cannot kill love."

"In some cases, it even strengthens it," replied Geraldine. As she ordered another sandwich, she acknowledged, "Of course, I prefer to live and enjoy the love we share right now."

Agreeing, Josie said, "Make the most of it."

"That's why I'm going with Evelyn as she lectures on the road," explained her friend.

Josie asked, "Where's she going?"

"Wherever they pay her," replied Geraldine laughing.

"That could be anywhere." In awe at the woman's success, she said, "She's built up an incredible following."

Geraldine smiled proudly. "I know. But we're just going across the country – mostly in the Midwest and then on to the Continent for a few months."

"That's a long trip," said Josie downcast as she realized she wouldn't see her friend for quite a while.

"In total, probably six months," acknowledged Geraldine. Putting her hand over Josie's she said, "I'm afraid it'll be hard for you to be in touch with me because we're going to be constantly on the move; she's got lectures booked in a different city almost every day when we're not in transit. But I'll send postcards."

"I'll miss you," said Josie seriously.

"I know, sweetie," replied Geraldine as she squeezed Josie's hand. "I'm really going to miss you too, and I hate leaving you with Charles away but Evelyn doesn't think she's got much time left. You know, she really needs me."

"You should spend all the time you can with her," said Josie emotionally as she hugged her friend. "I'm being selfish because you're my support and my dearest friend."

Geraldine said, "You know I feel the same way about you, Josie. But I keep telling myself it's just like the summer in the old days when you'd go to Europe and I'd be in Southampton and Newport. Except this time, you get to stay stateside."

"Don't rub it in!" replied Josie in mock anger.

"Just keep in mind, before we get to Europe that we've got many small towns to go through this side of the Atlantic," said Geraldine laughing. "You think Des Moines, Iowa is a hoot or Columbus, Ohio?"

"You might be pleasantly surprised," replied Josie with laughter in her eyes. Tapping her friend lightheartedly, she said, "You know you even could like it so much you won't want to leave."

"It's possible," said Geraldine skeptically. Then as she took out of her hip flask and poured its contents into their tea. She said, "But I doubt you'll get rid of me that easily."

Clinking her glass against Geraldine's, Josie toasted in jest, "Here's to trying." Choking on the strong, disgusting combination, she sputtered after taking just one sip, "What did you put in this?"

Geraldine laughed as she replied, "You don't want to know. But in a minute it won't matter because we'll both be flying."

Shaking her head, Josie said, "What am I going to do while you're gone?"

"Write lots of letters to Charles and hopefully have fun yourself! Carpe diem! Just promise me that you'll go out and laugh while I'm gone." While Geraldine reached for her handbag to dig out her spare flask to keep the mood jolly, James made the most of the situation.

"Don't worry Geri, I'll make sure she doesn't miss you at all," said James as he swooped down, kissing a stunned Josie on the cheek.

Geraldine narrowed her eyes in response and clasped her flask so tightly her fingers turned white.

Not giving Geraldine the chance to say no, James pulled over his chair from the nearby table and plopped himself down very close to Josie.

Irritated and not concerned about being rude herself, Geraldine said, "We were actually having a private conversation."

Turning to Josie for confirmation, he said bowing as he got up to leave, "My apologies. But I won't go until Miss Baxter-Browne agrees, barring her fiancé's return, that she will accompany me to the Crystal Ball."

Looking at Geraldine, Josie said laughing, "You wanted me to have fun while you're gone!"

Glowering, Geraldine replied, "Alone!"

Smiling at James, sweetly, Josie said, "Geri doesn't think I should agree."

"With all due respect to Miss Ashley, I wasn't asking her," stated James. Taking Josie's hand in his to kiss it, he said, "I promise we'll have a good time." Addressing Geraldine, he vowed, "I will be a gentleman."

After taking a big sip from her flask, Geraldine threw her arms up in exasperation. Her gesture suggested, "I don't like this, but do what you want."

After going between Geraldine and James several times, Josie finally consented with the promise he would make a substantial donation to the charity of Geraldine's choice

When he heard the sum she demanded, James said he understood what she meant when she said, "It's going to cost you."

Geraldine rolled in her seat laughing. As she raised her hip flask to Josie before downing the remnants, she thought maybe she didn't have to worry about her friend after all.

James was relieved Geraldine said she was leaving with Evelyn in a few days. As far as he was concerned, it couldn't be soon enough. His mood did not improve when he got home that night and found out he had to go to Boston for a business meeting.

* * *

CHAPTER XVII

Since Thomas' death, James had developed an aversion to Boston. He only went to the city when it absolutely was necessary and then he stayed as short a time as possible. After having completed the tedious business that took him back to the place he most loathed, on a Friday afternoon he found himself stranded there because of a late spring snowstorm. When it became apparent that he was stuck in the city, James decided to make the most out of a bad situation. After he realized he had left his gloves on the train on the way up, he decided to go to Filenes's to get a new pair. Unbeknownst to him, due to renovations that the company hoped to get done over the weekend, the store closed early. Never one to pass up a thrill and always figuring out a way of getting what he wanted, the cunning businessman managed to sneak past a group of exiting workers and shoppers. But much to his chagrin, despite his efforts, no one was left in the men's department to sell him any gloves.

James' mood improved when he saw a lone figure left in the store tidying up the cosmetics section. As he leaned over the counter, he was delighted to face a very pretty petite brunette with rosy red, cupid lips.

Her name was Rebecca Stanley and James was very happy to see her again.

Rebecca for her part was mortified. She had made the difficult adjustment from debutante to shop girl. With some effort she had become used to working full days. She even had come to terms with being treated poorly by wealthy customers. But on the rare occasions when Rebecca found herself on the wrong side of the counter facing someone who had known her before the Crash, she wanted to die. It was so terribly humiliating for her. Now, to see the man who was in her old social circle and who had financially donated to her as a charity case was more than she could take. Fleeing, she darted as fast as she could.

It wasn't fast enough.

In a few strides, James caught up to Rebecca and pulled her into him. Tears already were streaming down her face. Holding her close to him, James stroked her hair as he said reassuringly, "It's all right. Everything is going to be fine now."

After helping Rebecca lock up, James ushered her out. Once outside, as the cold air hit her face, she calmed down. He handed her his monogrammed handkerchief and gave her his arm. After ascertaining that she was not in contact with Josie and Geraldine anymore because she was too embarrassed to tell them what she was doing, he made her feel desirable.

First, James offered to take her shopping. He took her to all the best boutiques whose windows she had passed dozens of times but whose doors she never thought she'd be able to enter again. Whatever she wanted, he purchased. In the end she picked out over a dozen new outfits, an ermine trimmed coat and a gold necklace with a charm. She never questioned her benefactor's generosity. Having spent almost her entire life believing a man would always provide for her as her father had done until recently, she was perfectly happy to believe the fantasy could still be true. To think otherwise was too painful for her.

Rebecca was ecstatic when James invited her to accompany him to dinner and a movie. In a remarkable display of insensitivity, he suggested that they see *Bottoms Up*, a new release that spoofed the desperate times with stocks selling as cheap as groceries. But she didn't mind, the young shop girl was delighted to have a date.

James told the naïve girl he thought it would be a late evening. He suggested she phone her mother and tell her she was staying over at one of her co-workers' places because of the storm. When Rebecca informed him that Mrs. Stanley was out of town visiting a sick relative, James smiled to himself. He thought Boston won't be so bad after all.

Over dinner, James made sure the petite girl had a lot to drink. When she realized she was getting very tipsy, she tried to stop him from topping up her glass.

"I don't often drink," she explained.

He replied, "I can tell."

"I don't have much tolerance," she acknowledged.

Smirking, he said, "You don't say."

Getting serious, Rebecca recalled how she messed up her chances with J.D. Rockefeller the last time she was inebriated. Obviously she hadn't remembered James had been there. Starting to cry she said, "If I hadn't become drunk, he might have married me!"

James hushed her, as he thought to himself, not on your life! He thought if J.D. was anything like himself, his friend would have bailed when the scandal broke regarding her father. Even so, he had to admit she would have been better off because his friend would have felt obligated to leave her some financial compensation to end things quietly and because he pitied her. James knew this was more than he would have done if he had been in the situation. Of course, he rationalized, as rich as he was, he didn't have the resources of the Rockefellers or more importantly, live by their Christian moral code.

Cheering her up, James turned his attention to wooing Rebecca as he saw the snow falling and looked at the time. After some serious flirting, he convinced her that because of the inclement weather conditions, it would be better to sit by the fire in his hotel suite than go to the movies. He promised he'd be a gentleman.

As they walked into the hotel, Rebecca thought he was the most handsome man she ever had seen. She couldn't believe her luck that he had picked her even though she was now a financial liability. As James ushered her up to his suite, he told her he was the lucky one to be with her. She believed him until he started touching her as they sat on the sofa in front of the warm fire. Then she stiffened. Irritated by her response, he realized that he hadn't given her enough alcohol. After sharing a new bottle of champagne, Rebecca overcame her inhibitions.

While James sat on the sofa, he commanded her to get up. Claiming he was thinking of going into the movie business, he said he thought she had the look. Stringing her along, he said knowingly, "You could be the next Clara Bow or Mary Pickford."

"Really?" asked an excited Rebecca.

James couldn't stop himself from saying sarcastically, "Would I have said so otherwise?" After taking a long sip of his champagne, he said more gently, "Now let's see if you can take directions. I'll play the director and you'll be the actress."

"This should be fun!" exclaimed the giggling, hopeful starlet as she did glamour poses in the mirror.

Sipping his champagne as he enjoyed the show she put on for him, James said, "I'm glad you think so." Twenty-five minutes later, when they had emptied the bottle, he was ready to have his own kind of fun. His voice suddenly very serious, the "director" said, "Now convince me you're worth my time."

That night, as Boston was buried under a foot of snow, Rebecca lost her virginity to James. He came three times – once in each hole. When she woke up, he was gone. He left several hundred dollars on the bedside table. The cleaning woman found her vomiting in the bathroom.

* * *

A few days after James had seduced Rebecca, the bachelor escorted Josie to the Crystal Ball. New York's most eligible bachelor hardly could keep his eyes off her. She stood out in the ballroom crowded with ostentatiously gowned women, in a simple but elegant Marcel Rochas black-and-white Bali bias-cut evening dress that appeared as if it had been made just to flatter her silhouette even though it had been purchased at a second hand shop run to benefit a charity. As he escorted her around, he was delighted by the number of women who gave her jealous looks and men whose stares made it obvious they wished they were with her.

Surveying the group, James saw a pattern. The least attractive women wore the most beads and baubles and gaudiest of garments to divert attention from the assets they lacked most. Catching the eye of a particularly voluptuous blonde in a showy ensemble, he thought, of course there were the exceptions but they usually were new money that didn't know any better. But as his eyes lingered on the woman's torso, he appreciated the fact that shapeliness was back in vogue in the fashion houses of Paris and New York. While ordinarily he would have discreetly arranged to meet the well-endowed woman later, tonight he made sure he was on fine form the whole evening. James was content that he was showing Josie a good time and having one himself. He didn't want to jeopardize the progress he had made with her even at the expense of what he was sure would have been an incredible night.

As they danced, Josie playfully wrapped her lace Rochas' scarf around her escort. Twirling around, she was so carried away by the music she didn't notice in the least that her erotic moves caused quite a sensation both in his trousers and around the room. Oblivious as a society photographer flashed away, she instinctively continued moving to the beat. As she danced, she forgot all about the pain and suffering she saw daily on the streets of New York and the sadness she felt since the Crash. Rebecca, Henry Jay, even Charles' seemed far away.

Dancing was not only therapeutic for Josie, it energized her, melting away her deepest sorrow and the unresolved issues and fears in her subconscious. She just felt lightness and beauty. For one night, her world seemed carefree and beautiful again, and she was filled with the optimism of the endless stream of possibilities.

Walking back home after the ball with her arm wrapped around James', Josie freely laughed at the raconteur. He was so effortlessly amusing Josie couldn't help but enjoy his company. They had joked and teased each other the entire night. Her spirits rose because even the midst of what was becoming quite obviously a serious depression in America, there still was happiness in the air.

As she reached her doorstep, she thanked James for encouraging her to attend the ball. Pointing to the moon, she said emotionally, "Isn't it wonderful?"

Grabbing James and pulling him around so they spun in the street, Josie giggled as they spun faster and faster. The buildings and trees and cars started whirled around. Finally, when she couldn't take it any longer, she stopped and let James pull her close into him.

Turning so her back faced him, he held her, his arms wrapped around her waist. He rubbed his face against her hair, enjoying the softness and sweet smell of rosewater that she used when she washed it.

Her head was still spinning, as she pointed. Josie said, almost drunkenly although she hadn't had a sip of alcohol all night, "Look, the sky is so beautiful tonight and the air remarkably fresh!" As she spun around to face him, she said excitedly, her eyes dancing in the moonlight, "Life truly is wonderful!" Picking up his arms to spin around, she claimed girlishly, "You're *wonderful* and I'm *wonderful*, even cranky Lily Vanderhorn is *wonderful.*" Wanting to spin around some more, she had him twirl her as she declared, "Everyone and everything is absolutely fabulously *wonderful* this evening!" As he turned her towards him and reeled her in as she continued spinning, she exclaimed as she gestured, "The stars, the cars, even the bums on the street – oh *so wonderful.*" Her head now spinning from all the turns, she said giggling in a tipsy sort of sweet way, as she pointed to the milkman, "He's wonderful too!" Waving to the familiar man, she shouted, "Hello *Mr. Wonderful* ! "

James loved the sound of her voice. To him, it had a most dreamy, rich quality, so soft and sweet yet effortlessly affected, perfectly reflecting her educated upper class background. Josie's voice represented everything the old guard admired, standing out as a vestige of the disappearing gentility of her class. During a time when business lingo, immigration, and technological advances irreversibly disintegrated the English language and the acceptance of the new wealth of the twenties led to the toleration of bad accents and harsh, rough sounds, her voice resonated like the finest golden harp. As she spoke beautifully, he vowed to protect her and the old order from the onslaught of the swarming, screaming masses.

As Josie softly whispered good night, it took enormous effort on James' part to restrain his overwhelming desire to embrace her. Instead, he looked at her with great admiration and then gently kissed her hand. Fondly he smiled at her as she slipped inside her front door. He was delighted when almost immediately after she disappeared she reopened the door and came rushing out into the street to reiterate to him in an excited voice, "I had such a *wonderful* time."

Taking his hands in hers, she pulled him closer to her and reached up to his face. Her eyes sparkled as she kissed him on both cheeks and gave him a big hug. She said as she looked into his eyes, "Thank you so much." Then she darted back towards the house.

At the door she stopped and turned around once more to tell him, "You know, I think you're *absolutely wonderful?*"

James was still standing there smiling after she disappeared for the final time. Once again, with Josie, he actually had been more interested in pleasing a woman than in his own carnal desires.

Before moving away from the scene, he looked at his Patek Philippe wristwatch – the one he had absconded from Bentley. He had no trouble seeing the time because the sun was just starting to come up in the East. James was in such a good mood that he whistled the entire way back to his townhouse and slept well.

Sleep didn't come so easily for Josie. Over stimulated, she tossed and turned in bed for over an hour. She still had the adrenaline in her system and as much as she knew she needed to rest, she couldn't fall asleep. Unable to block out the sun that now streamed through her windows, she got up and started writing a letter to Charles. After re-reading what she had written, she ripped it up. She didn't want to write to Charles about what a *wonderful* time she had with James. It just wasn't right.

Although Josie knew she found James extremely attractive, she considered him just a very good friend. Loyal by nature, with every intention of being faithful to her fiancé, she tried to remember what a wonderful time she had with Charles dancing at Catherine and Junius' wedding. As she reread his letters to her, Josie felt she truly loved Charles and hardly could wait to marry him. There was no doubt in her mind that she wanted him to be the father of her children. With thoughts of the family they would have and the wonderful life they'd lead, she finally drifted off to sleep.

The following day, Josie thought about what she should do with James. Since she herself was taken, she decided to fix him up with one of her friends. After considering various matches, she concluded he'd be perfect for Rebecca. Josie frowned as she realized she hadn't heard from her dear friend for months. She vowed to find out what was going on. That night she wrote Charles that once she got back in touch with Rebecca, she would set up her friend with James. She thought if Rebecca hadn't already married, James would be eminently suitable.

Josie got her chance to approach New York's most eligible bachelor on the matter several weeks later as he escorted her back to her home following an Indian Raj inspired ball. They had had such an enjoyable time it already was almost three in the morning. Neither was tired as they stopped across the street from the Baxter-Brownes' residence to talk. James had Josie in hysterics as he made fun of all the women who had been at the party and lamented that there had been so few desirable ones. After he moaned about the dearth of attractive women in New York in general, she offered Rebecca as a possible solution to his problem.

A peculiar smile came across James' face as he informed her, he wasn't interested.

Undeterred, Josie pressed, "I don't understand."

He looked at her meaningfully and said, "She's not my type."

"I just don't get you!" Josie got up in frustration and said without disguising her irritation, "Becca's so pretty and sweet and vivacious. I don't see how you could possibly find her unattractive."

"I didn't say she wasn't attractive." His reply was curt and cold, "I just don't want to marry her."

Annoyed that he wasn't interested in her friend, she said, "I'm beginning to get the feeling maybe you're one of those men who should never get married!"

As he looked at her oddly, he said, "Perhaps." Then, as he moved closer to her, he claimed, "If you weren't engaged, I might change my mind."

Instantly moving away from him, her guard up, Josie replied stonily, "I love Charles desperately and I am getting married as soon as he gets back." Emphatically, she stated, "I can't imagine being with anyone else."

"Really?" remarked James his voice filled with disbelief. Probing, he inquired, "You've never been the least bit attracted to anyone else?"

"Of course not!" exclaimed Josie outraged at the suggestion.

"Are you sure?" said James as he reached over and pulled her towards him so she couldn't look away. He looked her deeply in the eyes as he brought her lips one inch away from his. As her body started to react, he pushed her away, laughing wickedly.

Josie was mortified. Collecting herself, she said frostily, "I don't think I should see you anymore." Humiliated, she started to quickly walk away from him and cross the street to her home.

Grabbing her before she had gone very far, he forcefully pulled her so close to him that she could feel his body pressed against her. He smiled as he felt her positively react to his touch. Letting his lips just touch her neck, he said, "I think you're attracted to me, Miss Baxter-Browne."

Her heart beat wildly. She tried not to look at him because she was afraid of what he might do to her if she did. But she didn't fight him when he pushed her chin up towards his so she no longer could avert him. In response, she blushed and dropped her pashmina shawl. His masculinity overpowered her. As their lips moved towards each other, she could feel her body aching. She groaned as he touched her. She wanted him to take her – right then, right there. Even with Charles, she had never felt this way. She wanted James and she knew he wanted her in the same way. Unable to stop, their passion erupted as they hungrily kissed and touched each other. Finally after several minutes, she forced herself to break away. Her fingers were cold but her face and body very much flushed. She rushed into the security of her family's home leaving him on the street outside with her shawl and the words, "Don't flatter yourself!"

That night, Josie found sleep impossible. Unable to stop thinking about James, she tried to rationalize the incident by telling herself it only had occurred because her fiancé had been gone for so long. Her love for Charles was never in doubt, but the longer he had been away the more distant he seemed. She missed the way he held her in his arms and talked to her at night. She missed everything about him – his smell, touch, humor, and most of all, his understanding of her. Josie had never expected to enjoy

James' company so much and to become so close to him. But with Charles, Geraldine, Rebecca, and Catherine away and Henry Jay dead, she kept thinking of New York's most eligible bachelor.

As she thrashed around in bed, Josie cursed James because he was so damned good looking and so terribly charming. Wickedly witty, he was always a laugh; she felt alive again when she was with him. Her body reacted as she kept reliving the night. Once again she envisioned him on the street in his midnight blue worsted "swallow-tailed" coat with faille revers that he had worn to the ball. She had held her breath at the party when he had taken off his jacket ostensibly to show her the decorative studs and cufflinks that he had purchased from Van Cleef &Arpels to match the pins she had worn to keep her Maggy Rouff sari closed. As she thought about how absolutely splendid he had looked in white tie at both the balls recently, Josie remembered what Texas Guinan jokingly had told her a few years back. The experienced woman had said, "Honey, never go to bed with a man who is wearing white tie. When you wake up the next morning, he won't look as good. Top hats and tails make even ugly men attractive."

But Josie knew James was one of the few men in the world who not only would not be a disappointment, but also might actually look better. Even though she sensed New York's most eligible bachelor was not a nice person, she found his masculinity overpowering. This evening, she had lost control. As she lay in bed unable to sleep, continuing to toss and turn, she vowed not to see him until after Charles returned. But after making the decision, Josie still couldn't fall asleep. Now that they had kissed, she wanted him even more.

* * *

Charles slept soundly as Josie restlessly struggled with conflicted emotions. After putting in another eighteen-hour day filled with manual labor and time spent pouring over the accounting books, he had fallen asleep at his desk writing a letter to his fiancée. Four hours later, the sound of the roosters and the piercing sunlight woke him up. As he reached for his work clothes, he knew it would be another difficult day. But Charles felt he couldn't complain.

Despite their troubles, the Blakesleys counted themselves amongst the lucky ones in Ada. They still had their land and a strong head of cattle when many others no longer did. Just the week before Charles and his Uncle had joined a group of ranchers and farmers who had buried old grudges to save some neighbors' homestead from foreclosure. It had been the seventh that week and they feared there would be many more in the future. Many others had simply loaded their beaten down trucks and motor cars with whatever they had left and headed west. Livestock, wheat and corn prices continued to plummet despite the withering crops and herds.

The government aid that had come from Charles' efforts was long since used up. It had been meant to as a temporary measure – to just help the farmers and cattlemen get through the winter and cover the spring planting. The subsidy had never been enough to last longer nor intended for that purpose. But now that the drought had worsened and was intensified by the Summer sun, despite repeated trips to Washington, Charles had been told by the politicians both local and federal, they could do nothing more than offer their best wishes to the farmers and ranchers in their area. None agreed to come out to tour the area again. They claimed things had been getting worse around the country for everyone- everywhere; there was no money left in the state budget for additional aid and the without a White House directive, Congress refused to allocate more federal funds.

Finally, just when the situation in Ada looked most dire, help came from Washington. Two months after Anna sent a hand-written appeal to the President for help, she received a personal letter from the Commander in Chief promising that his administration with the help of Congress was passing the Emergency

Relief and Construction Act and creating the Reconstruction Finance Corporation (RFC). Herbert Hoover explained that his plan was to have the RFC "provide government secured-loans not only to financial institutions and railroads, but also to farmers in need" like the Blakesleys. In the meantime, he expressed the hope that volunteers could be found to help the good people of Ada get through these tough times.

Although Charles felt the RFC was a great idea, as the months passed, his spirits sank as the program initially seemed to have a minimal impact on his community. Riding on the range, Charles also feared that the years of intense, aggressive exploitation of the soil by the farmers would come back to haunt them. As he led his horse through the parched acres of wheat fields that had been more suited to serve as grazing land, the howling wind stirred up the dust and dirt, pelting and beating his face with the dry land. Although he knew it should have been a bright day, he could hardly see the sun. The dust completely dulled and obscured its reddish hue. Through his world travels he had witnessed farmlands ruined by drought and desertification. Now as he surveyed the plains that he had loved, he feared the current low crop and livestock prices and even ruined crops might not be the end of their woes.

Shielding his face with a bandana as best as he could, Charles silently prayed his family's planting of a thousand acres during World War I to take advantage of the lucrative grain prices wouldn't be their undoing.

With the government unwilling to do more, Charles rode back home determined to get his Uncle to arrange a meeting with other ranchers and farmers and see if they could consult some agrarian scientists at the State University. He would soon learn few had any interest. Most of the Blakesleys neighbors, who hadn't moved or lost their land, were too pre-occupied with their current woes to worry about any questionable future problems. In fact, many planned to replant not only all their farmland but also even to tear up more grassland to make up for the low crop prices with greater volume. They didn't understand that increasing their oversupply only would lead to the further plummeting of prices.

For his part, Teddy Blakesley was willing to do whatever his nephew suggested. Morbidly depressed by his losses, feeling like a failure because he had let his wife and nephew down as well as his staff who had relied on him like a father, the old cattle rancher retreated to a barn where he spent his time talking to his favorite horses. There he didn't have to remember that his large house designed by Frank Lloyd Wright, with its dazzling array of art glass, screens, and embellished cabinets – once his pride – was stripped bare from the items of value and even many of the specially designed Wright furnishings. His garage, that echoed the Prairie styled masterpiece with its tented ceilings of sloping panels of geometric glass, lay empty except for the one vehicle the family kept. Charles would have sold the personally designed Pierce Arrow too if he could have gained any value out of it. But the few left with money in Ada didn't want to spend it, let alone flaunt it. Since gasoline was costly, the luxury motor car just collected dust in the specially built garage that used to house ten vehicles.

Particularly in front of visitors but when even just with his own family, Teddy hardly spoke. He was a broken man pre-occupied by the premonition that one day creditors would come after him for his land like they had done to so many of his friends. Knowing there were many in the town that had been jealous and would rejoice in his humiliation, Teddy had nightmares whenever he fell asleep. To prevent his haunting dreams, late at night, when the household was asleep, he crawled out of bed and slipped outside to sit on a swing that he had built years before for Charles. Although she didn't tell her nephew, Anna often found her husband there at dawn, swinging back and forth as he stared into the unknown distance, muttering incoherently.

* * *

Every evening, Charles, Teddy and Anna Blakesley gathered in their sitting room listening to the radio for entertainment. Anna darned socks as the President gave a radio address live from the nation's capitol. Yet again they found themselves furious that while the leader of the country supported farm subsidies, he still also continued to express the belief that the economy would soon turn around. Teddy actually stormed out of the room after he heard Herbert Hoover reiterate his belief that "while people must not suffer from hunger and cold, caring for them must be primarily a local and voluntary responsibility."

As Anna went after her husband who now suffered from hypertension along with his numerous other problems, Charles continued to listen in disbelief. When it was reported that the President had recently met with a hostile crowd that had thrown rotten fruit and eggs at him, he wasn't surprised.

Charles continued to sense others were out of touch when he read the morning paper. He felt terribly far away from Josie, his old college friends, and the world in which he used to circulate. Twice he had to reread a quotation attributed to J.D. Rockefeller. His friend had continued his plans for the extensive midtown development project informing reporters that his family considered the current market valuations a bargain and as a result had been buying stocks for some time. Charles sardonically laughed as he read in the same paper that when told about this comedian Eddie Cantor had retorted, "Yeah, who else in the country has any money left to buy them?"

That night Charles explained the desperate circumstances in Ada to Josie. Afterwards, he wrote:

My arms are heavy and my heart aches. I yearn to hold you.
Oh my love, I love you every day, more in each and every way.
It pains me more than you can know that it will be a very long time,
Before I can send for you.
Until then,

I give you – All I have - my love,
Your C.B.

Three times he re-wrote the note before sending it. Twice he tore up what he wrote – what he really felt like telling her, that the way things looked on the range, he couldn't imagine them ever improving and that she would be far better with someone else – someone more deserving. But as he stared at his favorite photo of her, the edges worn from the number of times he had held it, he vowed somehow he would find a way to ameliorate the situation.

* * *

As Charles sealed his latest letter to Josie, Albert Baxter-Browne peered over his bank's books. What he saw gave him a massive headache. Downing the rest of a bottle of whiskey did nothing either for the headache or the figures listed in front of him.

Although his bank had remained solvent following the Crash, as the Depression worsened, the number of defaulting loans rose to an unsustainable level. Albert didn't know what he was going to do. He asked himself how a prudent banker like himself could be in this situation. Through the early years of the boom, he had been so conservative in his lending policies that his own board criticized him for not taking advantage of the flow of easy money. By the mid-twenties, he found his institution under increasing pressure from the big banks that had moved into his territory because of the profit margins. Once considered a large lender, by 1928, his company had become a less significant player in the industry.

Briefly, Albert had considered an offer by A.P. Giannini who was building his TransAmerica bank based in San Francisco into a financial empire he would rename Bank of America. But Albert thought there always would be room for smaller institutions like his. He was wary of monopolies and didn't want to become a small cog in an impersonal behemoth. Although his board was furious that he had turned down the lucrative offer, he believed he was doing what was best for his employees and clients. He was sure no big institution would take care of them the way he did.

Although he hadn't told his wife and daughter, by remaining an independent bank, Albert's institution had, in fact, been forced to start taking on greater credit risks to remain competitive just as the market speculation spiraled out of control. Losing the Grade A investment loans to the big wheelers and dealers, he resorted to lending money to the savings and loans and smaller banks in the Midwest, as well as heavily leveraged companies. Because the default rate was so low and on paper the performing loans appeared to have assets, Albert didn't worry as long as the market kept rising. But following the Crash, he saw more defaults in the second half of the year than his bank cumulatively had over its entire history. Even so, initially, due to Albert's forethought, the bank had more than enough cash to cover these defaults. But as the outflow of capital continued quarter after quarter in rapid succession and by increasing amounts, he became apprehensive. As the winter passed into spring and headed towards the summer of 1930, he saw no signs of abatement.

Albert feared at the rate his bank was losing money, his liquidity would dry up within six months at the most. As he attempted a turnaround, he hid the extent of his bank's problems with bad loans. He knew he'd be doomed if word got out on the street that they were having liquidity issues.

But when Josie's father received a late afternoon call from the President of the People's Bank in Gary, Indiana, he knew he had to seek help from others. The People's Bank had the biggest loan on his books. Because of all the other defaults, the bank's payments now accounted for a sizable percentage of Albert's monthly revenues. Although occasionally late by a few days these past few months, the institution had been financially solvent and always managed to come through. The President informed him that this would no longer be the case. Barring a miracle, the People's Bank had just closed its doors forever. The millions of dollars the unsuspecting people had put into its vaults in the last fifty years of its operation had vaporized with the Great Bull market. As the bank president spoke to Albert, he clearly was shaken. He could hear the sounds of a panic stricken mob outside the temple of money. As the rain poured down on them, the good people of Gary – doctors, lawyers, mechanics, builders, housewives, assembly line workers and even the clergy stood outside the doors hoping their life savings really hadn't been lost.

Several hours later, the President emerged, bent and broken. A handful of the most desperate were still there. Several had no place left to go. A young girl, who had very dark hair and pretty features and was small for her age, came up to him. Her face looked gaunt; her eyes wide from the many days and night she had now lived without enough nourishment. Her tiny frame shook from the cold. Tugging on his sleeve, she said pleading, "Please, Mr. Sir, can I have my money so my little brother can get his medicine?"

Reaching into his pocket, the President took out his billfold and handed her a twenty and a five. He wished he had more to give, but it was all the money he had left himself. He had used his own money to support the bank the last few months. Now, it too had vanished.

As the Bank President walked past the distressed, destitute group, he bent his head low and muttered, "I'm sorry." There was nothing else he could do.

Albert had met the People's Bank's President several times over the years. He took a personal interest in all his clients. He wished that he could help the banker out of this malaise, but he knew the resources didn't exist. His own institution's survival hanging in the balance, Albert picked up the phone to call the one person he thought might be able and willing to do something. He had a "due" bill.

* * *

While Albert valiantly fought to save his bank, James sat in his home office with Vinnie Graves. The businessman was engrossed in a serious conversation with the goon when his houseman interrupted. James hollered at Bentley as the servant stood in the doorway.

Clearly annoyed by the interruption, James bellowed, "What do you want?"

The houseman replied, "Sir, a Miss Stanley is on the phone."

James snapped, "Can't you see I am occupied!"

Unemotionally, Bentley replied, "Yes." Then before James could slam the door shut in his face, he said quietly but firmly, "But sir, she says it is very important."

"Then you take care of it," retorted James smirking as he tried to kick the door shut.

"Sir, I don't think I can," replied Bentley as he put his foot in the door to stop it from closing. Still standing in the doorway with his foot serving as a doorstop, the houseman requested, "Can I speak with you for a moment *alone*, sir?"

As James walked outside the room into the hallway, the thug picked his nose. He put a particularly large booger in his mouth and chomped on it. Bentley would have been mortified if he saw what the goon was doing, but he was too pre-occupied by other matters.

To prevent the thug from eavesdropping, the meticulous houseman tightly closed the door to the office after his master had walked out. As they stood in the hallway Bentley whispered to James, "The young lady says she's pregnant."

His master growled, "That's not my problem."

"She says you're the father," said Bentley in a low, hushed tone.

Not bothering to keep his voice down, James replied, "Tell her I don't think so."

After clearing his voice, the houseman said, "Sir, she says she'll go to the papers."

"Inform her I'll meet her this weekend in the park by the swan boats," barked James, his expression and voice churlish.

When he came back into the room, Vinnie inquired, "Anything I can help you with?"

Frowning, James replied, "Unfortunately not. It's a woman."

As Graves used his teeth to clean his fingernails, he said, "Want her banged up or knocked off?"

Staring at the thug with the recognition that he was a total psychopath, James said carefully, "I'll think about it."

Chuckling, the goon stated, "She claiming you knocked her up?"

"It's none of your Goddamn business," replied James annoyed at how obvious the problem was. He was angry with himself for not being more careful and, he was furious at the thought he had only screwed her that one night. He wanted to believe that she was lying, but he knew that instinctively she just wasn't that kind of girl. She was too soft and naïve although, as he recalled, she had been very, very tight.

Handing Graves some papers, James said, "More importantly, I want you to take care of this matter. How long will it take?"

Looking through the list, Vinnie said, "That's a lot – six weeks at least."

"You've got four," stated the businessman emphatically.

Handing the thug an envelope with cash, James said, "I'll be in touch. If I need you for this other matter, you'll have to go to Boston.

* * *

CHAPTER XVIII

James hadn't seen Rebecca since he had seduced her. Since currently he had no business obligations in the city where she lived, he saw no need to be in touch. He ignored her letters and phone calls for as long as he could. Convinced she would no longer keep her mouth shut, James understood the trip to Boston was necessary. As they met on a perfect summer day, he did his best to pretend he cared. He thought she looked pretty for four months pregnant. Although she was a tiny girl, she hid the baby well. But when he put his hand over her belly, he could tell there definitely was a little lump. Her face was very pale, almost ashen. Even so, he still found her attractive physically.

Kissing Rebecca on the lips when he arrived, James appeared interested in her. On the way up from New York, he reasoned that it would be easier this way.

After walking Rebecca over to a secluded area of the park, he went straight to the point. "Have you told anyone other than my houseman?"

She whispered, "Of course not."

He pressed, "Not even your mother?"

"Definitely not her! She'd be the last one I told! She doesn't even know I met you!" Stressing out at the mere thought, she frantically said, "If mother finds out what has happened, she'd kill me! It's so shameful!" said the petite brunette breaking down.

Gently putting his arm around her even though he really wanted to strangle her, James said, "It's going to be all right."

"That's what you told me last time I saw you and then you disappeared!" screamed Rebecca as she pushed him away.

Trying to calm her down, James explained, "I've been very busy – traveling a great deal." He claimed, "I didn't even get your messages until earlier this week."

"Your houseman didn't give me the impression you were traveling," said Rebecca with an accusing tone. "He just said you were not available."

"My dear, when I'm away, I am not available," scoffed James as he started to lose his temper. After taking a deep breath, he said more softly, "But that's not the point."

Taking Rebecca's hands in his, he said gently, "Now I've got to take care of you."

"And the baby," she said looking up at him meaningfully.

James hesitated. Then he explained as delicately as he could. "I want to take very good care of *you*." Motioning for her to sit down, he said, "In the future, I'd like to get married and have a family." As he held her hand, he claimed, "I just can't do that right now."

As Rebecca started weeping, James attempted to calm her down. Sweetly, he claimed, "You know you mean so much to me."

After he got her back under control, he continued lying. He asserted, "It's not that I don't want the baby. But because of the guidelines in my trust and my uncle's will, I can't get married for another year." Having had practice before, he didn't falter once in his fabrication. As he held the troubled girl, he explained, "The men in my family were very concerned that I might marry too early and not concentrate on our businesses." As he stroked her hair, he said, "Don't worry. I'm going to take you to a very nice place that will take care of the baby and we can continue to see each other until I can get married."

"What exactly are you saying?" asked Rebecca confused.

"Darling, we can't have this baby." The words shocked the naive girl who had expected he would marry her once he saw her again. Realizing she wasn't going to take this as well as he hoped, he claimed, "Just because we can't have this child doesn't mean we can't have others in the future."

Tears rolled down Rebecca's face as she sobbed, "But I want this baby."

Lying, James said, "I do, too." Then he said what he really meant, "But we can't." As he kissed her tenderly on the forehead and pressed his hand against hers, he promised, "There will be others." Wiping the tears from her eyes with his handkerchief, he claimed, "I can tell you'll be a very loving mother one day."

James was determined to get the baby problem resolved that weekend. He wasn't going to leave Boston until it was aborted, and he didn't want to stay in the city longer than two days. So, relentlessly, he pushed the reluctant girl into agreeing. After his sweet approach fell on deaf ears, he threatened her. Finally, she consented. To get rid of her mother and Great Aunt, James gave Rebecca a pre-paid package deal for a week in New York for them. He instructed and drilled her on telling them that she had been rewarded with the trip for her family for her great work at Filene's. When she protested that this wasn't company policy, he grew irritated and insisted that she just follow through.

Once Mrs. Stanley and Rebecca's aunt had been taken care of, James gave Rebecca several new expensive outfits as presents. Then he made her go home with the garments and change into the worst dress she owned. Ever meticulous, he met her several blocks away from her residence after he himself changed into some clothes he purchased specially from J.C. Penny's and had taken off his crest ring and Patek Philippe watch. Then he took the trusting girl to a dubious practitioner in the outskirts of the city. Rebecca wavered outside the two- room shack. He finally got her inside after plying her with grain alcohol. James waited in the adjoining room as the procedure was done in the most unsanitary of conditions. It cost him more than he wanted to pay. Rebecca nearly died as the man who claimed to be a doctor butchered her. James left the place quite depressed after the "doctor" informed him that despite the significant loss of blood, the patient had pulled through.

When Rebecca turned up on his doorstep a few weeks later, James promised to marry her but made it clear she needed to keep it a secret until he could sort things out with his trustees. After promising his fiancée, the biggest Graf ring available and giving her a little spending money, Rebecca agreed to go back to Boston and wait for him. For the next several weeks, every time the phone or doorbell rang, the petite girl expectantly rushed to answer. It never occurred to her that another trip to New York City would be necessary. It wasn't.

Two months after he sent Rebecca back, James phoned her to make arrangements. As planned, after sending her mother out of town to visit her Great Aunt, an excited Rebecca, packed a bag with all the clothes and gifts James had given her as well as a few of her favorite things and stayed home alone to answer the special knock at the door she was expecting.

Wanting to look her best for her intended, when she heard the distinctive knock, she sweetly called out, "Just a moment, darling." Then she quickly changed into a special outfit, touched up her make-up and hair and checked out her appearance one final time in the mirror. Feeling pretty and in high spirits, Rebecca waltzed to the door humming Ted Weem's hit song, *My Baby Just Cares For Me*. She remembered the night he had seduced her, James had complimented her on her singing. She was certain she'd please him with the choice. She had been planning a little provocative dance act to accompany the lyrics that she had been practicing specially for him. Originally she had thought she would save it for her wedding night, but as James dragged things out, she decided to surprise him with it now.

Rebecca was midway through the refrain when she opened the door. Expecting a passionate kiss, she closed her eyes and puckered her lips as she continued her routine. But instead of being greeted by her much anticipated, handsome lover, she found herself facing a pockmarked thug that she had encountered once before – the night of the raid at Texas Guinan's. Vinnie Graves didn't even give Rebecca a chance to gasp – but he finished her song.

Several weeks later, without any press coverage, the Boston police closed the murder case of Rebecca Stanley. Her homicide was attributed to a serial rapist who had been terrorizing working class girls for over a year. They came to this conclusion after finding her mangled body floating in the harbor – the favorite dumping ground of the rapist. Familiar with the rapist's style from press coverage about previous cases, Graves made sure Rebecca's body bore consistent evidence with the other victims.

With so many unemployed, homeless, desperate people and an increasing crime rate, the police and media treated Rebecca as just another sad statistic. Shocked and bereft by the loss of her daughter, initially Mrs. Stanley blamed herself for being away. Then she took out her anger on their poverty and the lack of protection afforded the less affluent. Organizing a group for women who had lost family members to violence, brought some solace, as did the eventual death of the alleged rapist in a police shoot out.

Mrs. Stanley received mixed reactions when she contacted Rebecca's old friends to inform them of her daughter's untimely death. Relegating her social secretary to take Mrs. Stanley's call, Catherine seemed more horrified by the implications to her own social standing due to any association with the raped victim than with the actual death. For their part, Josie and Geraldine had the greatest sympathy for Mrs. Stanley and couldn't believe Rebecca was really gone. When the terrible reality sunk in, they cried a great deal and clung to each other for support. Charles' caring words of encouragement helped Josie as well. James did his best to offer her his condolences, trying to turn her friend's death into a vehicle for him to get close to the object of his affection again, but much to Josie's mother's distress, her daughter remained steadfast and refused to see New York's most eligible bachelor.

Claire enraged Josie by using Rebecca's death as a morality lesson. Her attempts to convince her daughter that the poor girl's fate was a result of her mother marrying a man who was incapable of continuing to support them in a privileged lifestyle as well as a result of Rebecca's failing to accept a suitable husband, and the obvious comparisons to Charles, were quickly and almost violently rebuffed by Josie. She left her mother in a fit of emotion when Claire pleaded, tears streaming down her face as she practically screamed, "You could end up like that if you don't marry appropriately!" Hysterically, she declared as damning evidence, "You're the same age!"

Josie and Geraldine, who chose to briefly take a break from Evelyn's tour, planned and paid for their dear friend's small funeral. The girls had expected to stay two weeks with Mrs. Stanley in order to sort through Rebecca's things and help her grieve. But because she was so mad at her own mother who had claimed her commitments in New York prevented her from attending the funeral, Josie stayed with Mrs. Stanley for almost two months after Geraldine returned to Europe to be with Evelyn. New York's most celebrated debutante visited her friend's grave everyday and prayed at the cathedral – looking for the divine. She desperately tried to understand why this had happened to her sweet friend. Every afternoon she knelt down in the same pew, asking God to take care of her friend's soul and hasten the time when she and Charles could be together again.

* * *

Busy cavorting with other women, James didn't mourn Rebecca's passing. With Josie away, New York's most desirable bachelor found other amusements to preoccupy him when he wasn't diligently working. He had every intention of continuing to pursue 1929's most celebrated debutante, but after meeting a feral red head with a most striking body and arresting green eyes at Henry Morgan's Adam and Eve Ball, he felt no immediate need to rush.

New York's most eligible bachelor had turned up at his friend's ball ready to have a good time. He had been working particularly hard the last few days. As he had talked with Doris Duke at the party, James had looked around the room. Initially he saw no stand outs, which is why he continued to converse with the shy but presentable United Tobacco heiress. His feelings changed when he saw *her* walk in on the arm of a Russian nobleman. As the red head and aristocrat chatted, he could tell *she* was as bored with her companion as he was with his. From across the room, James and the red head felt each other's presence. Instantaneously, their eyes locked in each other's gaze and they became oblivious to those next to them.

Catching on, Doris muttered, "Why don't you just go over there?" The chemistry between James and the red head was undeniable.

James dragged the United Tobacco heiress along with him as he walked purposefully towards the red head. She rolled her eyes when he joked referring to the alluring woman who interested him and the nobleman with her: "She has no chance against your money!"

Not amused, Doris replied, "You owe me!"

But James sensed Doris found the Russian attractive enough to pass the time. In fact the United Tobacco heiress had considered herself lucky that New York's most eligible bachelor had spent time talking with her this night. He wasn't the only one who found her a bit awkward. Since he had more than enough money of his own and had a reputation for only pursuing beauties, she knew her drawbacks were insurmountable impediments for any possibility of a serious romance between them to develop. Still, Doris couldn't help fantasizing about the witty, debonair bachelor that money couldn't buy.

After introducing Doris to the Russian, James turned to the red head. As he looked at her, his dark eyes penetrating her light, silk and chiffon evening dress, he thought she was the embodiment of sex appeal. He just knew she'd be great in bed.

Before he had the chance even to ask her name, she inquired with a sultry, low voice, "Would you like to dance?"

Smiling at her forwardness, he asked, "Is that *all* you'd like to do?"

She continued to hold his gaze as she gave him her hand so he could lead her onto the floor. As they tangoed, she replied, "We'll see."

Ten minutes later, not inconspicuously, James and the red head left the Adam and Eve Ball. As they walked into her apartment, he ripped off her clothes and enjoyed the best night of sex in his life. For her part, Alex Carleton, the red headed temptress, never had felt so satisfied by a man.

* * *

As the economy continued to defy the President, it spiraled downward with no end in sight. Those already not wiped out, behaved psychologically as if they were. This new period tested even the closest of relationships. Despite President Hoover's formation of the National Credit Corporation banking consortium and the subsequent RFC that was meant to provide government-secured loans to financial institutions, it took five phone calls and three meetings, all with the same person, just for Albert to save his bank. In these times, no "due" bill, regardless of its background, was honored without negotiations. It was a harsh awakening for the banker schooled in the days when a word was a bond and friendships meant more than money. But in the end, Josie's father was delighted that the man whose global business had been launched by his loan thirty-five years before had finally agreed to temporarily float his bank.

Financially secure for the moment, Albert immediately sought to improve his institution's image and bottom line. Subsequent meetings with Jack Morgan and the Rockefellers proved less difficult but not quite as cordial as in the Pre-Crash days. Because of Albert's friendship with the Morgans, Jack provided him with a line of credit and passed on some business. He made it clear, however, that he could not bail out his friend indefinitely. Given what Jack told him, Josie's father was left with no doubt that the slowdown had affected the House of Morgan as well. Albert's bank wasn't the only one with under-performing loans and stock losses.

After meeting with the Morgans, Albert returned home smiling. It was the first time in months that he had come back without a headache. The significance wasn't lost on his wife. Much as she had virtually no interest in business and had believed for years in her husband's abilities, despite Albert's assurances Claire had seen and recognized the worrying signs. She read the papers regularly and could not forget what happened to the Stanleys and so many others in their circle. More importantly, she had noticed the bags under her husband's eyes, the restless nights, heavier drinking, and recent muffled conversations on the phone. Claire hoped things would be fine for them in the future. But she wasn't as sure as she used to be, nor was she as certain of her husband's abilities. She thought he really could benefit from a son-in-law who understood business and was secure in his own right. Despite Albert's affection for Charles and liberal stance in letting his beloved only child choose her own mate, Claire had every intention of persuading her husband this had become a very bad idea.

Claire slept well that night, thinking how Albert frequently had joked, the secret to the Baxter-Brownes' happy marriage was that his wife always got her way.

* * *

While Josie was in Boston, James wasted no time making the most of the situation in New York City – with Alex Carleton at night and New York's most celebrated debutante's mother during the day. When business allowed, James met Claire for lunch or tea. Josie's mother made no effort in front of James to hide her disapproval of her daughter's choice. For his part, James went out of his way to impress Josie's mother that he would be the best son-in-law she could ever imagine. Attentive, thoughtful and amusing, in conversation and regularly surprising her with unexpected but appreciated gestures and gifts, James worked his charm on Claire so that Josie's mother would do everything she could to further the alliance they both wanted.

By the time New York's most celebrated debutante returned home, in Claire's eyes James could do no wrong. When Lady Ashley tried to enlighten her friend on the raconteur's reputation as a confirmed playboy and even told Claire she had heard James and Alex Carleton were caught in a compromising position at a party, Josie's mother still refused to see him as unsuitable. Several days later, when Lady Ashley pointed out the infamous red head to Claire as they dined at the Waldorf Astoria, Josie's mother simply responded, with a sniff, "She's not the type he'd ever marry." As far as Claire was concerned, she informed her confidante, until James and Josie were together there was no reason for him not to be a playboy. When pressed, she admitted, even if the playboy once married continued to do "things with other women that she wouldn't want him doing with her daughter," she felt, as long as they were done quietly, it really didn't matter. Financial security, social standing, sophistication, and charm, in that order, were the attributes Claire sought in a spouse for her daughter – particularly now.

* * *

One week after returning from Boston, while James and Alex Carleton made the most of the night, Josie stayed home with the flu. She felt so miserable she even didn't feel like writing to Charles.

Twice she picked up the phone in the hallway to call him, but both times she had to put it back down to go to the bathroom. Finally, she just crawled upstairs and went to sleep.

Josie didn't feel better until about five days later when she accompanied her parents to a dinner party Jack Morgan hosted in his New York City brownstone. The sumptuous five-course dinner was the first solid food she had eaten in close to a week. Her mouth salivated as she smelled the savory aromas. With difficulty she waited until everyone else was served before she dug into her starter. Because she hadn't eaten much the last few days, she was so hungry that she ate too fast. By the time the ladies withdrew to the drawing room and the gentlemen went to smoke, talk politics, and business, Josie felt stuffed and bloated. When they walked into the drawing room, Claire told her daughter she didn't feel well either. Feverish and achy, her hands cold, Josie's mother had all the typical signs of flu. After wrapping her mink stole around her mother, Josie went to the billiards' room to get her father so they could leave. As she stood in the doorway of the smoky room, she didn't see him anywhere. Not wanting to disturb the men, she waited where she was, thinking her father might have gone to the bathroom but would return shortly. There, although she wasn't trying, she couldn't help but hear everything the men were saying, as she stood unobserved.

While the men talked about the worsening state of the economy, J.D. Rockefeller played snooker with Junius and Henry Morgan. As Henry took his shot, J.D. leaned against a cabinet, talking to Jack and his uncle, Percy Rockefeller, who both sat in leather chairs smoking cigars as they watched the younger men play.

When J.D. went over to take his shot, he glanced around the room to see if Albert was back before saying, "You know I'm really worried about Charles."

Josie listened intently as she heard Junius agree that J.D. had valid reasons.

Having been fond of his son's former college roommate, Jack asked for an update on the Blakesleys.

Junius replied, "As you know, they over-expanded in the twenties and got hit pretty hard with the depreciation of crop and livestock prices."

"And their other assets?" inquired Jack who remembered they had had some money at the House of Morgan at one point.

"Practically wiped out," said Henry wiping his brow before he lined up his shot.

Josie gasped as Henry predicted, "I'll be shocked if their place isn't auctioned off by the summer. There's no near term future gains in agriculture in this country." From what her fiancé had written Josie knew his family's situation was terrible, but she hadn't realized until now just how dire it had become. As the revelation sunk in, she held her head in her hands and stared down at the carpeted floor. Had she been looking through the doorway, she would have seen Jack sadly shake his head as he thought of the numerous cases all over the country just like the Blakesleys. Then the financial titan spoke.

The young men looked up from their game as Jack made pointed inquiries. "How long has it been since it last rained in the Midwest?"

"It's been a record," reported J.D.

"The land has become unusable and is getting worse." Jack picked up a Cuban cigar, sliced off the end and lit it, then continued as he took a puff. "I understand Garrett Goldman just returned from a trip out there, Oklahoma in fact. I heard he met with some professors from the university. Now he's convinced that all that parched-up, dry dirt is going to be swept up and carried across the state – some kind of "dust bowl" he called it."

Surprised by the reference as well as the suggestion, Junius said, "I thought you didn't like Goldman, Father."

"I don't particularly." Between puffs, Jack replied, "But his sources are rarely wrong."

J.D. asked, "Who told you this?"

The older man replied, "Your friend, James." After putting out his cigar, he explained, "The Blakesleys are mortgaged to the hilt. They won't get anything out of their land and beef prices are at the lowest level since 1899." Softening his voice, he almost whispered, "This will finish them."

Josie's blood ran cold as she heard him say, "Much as I am fond of Charles, Josie's a beautiful girl with a lot of prospects. She and Charles won't last."

For several moments, the sobering news about their friend silenced the room. Finally Junius verbalized what all were thinking. "I just wish there was something we could do for them!"

As Josie held her breath and tried to come to terms with what she heard, J.D. spoke hesitantly. "I wasn't going to tell anyone, but since we're among friends, I've been helping Charles."

"How?" inquired Percy skeptically. "Nephew, you know the cardinal rule. Don't mix charity with business."

J.D. explained, "Charles met a land man who gave him the impression they might be sitting on oil."

As Percy scoffed, Jack sighed heavily recalling, "Teddy Blakesley didn't stint on getting all kinds of geological reports done years ago. He turned up nothing but more dirt."

"Apparently, there was one bit near the house they never checked." Glaring at his uncle Percy, J.D. said, "I don't expect a return on my investment but it's the least I can do for my friend."

Junius and Henry nodded their approval but waited for their father's response. For what seemed like an eternity, Josie could hear the ticking of the grandfather clock as the men waited for Jack to speak.

Finally, the esteemed banker gruffly replied, "There isn't a chance in hell that boy's going to get a gusher but he's too good to go to waste."

With deliberation he pointedly asked his sons and J.D., "That Charles, he likes to travel and he's good with foreigners, right?"

"He speaks six or seven different languages and from firsthand experience, I'll attest he can talk his way into and out of anything, anywhere," replied Junius excitedly as J.D. nodded in agreement.

"Good," said Jack to his encouragers. Thinking out loud, the powerful businessman stated, "He just might do. We need someone who can't be corrupted but will fit in down there. I sense he's loyal, honest, and quietly clever."

"What you have in mind, Father?" inquired Junius, hoping his father could offer his friend something.

Chuckling, Jack said, "A great opportunity for someone willing to work hard, live a little dangerously and be in love with adventure."

Junius, Henry and J.D. immediately said together, "That's Charles!" As they shared stories about their friend, Jack and Percy said he sounded like the perfect man for the job that required overseeing the Morgan's mining, shipping, and railroad interests throughout South America.

As they got serious, Jack said to his sons and the Rockefellers, "You do know that our last man was abducted by some bandits in Peru. They killed him before giving us a chance to decide whether he was worth the ransom money." Thinking of Charles' fiancée, he said, "I think he'd love the job. It certainly could make him a very wealthy man again, but it's dangerous and certainly not one worth considering if he's planning to settle down." Tears came to Josie's eyes as she heard Jack say, "We'd need at least a three or four year commitment from him."

Josie stood in the doorway, tears streaming down her face. While she silently cried, she heard J.D. say, "Too bad. There certainly isn't a job better suited for Charles that he'd enjoy more, but if it means giving up Josie, you know he'd sooner rot in hell."

Unable to listen anymore and realizing her father wasn't coming back to the billiards room, Josie decided to walk back to find her mother. The last thing she heard was Junius morbidly saying, "With the economy as it is, this really is his only hope. He's dead in Oklahoma and we all know Charles' has never been suited to an office job. He'd be so much better off if he wasn't engaged!"

Trying to hide her teary eyes, Josie tried to get her mother's attention from the hallway. Finally she succeeded and managed to tell her mother she'd wait for her parents outside. After asking Michael, the Baxter-Brownes' driver, to wait for her parents, she got into the back seat of the Bentley and sobbed. Twenty minutes later, when he parents sat down next to her she told them she didn't want to talk. The family rode back in silence. None of them felt well. Claire wasn't the only one with flu symptoms. The entire time Josie had been waiting for Albert by the billiards' room, he had been in the bathroom emptying his body from both ends.

Josie cried all night. She didn't know what to do. She loved Charles so much she didn't want to lose him. He was the only man she could imagine as her husband and the father of her children. He made her so happy and she was sure he truly felt blessed to be with her. But in her heart she knew as much as he loved her, he still was a free spirit. As she had listened to his friends describe the way he had been in college and she thought about how his eyes always lit up when he told her about his travel adventures, she recognized the Morgan offer was a once in a lifetime chance for him. Charles was so talented she knew he could make the most of it. But she also knew from what Jack Morgan had said he only could do it alone.

Josie felt tortured, torn between her desire to marry the man she loved and allowing him to have the job of his dreams. Her head spun as she kept asking why? Why did life have to be so complicated? Why did he have to lose his money? Why did he love exotic adventures in foreign countries where danger lurked? Why couldn't he be happy working for her father or taking some desk job in some country or place where she could live and they could raise a family? But she knew he found the Continent stale and New York City stifling.

Josie happily would have gone to Oklahoma and worked his family's fields just to be with him. She didn't care what people thought or would say about her, she was content in her love for him and his for her. But now, as she came to grips with the harsh reality that his family was on the brink of losing even that, she wondered how much more she could give up. She sobbed as she recalled Charles' words to her when he tried to break up after the Crash, "The greatest love is sacrificial, letting the one you love go, knowing it will be better for them if you do so." Josie knew Charles' friends were right. He never would take the South American offer unless she broke up with him. She cried herself to sleep knowing that's what she needed to do.

* * *

The next day Josie made an appointment to see Jack Morgan. The banker's secretary was extremely surprised by the debutante's request to meet with him. Few women came to 23 Wall Street, especially young ones. After conferring with her boss, the secretary told Josie to come next week at three in the afternoon. Jack had no idea why Albert Baxter-Brownes' daughter wanted to see him. He feared her father already was in financial trouble again. As she had done so many times before with others, 1929's most celebrated debutante pleasantly surprised the esteemed banker.

Not wanting anyone to know what she was doing, Josie drove herself to the bank. But as she walked through the halls of the House of Morgan, many gawked at the attractive girl wearing a cloche hat and a fetching black Chanel suit. She heard several whispering her name, but she knew there was nothing she could do about it. Because she was so nervous, she had butterflies in her stomach and ice-cold hands. But to Jack Morgan, as he offered her a chair in his office, she seemed perfectly poised.

Knowing how precious time was to the businessman, after exchanging brief formalities, Josie went straight to the point.

Bluntly she asserted, "I understand you need to hire someone to supervise your South American operations."

For a moment Jack just looked at the girl stunned. He was surprised she knew of the situation and even more shocked she had brought it up. Then he said, "Yes, that is correct."

After swallowing hard, she explained, "Charles Blakesley will take your offer." As she spoke, she thought the words didn't feel like they belonged to her. She felt numb, totally detached.

While the banker stared in shock at the girl in front of him, she reiterated quietly but firmly, "Charles Blakesley will work for you in South America."

After an awkward silence, Jack replied, "I'm glad to hear he wants to join us, although I did rather think he would be the one informing me of his decision after he received the offer."

Without pausing, she said, "He will shortly." Josie couldn't think about what she was doing. It would have killed her. To remain cool, she had instead imagined she was talking about something else, anything else, that didn't mean what he did to her.

Jack continued to stare at the young woman in front of him as he digested what was happening. He was a banker used to dealing with businessmen, making decisions solely based upon the bottom line. He didn't want to get involved in a soap opera. Getting a headache just from the thought, he rubbed his temples together with his hands as he tried to figure out what exactly she wanted. Never one for game playing, the financier said, "You've discussed things, then?"

She replied, "We will."

Thinking perhaps she was trying to convince him to let Charles take her along with him, he said, "You do understand I'd never send a family man down there to do this job."

Choking back tears, Josie replied, "Yes, I do." She explained as she twirled her engagement ring around her finger, "Charles doesn't know it yet, but I will break up with him so that he will take the offer." Her voice quivered as she said, "I know it's best for him."

Offering her his handkerchief, Jack said clearly touched, "You really do love him."

Softly, she whispered, "Yes, I do." Then despite her best efforts, the tears came down, as she couldn't stop herself from thinking about what she was doing. For several minutes she couldn't stop crying. The banker comforted her as best as he could. For some time, Josie sobbed, her head buried in his broad shoulders. Then she apologized profusely as she collected herself. The last thing she had planned to do was break down in front of Jack Morgan. She thought it was the worst possible scenario. In truth, it only strengthened her case.

A man of character above all else, Jack respected her greatly for hers.

The banker felt terrible that the couple faced such a predicament. He wished there was something he could do but he knew the job offer was perfect for the young man. Furthermore, given what the position entailed, the businessman had no intention of encouraging him to bring a wife or try to keep one in America when he'd be gone for several years. Given Charles' young age, the banker also thought several more years of bachelorhood was a good idea.

While Jack sat back down in his chair, Josie wiped her teary face and said, "Mr. Morgan, I want you to do me a favor because I am giving you the best man you could get to run your South American operations."

As Jack asked her to continue, Josie requested that he arrange financing for Charles' family's ranch so the Blakesleys' wouldn't lose it in bankruptcy. Jack chuckled when he realized that this is what she had been up to all along. He thought she was one of the cleverest girls he'd met and would have done pretty well in business if she had been a man. After shaking hands on the deal, Josie returned home to prepare for the inevitable. For several days, she considered various scenarios that would lead to the breakup. But the thought of actually ending the relationship made her so miserable she lost complete interest in everything. Unable to eat, sleep, functioning only on nervous energy, she started to believe she couldn't go through with her plan. Knowing Charles needed the Morgan job, and not one to go back on her word, she knew she had to end their relationship. But she wanted to see him at least one more time.

Just as the sun started to rise over Manhattan, one week after her meeting with Jack Morgan, and on the historic day when Americans, tired of Prohibition and Herbert Hoover's claims that economic prosperity was just around the corner, overwhelmingly elected Franklin Delano Roosevelt to the White House, New York's most celebrated debutante took decisive action.

As the dawn of the New Deal broke, Josie scribbled a hurried note to her parents, quickly phoned Charles, grabbed a few small bags packed with her dearest possessions and hailed a cab. She knew her parents wouldn't approve of her actions. Swiftly but not quickly enough for the impatient girl, she was driven down 5th Avenue, past the beautiful limestone apartment buildings and mansions she knew so well, into the midtown business district. Pausing as they hit a little traffic in front of the Plaza, Josie smelled the welcoming scent of fresh bread and croissants wafting through the dining room and kitchen windows – beckoning her nervous stomach. Had she any idea how long it would be before she returned to enjoy such pleasures she might have stopped. Instead, she jumped onto the first western bound train out of Grand Central, embracing the future as she watched all that had been familiar to her pass away into the great unknown.

Josie hardly slept during the entire trip. She wasn't even certain Charles would agree to see her let alone meet her at the station. He had made it abundantly clear to her when she had phoned that he did not want her coming to Ada under any circumstances until he called for her. But as nervous and unsure as she was about the reception she might receive, she took advantage of having a first class cabin to herself, by using the solitude, the space, to collect her thoughts on what she'd say once she saw him.

Over and over, she went through all her options and rehearsed what she'd tell him, what they'd do and how she'd create the situation that would make *him* want to break up with *her*. By the time her train rolled into the Ada station, Josie had a plan. But when she saw *her* Charles, leaner and clearly worn by stress and troubles, yet still standing tall, waiting on the platform for her, *her* golden boy, his soft blonde hair touched by the morning sun, his warm, penetrating blue eyes filled with love, she lost her resolve. In his strong arms, with his kisses, surrounded by his scent, filled with his love, she only could dream of having *his* children.

Despite his protests, she emotionally insisted that he hear her out before he said anything. Then she made it clear, no matter what, no matter how bad things were – even if he lost his land and they had to be migrant workers in California, she would follow him anywhere to be his wife.

When she finally finished, he grinned at her in the same way he had when she had discovered to her shock that he was not just a barman, but that he was actually Junius' best man. Calmly, quietly he informed her, "I guess you better start planning the biggest wedding Oklahoma has ever seen."

As she looked at him like he had lost his mind, she saw laughter in his eyes. She didn't get it until he pointed to a huge gusher in the distance and explained, "That's ours." As her jaw dropped, he told her, "Because of my love for you, I refused to give up. Everyone said I was mad. But despite the impossible odds we struck oil a week ago."

"But…"

Before she could finish, he said, "I wanted to surprise you and fix things up before you came out."

After recovering from the shock, she said teasingly, "You're not disappointed I'm here now, are you?"

Taking her into his arms, he hungrily kissed her, leaving no doubt as to his feelings.

That night, as Charles and Josie held each other close under the bountiful harvest moon, Josie once again smelled the sweet scent of summer and she felt a depth of love, she had never known before.

* * *

THE END OF BOOK I

AUTHOR'S NOTES
THE STORY BEHIND THE STORY

I have made an effort to remain true to the period in terms of the lifestyles, attitudes, events, and places in which the characters congregate. The music, books, magazines, movies, hotels, stores, clothes, automobiles, celebrities, artists, designers, and news discussed are authentic to the time. Although I am not a historian, the descriptions of events that occurred during the Stock Market Crash are based upon first-hand accounts and accredited histories.

For the sake of the story line, I marginally condensed the time period leading up to the Crash. While the book begins on the last day of summer, 1929, the high point of the Great Bull Market occurred slightly earlier on September 3rd. I also would like to note that the financier Clarence Hatry turned himself in on September 20th and Henry Ford's special commemoration of Edison's invention of the light bulb actually took place on October 21st. President Herbert Hoover, who did indeed speak at the commemoration event, did not have a booger hanging from his nose but did have his motorcade cheered by large crowds despite inclement weather.

It also should be noted that although psychologically much of America felt heartened by the election of Franklin Delano Roosevelt, unemployment remained an issue for several more years and many of the stocks of companies listed on the NYSE, in

1931, continued to slide until 1934. Some historians even assert that it was only World War II that fully ended the Great Depression and that the programs that President Hoover implemented in the last year of office started to work and were even incorporated into the much hailed New Deal.

In terms of the time frame, I have Josie listening to a prototype radio in her Bugati, in November 1929. This is possible although it was not until a few months later – in 1930, that the Galvin Manufacturing Company sold the first commercial car radios. Known as the Motorola model 5T71, the unit which could be installed in most popular automobiles, retailed between $110-130 in the United States.

Please note: I also have condensed the time period with regard to the programs designed to stimulate the economy that were initiated by the Hoover administration during 1930-1933.

Josie, Charles, James, Rebecca, Geraldine, Catherine, Bentley, Graves, Garrett Goldman, Evelyn Maker, Henry Jay, Alex Carleton, Lydia Kohler, Bigford, Mrs. Whitney Straight, Warren Bates, Charles MacVeagh, Prince Mikhail Stravinsky, Michael Mansfield, Mary, Suzie, Michael, Dexter, Edwin Baruch, Peggy Mitchell, Edmund Tates, Alfredo, Mr. Hedley-Dent, Lily Vanderhorn, and their families and friends are fictional characters. Although the history and main events during the course of the novel are accurate, I have created all encounters described between these fictional characters and those who actually lived during this time period.

It is my hope that this work will inspire readers to find out more about this fascinating period in history and those who lived it. With this in mind, on the next few pages please find a few facts on some of the real people mentioned in this book.

Prescott Sheldon Bush – The successful investment banker served as a U.S. senator from Connecticut from 1952-1963. His son, George Herbert Walker Bush became the 41st President of the United States and grandson, George Walker Bush served as the 43rd President.

Winston Churchill – The ex-Chancellor of the Exchequer and later famed Prime Minister of Britain – was an investor in the American market and really did witness part of the Crash. Undoubtedly considered one of the greatest public figures of the 20th century, the successful statesman was also an artist and acclaimed author. He passed away in 1965 at the age of 81.

Izzy Einstein and Moe Smith – Served as dry agents for five years before the government dismissed them due to their publicity, on November 13, 1925. Despite their unmatched record of arrests, convictions and seizures of bootleg booze, an official at the time of their firing claimed, "Izzy and Moe belong on the vaudeville stage." Izzy later wrote a book about his experiences entitled: ***Prohibition Agent Number 1.*** Five hundred seventy five copies were sold. Both agents subsequently worked in the insurance business and did well. A movie was released in 1985 called ***Izzy and Moe***, starring Jackie Gleason and Art Carney.

Texas Guinan – Born Mary Louise Cecilia in Waco, Texas in 1884 and educated in Catholic schools, "Texas Guinan" acted in 36 movies and on Broadway before getting her biggest role of all as the infamous night club hostess. She was so successful; she netted $700,000 in one ten-month period – close to $10 million in today's money. Like most businesses, her speakeasies suffered during the Great Depression. In 1931, she took her troupe of dancing girls on the road. After performing in France, Canada and other countries, she suffered from an attack of ulcerated colitis from which she died at the age of 49. It was November 5, 1933. Prohibition actually was repealed one month after her passing. It should be noted that although Texas did have a night club on West 54th Street, the interior as described in this book is made up. Furthermore, although the famous patrons mentioned in this book really did frequent Texas' speakeasy, the table numbers allotted to them are fictitious.

Joseph Patrick Kennedy – Despite the public slight he suffered on Wall Street at the House of Morgan, Joe Kennedy had a lasting impact on America. The banker who made money selling bootleg liquor during Prohibition and was a short-seller in the market, also was a film producer and made a great deal of money in real estate. After serving as the Chairman of the S.E.C. from 1934-35, he headed the U.S. Maritime Commission from 1936-37 and served as the U.S. Ambassador to Great Britain from 1937-40. Patriarch of a political dynasty that includes a former President, several Congressmen and other government officials, the Kennedy legacy in the political, social and cultural realms remains alive in America today.

John Pierpoint Morgan Junior – Known to his father and friends as Jack, Morgan continued working and providing philanthropy through the desperate days of the Depression. New York particularly is richer for the vast amounts of art, literature and other donations bequeathed by the Morgan family. After the Senate investigative hearings in 1933, he retired from active business. Following a number of strokes, he passed away on March 12, 1943 at the age of seventy-five. Through his efforts, his sons and capable managers like Thomas Lamont, the successors to the family's banking house, remain among the most powerful and esteemed in the world. Please note: in real life, Junius Morgan married but there is no reference in this novel to his actual wife.

Helena Rubinstein – Born in 1870 to middle-class Jewish parents in Krakow, Poland, Helena Rubinstein moved to Australia in 1902 where she started selling face cream based upon a secret family formula. After studying dermatology, she successfully opened salons in London (1908) and Paris (1912) before immigrating to the United States during World War I. In 1953, the "Empress of Beauty," as Cocteau called her, used a great deal of her wealth to establish a non-profit foundation to benefit women and children.

At the time of her death in 1965, at the age of 94, her international beauty empire was worth hundreds of millions of dollars. Now owned by L'Oreal, Helena Rubinstein's company continues to flourish in the billion-dollar beauty business. It should be noted that Helena Rubinstein really was a passenger on the *Berengaria* during the Crash and did lose a great deal of money on her stock investments during the trip. Davenport Pogue was her advisor but Lydia Kohler is a fictional character.

John D. Rockefeller III – After graduating from Princeton and taking a year to travel, the tall, apparently shy heir joined his father at their offices on 26 Broadway on December 2, 1929. On November 11, 1932, he married heiress Blanchette Ferry Hooker before 2,500 guests at Riverside Church. J.D. Rockefeller has been a most conscientious philanthropist behind numerous efforts including the Asia Society, Lincoln Center and Population Council as well as the Rockefeller Foundation. I would like to note that John's uncle, Percy Rockefeller, actually hosted the dinner for Winston Churchill described in the book. Please also note: All interactions between J.D. and the character Rebecca Stanley are made up.

Jacqueline Lee Bouvier Kennedy Onassis – Born on July 28, 1929 to Jack (who worked on Wall Street) and Lee Bouvier, "Jackie" went on to become one of the most adored First Lady's in history and an American icon.

Richard Whitney – Served as acting head of the New York Stock Exchange during the Great Crash. His actions then as well as during the Senate investigative hearings earned him respect on Wall Street. Unfortunately, while the Depression worsened, so did Richard Whitney's own financial situation. His firm bankrupt, personal accounts drained and real estate mortgaged, he resorted to speculating with his client's money. After his conviction, on April 11, 1938, he was sent to Sing-Sing to serve his sentence. Paroled in 1941, he lived for another twenty-seven years before he passed away at the age of 81.

Willy Messerschmitt – was a legendary German aircraft designer and manufacturer. His single most important design is most often considered the Messerschmitt Bf 109, which was designed in 1934 with the collaboration of Walter Rethel. The Bf 109 became the most important fighter plane for the German Luftwaffe as the country rearmed before World War II. This plane remains the most produced fighter in history, with some 35,000 built. Another later Messerschmitt aircraft broke the absolute world air speed record and held the world speed record for propeller-driven aircraft until 1969. The company Messerschmitt founded is also credited with producing the first jet-powered fighter to enter service. After World War II, Messerschmitt was tried by a de-Nazification court for using slave labor, and in 1948 was convicted of being a "fellow traveler." Following two years in prison, he was released and resumed his position as the head of his company.

John Jacob Raskob – was the son of a successful New York cigar manufacturer, who rose through the executive ranks of DuPont. He became an early investor in General Motors (GM) and helped engineer DuPont's 43% stake in GM, which was purchased from the financially strapped William C. Durant. Raskob held the top financial position both at GM and Dupont until 1928, when he resigned and sold his company stock due to a dispute with Alfred Sloan, the Chairman, arising out of Raskob's being named Chairman of the Democratic National Party (DNC). Sloan was a supporter of Herbert Hoover and insisted that his underling choose between GM and the DNC. Raskob was very bullish about the market and in the 1920's, did give an interview for *Ladies Home Journal* in which he suggested every American could become wealthy by investing $15 per week in stocks. The piece came out mere months before the Stock Market Crash of 1929. The businessman used much of the proceeds from his GM stock sale to finance the building of the Empire State building. During the Great Depression, the public was entertained by the development and rivalry over which building would be taller: the Empire State or Chrysler. Raskob had 13 children, donated a great deal to charities and was a vociferous opponent of the New Deal.

Bernard Baruch – was the son of a surgeon who pioneered physical therapy treatments. His mother's family immigrated to New York City in the 1690's and became successful in the shipping business. Before the age of 30, Baruch amassed a fortune through speculation. He was called the "Lone Wolf on Wall Street" because of his refusal to join other financial houses (he had his own seat on the New York Stock Exchange and was a partner in the firm of A. A. Houseman and Company). Baruch served as a Presidential Advisor to Wilson and FDR. During the First World War, he played an instrumental role in ramping up American industry in order for the country to reach full-scale war production. He also served as a member of FDR's Brain Trust and helped the National Recovery Administration. During World War II, he was a consultant on economic matters and was the first to coin the phrase "Cold War". He also supported numerous Democratic congressmen with donations.

Charles Schwab – was a self-made man who started out as a stake driver in Andrew Carnegie's steelworks and in 1897, and by the age of 35, became president of the Carnegie Steel Company. He was instrumental in negotiating the secret sale of the company to a group of New York based financiers that were led by J. P. Morgan. After the buyout, Schwab became the first president of U.S. Steel, which was formed out of the former holdings. Later, the industrialist became the head of the Bethlehem Steel Corporation. Under his leadership, it became the largest independent steel producer in the world. Schwab made a vast fortune and lived large. He was known for his high stakes gambling (which included: "breaking the bank" in Monaco) and numerous extramarital affairs. He built tremendous private residences, most notably the 75 room

"Riverside" in Manhattan. Schwab traveled in a $100,000 private rail car, in which Winston Churchill and his son really did ride. The industrialist businessman was a risk-taker who went bankrupt in the Stock Market Crash of 1929. When he died in 1939, his stakes in Bethlehem Steel were virtually worthless and he was in debt over $300,000.

Herbert Hoover - Due to the bad luck of presiding over the country at the time of the Crash and Franklin Delano Roosevelt's (FDR) negative Presidential campaign, Hoover has often been blamed for the Great Depression. Recent scholars have pointed out that a number of his policies started to work near the end of his term of office. Rexford Tugwell, New Dealer and member of FDR's "Brain Trust," even went so far as to claim, "Practically the whole New Deal was extrapolated from programs Hoover started." Certainly whether the President's actions helped or worsened the depression, his legacy in other areas is still impressive.

Orphaned at the age of nine, Hoover excelled through his own efforts. After graduating from Stanford, he traveled the world as a successful mining engineer and even co-founded his own company before working as a humanitarian in Europe. It is ironic that the man who helped organize the return of 120,000 Americans safely from Europe at the start of the First World War and then successfully administered the distribution of over 1 ½ million tons of food to 9 million war victims and provided food aid to post-war Germany and Russia, (despite opposition from his own party about feeding the starving people ruled by "Bolsheviks"), is often seen as uncaring about humanity due to the suffering during the Great Depression.

Hoover was the first and only President to date who rose directly from a full cabinet position (Secretary of Commerce). During his one term as President, a brief description of some of his achievements include: setting aside 3 million acres of national parkland and 2.3 million acres as national forests, advocating tax reduction for low-income Americans, doubling the number of veteran hospital facilities, drafting a children's charter that advocated the protection of every child regardless of race or gender, starting the building of the San Francisco-Oakland Bay Bridge and the construction of the Hoover Dam, re-organizing the Bureau of Indian Affairs, creating an anti-trust division at the Justice Department and having the IRS and Justice Department go after gangsters. Hoover also took a goodwill tour of South America, withdrew troops from Nicaragua and Haiti and in response to the Japanese seizure of Manchuria, created a doctrine stating that the United States would not recognize territories gained by force.

Franklin Delano Roosevelt (FDR) – So much has been written about FDR, I will simply state a few basics as related to this novel and the recent financial downturn. Born in 1882 to a wealthy family with a political history (Amongst other notables, President Theodore Roosevelt was his cousin), FDR succeeded Herbert Hoover as the 32nd President of the United States. FDR's legacy includes the fact that many of the programs he initiated during the Depression such as the Federal Deposit Insurance Corporation (FDIC), Tennessee Valley Authority (TVA), and the United States Securities and Exchange Commission (SEC), continue to have fundamental roles in the United States economy.

In the 1932 election, Roosevelt won 57% of the vote and carried every state bar six. After the election, Roosevelt refused the outgoing President's requests for meetings to come up with a joint program to calm investors. His reason was that to do so "would tie his hands." Certainly this decision preserved FDR from being associated with any of the "failed" policies of the Hoover Administration. However, it may also have helped to contribute to the continuation of the economy's spiraling downward and a near collapse of the banking system that resulted in a complete shutdown by the end of the Hoover administration.

When FDR was finally inaugurated (which in those days was not until March 4th – a full four months after the election), the country was unquestionably in the depths of the worst depression in its history. One quarter of the workforce was unemployed, 2 million were homeless and 32 of the 48 states and the District of Columbia had closed their banks. The New York Federal Reserve Bank failed to open the following day because of the amount withdrawn by panicky customers. FDR blamed the economic crisis on the bankers and financiers, "quest for profits and the self-interest basis of capitalism." To this end, he enacted a number of programs to redress these grievances, including the Glass Steagull Act which many financial experts believe helped build a more stable financial sector. It is interesting to note that many now blame the repeal of this in 1999, as a contributing factor to the Global Financial Crisis of 2008-2009. The repeal "allowed commercial lenders like Citigroup, to underwrite and trade instruments like mortgage-back securities and collaterized debut obligations and to establish structured investment vehicles (SIVs) that in turn bought those securities. It should be noted that while the year before the repeal sub-prime loans made up only 5% of all mortgage lending, by the time of the credit crisis of 2008, they were close to 30%."

In Presidential rankings, FDR is invariably ranked among the top 5. He is also the only President to have been elected to serve 4 consecutive terms.

The character Evelyn Maker was inspired in part by astrologist Evangeline Adams who was in fact called the Seer of Wall Street and did a great deal for the legitimization of her field of study. Evangeline Adams was married to a man but had no children. Amongst other predictions, she did in fact predict her own death (to the day) and she witnessed the flock of birds perish on Wall Street during the Crash.

The character Garrett Goldman was inspired in part by the famed securities speculator Jesse Livermore. Livermore made and lost several fortunes by short-selling during the stock market crashes of 1907 and 1929 and investing in the great World War I bull market.

While browsing in the beautiful main reading room of the Mount Holyoke College library late one night several years ago, I randomly came across the yearbook for the class of 1929. Within its spirited pages and several others from the 1920's, the smart set's Jazz Age came alive and I found the inspiration for a vivacious, amusing flapper named Josephine Baxter-Browne. I spent many hours writing her story in the former Duke Mansion, now New York University's Fine Art Institute on East 78th Street. Josie's parents' home is in part based upon this elegant mansion.

For more information on the period and real and fictional characters, please visit the novel's website: www.anupperclassaffair.com

I will be posting information on resources pertaining to the period, including a bibliography. I also welcome readers to post their own family's accounts of experiences during the roaring twenties, Stock Market Crash, Great Depression and subsequent market crashes. My hope is that this novel will provide some light entertainment and encourage the view that women of all ages can be attractive, smart, witty, and successful in their own rights as well as find love.

CREDITS AND ACKNOWLEDGEMENTS

I cannot thank enough Robert Hudovernik for his personal assistance and help as well as gratitude for his inspirational work: *JAZZ AGE BEAUTIES*. It was within the pages of his wonderful book, that I found the Alfred Cheney Johnson photograph of Dorothy Knapp which is on the cover of this novel. Additionally, I owe much to Nils Hanson and the Ziegfeld Club of New York for granting permission to use the photograph of Dorothy Knapp taken by Alfred Cheney Johnson. Many thanks to "Aaron1912," for his creative historical videos and help with research. I would also like to thank Diane Paradisco from the WPA Film Library, Matthew Giermala and John Leifert at Getty Images and all the staff at the Getty for preserving the image of the Wall Street sign used on the back cover. I appreciate the creative help offered by: Bruce Silversteen, Liyang Zhou and Andrew Harmon and all the edits by Margaret Rosalind Jones, Katy Kempf and Laurel Sharp as well as the read through by Cristina Spencer.

Finally, I would like to thank the following people for their support. In addition to my husband and parents, my sister Marianne, brothers: Michael, Mark, and Matthew, as well as Winberg, Henry and May-lee Chai, Arlinda Lam, Joy Madmai, Neil, Mary and Rod Clayton, Louise Bagshawe, Suzanne Messere, Desiree Mauer, Karen Nicholson, Ailinh Nguyen, M.H.T., G.E.R, Sandra R., J.N.R., Brigid, Rachel and George Hurn-Maloney, Mary and Philip McHale, Karen Holman, Shulamith Rubinfien, Naciba Balamane, Emily Margalit, Lena Miyamoto, Olga and Anna Gontar, Jessica

He, Carmen Hess, Karl Laughton, Jan Helbing, Nabil Balamane, Petro, Rosannah Harding, James Kyle, Katharine Manzini and every single person who reads this book.

For more information on the book and period, visit the website: www.1929anupperclassaffair.com

Cover photograph of Dorothy Knapp by Alfred Cheney Johnson, Courtesy of The Ziegfeld Club of New York, www.nationalziegfeldclubinc.com and www.alfredcheneyjohnson.com and with the assistance of Nils Hanson and the very talented Robert Hudovernik

Made in the USA
Lexington, KY
21 December 2009